DATE DUE

BRODART, CO.   Cat. No. 23-221-003

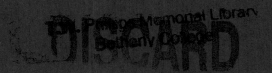

TEXAS

VILLE

A NOVEL BY

Larry McMurtry

Simon and Schuster ▪ NEW YORK

10 9 8 7 6 5 4 3 2 1
Library of Congress Cataloging in Publication Data
McMurtry, Larry.
    Texasville.
    I. Title.
PS3563.A319T48 1987   813'.54   86-31520
ISBN: 0-671-62533-0

For Cybill Shepherd

CHAPTER 1

DUANE WAS IN THE HOT TUB, SHOOTING AT HIS NEW doghouse with a .44 Magnum. The two-story log doghouse was supposedly a replica of a frontier fort. He and Karla had bought it at a home show in Fort Worth on a day when they were bored. It would have housed several Great Danes comfortably, but so far had housed nothing. Shorty, the only dog Duane could put up with, never went near it.

Every time a slug hit the doghouse, slivers of white wood flew. The yard of the Moores' new mansion had just been seeded, at enormous expense, but the grass had a tentative look. The house stood on a long, narrow, rocky bluff, overlooking a valley pockmarked with well sites, saltwater pits and oily little roads leading from one oil pump to the next. The bluff was not a very likely place to grow Bermuda grass, but six acres of it had been planted anyway. Karla took the view that you could make anything happen if you spent enough money.

Duane had even less confidence in the Bermuda grass than the grass had in itself, but he signed the check, just as he had signed the check for the doghouse he was slowly reducing to kindling. For a time, buying things he had no earthly use for had almost convinced him he was still rich, but that trick had finally stopped working.

Shorty, a Queensland blue heeler, blinked every time the gun roared. Unlike Duane, he was not wearing shooter's earmuffs. Shorty loved Duane so much that he stuck by his side throughout the day, even at the risk of becoming hearing impaired.

Shorty had the eyes of a drunkard—red-streaked and vacant. Julie and Jack, the eleven-year-old twins, threw rocks at him when their father wasn't around. They were both good athletes and hit Shorty frequently with the rocks, but Shorty didn't mind. He thought it meant they loved him.

Karla, Duane's beautiful, long-legged wife, came out of the house, a mug of coffee in her hand, and started walking across the long yard to the deck. It was a clear spring morning; she had already put in an hour in the garden. Her tomatoes were under threat from the blister bugs.

When he saw Karla coming, Duane took off the earmuffs. It annoyed her severely if he kept them on while she was complaining.

"Now you're ruining that brand-new doghouse, Duane," she said, sitting down on the deck. "I guess I'm trapped out here in the country with a man that's going crazy. I'm glad we sent the twins off to camp."

"They'll probably get kicked out in a day or two," Duane said. "They'll commit incest or something."

"No, it's a church camp," Karla said. "They'll just pray for their horrible little souls."

They were quiet for a minute. Though it was only seven in the morning, the temperature was close to ninety.

"You can die if you stay in a hot tub too long," Karla remarked. "I read it in *USA Today*."

They heard screams from the distant house. They came from Little Mike, Nellie's terrible two. In a moment the baby joined in.

"Nellie may not even hear them," Karla said. "She's probably got her Walkman on."

Nellie, nineteen, had just moved out on her third husband.

She liked getting married, but regarded the arrangement as little more binding than a handshake.

Karla wore a T-shirt with a motto stenciled on the front. The motto said, YOU'RE THE REASON OUR CHILDREN ARE UGLY, which was the title of a song sung by Loretta Lynn and Conway Twitty. Karla laughed every time she heard the song.

She had thirty or forty T-shirts with lines from hillbilly songs printed on them. Every time she heard a lyric which seemed to her to express an important truth, she had a T-shirt printed. Occasionally she took the liberty of altering a line in some clever way, though no one around Thalia seemed to notice.

Duane had once pointed out to her that their children weren't ugly.

"They got personalities like wild dogs, but at least they're good-looking," he said.

"That's true, they take after me," Karla said. Her complexion was the envy of every woman she knew. Karla's skin was like cream with a bit of cinnamon sprinkled on it.

Dickie, their twenty-one-year-old son, had been voted Most Handsome Boy in Thalia High School, both his junior and senior years. Nellie had been Most Beautiful Girl her sophomore year, but had lost out the next two years thanks to widespread envy among the voters. Jack and Julie were the best-looking twins in Texas, so far as anyone knew. Dickie made most of his living peddling marijuana, and Nellie—with three marriages in a year and a half—would probably pass Elizabeth Taylor on the marriage charts before she was twenty-one, but no one could deny that they were good-looking kids.

Karla, at forty-six, remained optimistic enough to believe almost everything she saw printed on a T-shirt. Duane was more skeptical. He had started poor, become rich, and now was losing money so rapidly that he had come to doubt that much of anything was true, in any sense. He had eight hundred and fifty dollars in the bank and debts of roughly twelve million, a situation that was becoming increasingly untenable.

Duane twirled the chamber of the .44. His hand ached a little. The big gun had a kick.

"You know what I hate worse than anything in the world?" Karla asked.

"No, and I'm not going to guess," Duane said.

Karla laughed. "It's not you, Duane," she said.

She had another T-shirt which read, I'VE GOT THE SADDLE, WHERE'S THE HORSE? It was, it seemed to her, a painfully clear reference to Mel Tillis's sexiest song, "I've Got the Horse if You've Got the Saddle." But of course no one in Thalia caught the allusion. When she wore it, all that happened was that men tried to sell her overpriced quarter horses.

"The thing I hate most in the world is blister bugs," Karla said. "I wanta hire a wetback to help me with this garden."

"I don't know why you plant such a big garden," Duane said. "We couldn't eat that many tomatoes if we ate twenty-four hours a day."

"I was raised to be thrifty," Karla said.

"Why'd you buy that BMW then?" Duane asked. "You could have bought a pickup if you wanted to be thrifty. A BMW won't last a week on these roads."

Their new house was five miles from town, dirt roads all the way. When they started building the house they intended to pave the road themselves, but the boom ended before they even got the house built, and it was clear that dirt roads would be their destiny for some time to come.

Duane had started hating the new house before the foundation was laid. He would have moved tomorrow, but he was surrounded by a wall of debtors, and anyway Karla loved the house and would have resisted any suggestion that they face up to straitened circumstances and try to sell it as soon as the paint dried.

He poked the barrel of the .44 into the water. Refraction made the barrel seem to grow. Shorty moved closer to the edge of the hot tub and peered in at it. Everything Duane did seemed interesting to Shorty. Many human actions were incomprehensible to him, but that didn't mean he couldn't watch.

"Duane, why are you poking that gun in the water?" Karla asked.

"I was thinking of shooting my dick off," he said. "It's caused me nothing but trouble my whole life."

Karla took that news with equanimity. She scratched her

shapely calf. Karla believed that the way not to have your figure ruined by childbearing was to have your kids young and then get tied off. Shortly after producing Nellie she got tied off, but ten years later something came untied. Intermittently religious, she decided it must be God's will that they have twins. It should have been medically impossible—and besides that, she and Duane only rarely made love.

But one afternoon, after ten days of rain, with the rigs all shut down, they did make love and the twins resulted. During the pregnancy Karla tried to cheer herself up by imagining that she was about to produce little human angels, perfect in every way. Why else would God give her twins when her husband wasn't even giving her a sex life?

The twins were born, and as soon as Jack grew four teeth he bit completely through his sister's ear. The angel theory was discarded—indeed, while sitting in the emergency room getting Julie's ear fixed Karla stopped being religious for good.

Jack and Julie were terrible babies. They bit and clawed one another like little beasts. They shouldered one another out of their baby bed, and stuffed toys in one another's mouths. As soon as they could lift things they hit each other with whatever they could lift. It seemed to Karla that she spent more and more of her life in emergency rooms—indeed, the twins were not safe from themselves even there. Once Julie grabbed some surgical scissors off a tray and jabbed her brother in the ear with them.

"My kids believe in an ear for an ear," Karla told her friends, who enjoyed gallows humor.

She learned never to take the twins to the hospital at the same time: there were too many weapons in hospitals.

In time Karla concluded that the twins' conception had nothing to do with Divine Will, and everything to do with medical incompetence. She wanted to bring a malpractice suit against Doctor Deckert, the young general practitioner who tied her off.

"No, you can't sue him," Duane said. "You might run him off, and if you do half the people in town will die of minor ailments."

"Shit, what about us?" Karla said. "We got a life sentence because of him."

Shortly after that Karla had a T-shirt printed which read, INSANITY IS THE BEST REVENGE. The line wasn't original with her, nor was it from a hillbilly song. She had seen it on a bumper sticker and liked it.

In fact, Karla found almost as many important truths on bumper stickers as she found in songs. One which hewed very closely to her own philosophy of life said, IF YOU LOVE SOME-THING SET IT FREE. IF IT DOESN'T RETURN IN A MONTH OR TWO HUNT IT DOWN AND KILL IT.

With more amusement than alarm, she watched Duane point the pistol into the water.

"Duane, I don't think you ought to try and shoot your dick off," she said.

"Why not?" he asked. "It don't work half the time anyway."

"Well, I wouldn't be the one to know about that," Karla said. "But it's a small target and if you miss you'll just ruin our new hot tub."

She laughed loudly at her own wit. Shorty, excited by the laughter, began to roll around on the redwood deck. He attempted to bite his own tail and came close to nipping it a time or two.

"Don't sulk, Duane," Karla said. "You left yourself wide open for that one."

She stood up and kicked Shorty lightly in the ribs. Shorty was too excited by the pursuit of his own tail to take any notice.

"I guess I'll go in and see if I can talk Nellie into acting like a parent for a few minutes," Karla said.

Duane took the gun out of the water. In the far corner of the vast yard the new white satellite dish was tilted skyward, its antenna pointed toward a spot somewhere over the equator. The dish was the most expensive one available in Dallas. Before they had even got it aligned properly Karla had gone to Dallas and returned with a Betamax, a VHS and four thousand dollars' worth of movies she had purchased from a video store. So far they had only watched two of them: *Coal Miner's Daughter,* which Karla and Nellie watched once or twice a week, and a sex movie called *Hot Channels.*

Duane pointed out to her that it was possible to rent movies. They could even be rented from Sonny Crawford's small convenience store, in Thalia.

"I know that, Duane," Karla said. "Just because I'm horny don't mean I'm dumb. The ones I want to see are always checked out, though."

However, on her next visit to Dallas she considerately bought only eight hundred dollars' worth of movies.

Duane had been in the hot tub nearly half an hour and was beginning to feel a little bleached. He climbed out and dried himself and his pistol. He felt weary—very weary. Sometimes he would wake up in the night needing to relieve himself and would feel so tired by the time he stumbled into the bathroom that he would have to sit on the pot and nap for a few minutes before going back to bed. Getting rich had been tiring, but nothing like as tiring as going broke.

The minute Duane climbed out, Shorty stopped rolling around on the deck and raced across the yard to park himself expectantly beside Duane's pickup. He knew it was almost time for Duane to go to town, and he was ready to roll.

CHAPTER 2

ON THE WAY TO TOWN DUANE GOT ON THE CB AND
tried to check in with Ruth Popper, his outspoken secretary,
who was actually no more outspoken than Karla, his wife, or
Janine Wells, his girlfriend, or Minerva, his maid.

While he was becoming rich, the women in his life had become outspoken. He had stopped being rich, but they had not
stopped being outspoken. Any one of them would argue with a
skillet, or with whatever was being cooked in the skillet, or
with whoever came by—Duane himself, usually—to eat what
was being cooked.

He didn't really want to talk to Ruth, but there was always
the faint chance that oil prices had risen during the night, in
which case somebody with a little credit left might want an oil
well drilled.

The CB crackled, but Ruth didn't answer. Shorty watched
the CB alertly. At first he had barked his characteristic piercing
bark every time it crackled, but after Duane had whacked him
with his work gloves several hundred times Shorty got the
message and stopped barking at it, though he continued to

watch it alertly in case whatever was in it popped out and attacked Duane.

Just as the pickup swung onto the highway leading into Thalia, Ruth Popper jogged off the pavement and began to run up the dirt road. Ruth was a passionate jogger. She passed so close to the pickup that Duane could have leaned out and hit her in the head with a hammer—though only if he'd been quick. Despite her age, Ruth was speedy. She wore earphones and had a Walkman, a speedometer, and various other gadgets attached to her belt as she ran. She also carried an orange weight in each hand.

She showed no sign of being aware that she had just passed within a yard of her boss and his dog. Feeling slightly foolish, Duane hung up the CB and watched her recede in the rearview mirror, her feet throwing up neat identical puffs of dust from the powdery road.

Ruth Popper was the only person left in Thalia who had preserved a belief in exercise, now that the oil boom was over. It had taken the greatest bonanza in local memory to popularize exercise among people who had worked too hard all their lives to give it the least thought, but once it caught on it caught on big.

Duane himself started jogging four miles a day, and devoted an evening or two a week to racquetball at the Wichita Falls country club. Roughnecks and farmers, finding themselves suddenly rich, floundered painfully over the county's gravelly roads in their expensive running shoes.

In the case of Jimbo Jackson, briefly the richest person in the county, a devotion to exercise had tragic results: a truckful of his own roughnecks, on their way to set pipe on one of his own wells, ran over him. Two or three trucks were ahead of them, carrying pipe to other wells, and Jimbo, flopping along patiently in the choking dust, not far from his newly completed mansion, accidentally veered into the middle of the road. The roughnecks thought they had hit a yearling—Jimbo was not small—but when they got out to look, discovered they had killed their boss.

The local paper, in a mournful editorial, advised joggers to keep to the bar ditches—a stance that infuriated Karla.

"The bar ditches are full of chiggers and rattlesnakes," she said. "What does he think this is, the Cotswolds?"

Duane wondered if it could be Cotswold, Kansas, she was referring to. During the virtually sleepless year when he had driven a cattle truck, Karla had sometimes come with him on his runs. He was just back from Korea; they were just married. It seemed to him he had passed through a town called Cots- wold, though it might have been in Nebraska or even Iowa. But it didn't seem to him that the bar ditches in Kansas could be that much better to jog in than the bar ditches in Texas.

"Duane, it's in England," Karla said. "Don't you remember? We read about it in that airlines magazine the time we took the kids to Disneyland."

Duane didn't enjoy being reminded of the time they took the kids to Disneyland. Jack had almost succeeded in drowning Julie on the log ride. Dickie, who hated to spend money on anything except drugs, got caught shoplifting. He tried to steal his girlfriend a stuffed gorilla from one of the gift shops. Nellie disappeared completely, having decided to run off to Guaymas with a young Mexican she met on one of the rides. They stopped in Indio so Nellie could call her boyfriend in Thalia and tell him she was breaking off their engagement. The boy- friend managed to reach Karla and Duane, and the runaways were stopped at the Arizona line.

Nine months later, having married and divorced the boy she had meant to break up with, Nellie had Little Mike, their first grandchild. He did not look Hispanic, or bear any resemblance to the husband she had had so briefly.

"They say travel's broadening," Karla remarked, on the flight home from Disneyland.

Duane looked up just in time to see Jack slip two ice cubes from his Coke down the neck of a little old woman who had been brought on board in a wheelchair and dumped in the seat in front of him.

"Whoever said that never traveled with our kids," Duane said as the old lady began to writhe in her seat. "I'm telling you right now I'll commit suicide before I'll go anywhere with them again."

He glanced at Julie to see what evil she might be contemplating. Julie wore dark glasses with huge purple frames. She had a teen magazine spread over her lap and her hand under the magazine. Duane decided to his horror that she was playing with her crotch.

"What did you say, Duane?" Karla asked. "I was reading and didn't hear."

"I said I'd commit suicide before I'd go anywhere else with these kids," he said.

"Duane, don't brag," Karla said. "You know you're too big a sissy even to go to the hospital and get a shot."

She noticed the little old lady, who was writhing more desperately as the ice cubes worked their way down her back.

"I hope that old lady isn't going into convulsions," she said.

Duane had been trying to decide where his duty lay. Should he try to help the old lady get the ice cubes out, which would practically mean undressing her? Should he grab Jack and break his neck? Should he demand that his son apologize? Jack was an ingenious liar and accepted no punishment meekly. The more blatant his crimes, the more brilliant he became in his own defense. Duane began to get a headache. He felt like strangling his son. He wondered if the stewardesses realized that his beautiful little daughter was playing with her crotch. Dallas-Fort Worth seemed very far away.

"Duane, don't sulk, it was a real nice trip in some ways," Karla said.

CHAPTER 3

DUANE WAS WELL AWARE THAT HIS IGNORANCE OF the world, and his unwillingness to go and see much of it, were shortcomings that particularly enraged Karla, though why they enraged her he had no idea, since she was every bit as ignorant of the world beyond Texas. He had been to California three times, and she had only been once. He had been to Las Vegas twice and had asked her to go both times. Both invitations had led to fits—the fit being one of Karla's favorite forms of self-expression.

"No, thanks, the only reason you're going is to get laid, and I'm not giving you a chance to accuse me of standing in the way of *that*," she said.

Duane knew perfectly well she wasn't standing in the way of it. Karla was a firm believer in sexual freedom, especially for her.

"I just thought you might like to see one of those shows," he said.

"If I wanta see tits all I have to do is take my bra off," Karla said.

She didn't really even have to do that, since her daughter

Nellie's fine young bosom was frequently on view around the house. For almost a year dinner had been eaten to the sound of Little Mike slurping at his mother. Nellie was too lazy to wean him, despite repeated entreaties from Karla, who had not cared for breast-feeding and didn't enjoy watching it take place.

Bobby Lee, Duane's number one tool pusher, was the only one who got much of a thrill out of watching Nellie nurse Little Mike or Barbette, the baby girl. With oil at twenty-one dollars a barrel and sinking, there wasn't too much drilling to do. Bobby Lee had plenty of leisure to devote to watching Nellie nurse her kids. His desire was obvious, but so far Nellie had refused him—and being refused by Nellie was virtually a unique distinction.

Bobby Lee had worked for Duane for over twenty years and made it plain that he hoped to marry into the family someday, although he was already married.

"I don't know why you'd want to, except that you never have been in your right mind," Duane said.

He had no serious objections, though. Bobby Lee would make at least as good a son-in-law as the first three Nellie had presented them with.

Karla, however, had plenty of objections, which she aired whenever she could get Bobby Lee alone. Unbeknownst to Duane, she and Bobby Lee had had a messy one-night stand several years back. Duane had been off deer hunting. It left Karla unaffected but caused Bobby Lee to fall madly in love.

The fact that she was completely uninterested in him as a boyfriend didn't mean—as Karla repeatedly pointed out—that she wanted him sleeping with her daughter, or daughters. Bobby Lee was a small man with mournful brown eyes. If Nellie wasn't around, the mournful eyes would frequently linger on Julie, who was just coming into bud.

"It does look like, with all the horny women there are in this country, you could find someone not related to me, if you'd just look," Karla told him.

"What horny women?" Bobby Lee asked. He liked to project an image of asceticism, although he could be found every night at Aunt Jimmie's Lounge, and Aunt Jimmie's was not exactly a monastery.

When Barbette was born, two months previously, Karla de-

cided she was going to have to take the weaning of Little Mike
into her own hands. In his two years he had shown no interest
in restraint, and if he felt his food source threatened there was
no telling what he might do to his baby sister.

Karla started kidnapping him every day. She drove him
around in her new BMW, plugged in via Walkman to the loudest music she could find in the hope of drowning out his
screams. Little Mike threw several bottles out the window, but
he eventually broke.

Duane had a deep fondness for the tiny, helpless Barbette.
She fulfilled his old longing for a quiet, gentle child. He would
sit with her for hours on the deck of the hot tub, shading her
with a cowboy hat. Sometimes he dreamed that he and Barbette were living somewhere else—where was never quite
clear, though it might have been San Marcos, where he and
Karla had once contemplated moving.

His urge to protect Barbette was very strong, and his biggest
worry was the twins, who pitched her around like a ball. One
day they left her on a kitchen cabinet and went outside to
swim. By a miracle of timing Duane came in from work just in
time to keep her from rolling off. The shock flooded him with
so much adrenaline that he began to tremble; it produced a
rage that frightened even the twins, who put on tennis shoes
and immediately ran off. They planned to hitchhike to Disneyland and get jobs as concessionaires.

Nellie and Karla, returning from a quick shopping trip to
Wichita Falls, accidently intercepted the twins just before they
reached the highway. They were in their bathing suits. Both
claimed that Duane had threatened to kill them.

"Oh, I doubt he would have," Karla said, not absolutely convinced. Duane did love that baby girl.

The twins were convinced, though. They didn't want to go
back home. Jack crawled through a barbed-wire fence and ran
off into a pasture. Julie calmed herself by appropriating her big
sister's Walkman and listening to a little Barbara Mandrell.
Little Mike, sensing an opportunity to regain a lost paradise,
clawed his way under Nellie's blouse and fastened himself
blissfully to a nipple.

"Let's go back to town and get the sheriff," Nellie said.

"Don't let that child nurse," Karla said. "What about his baby sister? She might want something to eat when we get home."

"I don't want to go home," Nellie said. Little Mike was draining her so fast she felt dizzy.

"Nellie, we have to go home," Karla said. "We live there."

Meanwhile, Jack had disappeared into the pasture.

"I want to stay with Billie Anne," Nellie declared. Billie Anne was Dickie's girlfriend. She worked in a savings-and-loan and had an apartment in the small community of Lakeside City.

Little Mike, not wasting a second, switched to the other breast.

Karla began to blow the horn, thinking it might make Jack come back. Instead, it caused Julie to open the door and slip out. Karla and Nellie were both too agitated to notice her departure. When they got home and discovered she wasn't in the car, they were dumbfounded. She had been right in the car, listening to Barbara Mandrell, except now they were home and she wasn't.

Nellie refused to get out until Karla determined whether Duane was still planning to murder his family.

"Don't kill the motor," she said. "I might be leaving quick."

Duane was out by the pool, giving Barbette a bottle. His rage has passed, leaving him only mildly irritated.

"I guess you'd all go off and leave this baby to starve," he said.

Karla quickly regained the initiative.

"Duane, the twins have run completely off because of you, and Nellie won't even come in the house," she said. "You'll have to go out to the car and promise not to murder her."

"Have I ever murdered anybody?" he asked. Giving Barbette her bottle gave him a lot of satisfaction.

"No, but you're not usually under this much stress," Karla said. "You could try calling that stress hot line in Fort Worth when you feel sort of pent up."

"That stress hot line is for broke farmers," he said. "It ain't for destitute oil millionaires."

It occurred to him, looking at the scrubby oil-stained acres below the bluff, that in a sense he did live on an oil farm, one that was about farmed out.

"Duane, it's for anybody that's feeling terrible, like people do when they go berserk," Karla said. "They ain't gonna ask if you're a farmer—they'll just give you helpful advice, like don't murder your children or anything."

"That baby could have been brain-damaged for life falling off the cabinet," Duane pointed out. "Where's Minerva? I thought we were paying her to watch this baby."

"I have no idea where Minerva could have got to," Karla said. Minerva had worked for them for more than a decade without becoming any more predictable.

"If she comes back I'm going to offer to trade jobs with her," Duane said. "She can run the oil company and I'll watch the baby."

Karla got a blue Magic Marker and wrote the number of the stress hot line on a piece of note paper. Then she stuck the paper onto the cabinet, right by the phone. Duane watched her with a disquieting look of amusement on his face. Karla remembered reading in *Cosmo* that people who were about to go berserk often seemed perfectly normal up until the moment when they started blasting away with a gun.

That very morning she and Duane had seen a TV report about a Midland oilman who had carbon-monoxided himself in the garage of his new mansion. He had thoughtfully turned off his brand-new security system so that if one of his kids happened to glance at a TV monitor they wouldn't see him turning black, or whatever you did if you monoxided yourself.

"Duane, Nellie's just sitting out there wasting gas," Karla said. "You're going to have to do something about the twins, too."

Duane walked Barbette until she went to sleep, and laid her gently in her baby bed. Then he went outside and whistled at Shorty, who was in the pickup in a flash, so excited at getting to take an unexpected trip that he barked his piercing bark a few times.

On the way to town Duane called the Highway Patrol to see if the twins had been picked up. They hadn't. He saw a dust cloud approaching and pulled well to the right. In a moment

Minerva flashed by, the back seat of her ancient Buick piled high with groceries.

Minerva had been their household help for the past ten years. Well into her eighties, she had been rich once herself. Her father made a fortune in the oil boom of the early twenties, and lost it a few years later. Minerva learned to drive in a muddy Pierce-Arrow and continued, from then on, to take her half of the road out of the middle.

This habit had resulted in five head-on collisions, all of which Minerva had come through without a scratch. As a result of these infractions Minerva spent most of her evenings at Bad Driver's School in Wichita Falls. She was indifferent to the traffic laws, but rather enjoyed Bad Driver's School, acquiring several boyfriends there over the years.

Most humans fantasized pleasures of one sort or another, but Minerva Hooks was different. She fantasized mortal illness. When Karla hired her she was fantasizing cancer in both lungs. Karla thought it would be nice to give the poor old soul a home during her last years. Now Minerva's soul was ten years older and she was fantasizing a brain tumor, the lung cancer, as well as several other cancers, having miraculously gone away.

"It might have been cooking on the microwave that cured me," Minerva theorized. "Or else it could have been watching TV. I've heard that TV gives off little rays that are good for curing up cancers."

She had been the prime mover behind the purchase of the satellite dish, in fact. A poor sleeper, she often felt the need for a dose of the little rays during the night. Sometimes Duane would have to get up at three or four in the morning to go deal with a problem at one of the rigs, and would often find Minerva in the den, watching a sex show that had been relayed through the heavens from Copenhagen or somewhere.

Minerva regarded sex shows with considerable skepticism.

"Now I've never seen one that big and I've lived eighty-three years," she said. "It's bigger than that girl's whole head. You think that's done with special effects, or what, Duane?"

"I have no idea," Duane said.

"You ain't really interested in it anymore, are you?" Minerva asked, switching her attention to him.

"Oh, sure," he said. "I'm interested in it."

"No, you ain't," Minerva said. "You ain't, but I am. Not this here show, particularly—I think one that big has got to be special effects. I'd rather watch them Jap wrestlers than stuff like this anytime."

Minerva was a passionate fan of sumo wrestling and would study the cable guide for hours in the hope of locating some.

Driving through the dark toward the rig that had developed the problem, Duane felt a little aggrieved. It was getting so he couldn't turn around without someone reminding him that he was off his feed, sexually. Karla reminded him, Janine reminded him, and now even Minerva was reminding him. His wife and his girlfriend might be expected to notice a lack of appetite, but why was it obvious to Minerva? Duane didn't know.

Next to watching sumo wrestling, the thing Minerva liked to do best was rip into town and charge a couple of hundred dollars' worth of groceries to Karla's account. That was what she had just done.

Duane found both twins playing video games at Sonny Crawford's small video arcade. It was in the rundown building that had once housed the town's pool hall and domino parlor. Sonny had done well with the arcade for a few years, but video glut soon became as widespread as oil glut, and Sonny had been talking of closing it. He had already moved a few of the more popular games into the Kwik-Sack, his convenience store.

Over the years, Sonny had acquired four or five of the buildings around the square, including the old hotel. He only operated the hotel a few nights a year, during the opening days of quail or dove season, when it would fill up with hunters. Otherwise it stood empty and dusty. Ruth Popper had lived on the top floor for a few years, after her husband had tried unsuccessfully to kill her, but then she bought a trailer house and moved out. For most of the year Sonny was the only person in the hotel.

He had no children of his own, and doted on Duane's. He had given each twin two dollars in quarters.

"Just because I threaten to kill you don't mean I'm serious," Duane said, on the ride home. "Running away from home in your bathing suits is not too smart."

"You can get arrested for child abuse," Jack reminded him.

"I wish Nellie would get married and move out," he added. "Those brats of hers squall all the time."

"Barbette is just two months old," Duane said. "She's a baby, not a brat."

"You're a brat," Julie said to her twin. "You're the worst brat that ever lived."

"Lick my dick," Jack said, his standard retort to almost anything his sister said.

Duane tried to imagine what possible discipline might work on the twins. None seemed to stand much chance.

"I'm going to put you out and let you walk home if you keep talking like that," he said. He realized it was an absurd threat, since he had just driven to town in order to prevent the twins from walking anywhere.

Jack still had several of the quarters Sonny had given him. Shorty dozed on the car seat with his head on Duane's leg. Jack grabbed Shorty's tail and began to yank it up and down.

"I'm pretending Shorty's a slot machine," he said, trying to stick one of the quarters up Shorty's ass. Shorty woke up and snapped at him but missed. Duane whacked Jack with his work glove. Shorty cringed, thinking the blow had been meant for him. He was too sleepy to know what was going on.

"Don't treat that dog that way," Duane said.

Jack snickered. The little pop with the glove hadn't hurt at all.

When they got home Karla was wearing a T-shirt that said, I'M NOT DEAF I'M JUST IGNORING YOU. Nellie lay on the couch talking to her boyfriend on the phone.

Joe Coombs, her boyfriend, was a slow talker insofar as he was a talker at all. Joe worked for a well-service company in Jacksboro. He was short and chunky—the work was so dirty that when he got home in the evening he was often almost indistinguishable from a barrel of oil. Home was a small trailer house on the north edge of Thalia, furnished with a bed and a TV set. Joe Coombs didn't believe in spending money on frills.

Joe had a good spirit, though. Just being alive seemed to thrill him, and talking to Nellie on the phone thrilled him so much that he often couldn't think of anything to say for ten or fifteen minutes at a time. Nellie didn't mind. She was not a big talker herself. Just having Joe on the phone gave her a feeling of peace, even though all they did was hold the phones to their ears for long periods of time.

Their nonconversation drove Karla almost crazy.

"Talk!" she said. "One of you talk! He's not saying anything! You're not saying anything! Why don't you get a message machine for a boyfriend? At least a message machine can say a message. That's more than Joe Coombs can do."

"I don't care, Momma!" Nellie said. "I love Joe a whole bunch and he loves me."

"Is Barbette his child by any chance?" Karla asked. Barbette, like Little Mike, bore no resemblance to any of Nellie's husbands.

"Of course not, I never even knew Joe way back then," Nellie said.

Nellie often thought of moving out so she could talk on the phone to Joe without her mother screaming at her. She could easily get an apartment in Wichita Falls, but whether she could get Minerva to come and help her with the kids was another question. Minerva was reluctant to leave the satellite dish. She liked having two or three hundred movies to choose from every day.

Unfortunately, Minerva was the only authority Little Mike respected, mainly because she would haul off and whop him with the *Cable Guide* at the slightest provocation. The *Cable Guide* was to Minerva what the work glove was to Duane—a handy, nonlethal weapon.

Although Karla had on the T-shirt that she wore when she wanted to ignore everybody, the sight of her daughter holding a silent phone to her ear for fifteen minutes at a stretch made it difficult for her to practice what her T-shirt preached.

"Say something!" she yelled. "One of you say something!"

Nellie remained firmly silent. She knew there was no use explaining to her mother how nice it was just to listen to Joe Coombs breathe. There was something very reassuring about the way he breathed when he was on the phone.

It was quite a bit better than the way he breathed in person, Nellie thought. In person he tended to get too excited. But over the phone his breathing had a wonderful effect. Nellie would be feeling tense and Joe would call and breathe into her ear for a while and help her relax. It was almost like magic how much better she felt sometimes if she could just curl up on her bed and listen to Joe breathe for a few minutes.

"Joe just breathes real sweet," she said, talking about it to her girlfriend Billie Anne.

CHAPTER 4

SOMETIMES, DRIVING INTO TOWN—AS HE DID JUST
after he met Ruth Popper on the road—Duane found it hard to
tell whether he was going forward or backward.

The pickup was going forward, of course. He was not yet so
crazy as to drive into town in reverse. And yet, internally, he
ran mostly in reverse. He spent hours replaying old conversations in his head, or reliving past events. If they had
been important conversations or crucial events, the habit might
have been understandable, but they weren't. They were just
ordinary conversations of the kind he had with Karla or
Janine or Sonny Crawford every day. Having such conversations once was enough, yet his brain would sometimes
play them back three or four times, as if his brain was a
cassette player that kept rewinding and replaying unimpor-
tant tapes.

Driving toward his office, he felt depressed by the knowledge that Ruth wouldn't be back for at least half an hour. If he
went to his office he would have no one to talk to and lots of
unpleasant things to think about. He had already thought about

most of them while sitting in the hot tub and had no desire to do more thinking that morning.

Just inside the city limits he passed his own pipeyard with the four towering rigs sitting in it, representing doom. They were all deep rigs and had cost nearly three million dollars apiece. One of them had occasionally been used to drill a well, but the other three had never been out of the pipeyard where they were built. Looking on the bright side—as everyone constantly advised him to do—he could tell himself how lucky he was that there weren't *ten* rigs sitting there accumulating rust along with interest he couldn't pay.

Lester Marlow, the president of the local bank—and recently indicted on seventy-three counts of bank fraud—had encouraged him to build ten rigs. That had been in the height of the boom, when every headline spoke of the energy crisis. It had been hard to get drills in the ground fast enough to meet the demand for West Texas crude. Duane's four small rigs operated around the clock, month after month, but they could only drill shallow wells. There was plenty of money to be made from shallow wells, and Duane was making as much of it as anyone in the area, but every banker he brushed elbows with assured him that deep oil was the wave of the future. Lester Marlow breezily offered to loan him thirty million dollars to build deep rigs with.

After much brooding, Duane decided to build four. Before they were even completed, the wave of the future knocked him right off the surfboard, along with plenty of other surfers. The energy crisis somehow changed into an oil glut. The four new rigs were dead in the water, or, at least, dead in the pipeyard, but the money it had taken to build them was very much alive, hungrily consuming interest payments of more than one hundred thousand dollars a month.

Lester Marlow's trial for bank fraud was coming up in three months. He was planning to plead ignorance. Everyone in town agreed that he was ignorant but cheerfully assumed that he was headed for prison.

Bobby Lee, who hated Lester for having once repossessed a pickup, argued strongly for the death penalty. Never having worn a white collar, he took a tough line on white-collar crime.

"I'd like to see Lester walk the last mile," Bobby Lee said whenever the subject came up.

"Why, he couldn't walk no mile," Eddie Belt said. "Too fat. I doubt he'd make it three hundred feet."

Eddie, who also worked for Duane, was the local realist.

It was true that Lester Marlow was substantially overweight. As bank president he had been too busy loaning money to participate in the exercise boom. Shuffling through mounds of loan applications was exercise enough. Never skinny, he soon became fat. Then, as the financial horizons darkened, he became fatter. He could be seen at the Dairy Queen every afternoon, eating banana splits in an effort to forget his problems.

Duane pulled up in front of his modest office, but didn't kill the motor or get out. Across the street were the new municipal tennis courts, the latest addition to the Thalia skyline. The west edge of town was so flat and ugly that a tennis net could legitimately count as an addition to the skyline.

The tennis courts were another product of the brief popularity of exercise. Built during the height of the boom, the courts were in constant use for several months. But tennis proved more complicated than jogging or sitting in hot tubs. Several marriages that were about ready to go anyway collapsed under the unaccustomed stress of mixed doubles. Now the courts were little used. Duane, who played decent tennis, kept a racquet in his office. Sometimes he would go over in the late afternoon and serve a bucket of balls at the tumbleweeds piled up against the north fence.

Rather than go into the empty office, he turned the pickup around and drove to the Dairy Queen. It was ringed with pickups, many of them belonging to his employees. Bobby Lee was there, and also Eddie Belt.

When Duane got out, Shorty put his front paws on the dashboard and watched him closely. Although Duane went into the Dairy Queen at least twice a day and always came out sooner or later, Shorty was anxious while he was gone. Shorty liked to keep Duane in sight, which was hard to do once he entered the Dairy Queen. By pressing his head against the glass of the windshield, Shorty could catch wavery glimpses of him through the plate-glass windows of the Dairy Queen. It was better than nothing.

The Dairy Queen was filled with the usual hard-bitten but dejected crowd—nouveau riche only a few months earlier, now nouveau bankrupt.

"I see you brought your land shark," Eddie Belt said, when Duane took his seat at the oilmen's table. Eddie was referring to Shorty, who could be seen through the big plate-glass window, his head still flattened against the windshield.

It was a remark Duane heard several times a week. Bobby Lee, whose wit was often indebted to *Saturday Night Live*, had once referred to Shorty as a land shark, and the phrase had caught on. Shorty was hated throughout the oil patch for his habit of unannounced attacks. He would lie motionless in the pickup seat for hours, looking like a dog that had had a sunstroke, but if some roughneck or old friend of Duane's so much as leaned an elbow against the pickup, Shorty would strike, instantly and unerringly. He preferred to nip heels, but would make do with elbows, as most of the people who worked for Duane had learned to their sorrow.

"Good morning," Duane said. He had no interest in defending Shorty or in talking about him at all. The thought that most of the people he knew could think of nothing to talk about except the bad habits of his dog often depressed him.

Junior Nolan was looking particularly low. Junior was fair-skinned, and his forehead had sunburned a fiery red. He wore a cowboy hat when he was in the Dairy Queen but often forgot to put it on when he was outside. It could usually be found on the seat of his pickup.

Junior had made so much money in the oil business that he had been able to buy a ranch and realize his lifelong dream, which was to be a cowboy. Unfortunately he had to run his ranch almost alone, since most of the cowboys in the area had long since given up and gone to work for oil companies. Junior made do with one ranch hand, an elderly chain-smoker named Mitch Mott, who was sitting beside his boss chain-smoking when Duane sat down.

"Mitch, I thought you quit smoking," Duane said.

"I did," Mitch said, lighting a cigarette off the one he was just finishing. "I quit for part of last week. But then I got down in the dumps and the first thing I knew I was smoking again."

Junior Nolan was well on his way to losing his oil company

and his ranch too. He was six foot five, one of the tallest men in the county. Karla had often expressed an interest in him, but so far little seemed to have come of her interest.

"I'll be damned if I'll make the first move," she told Duane, during one of the many discussions they had about her love life. "I don't see why I should."

"I don't see why you should either, honey," Duane said. Some of his lighter moments were spent in the hot tub with Karla, discussing her love life. It was her view that she didn't have nearly enough of one.

Duane felt vaguely guilty about it, but only vaguely. He was too worried about going broke to give even lip service to the notion that he should be providing someone with a love life.

Janine Wells, his girlfriend, was sitting a table or two away, having coffee with her girlfriends from the courthouse. Janine had got herself elected county tax collector. She was a petite blonde, and also a complainer on the subject of a love life.

Duane was glad that he and Janine had agreed to ignore one another in public. Or he guessed he was glad: sometimes he thought he would have done better to strike a deal allowing him to ignore her in private. Their last tryst or two had been uneventful from Janine's point of view, although Duane had taken two much-needed naps.

"You're not supposed to ignore me in private, just in public," Janine corrected, when he woke up from one of them. They were at an expensive hotel in Fort Worth, and were planning to go to a dinner theater and see a play starring Jack Palance.

"I'm not ignoring you, we're in Fort Worth," he pointed out.

"Duane, stop acting dumb," Janine said. "If you're worried about Karla, you don't have to be because she's having an affair with Junior Nolan."

"How do you know that?" Duane asked, wishing he hadn't agreed to go to the play. It would be delicious just to sleep for another few hours.

"Everybody knows it but you, Duane," Janine said.

Everybody would have to include Ruth Popper, who kept well informed about local love affairs. The Monday after his visit to Fort Worth, Duane asked Ruth if she thought Karla was having an affair with Junior Nolan. Ruth had worked for him fifteen years, and Duane was not afraid to speak frankly to her. Ruth herself was not afraid to speak frankly to anyone.

"No, he's too tall," Ruth said, when she heard the question.

"I thought women liked tall men," Duane said.

"That's a myth," Ruth said. She had extremely firm opinions on what was myth and what wasn't.

"Women like nice men," she added.

"Junior seems pretty nice," Duane said. "He's got a nice wife and nice kids. If wife swapping ever becomes a fad around here, like exercise was, I hope to swap for Suzie Nolan myself."

"Karla's an above-average wife," Ruth said.

She had been unhappy most of her life, but was being rewarded with a happy old age.

"Can't a tall man be nice?" Duane asked. He had always felt slightly envious of tall men in the belief that women liked them better.

"Any size man can be nice," Ruth said. "But a worried man is not going to be as nice as a man with peace of mind. I think what Karla needs is a man with peace of mind."

"I guess that leaves Sonny," Duane said.

Ruth looked at him sternly.

"Sonny has resignation," Ruth said. "He doesn't care whether he lives or dies. Resignation is not the same as peace of mind."

"I don't much care if I live or die, with things like they are," Duane said.

"Yes, you do, stupid," Ruth said. "You may think you don't, but you do."

CHAPTER 5

LOOKING ACROSS THE TABLE AT JUNIOR NOLAN, Duane could summon no feeling whatever regarding his presumed affair with Karla. Junior looked very worried, which, as he knew himself, could induce a certain apathy where once romance might have swelled.

The only cheerful person at the table was Luthie Sawyer. Luthie owned a small drilling company and was going broke like everyone else, but he talked so constantly and kept in such perpetual motion that he may not have noticed that detail. Luthie was an eternal optimist, and also an imaginative one. He was always coming up with novel solutions to problems that left everyone else totally stumped.

"I think I've got the answer to this oil glut," Luthie announced, stirring his coffee so rapidly he made a little whirlpool in his cup.

"Good," Duane said. "What's the answer?"

"Let's bomb OPEC," Luthie said. He was a small, vigorous man, deeply suntanned.

"Well," Duane said, noncommittally.

Bobby Lee and Eddie Belt looked thoughtful.

"Napalm it or use H-bombs?" Bobby Lee asked.

Luthie evidently hadn't got that far in his planning.

"I don't know if you could buy an H-bomb," he said.

"Why couldn't you buy one?" Eddie Belt asked. "It's still a free country, ain't it?"

"I don't think you'd need nuc-lar weapons," Luthie said. "I think regular bombs would do it."

"If this means getting drafted, I pass," Bobby Lee said.

"No army in the world would take you," Eddie Belt said. He and Bobby Lee were longtime rivals.

"Don't you remember Ross Perot?" Luthie said. "They stuck some of his engineers in jail and he just hired himself some mercs and got 'em out."

"What's a merc?" Mitch Mott wanted to know.

"You know, mercenaries," Luthie said.

The hated name of H. Ross Perot, the billionaire computer baron and educational reformer, rang like a bell in the dining room of the Dairy Queen.

Several people gave the oilmen hostile looks for having uttered it. Every time the door swung open they could all hear a low chant from the direction of the high school, three blocks away. Spring training was in progress and the squad members of the ever-hopeful Thalia Thistles were doing calisthenics under a blistering sun.

Thanks to the state's new no-pass, no-play law, students failing even one course could not participate in extracurricular activities during the six weeks following the failure. H. Ross Perot had done all he could to lobby the bill through, and it was ruefully admitted that he could do a lot.

What it meant for the Thalia Thistles was that many of the young men now sweating through calisthenics would fail off the team at the end of the first testing period, making it doubtful that the high school could even field a complete team.

Critics of the Thistles, whose record over the past decade showed three wins, two ties, and seventy-four losses, argued that Thalia seldom fielded a complete team anyway, but their mutterings went unheard. Rage like a wall of flame had swept the state in the wake of no pass, no play. The injustice of having teenagers sit in class all day learning boring things that their own parents often had not the slightest interest in was keenly felt.

"I'd rather just go bomb Ross Perot's offices," Bobby Lee said. His position on no pass, no play was not in doubt.

Duane, a closet advocate of the new law, kept his thoughts to himself. Occasionally he daydreamed about how nice it would be if his children got educations. He imagined Dickie becoming a lawyer instead of a criminal; of Jack and Julie being the first Texas twins to graduate from Harvard. Even in his sweetest daydreams he couldn't produce a diploma for Nellie, but there were the grandkids to hope for. Maybe one of them would want to get educated.

In public he confined himself to an occasional ambiguous murmur. The hometown newspaper argued that no pass, no play was the most serious issue to confront the town since the Civil War, ignoring the fact that Thalia had been blank prairie until two decades after Appomattox.

The fear haunting every parent's mind was that if their young ones were denied the right to play sports, twirl batons, lead cheers or blow horns in the band, they would quit school immediately and sit around the house forever, watching TV.

"How come Ross Perot ain't going broke like everybody else up here?" Eddie Belt asked. "You think he's a communist?"

"He's not in the oil business," Duane pointed out.

"I don't like no son-of-a-bitch that's that much richer than me," Bobby Lee said.

"It might not cost but a few hundred thousand to bomb OPEC," Luthie said, returning to his plan.

"I don't think OPEC is a place," Duane said.

Luthie looked hurt. He had always been thin-skinned. Bombing OPEC had seemed like a simple solution to everyone's problems. All the papers made it clear that OPEC was responsible for the oil glut. But Duane's remark shook his confidence.

"I thought it was over there by Kuwait somewhere," Luthie said.

"Mexico don't belong, but Venezuela does," Duane pointed out.

"Oh, shit, don't bomb Mexico, it'd just spread them germs," Eddie Belt said. He had been to Mexico twice and had caught inconvenient diseases both times.

"I don't want none of them germs coming around me," he said, as his memories grew more vivid.

After that, conversation lagged. It was as if the various patrons of the Dairy Queen had been overtaken for a moment by events too sobering for words. The only sound was the sound of Janine popping her bubble gum—a sound that made Duane feel tense, for some reason. Janine had never given up bubble gum, though it contrasted sharply with the polished, sophisticated image she felt was required of her as an elected official. Duane knew she was watching him. She watched him constantly, but without finding out much. Janine could not be said to be a very advanced student of male behavior.

"Do you think women want it more than men?" Junior Nolan asked suddenly, staring at a saltshaker.

The table was collectively stunned. Only Duane smiled. Everyone else stirred their coffee thoughtfully, embarrassed that Junior had seen fit to ask such a question.

"Want what more?" Bobby Lee asked, though he knew perfectly well what "it" meant.

"Uh, sexual intercourse," Junior said sadly.

The coffee in several cups was again thoughtfully stirred. Duane had already finished his, and chose to sit back and hear how the company responded to Junior's surprising question.

Just at that moment Sonny Crawford walked in, a copy of *The Wall Street Journal* tucked under his arm.

CHAPTER 6

TWENTY-SEVEN YEARS BEFORE, WHEN COACH POP-per, Ruth's husband, had found out that she and Sonny were having an affair, he had fired three shots at Sonny with his deer rifle as Sonny was crossing the street in front of the courthouse. The first shot hit Sonny in the elbow, causing damage that had never been completely repaired.

The coach's second shot missed Sonny but hit Ennis Lyons, who had been sitting on an old tractor tire outside his filling station. Ennis often took naps sitting on the big tire, which sat beside a largish pile of used tires that Ennis kept around because he could never find the time to haul them off. The shot knocked Ennis back into the tires and caused his greasy little cap to fall over his eyes.

Since Ennis could often be found sprawled out sound asleep on the tire pile, it was several hours before anyone noticed that he was soundly dead. Gene Farrow, an oilman needing gas, stepped over to complain about the slow service and made the discovery.

The coach's third shot went wild and, so far as had been

discovered, killed no one. He then drove around to the beauty parlor, where Ruth was getting a permanent, and fired two shots into it, hitting no one but ruining a dryer.

Gene Farrow and his wife, Lois, died four months later when their small plane crashed a few miles south of Ruidoso, New Mexico, where they had planned to take in the horse races.

While awaiting trial, Coach Popper was discovered to have lung cancer. He died scarcely a month later, a bitter man. His bitterness was compounded by the knowledge that not only had Ruth, his treacherous wife, had breast cancer and survived it, but had managed to have an affair with Sonny while she had it.

"I wish I'd shot straighter, but it was windy," he said to several people.

Nobody particularly missed the coach, though the whole county had been looking forward to the trial. That fall, to everyone's surprise, the football team blazed through its schedule like a comet and went on to win state in its division, a thing so unexpected that many felt it must have religious significance.

In a few years the shooting was all but forgotten, remembered principally by Sonny, who went to Dallas periodically to have his elbow operated on.

Now he got himself some coffee and came over to the oilmen's table, though he wasn't an oilman.

"Good morning," he said politely. Sonny was, by general agreement, the most polite man in town.

"Junior wants to know if women need more sex than men," Duane said.

"I didn't say need it, exactly," Junior said, blushing into his sunburn.

"Don't look at me, I'm a bachelor," Sonny said.

"We need the bachelor perspective," Duane said. "Mitch is a bachelor too. What do you think about it, Mitch?"

"Duane, I wouldn't know," Mitch said. "I've mostly done without, except during rodeos."

Duane glanced over at the ladies from the courthouse, avoiding Janine's steely blue eyes. He had an urge to invite them to join in the conversation, if it ever became a conversation.

He wondered what had prompted Junior to ask such a question. His wife, Suzie Nolan, was a lovely woman, quiet and seemingly demure. She had lived in Thalia all her life, graduating in the same class as Duane and Sonny.

In those years she had been overshadowed by Jacy Farrow, only child of Lois and Gene, and Duane's own first love. Jacy had overshadowed every female in town except her own mother, and had been Sonny's first love too. Their graduating class was planning its thirtieth reunion that summer, and everyone wondered if Jacy would attend.

Through the years she had only returned to Thalia for a weekend or a holiday now and then. She lived in Italy, where she had been a minor movie star. In March she had returned to Thalia, driven home, some said, by the death of her youngest child, a six-year-old named Benny, who had been electrocuted in a freak accident on a movie set.

So far Jacy had rarely been seen in town. She lived in the house of a friend, twenty miles in the country. The friend, a screenwriter named Danny Deck, lived in Europe and kept an eye on Jacy's two daughters, who were both almost grown. Danny Deck had grown up near Thalia but had not gone to high school there.

No one understood why Jacy was a movie star in Italy and not in America, or why she had had all her children by Frenchmen, if she lived in Italy, or why she had chosen to stay in the house of a man who lived in Europe with her daughters, while her own parents' large house stood empty. Besides inheriting the house, she had also inherited Farrow Oil, a solid little company Duane would have liked to buy. It consisted of the many leases Gene Farrow had managed to acquire during his lifetime—leases which still produced a few hundred barrels of oil a day.

In the flush years he had often thought of flying over to Europe and making Jacy an offer for the oil company. It was a plan Karla adamantly opposed—not the part about him buying the oil company, but the part about him going to Europe to see Jacy Farrow. Karla and Jacy had never met, Karla having moved to Thalia just after Jacy left.

Duane was careful to point out, as unemotionally as possible, that what he had in mind was strictly a business deal. He had a chance to get Gene Farrow's production, and if he didn't, somebody else would.

"No, they won't, she'll keep it herself and spend it in Paris buying clothes," Karla said. At that time her favorite T-shirt read, LEAD ME NOT INTO TEMPTATION, I'LL FIND IT FOR MYSELF.

"You don't need to go all that way to look for temptation, in case you've missed the point of my T-shirt," she said.

Duane was becoming a little irked at having to read a message every time he looked at his wife.

"There's not enough temptation in Thalia," he said.

"There's me," Karla said. "That's all the temptation you get, Duane."

Only Sonny Crawford had really seen Jacy since her return. Once in a while she would show up at his little convenience store in the middle of the night and look through the few magazines that Sonny stocked.

"Is she as beautiful as ever?" Duane asked.

"She never takes off her dark glasses," Sonny said. "She's beautiful, but she's older."

Just after they graduated from high school Duane and Sonny had had a terrible fight over Jacy, a fight that cost Sonny an eye. Since then they had tried to tread lightly where she was concerned—it wasn't hard, since she had been out of both their lives for thirty years.

Duane had glimpsed her only once since her return. He had been parked at a light in Wichita Falls and her Mercedes crossed in front of him. He had only a glimpse, but even a glimpse made him feel strange. He had been very in love with Jacy once. After glimpsing her he felt rather withdrawn—a fact that Karla noticed.

"What's wrong with you?" she asked.

"Nothing—more of the same," Duane said, though it wasn't more of the same, nor was it nothing. He was aware that he probably wouldn't know what to say to Jacy if they did meet. She was like a local Garbo—it was hard to imagine having a conversation with her.

Looking at the distressed Junior Nolan, Duane reflected that he had not really had a conversation with Suzie Nolan in thirty years either, though she had been right there in Thalia all the

while. She was one of the loveliest women in town, but for
some reason had made no mark on his imagination until her
husband asked the question about sex.

He remembered someone, Karla probably, saying that Suzie
had no personality, which probably just meant that she wasn't
like Karla. If there was such a thing as personality glut, Karla
had it. The night before, she had worn a T-shirt that said, LIFE'S
TOO SHORT TO DANCE WITH UGLY MEN, a motto that dated from
the days when Karla had first learned of the concept of open
marriage. She read about it in *Cosmo,* the source of many of
her concepts.

She had immediately opened theirs up by having an affair
with the carpenter who was redoing their kitchen. Then she
griped at Duane because he wouldn't go out and start a recip-
rocal affair.

"You'd rather sit there and make me feel guilty," Karla said.

The main result of that episode was that sloppy work got
done and nothing in the new kitchen really worked right. The
garbage disposal functioned more like a fountain, spewing
chicken bones and watermelon rind all over the place.

"I guess Richie was so in love he couldn't even put in a
garbage disposal right," Duane said, on occasions when he felt
aggrieved.

"Duane, he wasn't supposed to do the plumbing too," Karla
said.

The open marriage concept remained popular for several
years, during which time Duane often irritated Karla by his
refusal to find a girlfriend. But when he finally started the affair
with Janine, Karla accused him of being out of step with the
times.

"Duane, all that stuff was popular in the sixties," she said.
"How come you're doing it now? If you're planning to have a
midlife crisis you should have done it sooner, because you're
already past the middle by several years."

"I'm just forty-eight," Duane pointed out. "If I live to be
ninety-six, then I'm right square in the middle this year."

"I hope I'm not around when you're ninety-six, grumpy as
you are now," Karla said.

"You're the one that started all this," Duane reminded her.
"Why couldn't you just have picked a better carpenter?"

"We're supposed to be rich, why can't we just buy a new garbage disposal?" Karla countered.

Duane didn't answer, but the fact that he hated Richie's kitchen was one reason he had agreed to the building of the new house.

CHAPTER 7

JUNIOR NOLAN HAD NOT TAKEN HIS EYES OFF THE saltshaker since asking his unexpected question—a question which had given his tablemates a bad surprise. The specter of female need had been raised, and the response of most people at the table was to look discreetly away.

Junior himself abruptly decided not to wait for opinions, since none had been forthcoming in almost a minute.

"Mitch, we better hit it," he said. "It ain't getting any cooler outside." He got up and headed for the door, carrying his hat in his hand. Duane saw him toss it in his pickup.

"How come Junior only wears a hat inside?" Eddie Belt asked.

"He's always been a little eccentric," Sonny said.

Mitch Mott got up and ambled out, trying to walk bow-legged. He affected the walk of a lifelong cowboy, but for most of his life he had been a short-order cook who rodeoed a little on the side. Junior had gone up to the Panhandle to buy some calves, had met Mitch at a small rodeo, mistaken him for a cowboy and hired him on the spot.

Since he had lived in Thalia for a mere ten years, Mitch was not deeply versed in its lore, which only a lifetime's residence could make intelligible—and sometimes not then.

Duane had spent a lifetime there and still found much of what went on to be incomprehensible, but he didn't care. He was beginning to find the thought of Suzie Nolan interesting. After all, as he knew better than most, what looked demure from one angle might not look so demure from another. Janine Wells sat just behind him looking like the woman who invented Sunday school, while in fact possessing the heart of a slaver.

"Maybe Junior should call up Dr. Ruth," Sonny suggested.

One reason Sonny's little Kwik-Sack did such a booming business at night was because he took the night shift himself and kept the radio tuned to Dr. Ruth Westheimer's popular call-in show, *Sexually Speaking*. He kept the radio turned up loud so that all the customers could hear it, even if they were back in the far corner by the detergents. Roughnecks and truck drivers, stepping in to buy cigarettes or beer, would fall under the spell of Dr. Ruth's brisk Central European voice; often they lingered for fifteen or twenty minutes, piling up item after item they didn't need, while Dr. Ruth discussed the pros and cons of anal intercourse or offered helpful tips on how not to drip too much spit into one's partner's mouth while tongue kissing.

"Hell, let's get the women in on this," Duane said, suddenly feeling in an impish mood for the first time in months.

"They're the ones who know the answer," he added.

Sonny smiled when he said it. Sonny could smile without looking one bit less sad, a fact that had bothered Duane slightly during all the years of their friendship.

Elsewhere around the table the suggestion met with something akin to panic. Bobby Lee nearly swallowed the toothpick he had been masticating for the last ten minutes.

"I don't think we ought to ask them," he said. "They're women."

"Well, wasn't Junior asking about women?" Duane said.

Eddie Belt, who rarely agreed with Bobby Lee about anything, agreed with him this time. "If Junior wants to know, let

Junior ask them," Eddie said. "I ain't gonna ask one of them nothing."

He started to shut up, but then remembered the many injustices he had suffered at the hands of women.

"I wouldn't ask one of 'em for a Dr. Pepper if I was dying of thirst," he said. "I wouldn't ask them to connect the hose if my house was burning down. If both my legs was broke and one offered me a wheelchair I wouldn't take it."

"What's he raving about?" Janine said. She and her friends, Charlene Duggs and Lavelle Bates, were on their way out, but Eddie's outburst had been delivered in such a loud voice that they all stopped. Janine had the bold urge to chat with Duane a minute and felt that Eddie Belt, whom she couldn't stand, had provided her with a sufficient excuse.

"I wasn't raving about nothing, and if I was, it was none of your business," Eddie said. His memories had raised him to such a pitch of outrage that he forgot for a moment that he was talking to his boss's girlfriend.

"That's not very polite," Janine said crisply. "I just asked."

"You girls sit down," Duane said, jumping to his feet. He was not willing to be cheated of his first impish mood in months. Who knew when he would see another?

He secured chairs so quickly that the women were nonplused.

"Duane, we just got up," Charlene said. "We got jobs to do. We ain't allowed to sit back down."

"Yeah, you ought to been doing the jobs all this time instead of sitting there telling lies," Eddie said. Once he got up a headful of outrage, it took it a while to drain.

"What'd he do, take an ugly pill this morning?" Janine asked.

Some years earlier she and Eddie had been engaged for three months. Over the years Janine had indulged in a number of engagements, complete with rings and the selection of wallpaper. She had been responsible for some of the very episodes Eddie was remembering with such ire, but Janine had undergone two years of very helpful therapy with a psychologist in Wichita Falls. The therapist had taught her how unproductive it was to dwell on past mistakes.

One mistake nobody could ever accuse her of dwelling on

was Eddie Belt. She had traded in his engagement ring for a bracelet she liked, and when they met she treated him with cool formality. The one time he reproached her for this coolness she pointed out that she had only been practicing good mental health, and recommended that he try to do the same.

"You never cared no more for me than a bug," Eddie had said bitterly.

"We'll both get over it quicker if we try to keep a positive attitude," Janine said.

"I been over it for years, you whore!" Eddie said.

Janine realized then that he was a man on whom tact was wasted, and had refrained from wasting another ounce on him after that.

Therapy was the one thing she had in common with Sonny Crawford, who had driven to Fort Worth once a week and seen a psychiatrist. No one could tell that he was the least different as a result; the general view was that he would have done better to try and get a girlfriend.

Karla had gone to a psychiatrist twice and concluded that he was too bossy, which didn't surprise Duane.

"You won't take my advice either," he said.

"Why should I pay ninety dollars an hour to be griped at when you'll do it for nothing?" Karla said.

Since Duane had pulled up chairs, the ladies from the courthouse all sat down. All of them had worked there since graduating from high school. It occurred to Charlene and Lavelle that it was a fine opportunity to see how Duane and Janine behaved toward one another in public. At the very least it would provide meat for analysis.

Luthie Sawyer nodded to the ladies, got up and left, a hurt look on his face. The fact that his plan to bomb OPEC had bombed in Thalia was clearly a letdown.

"We hurt that old boy's feelings," Duane said. "He had a scheme cooked up to keep us from all going broke."

"Oh, you ain't going broke, you just like to feel sorry for yourselves," Janine said.

She knew that a person in good mental health didn't dwell on the bad things that might happen. Her view was that the oil business was just in a lull between booms. By the time she and Duane got married he would be richer than ever.

"What was you men talking about that's so important we have to neglect our jobs to hear about it?" she asked.

Bobby Lee had recovered from his moment of panic. He was one of the few men in town who had not been engaged to Janine. He felt she was nowhere near smart enough to get Duane away from Karla—therefore he had little to fear from her.

"We was talking about sex," he said.

"We knew that, we ain't dumb," Charlene said.

"Junior Nolan was wondering whether women want more sex than men," Duane said. "When I was growing up the boys all wanted it and the girls didn't. Now it's the other way around. I wonder why that is."

Charlene laughed. She had been married three times, but all three husbands had died after only modest use.

"We've got prettier and you'all have gotten uglier," she said.

It was certainly true that Charlene had gotten prettier. She had been overweight and sloppy as a teenager, but had turned into a good-looking woman.

"Men are all wimps anyway," Lavelle Bates said. She was a tall, raw-boned brunette who had recently become the first employee of the Thalia courthouse to go to a Club Med on her vacation. It gave her a slight aura of mystery, and even a slight aura had proven enough to intimidate local suitors. The Club Med had not been very eventful romantically, but at least she had got to snorkel. Since coming back she hadn't got to do anything.

"If any woman wants much she's out of luck around here," she said, looking pointedly at Bobby Lee, who had been flirting with her for the last several years in his languid fashion.

Janine tried to look thoughtfully aloof. It was the first time since the affair began that she had sat in public with Duane unless they were out of town. She found that she liked being in public with him. It was good for her self-esteem, the thing she had had to work on most assiduously with her therapist. The men she had been engaged to thought she had far too much self-esteem, while her therapist thought she had much too little.

"I think they should need it equal, the males and the females, don't you, Duane?" she asked.

Being able to sit in public with him raised her self-esteem to the highest pitch in her memory.

"There ain't a man alive that can think up as much dirt as a woman," Eddie Belt said.

"He must have taken two ugly pills this morning," Janine said. "Ugly as he is, he isn't usually *this* ugly."

Janine had a sense that she was finally getting the situation to swing her way. The sense was so strong that she casually put an arm across Duane's shoulder, a move not lost on anyone in the Dairy Queen. Even the cook was watching from behind a stack of taco shells.

"All I know is, men are scaredy-cats," Lavelle said.

"I figure the average man tells at least a million lies a year," Charlene observed.

"You women won't stick to the point," Duane said. "All we're trying to find out is whether you girls want it more than us boys."

"In the first place, you ain't boys," Lavelle said. "You look half dead to me."

"That's what being middle-aged means," Sonny said. "You're on the downhill slope."

"I ain't, and besides I've got my brakes on," Bobby Lee said. He was five years younger than Sonny and Duane and objected to being lumped with them. He didn't care for the downhill-slope concept either.

"What's it say about it in *The Wall Street Journal?*" Duane asked.

Sonny liked to buy penny stocks. He generally spent an hour or two each morning at the DQ picking through the *Journal*. He wasn't rich by any means, but he owned the laundrymat, the Kwik-Sack, the video parlor, four or five buildings and a recently installed carwash.

"It doesn't say a word about the problem," he said.

"I can't believe we have to pay taxes to the county so these women can sit here and talk about stuff like this," Eddie Belt said.

"Stuff like what?" Karla asked, materializing suddenly at Eddie's elbow.

CHAPTER 8

THOUGH EVERYONE ELSE AT THE TABLE WAS FRO-
zen with horror, Duane could hardly keep from laughing out
loud. He alone had seen Karla's BMW whip past the drive-in
window a minute earlier. Karla was impatient with the drive-
in window, as well as with other forms of service at the DQ.

What she usually did was park behind the building, come in
the back door, gossip a minute with the cook, sniff the nacho
dip to see if it met with her approval and pour herself some
fresh coffee before anyone in the dining room even knew she
was around. If there was no one there with whom she felt like
gossiping, she could cut back out the rear exit and be on her
way to wherever her mood took her.

Duane had decided to give Janine lots of rope and see if
Karla could hang her. He knew it wasn't a charitable thing to
do, but then he was not always in the mood to be charitable
toward Janine. Without bothering to ascertain whether he
planned to divorce Karla and marry her, Janine had told him
not to plan any custody fights because she had no intention of
living with his kids.

"Living with your kids wouldn't be my idea of a good time," she told him, as nicely as possible.

"It isn't anybody's idea of a good time," Duane said. "But they're my kids. I have to try and raise them."

"They're giving fathers real generous visitation rights," Janine pointed out. "Maybe Karla will move to Ruidoso and you can visit them up there."

In her thoughts Janine often moved Karla to some fashionable but distant place such as Ruidoso or Vail. Even during the brief conversation she had been vaguely moving Karla around, making it all the more a shock to see her standing behind Eddie Belt, very much present. Karla was wearing sunglasses, so there was no way of knowing what she was thinking, but then Janine didn't care to know what a person like Karla thought.

Duane, who just seemed to get the devil in him from time to time, wasn't a bit of help. He could have asked Karla what she thought she was doing, showing up at the Dairy Queen unannounced, but instead he just sat there grinning.

Janine withdrew her arm from Duane's shoulder as smoothly as possible, well aware that if Karla had happened to walk in with a chain saw the arm would be lying on the floor already.

"Hi, Janine," Karla said. "Haven't seen you in a long time."

"I hardly ever leave the courthouse," Janine said. "The only people who see me are people with overdue taxes."

Karla seemed to be happy as a lark, although she hadn't taken off her sunglasses.

"Why are you looking so red in the face, Eddie Belt?" she asked. "Were you talking about sex? I've noticed the mere mention of sex turns you red in the face."

"You don't have to call me by my whole name," Eddie pointed out. "You've known me all my life."

Eddie had a hard time concealing the fact that he was deathly afraid of Karla—more afraid of her than he would have been of a cobra. You could run from a cobra, but where could you run from Karla, if you happened to work for her husband?

"Now don't pick on Eddie," Duane said. "We've just been discussing whether women like sex more than men, or what."

"We didn't reach a decision yet," he added.

"In fact we haven't got very far in the discussion," Sonny said. It worried him that Duane would sit there practically egging on his wife and his girlfriend. Duane had that streak in him. In certain moods, he would take any risk. His daring made Sonny nervous—he didn't enjoy watching it operate. He himself preferred to avoid confrontations and had arranged his life so it didn't contain many.

"Bobby Lee's just a Peeping Tom, so he shouldn't get a vote," Karla said.

"I ain't, I'm married," Bobby Lee protested.

Pretending her finger was a piece of chalk, Karla marked a few scores in the air.

"Sonny's a bachelor, Eddie Belt's scared of women, and Duane says himself he's past his prime. I don't know if it's fair to judge the whole male sex by this ugly little bunch."

"Yes, it's fair," Lavelle said. "I lived in Olney twenty years, and men ain't no better down there."

"I ain't scared of women and you ain't no Gina Bardot yourself," Eddie Belt snapped, wishing he'd never stopped at the Dairy Queen in the first place.

"Brigitte Bardot," Sonny corrected.

Janine could hardly believe Duane would sit there and let his own wife insult him so bluntly. Ordinarily she would have thought it meant he suffered from low self-esteem, but Duane was tricky and couldn't really be understood in terms of self-esteem.

"I may get a second wind any day now," he said, grinning.

"Duane, you used up all your winds years ago," Karla said.

"I wish I could just sit here all day, but some of us have to work," Janine said, standing up. Charlene and Lavelle were reluctant to leave until they had heard what Karla had to say to Duane out of earshot of Janine, but they didn't have much choice. Fortunately the cook was still listening from behind the taco shells and they knew they could get a full report from her.

"If you ever figure out who wants it most, let us know," Charlene said. "I've often wondered."

Karla took Eddie Belt's dozer cap off and ruffled his hair to show him there were no hard feelings.

"I know you're not really scared of women," she said. "You're just scared of me, and that shows you got good sense."

"If I had good sense I wouldn't be here," Eddie said, though now that the horrible trio from the courthouse was gone his mood was improving.

"You oughta do like Duane, get you a girlfriend who chews bubble gum," Karla said, still the picture of good cheer.

Duane laughed.

"I don't know what you think you've got to laugh about, Duane," Karla said, smiling at him.

"I was just laughing at nothing," he said. "It's either that or cry about everything, and I wasn't in a crying mood."

Karla put an arm around Sonny, her old friend. From time to time, in years past, she had tried to penetrate his detachment at least enough to get him to flirt with her, but she finally came to accept that his detachment was impenetrable. Since then he had been a stable source of advice, though rarely a source of fun.

"It don't say much for your character that you'd let him sit here with that slut and not do a thing to save our marriage," she said.

"Your marriage isn't in any danger and it never has been," Sonny said.

"Wrong," Karla said. "You'd be surprised how many times it's been in danger."

But she knew it was pointless to talk marriage to Sonny, since his only marriage—to Jacy Farrow—had been one of the shortest, if not *the* shortest, on record.

Legend had it that Sonny and Jacy had only been married an hour when her parents had them picked up by the Highway Patrol. Jacy was immediately sent away and an annulment secured. Local cocksmen sometimes teased Sonny, urging him to try and get into the *Guinness Book of World Records*, but Sonny shrugged off the teasing. He said he imagined there had been marriages even shorter than his, and claimed to have seen an item in the Dallas paper about a bridegroom who dropped dead two seconds after he said "I do."

Karla could hardly imagine Sonny being married even for an hour—it just didn't seem like him. She sometimes called him

Luke, as in Luke the Drifter, because he reminded her of a great many Hank Williams songs.

Lately, to her consternation, and Duane's as well, the drifter part had begun to come true in an ominous way. Sonny's mind had begun to drift off.

Sometimes it only drifted for a second or two: he might be ringing up an item at the Kwik-Sack and forget what he was doing. Usually he would kick back in thirty seconds or so and finish ringing up the sale. But one or two lapses had lasted long enough and become embarrassing enough that the customers had just left money on the counter and gone away.

Several lapses had occurred in the City Council meetings that Sonny presided over once a month. Three or four times he had made a motion and then lost the train completely, sitting with a pleasant look on his face long after the motion had been voted on.

"It's like his brain slips out of gear," Buster Lickle, a Council member, said.

Usually, at such times, the Council could sort of move the agenda around Sonny, who always came back to himself after a few minutes. The general view was that lots of people's brains slipped out of gear more often than Sonny's, and with worse results. He was accorded the tolerance given to absentminded professors, although his college experience had only consisted of a few business courses at a small university in Wichita Falls.

There had been one big lapse, however, which only Duane, Karla and Ruth Popper knew about. Sonny had been in Wichita Falls, eating barbecue at a favorite haunt of his. Upon coming out, he had failed to find his own car—he assumed it had been stolen and called Duane to ask if he could come and get him.

"It was probably just some kids, joyriding," he speculated.

His car was a '72 Plymouth, not the sort of vehicle kids normally went joyriding in. Duane drove over to get him and arrived just in time to see the cops giving him a breath test. The '72 Plymouth was parked almost in front of the door of the barbecue joint. Duane thought the thief might have brought it back, but that was not the case.

"I guess I just sort of overlooked it," Sonny admitted.

The cops had already found out that the only thing Sonny had drunk with his barbecue was a glass of iced tea. He was very embarrassed, but he clearly wasn't drunk.

"Sir, are you on any medication that could affect your vision?" one of the officers inquired.

"No," Sonny said.

"Did you black out, or what?" Duane asked, once the policeman left.

"I don't know what I did," Sonny said. "I just didn't recognize my car."

"It's funny you could remember my phone number and not recognize your own car," Duane said.

Sonny was anxious for Duane to leave. It was the most embarrassing thing that had ever happened to him, and the truth was even more embarrassing than what was obvious. Before calling Duane he had wandered around the parking lot for fifteen minutes, looking for the '46 Chevy pickup he thought he was driving. He had driven such a pickup in high school, but it had fallen apart soon after he graduated; since then he had mostly driven Plymouths.

The most frightening part about his lapse was that his mind had made everything old. There was hardly a vehicle in the parking lot earlier than 1980; but he had wandered among them seeing cars and pickups from the fifties.

And yet, when he called the police, he had given them his current license plate number correctly.

It was as if the door of the barbecue joint—it was called the Dripping Rib—had opened into a former time. By stepping through it he had stepped back into the fifties for several minutes.

For the next few weeks he was careful to take a hard look at his car before going into a restaurant. He didn't want to step through that door again, and he began to avoid the Dripping Rib, although he had eaten there for fifteen years and was friends with all the help.

That night, back home, Duane and Karla discussed the incident at length.

"He could be on mood drugs," Karla said. "His psychiatrist might have given them to him."

"Sonny don't have moods," Duane said.

"Everybody has moods," Karla said.

"Sonny don't," Duane insisted. "He's had the same mood all his life."

"He must have had a mood that day you had the fight over Jacy," Karla said.

"No, *I* had that mood," Duane said. "Sonny just defended himself. He did a poor job of it, too."

"I wish I'd lived here then," Karla said. "I'd like to know what was so good about her."

"We were in high school," Duane pointed out. "There doesn't have to be anything so good about somebody to make you jealous when you're in high school. Look at Dickie. He bought a machine gun just because some old boyfriend sent Billie Anne flowers for her birthday."

"He's still dying to massacre somebody, too," Karla said. "Maybe Sonny's on pills. His father was a pillhead."

"Anything's possible," Duane said, though he didn't think Sonny was on pills.

"If you two were both in love with her, why did Jacy go to Italy in the first place?" Karla asked. The events of Duane's high school years interested her a lot.

"I think she just went with some of her sorority sisters from SMU," Duane said. "I guess she must have liked it."

"They just let her be in Tarzan movies," Karla said.

At times she became obsessed with Jacy Farrow, her unseen rival. About all that anyone in Thalia knew about Jacy's movie career was that she had gained fame playing a character called Jungla in a series of Italian movies. She wore a leopardskin bikini and swung through the trees—or so Bobby Lee said. He had seen one of her movies on late night TV in a motel in Texarkana, while returning home with a load of pipe. No one else in Thalia had ever seen one.

The next morning Duane told Ruth about Sonny's failure to find his car.

Ruth was at her desk, rapidly throwing away the morning's mail. She believed in keeping a clean desk and speedily threw away anything that seemed likely to create clutter. If the drilling company received a hundred letters, Ruth would immediately throw away ninety-five unopened after no more than a cursory glance at their postmarks.

The sight of her blitzing the mail always made Duane nervous. He could never grasp her method, if she had one. Once, when she was out to lunch, he went through the wastebasket himself to see if she could possibly have thrown away any letters with checks in them. She hadn't. When she returned from lunch she glanced at the wastebasket and gave him a severe look. Nothing was said, but from then on, as soon as Ruth went through the mail she put the rejects in a garbage bag and carried it right to the dumpster.

"I think Sonny wants to die," she said, when told about the car incident. "He's never found anything that interested him."

"I thought you interested him once," Duane said.

Ruth looked sad for a moment.

"No, he interested *me*," she said. "He was my only chance at love. I was lucky. He was a very nice boy. But he shouldn't have settled for me. He should have got out of here and looked around."

The Sonny Duane knew seemed only mildly unhappy. Duane found it hard to believe he wanted to die.

"Karla agrees with me," Ruth said, seeing that he looked skeptical.

"Oh, well," Duane said, "if Karla and you agree on something there's no point in the rest of us even having an opinion. There's only about a chance in a million that you and Karla could be wrong."

He wondered if they agreed on anything having to do with him, but Ruth was typing a lease and he didn't ask.

CHAPTER 9

"KARLA'S CHASED OFF ALL THE WOMEN EXCEPT herself," Duane said. "I guess it's time to go to work."

"As soon as you leave I'm gonna pump Sonny like he was an oil well," Karla said.

She made a pumping gesture with her right hand.

"I'll pump until I get you to have total recall of everything Duane said to his girlfriend while I wasn't here," she said.

"That won't take long," Sonny said. "They barely spoke."

"Do you think morals have declined?" Karla asked. "Ten years ago a married man like Duane wouldn't have dared sit right in this Dairy Queen with his girlfriend."

"Ten years ago this Dairy Queen wasn't here," Duane observed.

"There's never been a dollar's worth of morals in this whole county," Eddie Belt volunteered. He was perking up a lot. The decline of local morals was one of his favorite topics.

Duane got up and stepped over to the window. Shorty, ever loyal, still had his head pressed against the windshield although the sun was blazing down. Duane waved at him.

60

Shorty, overjoyed, jumped straight up, bonking himself against the roof of the cab. Then he went into a frenzy, trying to scramble onto the dashboard to be closer to Duane. In his frenzy he knocked pliers, receipts and everything else Duane kept on the dashboard onto the floorboards. Duane laughed. It always cheered him a little to see Shorty leap up like a fish and bonk himself on the roof.

"Laughing at animals is a sign of bad morals, too," Karla said. "Shorty can't help it that he's the stupidest creature on earth."

"What do you expect when a place is nearly a hundred years old?" Sonny said. "Decadence sets in."

"Who's going to the centennial meeting tonight?" Duane asked, since Sonny had mentioned the county's age, a topic on everyone's mind.

Duane was chairman of the Centennial Committee, a position he had accepted at the height of his affluence, when it seemed likely he himself would finance the whole centennial as a charitable act.

Now that his financial position was shaky—a fact known to every single person in Thalia—it was obvious that the centennial would have to be financed some other way. Tickets would have to be sold to the various events, and souvenirs vigorously marketed. Centennial T-shirts were already being made, as well as centennial ashtrays, dozer caps and key chains. There would be concessions, raffles, a carnival, street dances, a pageant that would run for a week, and even a centennial calendar.

The very thought of the centennial had begun to depress those actually responsible for planning it—mainly Duane and Sonny. It had become increasingly difficult to get people to come to the planning meetings, although the celebration was only three months away. "Who's coming to the centennial meeting tonight?" Duane asked again.

Only Sonny raised a hand. As mayor of the town, he spent most of his evenings going to one meeting or another. The week before, in the City Council, there had been hot debate over street names, a flourish the town had done without so far. Some wanted to name streets after pioneers, others after trees. The tree faction won by three votes.

Everyone else stonily ignored Duane's question.

"What happened to the pioneer spirit?" Duane asked.

"Who cares what happened to it?" Eddie Belt said. "I ain't growing no beard, either."

It had been decided to require all adult males in the county to grow beards for the centennial. Many neighboring counties had had their centennials already, and had had a beard requirement. For this one, those refusing to comply faced the danger of being ducked in a water tank situated on the courthouse lawn for that purpose.

"You'll get ducked if you don't grow a beard," Duane warned.

"You're not a dictator, Duane," Karla said. "You can't make people grow beards just because you're chairman of that stupid committee."

"I hate beards," Bobby Lee said. "The whiskers kind of stick into you when you try to sleep at night."

"The people of this county don't deserve a centennial," Duane said. "They're too uncooperative."

"Who asked for the damn thing anyway?" Eddie Belt asked. "I wasn't here a hundred years ago and nobody else was either. What do we care about how the thing got started up?"

"You're supposed to care about your history," Karla said.

"I'd rather forget mine," Bobby Lee said.

The pay phone rang and Louise, the cook, came out from behind her shield of taco shells and answered it.

"It's for Duane or Karla," she said, holding out the receiver.

"I just left," Duane said. "Me and Shorty have urgent business on down the road."

"It could be good news," Bobby Lee said.

"No, it's the police," Louise said.

Karla got up and took the call. Duane looked out the window at Shorty, who was still jumping around.

"Why would you want a dog like that?" Eddie Belt asked. "He's just about torn your whole pickup up."

"He means well, though," Duane said.

Karla hung up and came back to the table, looking only mildly peeved.

"Dickie got arrested for going eighty-five in a school zone," she said. "Not only that, he was pulling a trailer."

"What was in the trailer?" Duane asked. "Bales of marijuana?"

"Dickie might be the first man in history to get longer sentences for traffic offenses than he would for selling dope," Bobby Lee observed.

"You get him out," Duane said to Karla. "I got him out the last three times."

"I might get him out this afternoon," Karla said vaguely.

Duane went to the counter and bought a chocolate milk shake. Shorty loved chocolate milk shakes, and Duane thought he deserved some reward for the long days of boredom spent in the hot pickup.

Karla was wearing her WOMAN'S PLACE IS IN THE MALL T-shirt.

"I think I may go to Dallas and spend a few thousand dollars," she said.

Duane just waved and went out. Shorty jumped out of the pickup to have his milk shake. He was overjoyed to have been remembered. He plunged his nose into the milk shake and pushed the cup all around the parking lot, trying to get the last drop. By the time he had the last drop Duane had already started the pickup and Shorty had to race or be left behind. Sometimes he didn't make it back in time and had to run all the way to the office. It was only four blocks, but it seemed like a long way to Shorty. Fearful that he might never see Duane again, he raced like the wind on his short legs.

But this time Duane waited and Shorty leaped back in the cab.

Karla came out as they were about to drive off.

"Eddie Belt looks depressed," she said. "Do you think he's stable?"

"Do you think *I'm* stable?" Duane asked.

"Duane, you're too stable," Karla said.

CHAPTER 10

RUTH WAS BACK WHEN HE GOT TO THE OFFICE. SHE had taken a shower after her run. Duane thought she looked younger than she had thirty years earlier. Then, marriage to the coach had caused her to seem prematurely aged. Now, at seventy-two, she seemed girlish—a living example of how seldom life turned out to be as advertised.

"Any checks?" Duane asked.

"We finally got thirty-seven thousand from those crooks in Oklahoma, but it's a drop in the bucket," Ruth said. "What do you want me to do with it?"

"Hide it till after lunch," Duane said.

"Lester's called three times," Ruth said. "He said please send over a check for twelve million. He said the Federal regulators are coming today and he needs it."

"He gets nervous at the thought of going to prison," Duane said.

"He said he'd rather have a hot check than none at all," Ruth said. "I feel sorry for Lester."

"I doubt if those Federal regulators are within a hundred miles of here," Duane said.

He went in his office and sat waiting for the phone to ring. While he waited he stared at the beautiful color pictures of his children and wife that filled the office. On paper, particularly photographic paper, his family looked wonderful. All of them were amazingly photogenic. The disparity between how they looked in pictures and how they behaved in real life was a subject for much thought, and Duane had given it not a little in the many long days when the phone rang only once or twice. His conclusion was that the camera lied, although Karla claimed it didn't.

Toward noon, when Duane was still sitting, numb with boredom, the phone did ring. It was Lester Marlow, the beleaguered bank president.

"Wanta have lunch?" he asked. "I'll buy it."

"I'm on a diet," Duane said. "I'm just gonna have a glass of grapefruit juice."

"We need to talk," Lester said.

"We talk every day," Duane reminded him. "I don't have twelve million. If you want my rigs, take them—just leave me in peace."

"You're no help," Lester said, sounding a bit peeved.

"I could send you a check if it wouldn't hurt to postdate it a few years," Duane said.

"Jenny left me this morning," Lester said. Jenny was a tall, frenetic brunette, easily the best female softball player in town.

"Left you and went where?" Duane asked, feeling a flicker of sexual curiosity for the second time that day.

"Well, she hasn't actually moved out of the house yet," Lester said. "She made me take my sleeping bag when I came to work. She says I can sleep on the floor of my office for all she cares."

"Women have a heartless side to them, don't they?" Duane said.

"This whole town's heartless," Lester said. "Nobody's losing any sleep over the fact that I have to stand trial for trying to protect their interests."

"It's about time for my grapefruit juice," Duane said. He didn't think he could stand to listen again to Lester's stories about how hard he had tried to protect people's interests.

"I wish you'd talk to Jenny," Lester said. "She respects you, Duane."

"She's on the Centennial Committee," Duane said. "I guess I'll see her if she comes to the meeting tonight."

Duane had often sat through softball games that he had no interest in, just to watch Jenny Marlow pitch. She had single-handedly increased the attendance at local softball games by several hundred percent. Even people who considered Jenny too opinionated enjoyed watching her pitch.

As a committeewoman she was, if anything, too fertile with ideas. She was in charge of floats, and thought there ought to be a float of the courthouse. Others took the view that there was no need for a float of the courthouse, since the courthouse itself was there for all to see. Jenny was one of the few Republicans in town, and her sense of patriotism extended all the way down to the county level.

"That courthouse is the oldest building in the downtown area," she pointed out. "It's the symbol of the county. It's what unites us as a people. There has to be a float of it."

"I didn't notice that we was even united as a people," Duane said, but he had no real objection to the courthouse float, since Jenny herself would do all the work. She was a whirlwind of energy and for that reason was rarely left out of any civic undertaking. She ran the concessions at football and basketball games with relentless efficiency.

The fact that Duane voted for the courthouse float irritated Karla, who took it as a sign of weakness. Karla thought floats were boring.

"You just let women trample all over you," she said.

"Well, I let *some* women trample all over me," Duane said.

"That's right, pretty ones," Karla said. "I don't notice you doing many favors for ugly girls."

CHAPTER 11

In order to get Lester off the phone, Duane promised to drop by the bank that afternoon. He knew it was in his interest to keep Lester soothed as much as possible.

There was absolutely nothing to do. Two years earlier there would have been fifty people passing through the office every morning—promoters bringing him investors, investors trying to get him to take their money. Now they had vanished, leaving only Ruth.

Duane went out to see what she was doing. As usual, she was writing letters at a furious pace. There was a large stack of letters on her neat desk, each with its envelope stamped and ready beside it.

"Do I need to sign any of these?" Duane asked. He had not dictated any of the letters and had no idea what they concerned.

"If you do I'll ask you," Ruth said, giving him a testy look. She didn't like him interfering with the mail in any way.

Since he rarely saw any of it, the mail Ruth produced worried Duane almost as much as the mail she threw away. She seemed to conduct an elaborate business from his office, but there was no indication that it was *his* business.

Though she knew the secrets of everyone in town, Ruth herself was a total mystery. Since leaving Sonny, nearly twenty-five years before, she had had no visible love life, but she seemed happy and looked fresher every year.

"Maybe she just has hundreds of friends we don't know about," Karla said, when Duane brought up the matter of Ruth's voluminous correspondence.

"She never leaves town," Duane said. "Where would she get hundreds of friends?"

"She leaves town," Karla said. "I see her running up and down these dirt roads all the time."

Duane knew he should just shut up. Nevertheless, he didn't shut up. Little Mike was toddling around trying to hit the cat with a pair of pliers somebody had left in the kitchen. The cat, whose name was Leon, easily eluded Little Mike.

"I don't think Ruth Popper makes hundreds of friends jogging on these roads," Duane said.

Minerva passed through unexpectedly and swatted Little Mike with the *Cable Guide*. He was too surprised to cry.

"I don't know why you think a baby that small needs to play with pliers," she said.

"Duane don't trust Ruth," Karla said, attempting to draw Minerva into the argument.

"Me neither," Minerva said. She flopped down in a chair and began to scan the *Guide*, hoping to find some sumo wrestling.

"Why don't you trust her?" Duane asked.

"Because she lives in a trailer house," Minerva said. "Anything could go on in a trailer house."

"But anything could go on anywhere," Duane said.

Sometimes the arbitrariness with which women took positions made him feel like he might go crazy. Both Minerva and Karla excelled at arbitrary positions.

Little Mike abandoned the pliers and hurried out of the room. He liked to put space between himself and Minerva whenever he could.

Minerva got up, took inventory and discovered they were out

of barbecued pork rinds, a necessity of life as far as she was concerned. She ate them by the thousands while watching TV, washing them down with vodka and grapefruit juice.

"If you're even suspicious of Ruth, I think you ought to get help," Karla said. "There must be a psychiatrist somewhere that you'd like."

"You sure didn't like the one *you* tried," he reminded her.

"I liked him," Karla said. "I just decided I wasn't crazy enough to spend that kind of money on advice. I can get plenty of advice down at the beauty parlor when I want it."

"Having nobody to talk to but you and Minerva and Ruth would drive anybody crazy," Duane said.

When he stepped out of his office, Ruth stopped typing instantly. She insisted on total privacy when she was typing.

"Jenny kicked Lester out," he said.

"I knew that several hours ago," Ruth said. "I saw Jenny at the post office. I think it's a mistake. Jenny's a little vain, and vanity comes before a fall."

She stared at him sternly.

"That makes one more footloose woman in this town," she said. "Suzie Nolan is also footloose now."

"I intend to give them both a wide berth," Duane assured her.

"I don't know why we're even talking about this," he added.

"Because the oil business has gone belly up and there's nothing for you to do except sleep with every woman you can find," Ruth said.

"Could I have a check?" he said. "I think I ought to give Lester a few thousand."

Ruth tore a check out of the checkbook but didn't hand it to him.

"How many thousand?" she asked.

"I haven't decided," Duane said.

"Why don't you go see Jacy?" Ruth said.

Duane was very surprised. Ruth had never so much as mentioned Jacy before.

"I doubt she wants company," he said.

"She might, though," Ruth said. "I would, if I'd lost a child."

"I thought you hated Jacy," he said.

"I don't hold grudges for thirty years," Ruth said. "She was just a girl then. Besides, tragedy changes people. She just sits there alone in that man's big house, grieving for that child. The thought of it preys on my mind."

"I doubt she'd even remember me, Ruth," Duane said.

"You remember her, don't you?" Ruth said. "Why should her memory be worse than yours?"

"I just meant we aren't friends anymore," Duane said, feeling that he was losing an argument he had not expected to be having.

"I think you'd rather pick on footloose wives than go help out a woman you used to love who's had a tragedy," Ruth said. "You're scared you'll fall in love with her again, aren't you?"

"I wouldn't know how to fall in love with anybody," Duane said. "I'm too old for it."

"You never get too old for it," Ruth said.

"I haven't noticed you falling in love lately," he said. "If it's such a fine thing, why don't you do it?"

Ruth just looked at him and smiled. She had long had a little crush on him, and because she was so much older they both were free to enjoy its products.

"I'm too broke to fall in love," Duane added. "I can't get the fact that I owe twelve million off my mind long enough to get serious."

"Ten years from now you might not even remember you had this debt," Ruth said. "But you'll always remember Jacy, and you'll always remember me."

"Why will I have to remember you?" he asked. "Where will you be?"

"I'll be in the afterlife," Ruth said quietly. "I just hope you can find someone competent to keep your books."

Duane took the blank check and stepped out into the blazing sun. Shorty immediately began to jump up and down in the seat and bark his piercing bark.

CHAPTER 12

Duane chickened out on his date with Lester Marlow. He gave the five-thousand-dollar check to the drive-in teller and told her to give it to Lester's secretary. He could see Lester through the bank's big plate-glass windows. He was running his fingers through his hair, and he looked very unhappy. Duane sped off before Lester could spot him—otherwise he might have rushed out and jumped in the cab, annoying Shorty.

Shorty hated it when people rode in the cab. He regarded it as a place that belonged exclusively to himself and Duane. When someone got in he would often snarl ominously and keep on snarling even while Duane was beating him vigorously with the work glove. If it proved impossible to silence him, Duane would sometimes stop, get out and fling Shorty in the back of the pickup for the remainder of the trip.

For Shorty, having to ride in the back of the pickup was the worst conceivable humiliation. The minute Duane flung him in the back, he would press his face against the cab and keep it there, no matter how long the ride, hoping Duane would give him a chance to atone for whatever he had done.

Eluding Lester gave Duane a brief sense of freedom. He decided to skip lunch, since if he went to lunch he would just have to have familiar conversations with familiar people. Not having to sit in the bank and talk to Lester about his debt was such a relief that he felt a little lightheaded.

Lacking firm plans, he spent the afternoon driving idly along the dirt roads of the county, as he often did when he wanted to avoid everyone. It had been a dry spring and the pastures were parched. Even traveling slowly, the pickup threw up clouds of dust. Duane remembered Jimbo Jackson, with whom he had umpired many a Little League ball game. It was in just such dust that Jimbo had met his death. What kept bothering Duane was that Jimbo had been jogging at all. It spoke of sad hopes. Probably Jimbo thought that if he could get slim he could also become happy, and even out of debt. It seemed so sad to Duane that sometimes his eyes would fill up when he thought about it.

Duane could drive for hours with his mind totally blank. The blankness was very restful, a welcome change from the familiar contest in which his mind pitted what he owed against what he could pay. Sometimes, if he crossed a creek that actually had water in it, he would stop and fish a little. Occasionally he caught a sluggish catfish, which he usually threw back. He fished for peace, not for fish.

But even on the backroads of the county it was not possible to get very far from people he knew. The road cut through one of Junior Nolan's pastures, reminding him of Suzie Nolan. In the morning the thought that both she and Jenny Marlow had become, in Ruth's phrase, footloose, aroused a flicker of interest. But it was now afternoon, and when he tried to fantasize something sexual involving either one of them, his imagination was depressingly chaste. It rendered them topless, but not bottomless. He had seen both women hundreds of times, at picnics, barbecues, ball games. He had seen them water-skiing, danced with them at rodeo dances, sat with them at high school plays. Despite it all, he had a paltry stock of images from which to create fantasies—their bosoms faded from view after only a few seconds and a sexless blankness returned.

"I don't know what's wrong with me, Shorty," Duane said out loud.

Shorty was in the middle of a deep nap and merely flicked an ear when he heard his name.

All of Duane's small rigs were working. From time to time he liked to drop in on his crews unexpectedly to see how many he could catch loafing on the job.

Bobby Lee's rig was down in the post oaks near the bottom of the county. When Duane drove up, Bobby Lee and four roughnecks were standing around looking dejected. The very sight of them made Duane wish he hadn't come. No matter when he went out to one of his rigs, day or night, winter or summer, the crew would be standing around looking dejected.

"If I wanted to see depressed people I could have stayed in the bank," Duane said. "At least it's air-conditioned."

"Broke a bit," Bobby Lee said hopelessly.

"Unheard of!" Duane said, trying to joke a little. Broken bits were a fact of life in the oil business.

Bobby Lee looked near tears, and the four roughnecks stared at Duane dully. A red ice chest full of beer sat on the tailgate of Bobby Lee's pickup. The roughnecks were very oily. Duane decided that one advantage to going broke would be that he wouldn't have to look at so many oily people in the course of a day.

"We were just a hundred feet from being down—why did that sonofabitch have to break?" Bobby Lee said.

Duane wondered if Bobby Lee were still stable. Commonplace setbacks seemed to leave him overwhelmed.

"I wish I'd become an airline pilot," Bobby Lee said.

"I don't," Duane said. "You can't see twenty feet. With my luck I might end up on a plane you were flying."

Bobby Lee's myopia was legend. Though only moderately good-looking, he was far too vain to wear glasses. As a result he had had so many accidents that it was more and more difficult to get a crew to work with him. He could not see wire at all and was constantly driving through barbed-wire gates.

Duane had not killed his motor or stepped out of the pickup. He felt disinclined to do either, but at the same time did not want to drive off and leave his crew mired in depression. As the head of the company it was his duty to do what he could for group morale.

"It's not the end of the world if a bit breaks," he said. "Fish it out."

"They never break on Eddie's rig," Bobby Lee said.

One of Bobby Lee's problems was that he was convinced Eddie Belt had a better life than he did. Eddie Belt was just as firmly convinced that it was the other way around. Duane spent a lot of time trying to persuade them that their lives were almost identical, which was, in fact, the case.

"Eddie's broken forty-two bits since he came to work for me," Duane said. "How many have you broken?"

"I don't believe in statistics," Bobby Lee said haughtily.

"I can probably have Turkey Clay out here in an hour," Duane said. Dickie, his son, and Turkey, a sixty-year-old roughneck, constituted his trouble-shooting unit. Turkey had been a hard-working, reliable employee until Dickie introduced him to the pleasures of cocaine. Turkey's response was euphoric.

"All them years I got by on beer and pussy, they just seem like wasted years," Turkey said. In his euphoria he ran over almost as many gates as Bobby Lee.

"That old man practically eats cocaine," Bobby Lee said. "Maybe we'll try fishing that bit out ourselves. I get nervous working with people who eat drugs."

Knowing that that was about as upbeat as Bobby Lee was likely to get, Duane hastily drove off.

Eddie Belt's rig was only ten miles to the north. Long before he reached it he knew something was wrong. The generator they used made a noise like an attacking warplane and it wasn't making its noise.

The only noise that came from the vicinity of the rig was the noise of gunshots. The shots caused Duane to speed up. Eddie had been known to fire a whole crew of roughnecks if he found them incompetent. There was always the possibility that he had just decided to execute them rather than fire them.

Duane's first glimpse of the location was not reassuring. Four bodies lay motionless under a mesquite tree. It was only when he skidded to a stop that one of the bodies raised its head. The other roughnecks continued to nap.

The gunfire seemed to be coming from a small stock tank about a quarter of a mile away.

"What's he shooting at?" Duane asked the one roughneck who seemed to be awake.

"Frogs," the man replied, before lying back down.

"Why isn't the generator running?" Duane said. "We're drilling an oil well, aren't we?"

The roughneck, a spindly lad of about nineteen, seemed annoyed at having to carry on a protracted conversation at a time when he would rather nap.

"The generator ain't running because there's baling wire in it," he said. He pulled his dozer cap over his eyes to indicate that the conversation was over.

"Baling wire?" Duane said. It sounded like fiction to him.

He got out and walked over to the stock tank. It was a good year for bullfrogs. Fifteen or twenty healthy specimens were lounging in the mud near the water's edge.

Eddie sat on the bank, reloading the customized deer rifle Duane had given him as a Christmas bonus several years before.

"How come there's baling wire in the generator?" Duane asked. "We don't bale our oil, we barrel it."

"I did not put no baling wire in that generator," Eddie said.

"Do you always hunt frogs with a deer rifle?" Duane asked.

"It's the most humane way," Eddie said. "You shoot just under them."

He proceeded to shoot just under a large frog.

The bullet produced an explosion of mud, which kicked the frog some ten feet in the air. When it came down it didn't move.

"Now that frog was not even nicked," Eddie said. "He's just knocked out. If I wanted to I could go get him, put him in a sack and take him home with me. I could use him as a breeder and he'd do fine."

"I didn't know you bred bullfrogs," Duane said.

"I don't, but I could," Eddie said.

"You're gonna have to breed 'em for a living if you don't get that generator going pretty soon," Duane said. "I don't like paying roughnecks to take naps."

"That generator will probably have to be taken apart, and I'm not mechanic enough to do it," Eddie Belt said. He shot again, and another frog flew high in the air.

"I'm going back to work in a minute, though," he said.

"This is a strange oil company," Duane said. "I wish there was real money in bullfrogs."

He got up and went back to the well. The roughnecks were still napping. As soon as he got in his pickup he honked the horn loudly. The roughnecks all jumped up, groggy from the heat. Shorty also jumped up, no less groggy.

Duane drove closer to the roughnecks. Two or three were rubbing sleep out of their eyes.

"If that generator ain't running before I'm out of hearing distance all you lazy sons-of-bitches are fired," he said. "And I don't want to hear any more lies about baling wire."

As he was bumping out of the pasture back onto the county road he heard the generator whine like a jet.

CHAPTER 13

DRIVING HOME, DUANE PASSED THE LARGE HOUSE where Jacy Farrow was staying. It was adobe and, from a distance, blended in with the rocky bluff on which it sat. So far as he knew, no one in Thalia had ever been inside it. Danny Deck, the screenwriter, had had it built nearly fifteen years before. A group of Indians from New Mexico, who knew how to work with adobe, had lived on the bluff in trailer houses for almost a year, building it.

The house overlooked a valley known locally as The Sorrows. Long before, Indians had traded captives in the valley. Many sad scenes had been enacted there. A mailbox near the house had Los Dolores written on it.

When the house had first been built, excitement ran high in the county. There were rumors of movie stars having been glimpsed going to or from the house. Bobby Lee thought he saw Steve McQueen drive through town.

But the rumors all remained rumors. No one managed to establish that Steve McQueen, or any other movie star, had actually been to the house, or even to the county.

The mailman who served that route reported that he delivered more mail to Los Dolores than to all the rest of the route put together. Sometimes the big mailbox—it was also adobe—got emptied regularly, but other times it filled and overflowed, and mail had to be stacked in the post office for weeks, or even months, until the writer reappeared.

No one kept house for him, and no one looked after the yard. In summer grass and weeds grew thick around the adobe.

Danny Deck himself was never seen in Thalia. Roughnecks going out for the midnight shift would sometimes see lights in the house. Then it would be dark for months at a stretch.

The excitement that had prevailed when the house was being built had long since faded. People who moved to the county during the oil boom didn't even know of its existence. There were only a few die-hard ranchers left in the part of the county where the house stood, some of them glimpsed almost as rarely as Danny Deck.

Prior to Jacy's return, the only person who had expressed much interest in Los Dolores itself had been Karla, who wanted to buy it.

"I bet he'd sell it if you made a high enough offer, Duane," she said every few weeks for a couple of years when they were richest.

"How do you know what he'd do?" Duane asked. "You've never met him."

"I saw him once, though," Karla said. "He was getting gas at the same station I was getting gas at. He looked real friendly."

"That don't mean he wants to sell his house," Duane pointed out.

"Duane, it don't hurt to ask," Karla said.

For a while she drove by Los Dolores often, though she had no earthly business in that part of the county. Nobody had any business there except a few drillers and one or two cowboys. Karla's hope was that someday Danny would be standing outside. If he waved, she could wave back. Then the next time they stopped at the same gas station they could strike up a conversation.

Karla prided herself on her friendliness. She often struck up conversations with total strangers for no reason at all and was eager to strike one up with Danny Deck. She had never met a writer, unless you counted the reporters who covered the petroleum industry for various Texas papers. From her one glimpse of Danny Deck at the filling station she was convinced they would like knowing each other. For a while she drove past Los Dolores three or four times a week, hoping to see him puttering around in the yard.

"It doesn't have a yard," Duane said. "The house is just built out on that bluff."

In fact, the absence of a true lawn was the one thing that drew comment from people who passed the house. In Thalia, even the humblest dwelling had a yard with a few sprigs of Bermuda grass out front. The houses of the more affluent were completely surrounded by lawns.

But Los Dolores, which must have cost hundreds of thousands of dollars to build, had buffalo grass and broom weeds growing right up to its walls. It was the only house in the county without a lawn, a fact that drew adverse comment in some circles.

"I'm glad it's way off down there because he must be a weirdo not to have a lawn," Wanda Hawkins said. Wanda, the wife of the town's lone insurance agent, had reigned for a time as Karla's best friend.

"It could have an inside patio, it's a real big house," Karla pointed out. Despite her irritation at Danny Deck for not puttering around outside so she could meet him, Karla had appointed herself his defender. She defended him vigorously even against the mild criticisms of her best friend, Wanda.

"I've got a patio, and a lawn too," Wanda pointed out. "I don't know what to think of people who don't have enough self-respect to have a nice lawn."

"Broom weeds are pretty from a distance," Karla said, not about to concede any point to Wanda.

Privately, she grew more and more irritated with Danny Deck for not appearing. She had thought about the conversation she planned to have with him so many times that it was frustrating not to get to have it. It all took place at a filling station and ended with their becoming such good friends that he agreed to sell her his house.

But months passed, and he didn't appear. One day, passing the house, she decided just to ring the doorbell and pretend she had to use the telephone. She even invented an excuse, which was that her father was having a kidney transplant and she needed to check on him. Her father had been dead for years but she sometimes resurrected him and pretended he was in some emergency room if she needed an excuse.

Los Dolores didn't have an ordinary doorbell. It had a little screen you spoke into. The screen hummed a little, and Karla promptly spoke into it.

"Hello, I'm Karla Moore, I have an emergency and need to use the telephone, please," she said, but then the screen stopped humming and no one came to the door.

Karla was disgusted. It had taken a certain nerve to march up and speak into the screen. Karla didn't like to waste nerve, much of which she needed just to manage her home life. She went around in a sour mood for several days.

"Write him a letter," Duane suggested.

"Fuck you," Karla replied.

"It was just a suggestion," Duane said, grinning. "Maybe the man's shy."

"If he's too shy to open his own door he's too shy for me," Karla said. "He could at least hire a housekeeper so we'd have some way of finding out what's going on."

Her friend Wanda was horrified when told that Karla had just gone up and rung a strange man's doorbell.

"You could have been dragged in and raped," Wanda said. "I've never rung someone's doorbell in my life unless I knew them first."

"At least I would have got to see the house," Karla said.

Her mood remained sour. The existence of a house she couldn't buy was a major frustration to her. It looked as if it might be the perfect house, too.

"He might as well sell it to me, everyone around here thinks he's a weirdo," Karla said.

"I don't see why he would care," Duane said. "He don't know any of them."

"He could know me if he'd just stay home," Karla said.

"Why don't you just go tack an offer on his door?" Duane said. "That might get his attention."

"I might do that," Karla said. "I might leave a note offering half a million and see what he says."

Duane shut up. He had often suggested obviously ridiculous courses of action to his wife only to have her adopt them immediately.

Nothing was said for a few weeks and Duane thought Karla might have lost interest. He was wrong. Karla had a friend named Randy Royt, with whom she liked to flirt—or possibly do more than, for all Duane knew. Randy was a helicopter pilot —he mostly helicoptered investors or oil company officials to remote oil wells. Karla had the brilliant idea of hiring Randy to fly over Los Dolores.

"It's got an inside patio and a swimming pool too," Karla reported, when she returned from the flight. Her eyes were dancing. Duane had never been particularly fond of Randy Royt and he began to feel even less fond.

"Did you go in and check out the bedrooms?" he asked. "Has it got waterbeds, by any chance?"

Karla was a passionate advocate of waterbeds. She had bought the first one ever seen in Thalia, and had had forty or fifty since.

"Duane, are you jealous?" she asked.

"It could be I just wish you had better taste," he said.

Karla laughed. "Randy's just the best-looking helicopter pilot in north Texas," she said. "We didn't land, though. How would you like it if somebody landed a helicopter in our patio?"

"I didn't even know we had a patio," Duane said, looking out the window at their lawn. It was a modest lawn, by Thalia standards. Karla watered it lovingly every day in the summertime and it produced a modest covering of Bermuda grass and a splendid crop of grass burs.

"We don't," Karla said. "But we will in our next house."

CHAPTER 14

AFTER HER TOUR BY HELICOPTER, KARLA RAPIDLY lost interest in Los Dolores.

"It's too spread out," she said. "Minerva could never keep it clean even if she tried, and she probably wouldn't even try."

The next year they bought a small ranch on the rolling plain northwest of town. The ranch had several low bluffs on it. Karla replaced Randy Royt with an articulate young architect from Fort Worth who soon designed them the house they had just moved into.

Duane reminded his wife several times that she had rejected Los Dolores on the grounds that it was too spread out for Minerva to clean. The new house—stucco over brick—was much larger than Los Dolores, weighing in at twelve thousand square feet.

"I thought you wanted adobe," Duane said. "It's all you've talked about for years."

"I don't want that writer to think I'm copying him," Karla said.

"He's never heard of you," Duane said. "Why would he care what kind of house you build?"

"Arthur says Italian style looks better anyway," Karla said. Arthur was her young architect.

"I think we ought to build two houses," Duane said. "One for us and one for the children and grandkids. We could put the one for the children and grandkids several miles away."

"Duane, you should have read that article I showed you that said kids really want discipline," Karla said. "If you'd ever disciplined them they wouldn't be like this."

"If you believe our kids really want discipline, you'll believe anything," Duane said. "I still think two houses is a great idea."

But he soon gave up on that idea, or any idea having to do with the house. Karla would listen to no one but Arthur, her new love slave. The result was a house covering most of the top of the bluff it was built on. It had several wings, each one meant for a different child. The children ignored their spacious wings and spent most of their time clustered in the den off the kitchen, screaming at one another.

"Go scream in your own rooms," Duane screamed at them from time to time. "The reason we built this house was so we'd each have our rooms to scream in."

"When I scream in my room I get scared," Julie said. "It's so big I hear echoes."

"I hate this house," Jack said. "You shouldn't have built it so far from town. We can't get any kids to come and play with us."

"That's not because of the house, it's because of the way you play," Duane said.

Only the week previous they had lured a little playmate out, tied him hand and foot and thrown him off the diving board.

"We just wanted to see if he could do magic," Jack said. "We were pretending he was Houdini. Besides, we know lifesaving."

"Why didn't you use it, then?" Duane asked. "Minerva had to jump in with all her clothes on and pull him out."

"He's not a very nice kid," Jack said. "He talks back and stuff."

"Your mother talks back to me but I don't try and drown her," Duane said.

"Anyway, Arthur's a wimp," Julie said. "He always wears those dumb bow ties."

That night Duane was unable to resist passing along Julie's judgment.

"Your youngest daughter thinks your new boyfriend's a wimp," he said. "She don't like his bow ties."

Karla had just returned from a little shopping trip to Fort Worth. She wore a T-shirt that said, PEOPLE WHO THINK MONEY CAN'T BUY HAPPINESS DON'T KNOW WHERE TO SHOP. Her eyes were dancing again.

"Go tie a knot in your dick, Duane," she replied cheerfully. Her hands were full of shopping bags.

"Don't you think we oughta build a guesthouse while we're at it?" she asked, a moment later.

"Who for?" Duane asked. It was one of those moments when life seemed unfair. Karla got better-looking every year, whereas he just got more tired.

"For guests, Duane," Karla said. "That's who you need a guesthouse for."

"This house will sleep about a thousand people," he pointed out. "And the only guest we ever have is Bobby Lee, when he passes out after supper."

"He might like privacy, though," Karla said.

"All he'd have to do is walk off down any hall," Duane said. "He'd have so much privacy we'd have to call the Highway Patrol to find him."

"It's not the same as a guesthouse, though," Karla said. "A lot of people wouldn't care to be surrounded by our family."

Duane was lying on their most recent waterbed, which was larger in terms of square footage than the little house he and Karla had lived in when they were first married. He was watching cable news with the sound off. A tidal wave had hit somewhere in India, washing hundreds of thousands of people into the sea.

"I don't care to be surrounded by our family, either," he said. "I might build myself a guesthouse. We could buy a golf cart and park it in the kitchen."

"Why would we want to park a golf cart in the kitchen?" Karla asked, momentarily intrigued by her husband's line of thought.

"Then if any guests show up they could drive around in it until they find a bedroom," Duane said.

"I guess we could use a golf cart," Karla allowed. "Little Mike's too speedy for Minerva. She could use it to chase him down."

"Karla, I was just kidding," Duane said.

"Sometimes you have your best ideas when you're kidding," she said.

"I've had another one," he said. "Let's don't build a guest-house, let's build a jail. It can be Jack and Dickie's room. We'll have real bars on the windows. It will be good to give those boys a taste of prison life right here at home so they'll know what to expect when they wind up in Huntsville."

"The reason there's women's lib is because husbands don't take their wives seriously when they want to build guest-houses," Karla said.

She changed T-shirts, slipping into one that said, MARRIED BUT STILL ON THE LOOKOUT. Duane wondered if there was any significance to the fact that she hadn't worn a bra to Fort Worth. He wondered if there was any significance to anything people did with their bodies. The older he got, the more he doubted that there was. Who people slept with seemed too circumstantial to worry about. It wasn't the fact that Karla had boyfriends that annoyed him—it was the boyfriends she picked, none of whom made any effort to be friendly to him, or even civil. Arthur treated him like a yardman.

Meanwhile, on the big screen of the TV, in vivid color, the survivors of the tidal wave wandered around looking stunned, on a white beach. They had lost everything: their homes, their loved ones, their meager possessions had all been swept into the sea.

"There's some people with real trouble," Duane said aloud, half to himself.

Karla was brushing her hair. She could see the TV in the mirror.

"I know, don't lay there and watch it," she said. "Turn the channel."

"A hundred and twenty thousand people got washed away," Duane said. "That's more people than there are in Wichita Falls."

"It's way over there and we can't do a thing about it, Duane," Karla said. "It's what can happen if you live too near the ocean."

"It wasn't two years ago that you wanted to buy a beach house on Padre Island," he reminded her.

Karla brushed her shining brown hair for a while.

"You once told me you'd give me anything my heart desired," she reminded Duane.

"I must have been drunk when I said it," he said.

"You were not—it was about twenty years ago," Karla said.

"Oh, no wonder," Duane said. "A young man's even more unreliable than a drunk."

"Arthur's young and he's reliable," Karla said. "I should go snatch that child baldheaded for calling him a wimp."

"She's got a right to freedom of speech," Duane said.

Shorty was standing just outside the glass doors that led to the deck and the hot tub. He often stood there for hours, staring longingly into the bedroom. It was a sand-stormy day—pellets of West Texas grit occasionally peppered the glass.

"I can't stand the way that dog stands there with his tongue hanging out," Karla said. She left the room.

Duane continued to look at the wet, stunned people wandering dejectedly along a beach on the other side of the world. One hundred and twenty thousand of them had been washed away forever, which should have brought his own troubles into perspective, only it didn't. He felt just as depressed as ever. His huge debt depressed him, his unruly children depressed him, his smug girlfriend depressed him, and the huge house that he didn't like and would probably never manage to pay for depressed him most of all. He even hated the bed he was lying on—it was so vast that he often had to crawl twenty feet just to answer the phone.

The survivors of the tidal wave actually seemed to inhabit a more beautiful world than he did. The sea that had swallowed their loved ones was a vivid blue. The palm trees that had been spared were a lush green. The large new Sony TV transmitted all the colors perfectly—the scene of devastation actually looked like a South Seas paradise, whereas out his window all he saw was grayness, grit, and Shorty with his tongue out.

The sand the survivors walked around on was brilliantly white and far more beautiful than the sand that peppered his glass doors. West Texas sand looked and felt like ground rocks. Duane had felt it often and hated it. He often thought it would be nice to live in a place where the wind wasn't strong enough to blow little rocks around.

His imagination refused to accord the Asian tragedy anything like the gravity it deserved. Despite himself, he imagined a freak tidal wave, in the form of a waterspout, arching over four hundred and fifty miles of Texas and striking the Thalia court-house dead center, washing away the courthouse and everyone in it. He knew it was an unworthy thought, since many inno-cents would die; on the other hand, it was an appealing solu-tion to the problem of Janine—a problem he would have to face up to pretty soon.

As he drove past Los Dolores, its brown adobe walls somber even in the bright sunlight, Duane's mind chose to replay the afternoon he had watched the tidal-wave coverage. When he was depressed, his memory proved particularly uncooperative. Instead of replaying scenes of happiness and mirth—of which there had been many in his life—it only replayed other depres-sions. Though he had been happy for most of his life, and seriously depressed only for a year or two, it was an effort for him to remember much of what had happened during his forty-six happy years. His mental processes seemed to be the oppo-site of Minerva's, with whom he had discussed the problem several times.

"Shoot, I just remember the good," Minerva said. "I forget the bad right off."

At the time she was convinced she was getting spinal men-ingitis, though so far she had none of the symptoms.

"I guess you're more of an optimist than me," Duane said.

"No, I'm crazier," Minerva replied. "You're too sane, Duane. There's not a saner man in this county, and right there's your problem."

CHAPTER 15

LOOKING AT LOS DOLORES, DUANE WONDERED what Jacy felt. It occurred to him that he could just stop and ring the doorbell, as Karla had. Perhaps Jacy was inside, depressed, hoping someone *would* ring the doorbell.

She might be lying on a bed as vast as his own, watching TV coverage of some disaster and sinking ever deeper into her own depression. She might enjoy talking over old times, even though the old times just consisted of a year or two of dates and a few brief weeks of lovemaking, thirty years before.

Duane could remember thinking that he would never get over her; but long before he had returned to Thalia from Korea he was over her. Karla had moved to town in his absence. She worked as a checker in the grocery store. They had a few dates, got married, stayed married.

Even Sonny Crawford had finally gotten over Jacy, and, of the two of them, he had been the more in love.

Duane thought Ruth Popper's theory was wrong. He wasn't afraid of falling back in love with Jacy. Nothing was much less likely than that they would ever be in love again. He was just afraid of violating her privacy. He had almost no privacy himself, and valued it so highly that he would drive around on dirt roads all afternoon just to have a little. He was not about to interfere with Jacy's, and he watched Los Dolores disappear in his rearview mirror without remorse.

On his way back to town he stopped at Aunt Jimmie's Lounge for a few minutes to meditate over a beer. Aunt Jimmie's was a dilapidated little county line honky-tonk. The clapboards it was made of hadn't been painted in thirty years, and neither had the proprietress, Aunt Jimmie, a plain, solemn little woman who sat by the cash register all day and much of the night, smoking cigarette after cigarette and ignoring what went on around her. She had gone broke running a dime store in Thalia. Aunt Jimmie's did a booming business, but Aunt Jimmie herself still looked like a woman who ran a dime store.

Duane was relieved to see that for once none of his employees were getting drunk on his time. Why would they need to, when they could take long naps in the shade?

"The waitress is gone to the beauty parlor, you'll have to get your own beer," Aunt Jimmie said. She was not liberal with conversation, which suited Duane fine.

The bar was empty except for the local highway patrolman, a mournful widower named P. L. Jolly. P.L. was rumored to have designs on Aunt Jimmie, but, so far as Duane could observe, had done little to advance them.

Duane got a beer and sat down by P.L. He tried to maintain good relations with the local police, since the day seldom passed without a family member or an employee being arrested for something.

"Hi, P.L.," he said. "How's Dickie behaving?"

"Terrible," P.L. said. "He says he's gonna organize a prison riot if we don't let him out. It's a good thing for us there's nobody else in jail but a nigger and the nigger's in a coma."

"That doesn't sound good," Duane said. "How'd he get in a coma?"

"He just slid into it in the night, some way," P.L. said. "The doctor was gonna come have a look at him this afternoon."

"Was Dickie really going eighty-five in a school zone?" Duane asked.

"Yep," P.L. said. "That little sucker sure flies along, don't he? I like Dickie, though. He don't mean no harm. It's just he's lively."

"I hope that other prisoner's okay," Duane said. "We've got this centennial coming up. We don't want to get any bad marks if we can help it."

P.L. smoked for a while. The thought of black marks made him seem more depressed than ever.

"We get quite a few that do go into comas," he said. "They get their heads beat in, but it don't take hold for a while. Then they wind up in jail over here and the next thing you know they slide off into comas. It's a big strain on our personnel."

"I wouldn't try to tell you how to run your business," Duane said. "But couldn't you just call an ambulance and have them sent to the hospital?"

"Well, we can," P.L. said, "but I like to give them a day or two to see if they're faking. If they're faking, and you send 'em to the hospital, they might get after the nurses or something. Or else you have to send a guard with them, and that means overtime wages."

"I thought Karla was gonna bail Dickie out," Duane said.

"She came by, but Dickie popped off and got smart with her and she changed her mind and left him in," P.L. said. "That little sucker don't care what he says, does he?"

"Nope," Duane said. "And if there's anybody who could get a man in a coma to help out with a riot, it'd be him."

P.L. grinned an approving grin.

"That little sucker, he livens things up, don't he?" he said.

CHAPTER 16

Dickie was not particularly grateful when Duane came by and got him out of jail. He was a tall, rangy boy with spiky, oat-colored hair and lively blue eyes.

"I could have done a day's work if you'd got me out sooner," he pointed out.

"A day's work for who?" Duane asked.

In the course of racing eighty-five miles an hour through a school zone, Dickie had also managed to crack the head on his pickup. He seldom drove at anything less than top speed and went through three or four pickups a year. The local Ford dealer kept a pickup with Dickie's specifications sitting on the lot at all times.

The injury to his pickup forced Dickie to ride home with Duane, which delighted Shorty. He loved Dickie almost as much as he loved Duane. He tried to show his affection by giving Dickie a playful bite on the elbow, but Dickie didn't enjoy such love play. He promptly threw Shorty out the window.

Fortunately they had just turned off the pavement onto the

dirt road, and were not going fast. Shorty was more puzzled than hurt. Like the twins, Dickie played strange games. The twins threw rocks at Shorty, whereas Dickie threw him at the road. Shorty thought it was all love, of a sort. He picked himself up and raced along after the pickup as if nothing had happened.

"Don't be throwing that dog out of the pickup," Duane said. "He's not your dog."

"He's not going to be anybody's dog if the little blue fucker bites me again," Dickie said. He was wearing one of his mother's T-shirts. It read, WHEN THE GOING GETS TOUGH, THE TOUGH GO TO COZUMEL.

The Moore family had once made one of their frequent attempts at an idyllic family vacation in Cozumel. Dickie had got in a fistfight with the doorman of the hotel before their luggage was even unloaded. He claimed the doorman sneered at him, but Duane thought that several hours' contact with his siblings had caused Dickie to hit the first person he saw.

That same afternoon Nellie took some kind of strange drug, the nature of which could never be determined. She turned greenish and stopped breathing several times without warning. The twins were their usual selves. Only Karla enjoyed Cozumel. She played on the beach all day, while Duane dispensed a fortune in bribes in order to keep his children from being deported.

Duane kept an eye on Shorty, who raced along two or three hundred yards in the rear. The local coyotes regarded Shorty as their plaything and frequently ambushed him, though they seldom did more than rip up his ears.

It depressed Duane that he didn't know what to say to his son on the few occasions when he actually had the opportunity to talk to him. He felt he ought to give Dickie some sound fatherly advice, but when presented with an opportunity— such as just getting him out of jail—he rarely came up with any.

"You've got a world of opportunity ahead of you," Duane said. Dickie might not be listening, but *he* felt better if he thought he was at least trying to influence his son for the better.

"You could be anything you want to be," he added. "You've got energy, and that's a wonderful resource."

"Money ain't a bad resource, either," Dickie said. "Let's buy some airplanes and sell cocaine for a while."

"No, I'm not going to sell cocaine and neither are you," Duane said. "You ought to try and do something useful while you're young."

"Selling dope is useful," Dickie said. "It cheers people up when there's northers and sandstorms and they're going broke."

"You'll think useful when a Mexican catches you and chops you up with a chain saw," Duane said, but he felt boring even to himself, and shut up.

Just then Karla came blazing around them in the BMW, burying them in dust. She honked, and her horn played the theme from *Urban Cowboy,* one of her favorite movies. She had stopped and picked up Shorty, who looked at them inscrutably as he passed.

"Mom drives faster than I do," Dickie observed.

"BMWs run faster than pickups," Duane said. He still felt depressed. Being with Dickie often depressed him. Dickie was likable, lively and competent. Practically everyone in the county, male and female, doted on him. He was sort of the star of the county. What bothered Duane was a sense that he had never managed to give his son a clear sense of what ought to be, of how life ought to be ordered or even of what to expect of it. He himself had proceeded into adulthood without such a sense, but his father had had no time to influence him, and his mother was too bewildered to try.

But he had been Dickie's father for twenty-one years and yet didn't feel that he had made any constructive impression on the boy at all. He couldn't tell that he had made any impression on any of his children. It was a haunting feeling, because in most respects he knew he had been a fairly effective man. He had started with nothing and built a successful little oil company. Building the rigs had been a mistake, but a mistake he didn't reproach himself for. Booms induced such behavior, and thousands had made worse mistakes than he had.

But he did reproach himself for his inability to civilize his children. Collectively or individually, they seemed as uninfluenceable as wild animals. You could yell at them or put them in cages, but how could you make them less wild?

"They've got your genes," Ruth Popper often said, whenever one of his children did something particularly outrageous.

"They've got Karla's too," he always said plaintively, not wanting his genes to have to shoulder all the blame.

The longer he contemplated the children, the more he wondered about genes. He bought two books about genes and tried to understand how they worked, but the more he tried to apply what he read to his children the more puzzled he grew. Looking at the kids, he couldn't detect any signs of his genes at all. They all had Karla's sharp blue eyes, her oat-colored hair, her perfect teeth. His mouth was filled with bridges, but Karla had never had a cavity in her life, and neither had any of the kids.

But the principal thing the children seemed to have taken from Karla was a kind of unstoppability. You just couldn't stop any of them from doing anything they wanted to do unless you met them with superior force, and that had become increasingly hard to do. They were all totally convinced by their own impulses and acted accordingly. In a way, Duane supposed, such conviction was a form of integrity, but if so, it was a frightening form. The children were true to their natures, but what natures!

Duane couldn't remember when he had been as convinced by one of his own impulses as his children were by their most vagrant whims. At times he envied them. It must be nice never to be indecisive. But then he would have to spend half a day undoing the results of one of their decisions, and envy would be replaced by a murderous feeling. They could all sense it when he got the murderous feeling, too. They weren't dumb.

"Oh, shit, Billie Anne's here," Dickie said, when they turned into what Karla liked to call the driveway—in reality an old feed road that ran along the bluff for a quarter of a mile before it dead-ended at a basketball goal. There was a concrete parking space between the basketball goal and the six-car garage.

Dickie could tell Billie Anne was there because he could see her pickup looming over the scrubby mesquite that lay between them and the house. Billie Anne's pickup had a small cab, but giant wheels of a type more commonly found in the desert country of Arizona. Billie Anne, though born and raised in Thalia, had spent her first two marriages in Benson, Arizona.

"One advantage to big tires is you're up high enough that you can tell if the truck drivers are good-looking," she said, when kidded about her pickup, which looked, from a distance, as if it were on stilts. "If they ain't, then that's that."

Dickie treated the remark as a joke. Karla didn't think it was a joke and occasionally needled her son about his girlfriend's independent ways.

"What would you do if you caught her with a cute truck driver?" Karla asked.

"The same thing I'd do if I caught her with an ugly truck driver," Dickie replied. "And you don't want to know."

"Let's stop a minute," Dickie said to Duane. "I need to think this out."

"Think what out?"

"That woman's got a temper," Dickie said. The lights had stopped dancing in his blue eyes. He kept looking nervously in the rearview mirror.

"I might want to hitchhike back to town," he said. "I don't think I want to go home right now. Take me back to jail so I can pay my debt to society."

Dickie showed traces of panic, a sight Duane found mildly exhilarating. Just as he had concluded that his children were all inhuman monsters, one of them exhibited slight traces of vulnerability.

He stopped the pickup.

"Are you scared of Billie Anne?" he asked. Billie Anne was a tall, fairly good-looking girl with lank brown hair and a demeanor that could fairly be described as comatose, unless she happened to be water-skiing. Water sports were her passion. After a few hours spent skimming over the brown surface of Lake Kickapoo behind Dickie's speedboat she became voluble and talked a blue streak.

"Back up," Dickie said. "She might spot me."

"Now look," Duane said. "I'm tired and I wanta get home. Billie Anne's probably in the hot tub. What are you so worried about?"

"She's been taking shooting lessons," Dickie said. "Remember, I gave her that Thirty-eight Special for her birthday so she'd have protection when I'm not around."

"What's she so mad at you for that you're worried about getting shot with your own birthday present?" Duane asked.

"Gossip," Dickie said. "I wish we lived in New York, so people wouldn't gossip so much. They should pass laws against it. Gossip does a lot more damage than drugs."

Duane wanted to laugh. "Who are you sleeping with that Billie Anne's found out about?" he asked.

Dickie kept up a nervous surveillance of the hill as if he feared Billie Anne might be crouched behind one of the many mesquite bushes with her .38 leveled.

"You know that song called 'War Is Hell on the Home Front Too'?" Dickie asked, glancing at his father.

"I've heard it," Duane said.

"It's about wives that don't get enough because their husbands have gone to war," Dickie said. "And this ol' boy—he's not very old—has to help them out of their suffering."

"I didn't know there was a war on," Duane said. "Who are we fighting?"

"I just used that as an example," Dickie said. "The same thing can happen even if there isn't a war on."

"Are you involved with a married woman?" Duane asked.

"I tell you what, loan me the pickup," Dickie said. "I think I wanta go to Ruidoso, and this is a good place to start from."

"Which married woman are you involved with?" Duane asked.

"It's not necessarily just one," Dickie said. "There's more of them than you think who have that war-is-hell-on-the-home-front-too attitude."

"Yes, I know," Duane said. "Your mother's explained that to me. So which two married women are you involved with?"

"Mrs. Nolan and Mrs. Marlow," Dickie said.

Duane killed the motor.

"Say it again, just so I'll know I'm not going crazy," he said.

"Mrs. Nolan and Mrs. Marlow," Dickie said. "I don't know how it got started, but now Mrs. Marlow's left her husband and Mrs. Nolan's fixing to."

"Do Junior and Lester know about this?" Duane asked.

"Yeah, because Billie Anne called them up and told them this afternoon," Dickie said.

"You were in jail this afternoon," Duane pointed out. "Maybe she changed her mind. Maybe she even plans to forgive you."

"This ain't a good time to sit around and talk," Dickie said. "I figured she'd just take all the dope money I got hidden and go to Fort Worth and buy clothes with it. But if she's out here, it probably means she wants revenge."

"You know, Ruidoso ain't the worst idea in the world," Duane said. "It might be a good idea to let the dust settle for a day or two."

He stepped out of the pickup, and before he could even close the door, Dickie was in the driver's seat and gone. The pickup spun around like a top, throwing up a cloud of dust that could be seen ten miles away. Duane walked through the dust cloud toward the basketball court. In a minute Shorty came racing along the road. Then he stopped and looked puzzled. His beloved master had returned, but where was the pickup?

"That's okay, Shorty," Duane said. "It ain't the only pickup in the world."

CHAPTER 17

As he was walking into the garage, Duane heard shots from the backyard. He began to run, causing Shorty to grow excited and bark his piercing bark. Because of the ingenuity of Arthur the architect, it was necessary to run most of the length of a twelve-thousand-square-foot house in order to reach the backyard.

When he finally reached it, he saw that Karla and Billie Anne were in the hot tub, delicately sipping the quart-sized vodka tonics that Karla favored in hot weather. Minerva, shooting from a prone position, was trying to hit several balloons that floated over the new doghouse. The balloons were left over from the twins' last birthday party. She was hitting them, too, popping the last one just as Duane trotted up.

"It's about time you came home," Minerva said. "Where's that boy?"

"Gone to Louisana," Duane said, lying with what he thought was passable casualness.

"I don't guess he cares that he broke this girl's heart," Karla said.

Billie Anne didn't exactly look like a tragedy victim. She giggled as she might if she had just had a nice swirl around Lake Kickapoo on water-skis.

"I like shooting this little gun," Minerva said, still in the prone position.

Then she got up, laid the loaded gun beside Billie Anne's quart-sized vodka tonic and sauntered back to the house. As she went in, Nellie came out, carrying Barbette under one arm and dragging Little Mike with the other hand. Little Mike was holding the pliers with which he liked to try to hit the cat.

Nellie wore a string bikini so brief that Duane felt embarrassed. The bikini would barely conceal a clitoris. Nellie, oblivious to his embarrassment, handed him Barbette and dropped Little Mike in the pool, pliers and all.

"They say the best way to teach kids to swim is just to drop them in the water," she said.

Barbette cooed, as she often did when Duane was holding her.

Little Mike was not making rapid progress as a swimmer, though. The top of his head was all that was visible. Duane placed Barbette carefully on the deck and went over and fished him out. Little Mike still clung to his pliers. He began to trot toward the house. He had once been stung by a wasp and hated being outdoors.

"Guess what, Daddy, me and Joe got engaged today," Nellie said as she sank into the hot tub. "Momma wants you to build us a house as a wedding present. It don't have to be very big."

"I think that doghouse would make a nice residence for a young couple just starting out," Duane said. "It's one of the few two-story doghouses around."

He looked at Karla, to see what her mood might be. Her mood seemed to be noncommittal.

"I suppose you know that Dickie has wrecked two homes," she said, without much outrage.

"Three," Billie Anne said. "He wrecked ours too, and we hadn't even started it yet."

"I wouldn't pay too much attention to rumors," Duane said. "A lot of idle gossip gets gossiped in Thalia."

"They carried Lester off to the quiet room today," Karla informed him.

"Why?" Duane asked. "I talked to him this afternoon and he didn't seem any nuttier than usual."

"He went crazy and threatened to cut his own throat with a razor," Karla said. "He said he'd had about enough."

"He probably just felt like a day in the quiet room," Duane said. "He won't cut his own throat."

"Junior Nolan was last seen buying shells for his deer rifle," Karla added. "It ain't deer season, Duane."

"It's Dickie season," Nellie said cheerfully.

Duane picked up Barbette and walked across the sparse yard to where the bluff dropped off. The sun sank majestically toward the western plains, turning the lower sky golden as it sank. The sunset made the country seem beautiful, a transformation Duane loved to watch. Sundown brought with it a quality of peace that belied almost everything that happened during the day—not to mention the night.

He sat on the edge of the hill, his grandchild in his arms, and watched until the sun sank below the horizon and the first stars came out. It occurred to him often that he might have been happier if he had decided to be an astronomer rather than an oilman. Watching stars seemed a pleasanter way to make a living than watching roughnecks.

He indulged in a little fantasy in which he and Barbette were the last survivors of the human race. They lived peacefully, raising goats and watching lots of sunsets. In their world there was no adultery, no bankruptcy. Barbette grew up to be a sweet, beautiful young woman who wore respectable bathing suits.

The fantasy was soon nudged out of his consciousness by the knowledge that Nellie was apparently engaged to Joe. Duane had nothing in particular against Joe, not even the fact that he looked like a barrel of oil. His main objection was that he doubted Joe's staying power.

The group had left the hot tub but not the deck, when he returned. Minerva had just come out with more quarts of vodka tonic.

"I didn't know you were divorced from Hal yet," Duane

said. Hal's staying power had run out during the honeymoon, apparently.

They heard a pickup coming.

"I bet that's Junior," Karla said.

"I think Junior's cute," Nellie said. "I wouldn't even much mind marrying *him.*"

"Ick, I hate baldheaded men," Billie Anne said.

"I knew a man who was bald everywhere," Nellie said. "He didn't have a sprig of hair on him."

"Ick, that makes me sick just to think about," Billie Anne said.

In a moment Junior Nolan, hatless and somber, walked into the yard carrying a .30-.30.

"It won't do no good to hide him, I'll get him eventually," Junior said.

"Have a vodka tonic, Junior—I haven't drunk much out of it," Karla said, offering him hers.

Junior took the vodka gratefully.

"You can sue for alienation of affections," Junior informed them. He sat down in a lawn chair.

"Of course you can't sue a corpse," he added. "But if he gets plumb away I can at least sue him."

There was a click from the vicinity of the hot tub. Billie Anne pointed the .38 at Junior Nolan, who looked disconcerted.

"Don't you threaten my fiancé, you old baldheaded horse's ass," Billie Anne said.

"Put the gun down, Billie Anne," Karla said. "Little Barbette might have a trauma for life if you shot somebody right here by the hot tub."

"Let's all put the guns away," Duane said, as soothingly as possible. "Let's talk this over like civilized people."

Having drawn a good bead, Billie Anne was reluctant to undraw it. Junior hid his sunburned head in the vodka tonic and kept quiet.

"Billie Anne, don't shoot him, it's too horrible in prison," Nellie said. "Remember that TV show we saw where the warden's a lesbian?"

"First offenders don't usually get too long a sentence," Billie Anne said. "It would be worth it if it would save Dickie."

"Save him? I thought you wanted to shoot him yourself," Karla said.

"You folks got any steaks?" Junior asked. "I'd love a good steak. This thing's had me torn up so much I can't keep down but one meal a day and I normally have it about this time of an evening."

"Well, it's tore me up too, I know just how you feel," Billie Anne said, laying the pistol down.

Duane quickly collected it and the rifle too. No one seemed to care.

"We could all go to the Howlers," Karla said, referring to a steak house they frequently ate at. "Our steaks are in the deep freeze and we'd all be so drunk no telling who would get shot by the time they thawed out."

"I'm so hungry I could eat one froze," Junior said. The extent of his own hunger seemed to have just dawned on him. Karla took him by the arm and led him into the house.

"Minerva might let you have some pork rinds or something," she said.

Duane followed them in.

"I got that centennial meeting," he reminded Karla. "Maybe I could meet you at the Howlers later."

Both Suzie Nolan and Jenny Marlow were on the Centennial Committee. Only that morning he had briefly thought that one or another of them might be his new love. He had felt inclined to flirt a little. Now, it turned out, both were his son's girlfriends, and the possibilities of flirtation had been bashed.

Karla sent Junior on to the kitchen and stopped with Duane a minute.

"Duane, things are getting a little too unruly around here," she said. "I guess it's a good thing Nellie's marrying Joe. Joe's stable."

"Joe's dumb," he said, but he didn't want to argue about anything as ephemeral as sons-in-law. He put Barbette to bed. When he came back, Karla had already dressed for the steak house. She wore armadillo-skin boots, a fifteen-thousand-dollar concho belt and a T-shirt that read, YOU ME DINNER MOTEL.

"I hope this is a short meeting," Duane said. "Order me a T-bone for about nine o'clock."

"I feel sorry for Junior," Karla said. "I think it's real sweet that there's one husband left who really loves his wife."

"There's probably lots of husbands who love their wives enough not to want them sleeping with Dickie," he said. "Lester, for example."

"I've got to get Billie Anne out of the hot tub," Karla said. "She's so drunk she could drown and never notice."

"That T-shirt you're wearing could give someone the wrong idea," he said.

"Oh, hush, Duane," Karla said. "I never see anyone with an idea."

Duane washed his face, which was about all he had time to do. When he came out, Karla had changed the T-shirt to one that read, PARTY TILL YOU PUKE.

"Maybe they could have a double wedding," she said.

"Who?"

"Dickie and Billie Anne, and Nellie and Joe," she said.

"Dickie and Billie Anne aren't speaking," he informed her. "He was afraid to come in the house for fear she'd shoot him."

"We could get worse as a daughter-in-law," Karla said. "He could go off and marry somebody we don't even know."

"It must have been ten years since I've seen you wear anything I didn't have to read," Duane said, but Karla was ready to roll and was thirty feet down the hall by the time he said it.

CHAPTER 18

WHEN DUANE GOT TO THE MEETING, SONNY WAS the only person there. The meetings were held in a little meeting room that for some reason was painted the color of an egg yolk. Walking into it was like walking into an egg.

"What's the news on Lester?" Duane asked. He felt a little guilty for having skipped out on the afternoon chat he was to have had with Lester.

"I think he's just down at the hospital doing crosswords," Sonny said. "He gets a little stressed out now and then."

Sonny always dressed neatly, doing his own laundry every Sunday in his own laundrymat. He washed his car every Sunday, too, in his own carwash. But it seemed to Duane his cleanliness only exposed his sadness.

Looking at him, Duane wished someone else would show up at the meeting soon. He and Sonny had been friends virtually all their lives; the friendship still had its moments, but on a day-to-day basis their interest in one another had faded and they found it hard to make conversation.

"I guess the softball game must have gone into extra innings or the women would be here," Duane said.

They heard a shuffling sound, and Old Man Balt shuffled in carrying an empty tomato-juice can. During the course of the meeting the can would gradually fill up with tobacco juice. Old Man Balt was a big chewer.

He was the oldest living citizen of the county, and looked forward keenly to the coming centennial. Apparently he had been the first citizen born in Hardtop County, and his hundredth birthday would be celebrated during the festivities. He had been made an honorary member of the Centennial Committee in hopes that he could help keep historical inaccuracies from popping up, but he had proven to be entirely useless where the county's history was concerned.

For the past twenty years he had lived with his only surviving child, a woman named Beulah, herself in her late seventies. They watched soap operas and game shows all day long. Two decades of what Minerva called the little rays had obliterated all traces of the county's history from the old man's mind. The only thing he could remember from a hundred years of exposure to Hardtop County was that a building had somehow blown up in the twenties and killed a blacksmith.

But he was a lively old man, and would often spit and cackle throughout the committee meetings, finding humor where no one else found anything but boredom. It was as if, mentally, he was still tuned in to a game show.

"Here I am, boys," he said. "What are we gonna meet about tonight?"

"Oh, the pageant, I imagine, Mr. Balt," Duane said.

It had been decided that a pageant would be put on, to run for a week in the local rodeo arena. The pageant would depict the county's history from the creation of the earth until roughly 1980.

There had been prolonged debate about what time span such a pageant should attempt to cover. Since for several million years the only action in the county had been geological, some were for omitting those slow epochs entirely. Others felt that just to leave out several million years left the pageant open to charges of superficiality, or lack of comprehensiveness.

The script of the pageant was the work of many hands, several of which had not written a word. But the local churchmen —who felt that theology, not geology, should dictate the begin-

ning—were not among the idle. A long skit based on Genesis
was already in hand. Karla had been approached about playing
Eve, but was not enthusiastic.

"If they think I'm gonna stand out in the rodeo arena naked
and talk to a snake, they're crazy," Karla said, although at the
time she was wearing a T-shirt that said, YOU CAN'T BE FIRST
BUT YOU CAN BE NEXT.

Bobby Lee, an inveterate mocker of established truth,
scoffed at the notion that the Garden of Eden had been located
anywhere near Thalia.

"I think we oughta have a Hell-on-Earth skit," he said. "If
they're holding the thing in August, it's gonna seem like hell
on earth anyway."

"I could write a skit about how miserable it is to work all
your life in the fuckin' oil fields," Eddie Belt said.

Debate still raged about how to handle other periods of history. Jenny Marlow felt that the skits should include the Boston
Tea Party and the signing of the Declaration of Independence,
although at the time those events took place only a few starving
Indians inhabited Hardtop County.

"I know, but it's all good background, and we're part of
America, just like Boston is," Jenny argued.

Jenny soon wore them all down on that point—she generally
managed to wear them down—and Sonny had even been persuaded to play Benjamin Franklin.

There was widespread agreement that as many wars as possible should be covered in the skits, and that the pageant
should end with the boom of two years back. To end with the
present recession would upset performers and audiences alike,
since so many of them were being carried into bankruptcy by
it.

More out of boredom than conviction, Duane argued against
ending with the boom.

"I think we oughta build a replica of the bank and the last
scene oughta be people shooting themselves or cutting their
throats outside it," he said. He found that he had acquired a
fund of gallows humor since his debt had begun to grow.

Despite his pleas, a proposal to end the pageant with an oil-
boom skit passed the committee with only one negative vote.

The skit was to involve a gusher spouting colored water rather than oil. Duane had cast the negative vote.

"Oh, let's just use oil," he said. "It might be cheaper than water by the time we put on the pageant."

"I think the final scene should be like a grand entry in a rodeo," Jenny said. "Only instead of riding around the arena on horses we could all ride around it in Cadillacs. That'd be a wonderful way to end. It would suggest prosperity."

"By then every Cadillac in town will have been repossessed," Duane said peevishly. It annoyed him that no one had voted with him to end the pageant on a recessionary theme.

Just as he was working up to adjourning the meeting for lack of a quorum, Suzie Nolan walked in wearing a startling new hairdo. She had had her brown hair frosted and cut in a manner reminiscent of Tina Turner. She was also chewing gum in a rather energetic fashion. That was even more un-Suzie-like than the hairdo. It was a small thing, but it made Duane feel apprehensive.

She was followed almost immediately by Buster Lickle and the Reverend G. G. Rawley. Buster, in addition to being a Council member, was the local merchant prince. He owned several businesses of various natures in Thalia and neighboring towns, including the Dairy Queen. He was short and energetic, and he devoted his leisure time to historical pursuits.

G.G. Rawley was a horny-handed old man who had clawed his way onto the committee over the feebler efforts of other local churchmen. G.G., who had been called to the ministry from a life of lust and alcoholism, ministered to a Baptist splinter group called the Byelo-Baptists. Duane had never been certain what a Byelo-Baptist believed, but whatever it was, they believed it fervently. At one time the Byelo-Baptist creed had had a strong appeal to the ladies of Thalia, many of whom had left their normal churches to join G.G.'s.

Buster and G.G. had hardly taken their seats before Ralph Rolfe, a local rancher, and Jenny Marlow came in. To everyone's astonishment Jenny Marlow also had a new hairdo. She had always worn her hair in a short boyish cut so it wouldn't interfere with her pitching motion. It was still short, but now managed to stick out every which way in a spiky fashion. Jenny was also wearing a good deal of vivid blue eye shadow.

"Well, I guess we're all here," Duane said, with a sinking heart. He wished he knew what the new hairdos meant. When Karla changed hers it usually meant a new boyfriend.

The main reason his heart sank, though, was that the whole committee was present, and the more members who came, the longer the session. Arguments tended to flare up like grass fires. Just thinking about all the arguments that might flare up caused him to experience a sudden energy loss.

"This should be a short meeting, folks," he said, trying to sound brisk. "The T-shirts and ashtrays and bumper stickers should be coming in next week. That'll be one worry off our minds."

No one seemed to be too interested in that particular worry, so Duane went on to the next one.

"The first thing we need to vote on is whether to hire an outside person to direct the pageant," he said. "We're gonna need to start rehearsals in about another month."

The committee remained silent. The question of hiring an outside director for the pageant did not seem to interest them deeply. Duane felt like hitting them with his work glove, as he did Shorty, to make them talk.

"I have the name of a man from Brooklyn who directs pageants," Duane said. "He did one down in Throckmorton County and they were real pleased with him."

"Is Brooklyn over near Tyler, or where would it be at?" the Reverend Rawley inquired.

"It's part of New York City," Duane informed him. "He comes with a crew of three, to help him with special effects. We're gonna need a little light show when we're doing the Creation."

"The Lord didn't employ electricity," G.G. pointed out. He saw it as his duty to fend off any skits that might lead to a liberal interpretation of the Bible.

"He employed lightning," Sonny said. "That's electricity."

"He didn't employ nobody from Brooklyn, New York," G.G. said. "The man might be a Catholic."

Duane sighed. "He's supposed to be real good with fight

scenes," he said. "We're doing about ten wars, we need somebody who knows how to stage fight scenes."

"Most people around here already know how to fight," G.G. said.

"But they won't be fighting, they'll be *pretending* to fight," Duane said. "At least I hope they'll just be pretending."

The necessity of staging the Revolutionary War, the Texas war of independence, the Civil War, the two World Wars and possibly Korea and Viet Nam worried him a good deal, considering the stressed-out condition of the people who would be simulating all that combat.

It was agreed to place a call to the man from Brooklyn to find out how much he would charge the county to direct their pageant.

Duane had recovered a bit from his energy loss. He decided to move at once to adjourn the meeting while he still felt vigorous enough to walk to his pickup; but before he could act, Buster Lickle hunched forward, a passionate gleam in his eye.

"Now that that's out of the way, can we talk about Texasville?" he asked. "We got to settle that question pretty soon, don't we?"

"I guess we do, Buster," Duane said. He had lost his appetite for a steak and wished he could just be at home, eating a bowl of Cheerios.

CHAPTER 19

UNFORTUNATELY FOR THE PLANNING COMMITTEE
of the Hardtop County centennial, Thalia had not always been
the county seat. That honor had not fallen to it until 1906.

The original county seat had been called Texasville and had
consisted at first of nothing more than a clapboard post office
constructed on the stark prairie by two land speculators, Mr.
Joe Brown and Mr. Ed Brown, who were not related. They had
needed a post office so land-hungry suckers could mail them
checks, and had managed to get the state to authorize one.

Texasville, by all accounts—and from the point of view of
the Centennial Committee, there were far too many accounts
—had never developed into much of a town, though the two
Mr. Browns had chosen a site that offered anyone who cared to
look an almost unlimited view of the commodity they had for
sale.

Unfortunately for the two gentlemen, not many cared to look,
and of those who looked, even fewer liked what they saw. The
Comanches had been officially whipped a few years previously, but there were still those who doubted that the whipping would take.

Another discouraging factor in the eyes of early settlers was that the sun around Texasville was a good deal too bright. The nearest shade tree was a half day's ride to the south, and the nearest creek as well. Though Joe Brown and Ed Brown printed up flyers assuring settlers of abundant water, most were in a thoroughly parched condition long before they reached the little post office. The two Browns dug a well and dispensed free water lavishly, but despite their generosity a land boom failed to develop. Even once there was an official county—named Hardtop because of the flintlike nature of the topsoil—settlement remained sluggish. The few pioneers who straggled in ignored Texasville and homesteaded near one of the county's five or six anemic creeks.

The two Browns were resourceful men, not easily discouraged. They soon gave up on land and turned their attention to sin. They tacked a saloon onto their little post office and procured a shady lady or two from the fleshpots of Fort Worth.

Sin didn't really boom either—the homesteaders couldn't afford it—but enough cowboys and drummers passed through to support Texasville for another twenty years. Mr. Joe Brown and Mr. Ed Brown became their own best customers. Mr. Joe Brown drank himself to death in 1915, and Mr. Ed Brown married a toothsome little shady lady in the same year.

When oil was discovered in the county a few years later, Mr. Ed Brown rapidly converted his windmill into a drilling rig and began to puncture, more or less at random, the large tract of land he still owned.

Instead of striking oil, he struck rattlesnakes. He positioned his drilling rig a bit too close to one of the many rocky bluffs in the neighborhood and drilled right into what was then believed to be the most populous den of diamondbacks in the world. It was conservatively estimated to contain ten thousand snakes and made headlines as far away as Waco.

The veracity of the count was soon called into question by envious snake hunters in neighboring counties, several of whom claimed to have uncovered dens containing fifty or even one hundred thousand snakes.

Claims and counterclaims filled the pages of small prairie newspapers for the next several years, but when the excitement subsided it became evident that the proximity of ten thousand snakes would do little to spur land sales around Texasville.

Mr. Ed Brown racked his brain for the next year or two, trying to think of a way to market the snakes, or to turn the den into a profitable tourist attraction. Unfortunately it was necessary to crawl into the den itself in order to appreciate the magnitude of the discovery, and not too many could be found who were willing to pay money to crawl into a den containing ten thousand snakes.

Ed Brown grew increasingly discouraged. Despite his hopes, the prosperous little community he had envisioned refused to develop. Texasville continued to consist of one building, his own saloon—post office. He tacked on a third room and made it a general store, but three rooms didn't make a town.

Meanwhile, in another part of the county, just the sort of community he had envisioned *did* develop. It was called Thalia. It, too, started as a post office. The site was no less barren than the site of Texasville, but for some reason houses were built and businesses started. There were even churches.

Ed Brown was consumed with envy, and had other problems as well. Belle Brown, the little shady lady he had married, proved more toothy than toothsome. Ed Brown was frequently heard to say he would rather go crawl in with his rattlesnakes than share a bed with Belle.

Desperate to utilize the one resource that remained to him, he made an expensive trip to Chicago to see if the meat-packing interests would be interested in packing rattlesnakes. He was promptly assured that they wouldn't, and returned to Hardtop County a broken man, only to discover Belle dancing gaily with three cowboys. He promptly found a pistol and emptied it at his wife and the cowboys, but the shots did no damage. Then he found a shotgun and again approached his victims, who were cowering behind a barrel of molasses in the general store.

"I curse the goddamn fate that caused me to start up this goddamn place," he said. "It's ruined me to the point where I can't even shoot straight. I would like to see a plague of scorpions descend on Texasville and sting you skunks to death."

Having delivered that chilling hope, Ed Brown walked out

with his shotgun and was last seen, about sundown of that day, standing pensively at the entrance to the snake den.

Attempts to recover his body were half-hearted. Hooks were dropped into the den in hopes of snagging it, but when the hooks were pulled up they were usually covered with a dozen or so writhing diamondbacks. The crews soon grew discouraged.

Belle Brown, his bereaved widow, didn't press the search.

"A grave is nothing but a hole in the ground, anyway," she observed.

A year later oil was struck on the old Brown & Brown tract, of which Belle was sole owner. The tract soon had one hundred and fifty producing wells. Belle moved into Thalia and built a mansion. Though by far the richest person in the county she refused to have any truck with high society, such as it was then. She rode her mule to town to get her mail and let her coon dogs sleep in her big Packard automobile. Her passion was chicken-fighting; she often had a few cronies in and held cockfights in her vast living room. She drank heavily and went from toothy to toothless within a few years. She was quick to take offense and flung unintelligible threats at almost anyone who crossed her path.

Meanwhile a legend grew around the unhappy Ed Brown. Cowboys crossing the plains at night near Diamondback Hill, the bluff where the den was located, reported hearing singing that seemed to come from under the ground. Ed Brown had had a fine tenor voice.

Once or twice a figure was seen strolling around the bluff. There were people who felt Ed Brown wasn't dead at all. He was living with the snakes, they said. Travelers reported that the snakes encountered on Diamondback Hill were unusually testy, as if protecting a secret. Old-timers speculated that Ed Brown was just biding his time, waiting to get revenge on Belle.

If that was true, he waited too long. Belle Brown wandered out on her second-story porch one night, deep in her cups, fell off and broke her neck. The whole fortune went to her three nephews, who sued one another for more than twenty years, each trying to secure the lion's share.

Texasville thrived during the boom. Boomers gladly paid Belle five dollars a night just to be allowed to bed down on the floor. Five or six more clapboard shacks were built, and it looked as if the place might become a town after all.

But when the boom died all forward progress stopped. Texasville soon lost its post office, and when the county voted itself dry the saloon had to close. The general store failed and the clapboard shacks were soon pulled down by people needing lumber. The only visitors were cowboys who would occasionally stop and nap in the shade of the old porch.

The original building began to sag, and eventually it collapsed. A small tornado passed through in the late thirties and scattered the remains far and wide. The floor was all that was left. Scorpions bred plentifully under the sandy floorboards, but no skunks, human or otherwise, got killed.

In the fifties a bulldozer cutting a pipeline trench along the side of Diamondback Hill bored right through the snake den. It happened in March, and a couple of hundred sluggish snakes were killed by the pipeline crew. They found a few bones, but none of the pipeliners had ever heard of Ed Brown, so the bones were let lie. A month or two later one of the pipeliners casually mentioned the snake den to the local newspaper editor, who rushed to the site at once hoping to find the skeleton of Ed Brown, the father of Hardtop County.

The only bones that could be found turned out to belong to a calf. The editor, who had little enough to write about, rehashed the whole legend of Texasville and the two Mr. Browns for a week or two and then forgot about it.

Another quarter century passed and the centennial loomed on the horizon. Buster Lickle, who had only lived in the county a few years, began to agitate for a celebration. He took more interest in the county's history than many people who had lived there all their lives.

By the time the actual planning for the centennial began, almost no one was left who could say with certainty where Texasville had been. Old Man Balt, whom everyone had counted on for help, couldn't remember the place at all. When pressed he grew defensive and denied that it had even existed. Family albums were canvassed and a number of pictures of

Texasville collected. These were shown to Old Man Balt, who said it looked like someplace in Arkansas to him.

The indefatigable Buster Lickle made an exhaustive search of the prairie south of Diamondback Hill and eventually managed to kick up a few rotting boards that he claimed were the remains of Texasville. The boards were only a few hundred feet north of Aunt Jimmie's Lounge.

A dispute soon arose over the boards. By this time it had become clear to many people, Duane foremost among them, that putting on a county centennial was no simple matter. Hardly anything of interest had ever happened in Hardtop County, but the few things that undeniably *had* occurred were almost all subjects of dispute.

Duane felt a little betrayed. Until the Centennial Committee started its work, the people of the county had been blithely indifferent to their own scanty history, but as soon as he committed himself as head of the project everyone came alive and started arguing like wildcats. Rumors casually passed down by grandparents thirty and forty years previously took on the weight of Scripture—and the weight of the real Scripture, as invoked by G. G. Rawley, was heavy enough.

So far no issue had proven more explosive than Texasville. Hoyce Howell, editor of the *Thalia Times*, and himself a relative newcomer to the county, had never liked Buster Lickle. Hoyce set out to debunk Buster's discovery of the remains of Texasville. In a front-page article he claimed that the boards Buster had kicked up were only the remains of an outhouse.

Buster Lickle was so outraged by this slur on his archeology that he threatened to pull all his advertising out of the *Times*.

The threat of economic sanctions soon became a common tool. Karla despised Buster Lickle and was outraged by his pretensions to historical expertise. She threatened to organize a boycott of the Dairy Queen if he didn't stop bugging people about things they weren't interested in.

"He could have planted those boards himself, and aged them to look old," Karla said.

"Even Buster wouldn't be crazy enough to age boards in a place where there's lots of old lumber," Duane argued.

"I don't like his attitude anyway," Karla said. "I'm gonna print a T-shirt that says, TEXASVILLE SUCKS."

"Please don't do that," Duane pleaded. "I've got enough trouble without you doing that."

They were bobbing on the surface of their vast waterbed at the time, watching David Letterman.

"I might relent and not do it but there's no telling what else I will do if you start censoring my T-shirts," Karla said.

Duane had never liked the waterbed.

"If they're gonna make waterbeds this big they oughta provide life jackets, just in case," he said.

"You didn't used to complain about any bed as long as I was in it," Karla said. "What do you say to that?"

Duane didn't say anything to it. He tried to feign sleep.

"I've never heard of half the people on these interview shows," Karla said.

She had graciously refrained from printing the TEXASVILLE SUCKS T-shirt, but the many issues raised by the fact that Texasville had been the first county seat continued to bedevil the committee. There was no getting around the fact that the place had once existed—any comprehensive celebration dealing with the history of the county would have to take it into account.

Buster Lickle, Texasville's most vigorous sponsor, wanted a full-scale re-creation, with tourists being taken out to the site —to be called Old Texasville—on buggy rides which would start at his Dairy Queen.

Opposed to this plan was the Reverend Rawley, who was for ignoring Texasville entirely. After all, it had been a saloon and bawdyhouse, and G.G. stood ready to take the Byelo-Baptists to the barricades rather than have a centennial that glorified what he called "lowlife riffraff and persons who sold whiskey."

It was the necessity of reconciling these two apparently unreconcilable points of view that now faced the committee.

CHAPTER 20

"I WONDER IF WE CAN'T COME TO A COMPROMISE about Texasville," Duane said. He felt that he would almost rather be on a trip with his children than to be doing what he was doing.

"Not me," G.G. said. "There's no compromising with what's right."

"But what we're proposing ain't wrong, G.G.," Buster said. "This is gonna be a big celebration. We've got to give it the Old West flavor."

"Not if the flavor's Bourbon whiskey," G.G. said. "I ain't voting to build no replicas of saloons or whorehouses."

"But it's history!" Buster said.

"The only history worth putting on a show for is the Lord's history," G.G. said, his heavy jaw thrust forward.

"We're gonna get Adam and Eve in the pageant," Buster reminded him. "I don't see why we can't have a little of the Old West too."

"It could create alcoholics if you start people at one saloon and give them a free buggy ride to another one," the minister said.

Duane himself was dubious about the buggy rides, though on practical rather than moral grounds. The proliferation of events already had him worried. There was going to be a mini-marathon and a wagon train; the Governor was going to come and make a speech. There would be an art show, a visit to an oil rig (his), street dances, barbecues, class reunions and organized trips to every place of interest in the county. Buggy rides might be too much—besides, who knew how to drive a buggy?

"What if we just build a small replica of the Texasville post office and put it on the courthouse square during the festivities?" Sonny suggested. He and Duane had discussed such a compromise at length.

"I think that's a good idea," Duane said. "People aren't going to drive way out in the country to see a replica of a post office."

"Put a saloon right here in the heart of town?" G.G. said, not taken in by the pretense that the replica would merely be that of a post office.

Duane looked around the room, hoping for a show of support. Instead he found a show of indifference. Ralph Rolfe, the rancher, was carefully slicing a corn off his thumb with a large pocketknife. Old Man Balt watched the proceedings intently, waiting to burst into cackles if anything funny happened. Suzie Nolan and Jenny Marlow both seemed lost in thought. Duane was sure they weren't thinking about Texasville either. They had a smoldering look beneath their new hairdos and vivid eye shadow. He wondered briefly if Dickie had actually had the good sense to proceed on toward New Mexico. It didn't seem likely.

"We've got to make some progress here, folks," he said. "Time's running out. We just have to settle some of these issues as best we can."

He felt himself building a considerable head of annoyance with G. G. Rawley. Behind the Texasville question lurked the larger issue of liquor sales during the centennial. The county was wet only to a degree. Liquor could only be sold in package stores. If people wanted to sit at a table and drink they had to drive out to Aunt Jimmie's, just across the county line.

It seemed obvious to him that people who were gathered for

a once-in-a-century event would want to dance, holler and
drink by way of celebration. Duane had thought the matter
over and had decided to propose the radical step of allowing
the sale of beer on the courthouse square during the time of
the festivities, after which the county would have to return
immediately to its sober ways.

The rationale he planned to advance was that most people
would be drunk before the nightly street dance even started,
and if they had to go racing off to Aunt Jimmie's or some of the
far-flung package stores to replenish their supplies, the roads
of the county would soon be littered with car wrecks.

Toots Burns, the sheriff, was prepared to back Duane's argument to the hilt.

"Let 'em dance and have fistfights," he said. "If they get to
chasing around in pickups there won't be enough wreckers in
North Texas to handle it."

Still, it was obvious that the proposal would meet with the
furious opposition of G.G. and the teetotaling Byelo-Baptists.

Duane had been postponing a vote in the hope that G.G.
would be called away to preach a revival or something, allowing them to sneak it in behind his back.

But time had grown short, and anyway Duane had ceased to
care about avoiding a fight.

"What this whole celebration is about is history," Duane
said. "It's about the history of this county of ours. We can't just
put in the good history and leave out the bad."

"Why can't we?" G.G. asked. "The Lord don't want nobody
exhibiting any bad history."

Buster Lickle, who had been pouting anyway, suddenly
flared up.

"It ain't the Lord that's blocking this," he said. "He don't
care what kind of little show we put on down here. You Baptists just don't want normal people to have any fun."

"Buster, I'm trying to make a motion," Duane said. "I move
that we build the replica of Texasville right here on the courthouse square."

"I second that," Sonny said.

"We can still do the buggy rides," Duane said, noting that
Buster was so disappointed that he was about to cry. "We can

put the buggies at the Dairy Queen and people can just ride through town. All in favor of the replica motion raise their right hands."

Five hands went up immediately and Ralph Rolfe raised his as soon as he finished slicing off his corn.

"Opposed?" Duane asked.

G.G. glared at the two women. "I'm looking right at two people who just voted against the Lord," he said.

"I didn't," Jenny Marlow said. "I just voted against you, G.G."

"That's just as bad," G.G. said. "I'm the shepherd of your flock. You're nothing but a woman that's pitched softball until she's got the big head."

"Now let's not get into stuff like this," Duane said. "The motion carried and I want to make another one. I propose we authorize the sale of beer on the courthouse lawn while the centennial's going on. I make this motion in the interest of public safety."

"I second it," Suzie Nolan said.

G.G. seemed thunderstruck. Suzie had led his choir for many years. But G.G. recovered quickly.

"Thou shalt worship no graven images!" he thundered. "Now that's one of the Lord's commandments."

"We're not talking about engraving no images," Buster Lickle protested. "Just maybe putting Sam Houston on some of the T-shirts."

"Hadn't been for old Sam I doubt there'd even be Texas," Ralph Rolfe commented.

"The motion was seconded," Duane said. "Let's vote."

G.G. showed signs of bewilderment. Things were moving too fast. He had been about to preach a little sermonette demonstrating to the committee that building a replica of an old saloon was the equivalent of erecting a graven image, but before he could get his sermon untracked, an even worse proposal had been made, and seconded by another ewe from his own flock, the normally reliable choir leader, Suzie Nolan. He looked around in dismay. Sin was accumulating so fast that he hardly knew where to strike at it.

"What's that about public safety?" he asked. "How's the

public gonna be safe if it's allowed to get drunk right in the middle of town?"

"What we hope to do is cut down drunk driving, G.G.," Duane said. "The sheriff thinks it's best to keep people off the roads as much as possible."

"Toots Burns is a fat sot himself," G.G. pointed out. "You can find him stretched out dog-drunk in his police car any night you care to look. Besides, letting people pour beer down their gullets right on the courthouse lawn won't keep people off the highways. They don't all live at the courthouse. They have to go home sometime, and I doubt they'll want to walk."

Duane had seen that objection coming and was ready.

"We're gonna provide army cots so people can just sleep it off and go home in the morning," he said. "All in favor of the motion raise your right hands."

Six hands went up.

"Opposed?" Duane asked. Old Man Balt had been seized by a spasm of amusement and was cackling so loudly nothing else could be heard.

G.G. Rawley got to his feet.

"You can floorboard these votes through all you want to, Duane," he said. "You're a sinner and your wife's a sinner and your kids fornicate and sell dope."

"I don't claim to be perfect, G.G.," Duane said.

"Well, we won't discuss personalities," G.G. said with an air of dignity. "This is just a tawdry little old committee and it can't vote to sell alcohol nowhere. I know that much."

"No, but the City Council can, and several of us are on it," Duane said. "I think we can get the liquor provision approved."

"Well, now you're flirting with hell, all of you," G.G. said.

"Sit down," Duane said. "You don't have the floor."

"I may not have the floor, but I've got the Lord," G.G. said.

"Oh, stop bragging, G.G.," Jenny said. "All you've got's a big old swelled-up ego."

"At least I ain't married to a sinner that's been indicted on seventy-two counts of crime," G.G. said. "If you've got any shame you'll get over to church and rededicate your life the first chance you get, which will be this coming Sunday."

"If we don't move along with the agenda, this meeting will still be going on Sunday," Duane said.

"You blasphemers and idol-makers can sit here and propose all you want to," G.G. said. "All this committee's done so far is think up sins and temptations to put before the public."

He paused, to give the committee a moment to contemplate the enormity of their error. Suzie Nolan was filing a nail. The rest of the committee looked back at him sullenly.

"I'm going home and pray," G.G. said. "I'll tell you one thing though. You won't be selling no spiritous liquors on the courthouse lawn. If we have to fight the Alamo all over again, then so be it."

With that he stalked out.

"That man's got too bad a temper to be a preacher," Suzie said.

"I don't understand what he meant about the Alamo," Buster Lickle said. "Would we be the Mexicans or the Texans?"

"I think he means for us to be the ones that get slaughtered," Duane said.

CHAPTER 21

THE FINAL VOTE OF THE EVENING HAD TO DO WITH the time capsule—Sonny's idea. He thought it might be interesting to let people write notes to posterity. The notes could then be put in a bottle and buried on the courthouse lawn for a hundred years. At the bicentennial, which would surely be held if there wasn't a nuclear war, the time capsule could be dug up and the celebrants could read what people in Thalia had on their minds in the late twentieth century.

"Sex and dope and making money," Karla said, when she heard about the idea. "That's all people around here ever have on their minds."

"We write it on a piece of paper and put it in the time capsule," Duane said.

"I will not," Karla said. "I might have great-grandchildren alive. Do you want our great-grandkids to think I was a horny old woman?"

Duane didn't answer. At the rate Little Mike was growing, several generations of Moores might sprout before the bicentennial. One of Little Mike's grandchildren might be sitting

123

where he sat, at the head of a committee designed to organize appropriate festivities.

The committee took an enthusiastic view of the time capsule, approving it unanimously.

"I guess we all better be thinking about what we want to say to posterity," Jenny Marlow said, looking at Duane again.

"Yes, and I hereby adjourn this meeting so we can get started thinking right now," Duane said.

Beulah Balt, the old man's daughter, was at the curb in their ancient Plymouth, waiting to take her father home. Duane helped the old man down the courthouse steps and inched along with him as he made his way along the sidewalk. He liked Old Man Balt and enjoyed watching him in action. The old man carefully emptied a half can of tobacco juice onto the courthouse lawn.

"Hurry up and get in the car, Daddy," Beulah called. "We're missing *The Waltons*."

Before they made it to the curb, Suzie Nolan strolled past on one side and Jenny Marlow passed on the other side. Old Man Balt didn't increase his speed and Duane felt momentarily like a stalled car on a freeway, but they eventually reached the car and got the old man settled.

"Take it easy, Mr. Balt," Duane said. "We're counting on you to make this centennial work."

"Daddy'll help you out," Beulah said. "It'll be a good distraction for him."

Suzie and Jenny left at the same moment. They both caught the red light at the corner, the only traffic light in town. When it changed, Jenny turned right and Suzie left. Neither of them was headed in the direction of her home.

Duane drove down to the little six-bed hospital, parked and went in. Though he tried to walk quietly, his boots rang on the hard waxed floor. No nurse appeared, so he walked on down the hall until he saw a room with a light. Lester Marlow was sitting up in bed, reading a paperback spy novel.

"How you doing?" Duane asked.

"I'm dulled out," Lester said. "I don't think I can sleep, though."

Lester didn't look dulled—he looked wired. His brown hair,

which had always run to cowlicks, now seemed to consist of nothing but cowlicks. It stuck out in all directions, and his big feet stuck out from under the covers.

"If I'd finished college I could have worked for the CIA," he said. "They say ordinary people like me make the best spies. It's probably a lot less stressful than being a bank president in a small town."

Duane sat down in the one chair.

"Why would you want to be a spy?" he asked.

"I'd rather be anything than what I am," Lester said, ruffling his cowlicks. He had a large head, a large face. It struck Duane that large faces could look sadder than small faces. Lester's looked quite sad.

"Do you think I'll get raped in prison?" he asked.

"I doubt you'll even go," Duane said. "Maybe they'll let you do community service. You could mow the grass on the football field."

"Butt-fucking doesn't appeal to me," Lester said plaintively.

"Or it'll probably be one of those country-club prisons," Duane said.

"You're not going to take bankruptcy, are you?" Lester asked.

"No, I don't plan to," Duane said.

"Why not?" Lester asked. "Your position is hopeless. A lot of people in your shoes would have jumped into Chapter Eleven."

"Luthie's got a plan to bomb OPEC," Duane said. "Once he does that, the oil business is bound to pick up.

"Nothing's hopeless till you're dead," he added cheerfully.

"My marriage is hopeless," Lester said. "Jenny says I have no common sense. We haven't slept together in months. She goes off in a car at night and I don't know where she goes.

"But we have sweet children," he added. "I hope the girls don't turn against me while I'm in prison."

"Those girls aren't going to turn against you," Duane said. Lester and Jenny had two daughters, Missy and Sissy, both teenagers. They were among the best-liked children in town. They were lively and talkative but also well-behaved, and they already showed promise in softball.

"I wish the ax would fall," Lester said. He looked at the ceiling as if he expected an ax to come dropping right through it.

"Which ax?" Duane asked, not sure whether Duane was talking about his marriage, his bank or his prison sentence.

"Any ax," Lester said. "I'm tired of thinking all day long. Maybe I would be better off in prison, making license plates. I think I could handle a simple job like that. I just wouldn't want to get raped."

"You worry too much," Duane said. "I was thinking of going fishing. Go with me. The crappie might be biting."

"With my luck, they'd bite me," Lester said gloomily. "What do you think's the matter with Jenny?"

"I have no idea," Duane said.

"Jenny likes excitement," Lester said. "She says I'm not exciting anymore. She says I haven't been exciting since Missy was born."

"It's hard to stay exciting for a whole lifetime," Duane said, standing up. "I hope you get to feeling better."

CHAPTER 22

SUZIE NOLAN WAS WAITING IN THE PARKING LOT
when Duane walked out of the hospital. As he approached the
car he could see the shine of tears on her cheek. He leaned
down and looked in at her.

"Now what's the matter with you?" he asked.

"I just feel lost," Suzie said. "I just love Dickie so much,
Duane. I just love him heart and soul."

"Suzie, I wish you'd picked me," Duane said. "I don't know
if you can count too much on a boy like Dickie."

"I can't count on him at all," Suzie said. "I know that. It's
why I'm so lost. It's just good fun to him but it's heart and soul
to me. Now Junior's going broke, and it's just all going to break
down."

She began to sob and laid her head on his arm. Duane let
her cry, occasionally stroking her hair. He thought briefly of
what a terrible thing it must be for a woman of Suzie's age to
be madly in love with Dickie, but his thoughts kept drifting
elsewhere—specifically, they drifted to his own girlfriend, Janine Wells, for whom he had conceived a growing distaste. He

tried to remember whether he had always felt a distaste for Janine or whether he had just begun to feel it lately. If he didn't like her, why had he started sleeping with her? She was probably sitting on her couch in a negligee at that very moment, waiting for him to come by. He hadn't told her he would come by, but sometimes he did after centennial meetings. On such occasions Janine always dressed in a negligee, usually lavender.

Duane decided it was probably the negligees, and not Janine's grasping ways, that were causing the distaste. He was certainly no stranger to grasping ways, and had long since concluded that it didn't pay to be too fastidious in this life.

He looked across the top of Suzie's car and saw that indeed the lights were on at Janine's house. She lived two blocks from the hospital in the little house her parents had lived in.

Her parents had been killed in a car wreck while Janine was in high school. Janine had gone to work in the courthouse the minute she graduated from high school. She had been married briefly to Joe Bob Blanton, a local minister's son. They had become close after her parents' funeral. Janine was not popular and had no one else to be close to.

But the marriage only lasted a summer. Joe Bob had first gone to college in Wichita Falls, then had switched to Denton, then to the University of Oklahoma, then to the University of Kansas, at which point people in Thalia finally lost track of him. He removed himself one college at a time—someone had heard that he had finally reached Syracuse, New York, but that was just a rumor.

Duane began to feel guilty. He didn't want to go to see Janine. At the same time he knew it must be sad to sit in the little house your parents had lived in, in a lavender negligee, and have your boyfriend drive right past and not come to see you. He wondered what was going on at the Howlers—maybe Karla and Junior had finally fallen in love. But the thing that bothered him most was that he had ordered a steak and was not going to get to eat it.

While he weighed his sense of duty to Janine against his hunger, depression and various other feelings, Suzie Nolan began to bite his hand. She had been crying on his arm while

he stroked her hair. One of his hands was beneath her cheek
and she turned her head and began to suck her tears off his
hand. Then she bit the fleshy part of his hand. Her bite was
soft at first, but then she bit harder. She moved up to his fingers
and bit one, fairly hard.

When Duane tried to pull his hand away, Suzie held the bite.
She was looking at him out of wide, determined eyes, her teeth
clamped on his finger, reminding him for a moment of how
Shorty might look if he tried to remove a bone Shorty was
eating.

Shorty himself watched the scene from the front seat of Minerva's Buick, which Duane had borrowed. Shorty was happy
that Duane was so close. The periods when Duane had been
in the courthouse and the hospital had been agony for Shorty,
but he didn't mind at all if Duane stood by the car, feeding his
hand to some woman. Shorty accepted everything about Duane
except his absences.

Suzie turned her head so she could take the finger she was
biting into her mouth. Duane tried once more to slide it away
but Suzie set her teeth in it and bit harder. He looked around
nervously to see if anyone was coming. People were always
getting sick in Thalia—anyone could drive up.

Duane felt a confusing mixture of surprise, dismay and desire. Suzie's passionate bites were having an effect. At the same
time it was not lost on him that she was in love with his son—
she was Dickie's girlfriend, or one of them. Of course she was
Junior Nolan's wife, but Junior crossed his mind only briefly.
He had long since reconciled himself to adultery—but sharing
a lover with one of his own children was a different matter.
That *had* to be different, but in his nervousness he was not
exactly sure where the point of difference lay, or what it meant.

He had a sense that life was about to jump the fence of
credibility and become completely unbelievable. He wanted
to stop it, to keep it from racing into hopeless emotional chaos,
but, unfortunately for his ethical sense, desire was growing
faster than dismay. It was growing urgent, which added to the
surprise and confusion—he hadn't felt an *urgent* sexual need
in two or three years. It was all he could do to make an effort
to check himself, but he did try.

"Suzie, stop," he said. She was still mouthing his fingers. "Don't do that. It's Dickie you're in love with."

Her mouth made a little pop as she released his finger. The small, intimate sound was more affecting than the bites and all but undid his resolve.

"He don't love me," Suzie said. "It's just good fun to him. I do love the little rat something terrible—but don't leave me, Duane. I don't want you to leave."

She pulled his wet hand down into the heat of her bosom and raised herself half out of the window to kiss him. In contrast to the aggressive biting, her mouth was soft and shy—her breath tickled his cheek. He ceased trying to stop and followed her through the window when she drew back to loosen her blouse. She began to unbutton his shirt but kept an arm around his neck, apparently thinking he could just slide in through the window. She twisted backward far enough to get her legs out from under the steering wheel.

Duane was not so limber. His erection, of which he was very aware, was jammed against the door handle and both his feet were off the ground. Suzie managed to get her legs up on his shoulder and to loosen his belt, but it did her little good because the rest of him was still out in the parking lot. Meanwhile she was still smothering him with quick, breathy kisses, and she seemed puzzled by the delay.

"I don't know if I can get in through this window," Duane said. He had rarely felt so horny and at the same time so silly —his legs were sticking straight out the window. By a desperate wrench he had managed to free his erection from the door handle but it still wasn't inside the car.

"Shoot, I told Junior we needed a station wagon," Suzie said, vexed by the logistics but unwilling to stop kissing him. She caught his hand again and thrust it between her legs, hoping that a touch there would inspire him.

Duane could not have been much more inspired, but his inspiration could not widen the window or eliminate the steering wheel or raise the roof. He was about to try to wiggle out and simply open the door when a flicker of light struck the windshield. A car was racing along the little road toward the hospital. Suzie saw it too.

"Oh, no!" she said. "Bad timing!"

"Terrible timing," Duane said. "I'm stuck."

Indeed, getting back out the window was no simpler than getting in. For a moment he wished he had paid a little more attention to the various diets Karla read to him while he was in the hot tub ignoring her.

His exit was not made easier by the fact that Suzie, bent on assuring herself as thorough a caress as possible, held his hand tightly to her crotch. She lay back in the seat and covered her eyes with her forearm.

"Just do that for a second," she said. "That car's not here yet. Just do that. That's nice.

"I thought you'd be nice," she added. "You know how you think about how people will be?"

Before Duane could comment, Suzie bit her forearm to stifle a nice cry of pleasure. Duane felt that it would also be very nice to have his feet back on the ground before the car arrived. He could hear it rattling as it raced up the bumpy road.

He got a crick in his back, twisting out, but left his hand with Suzie for a bit as he leaned against the door and caught his breath. A couple more nice cries of pleasure were imperfectly stifled. Duane felt sharply frustrated, but still glad to be out of the window.

Suzie sat up, her eyes gleaming, just as the car came skidding to a stop.

It was Beulah Balt, so crazed with shock that she immediately yanked the car into reverse rather than park, and almost ran over Duane, who was not at his most nimble.

"Daddy's dead!" she said. "He fell out of the car and rolled off into the ditch."

"Oh, no!" Suzie said, getting out of the car to comfort her. "He was gonna be the star of our centennial."

Duane raced into the hospital to see if Buddy, the ambulance driver, was anywhere around. May, the night nurse, a woman as secretive as a mouse, was sitting in one of the closets counting packages of Q-tips.

"Buddy's gone crappie fishing but he left the ambulance, help yourself," May said, when Duane ran up.

"You better call the doctor," Duane said.

"I will, but don't make me lose count, I'm taking inventory," May said.

Lester came out of the hall to see what all the excitement was about and just had time to grab his shoes.

They got the two women into the ambulance and went racing out the highway. Old Man Balt and his daughter lived about ten miles out.

"It's my fault," Beulah said, weeping. "I get on him for missing his tobacco can when he spits. He can't hit the can in the dark in a moving car. I got on him and he opened the door and tried to spit. The next thing I knew he was gone."

"It might not be that serious," Suzie said. "He might just have a few broken limbs."

"I was in this ambulance earlier in the day," Lester remarked. Suzie Nolan made him nervous.

Beulah had only a loose idea of where she had been when her father rolled out.

"I had the radio on and didn't notice it when he fell out," Beulah said. "I'll never forgive myself for any of this. If he could just have lived three more months he would have got his letter from the President. The President writes everybody who gets to be a hundred years old."

Precious minutes were lost in trying to pinpoint the spot where Mr. Balt fell out. Beulah thought it must have happened somewhere between Onion Creek and the next creek, which had no name. Duane finally got out and walked up the bar ditch. Lester was feeling nervous, so Suzie drove the ambulance and worked the spotlight. Duane had scarcely walked a hundred yards when he found Old Man Balt flat on his back in the ditch. He looked quite dead, but in fact was only sleeping.

When first awakened he seemed docile—"What's on TV?" he asked—but when told that he had to come back to town and submit to a physical examination he began to show fight. It was soon clear that his arms and legs still worked because he proceeded to kick and strike with all of them. Duane finally wrestled the old man into the ambulance and clutched him in a kind of bear hug on the ride back into town.

"Mr. Balt, if you was any younger I believe we'd have to let you go," he said.

"If I want to sleep in a bar ditch, whose business is it but mine?" the old man wanted to know. "This was a free country back before Roosevelt."

"Hush, Daddy," Beulah said. "You might have internal bleeding."

"We'll all have internal bleeding if Suzie doesn't slow down," Lester said. "External bleeding too."

Suzie, looking flushed and competent, didn't reply, nor did she slow down.

"She tries to get me to give up tobacco," the old man said, glaring at his daughter.

"Daddy, I'll settle for you just getting a bigger can," Beulah said.

At the hospital it was soon determined that a skinned hand was the extent of Mr. Balt's injuries. In their absence the emergency room had filled up. Three roughnecks had turned a truck over. They had bled all over themselves, though none was seriously hurt. Toots Burns, the sheriff, had brought in a runaway girl who seemed disoriented.

"She thinks she's in Georgia," Toots said sympathetically. He did not look in top form, but he looked better than the girl, who sat crying listlessly on a couch across from the bloody roughnecks.

Suzie soon left to pick up her children, to Duane's profound relief. The brightly lit emergency room filled with depressed people made what had just occurred in the parking lot seem particularly absurd. Though Suzie did nothing more than try to comfort the miserable Beulah Balt, her behavior struck Duane as intolerably cheerful. She didn't look at him when she left, either, which irked him, though it was illogical to feel that way when he couldn't wait for her to leave.

He sat on the bench by the runaway girl for an hour, until it was determined that Mr. Balt could be released. He offered to drive the Balts home, but they refused his help and, after another slow trip down the sidewalk, they set off again.

Through the whole experience Duane had been nagged by the thought of the lonely Janine in her lavender negligee. Once the Balts were finally gone he went back in and called her on the pay phone.

"Well, Old Man Balt nearly got killed," he said. "That's why I couldn't come by."

"I'm already in bed," Janine said in a small, beaten voice, the opposite of the triumphant voice she had used that morning in the Dairy Queen.

"He fell out of the car," Duane said. "It's a wonder he didn't break into fifty pieces. I didn't have a chance to call sooner."

"You don't have to apologize, if that's all that happened," Janine said, in the same hopeless voice.

"I could still come by for a minute," he said.

"No, I've got grease on my face, and anyway you don't really want to," Janine said.

She was on the edge of tears. Duane tried to think of something he could say that would keep her from crying, but he didn't feel very inspired.

"Maybe we can sneak off this weekend," he said.

"You don't really want to," Janine said again, in toneless despair. Then she hung up.

CHAPTER 23

DUANE STOOD BY THE PAY PHONE A MOMENT WON-dering why he had tried to persuade Janine that what was actually true wasn't true. She was an expert at hanging up in a way that would produce the maximum guilt feelings in him, but it was a trick she had used too often. He didn't feel very guilty, and he knew that by morning Janine would have stopped despairing and be mad as hops.

It was far too late to go to the Howlers, but he didn't partic-ularly feel like going home either. He put another quarter in the pay phone and called his house.

"Who's calling?" Minerva snapped.

"Just me," Duane said.

"Well, I'm watching a movie, what do you want?" Minerva said. She loathed being interrupted when watching a movie, by casual callers or any callers.

"Is Karla home?" Duane asked.

"No, ain't seen her," Minerva snapped.

"Must be a pretty good movie," Duane said.

"It's Woody Allen, I laugh every time I see that man," Minerva said, softening slightly. "All he has to do is walk around and I laugh till I flop on the floor."

"If Karla shows up, tell her I went fishing," Duane said.

"I will. 'Bye," Minerva said, hanging up.

"I wonder who else I could call who would hang up on me," Duane said to himself.

He started to drive out to the lake and realized he had no bait. He turned around and drove to the Kwik-Sack. Sonny sat behind the cash register, watching a talk show on his little four-inch Sony. He glanced up and smiled, but he looked depressed.

Duane went over and got a package of baloney, some cheese, a jar of pickles and a loaf of bread. He could dine on a baloney sandwich, with pickles and cheese, and use the rest of the baloney for bait. It wasn't good bait, but then he wasn't that serious a fisherman—just serious enough that fishing with no bait at all made him feel guilty.

"We almost lost our star pioneer tonight," Duane said.

"What happened?"

"Old Man Balt fell out of his car and rolled off in the bar ditch," Duane said. "He wasn't hurt, though."

"I think I'm losing my mind," Sonny said.

"Why? You're not in the oil business," Duane said. He was joking but Sonny wasn't.

"I'm having these lapses more often," Sonny said. "I had one an hour ago. I started ringing up a sale and then I just forgot what I was doing. Toots wanted to buy some sandwiches for that girl he caught and I just completely forgot how to work the cash register. Toots finally had to ring up the sale himself."

"You're probably just cranky, like Minerva," Duane said. "Don't like to be interrupted when you're watching TV."

"I don't mind being interrupted at all," Sonny said. "It's my mind that's being interrupted. It just goes blank sometimes."

He looked really worried. Duane didn't say it, but the worried look was actually an improvement on the look of courteous neutrality that Sonny had worn for most of his life.

"Try ringing these groceries up," Duane suggested.

Sonny looked at the cash register a moment, and then rang Duane's purchases up perfectly.

"I don't usually have two lapses in one night," Sonny said.

"But I've had two lapses in one week. Last week I had three or four. Maybe I have a brain tumor."

"Now you're really sounding like Minerva," Duane said. "I don't think you have a brain tumor, and I hope you won't lose your mind before the centennial's over, because we've still got a lot of organizing to do."

"I think about Sam and Billy a lot," Sonny said.

Sam was a man who had been a great help to Sonny in his youth, and Billy a simple-minded boy who had worked for Sam. Sonny had idolized Sam, and Billy had idolized Sonny. Both Sam and Billy had been dead for thirty years.

"I wish we could work them into the centennial, somehow," Sonny said. "Sam kind of kept the town going at one time. Maybe there could be a skit or something."

"There's not too many left that remember those two," Duane said, thinking that a skit about Sam the Lion, which was what everyone had called him, would be even more incomprehensible to most of the audience than those already planned. People had heard of Adam and Eve, and had some vague idea of who Ben Franklin was, but local figures, dead so long, were almost as lost to memory as Texasville itself. Duane couldn't remember Sam and Billy very well himself.

"I just hate for them to be forgotten," Sonny said.

"Most people are forgotten," Duane said.

It struck him that Sonny's problem was that he had forgotten himself throughout most of his own life. Only now, with his mind developing a tendency to wander, had he finally begun to remember that he was alive.

"Sam and Billy lived here," Sonny said. "They were part of this place. Adam and Eve didn't live here. Ben Franklin didn't live here. It seems like the pageant ought to be more about people who did something for the county."

It had taken months of discussion to get the pageant into even rough shape—the last thing Duane wanted was for it to unravel before they could even begin rehearsals.

"I just want it to be enough of a pageant that people will enjoy seeing it," Duane said. "I think I'll go find out if the crappie are biting."

Sonny gave Duane his change and turned without comment back to the TV set.

CHAPTER 24

SHORTY HATED FISHING TRIPS. HE DIDN'T LIKE TO stay in the pickup worrying that Duane might never return, nor did he like riding in boats, with water all around. He didn't like water at all. It was hard to chase anything in it. Once he had jumped out of the boat to chase a turtle and had promptly disappeared. The turtle also disappeared. Another turtle appeared and he tried to chase that, but it, too, disappeared. Turtles kept appearing and disappearing. When he tried to bark at them he almost drowned. Then he lost sight of the boat and had to swim all the way to shore, an effort that left him prostrate with exhaustion.

When he saw that they were approaching the lake, he began to whimper unhappily. Duane hated to hear him whimper.

"The last thing I need, after a day like this, is to listen to you whine, Shorty," he said.

In fact, the day had not been notably more stressful than most other days. Every time he thought he had at last experienced every possible variation of stress, new variations appeared to surprise him. The effect of all of them was to make the prospect of a night on his boat, floating on the calm if smelly bosom of Lake Kickapoo, seem amazingly restful. All he would have to do was eat baloney-and-cheese sandwiches, watch the moon and occasionally put a new piece of baloney on his hook for the turtles to nibble.

The prospect lifted his spirits and he sped along through the dark mesquites, eating a sandwich he had put together with one hand under the very nose of Shorty. He gave Shorty a pickle as a consolation prize, and Shorty ate it.

The lake was low, thanks to a dry spring, and smelled muddy. A coon had cracked a mussel and was eating it on the boat dock when Duane drove down to the water. Shorty had gone to sleep and didn't notice the coon, which ran off.

Duane took his fishing gear and little sack of groceries down to the boat, started the outboard and was soon out in the middle of the lake. The shore was rimmed with small houses, many with a vapor light stuck over the carport or dock. The lights at the far end of the lake, several miles away, seemed as remote as stars.

Duane decided that even the pretense of fishing was too much trouble. He cut the motor, ate another baloney sandwich and let the fishing go. He napped for an hour, but had a heavy dream about trying to check into a motel somewhere with Janine. The dream woke him. It seemed more restful just to lay in the boat and watch the stars.

All night he drifted on the lake, dozing now and then. Not long before dawn he heard a car, then saw it moving along the north shore of the lake, its headlights slanted across the water. The car pulled down to a dock, and the lights went out. Duane decided it was probably just teenagers looking for a place to do what he and Suzie Nolan had been about to do. If it had been burglars waiting to break into one of the lake houses, they wouldn't have waited until almost daylight.

He lay back in the boat and watched the gray light spread over the water. The sky was absolutely clear, and soon the horizon turned a fiery gold, as if a forge stood just beyond the hills.

Duane was making himself a sandwich when he heard a soft sound in the water, a little splashing. He looked around, thinking the fish might be jumping, and saw a woman swimming right toward the boat. A Martian wouldn't have startled him more. The woman was a powerful swimmer. She wore goggles and a swimming cap and evidently hadn't noticed the boat. She was swimming right across the lake, which at that point was not quite half a mile wide.

Duane decided it must be some girl from Wichita, training for a swim team or something. When it seemed as if she would swim right into the boat, he started to call out, but then saw that she would miss it by five or six feet. He said nothing.

Just as the swimmer passed across the front of the boat, she saw it or sensed it and stopped swimming. Probably she was as startled as he was.

"Howdy," Duane said. "I didn't mean to scare you."

"I'm not scared," the woman said. "I guess I just assumed I had this lake to myself."

She lifted her goggles and Duane saw that it was Jacy. To the north, a black Mercedes, the one that had passed him at the stoplight, was parked at the dock below the old Farrow lake house, unused, so far as he knew, since the death of Jacy's parents, Lois and Gene.

The boat had drifted toward her. She stroked once and caught the side.

"Don't I know you from somewhere?" she asked, looking at him closely.

"Jacy, I'm Duane Moore," he said. "We went together in high school for a while."

"Duane?" she said, smiling. "My lord, what a place to run into an old boyfriend. Do you live in a boat now, or what?"

"No, I just hide out in one now and then when I'm depressed," Duane said.

"I heard you got rich," Jacy said. "What are you depressed about?"

"Nothing serious," he said, remembering her loss.

"Did you get rich?"

"Yeah, pretty rich," he said.

Duane had often wondered how Jacy might have changed, but with swim goggles on her forehead and her hair under a cap, all he could be sure of was that she still had the large blue eyes that had once mesmerized him. His memories of the flirty girl she had been didn't go far toward describing the woman who looked up at him from the brown lake. The swim goggles had left marks on her face. He remembered how vain she had once been, studying her face or body for the slightest blemish. She bruised easily, and though she liked wrestling and rough-housing, she always scolded him fiercely if a bruise resulted.

Looking at her made him feel a little foolish—through the years he had been imagining that she was still the most beau-tiful woman in the world, forgetting that those same years might have roughhoused with her more decisively and destruc-tively than he ever had. Though amply good-looking, she was no longer the supreme beauty of his fantasy, and he felt silly for having held it so long.

"Were you going to swim all the way across the lake and back?" he asked.

"Yeah," Jacy said. "I lived on the Mediterranean a long time and got used to swimming in open water. This is about the best I can do around here."

"I drive by Los Dolores once in a while," he said. "I've often thought of ringing the doorbell since I heard you were there."

"Why didn't you?" she asked.

"I have to sit in a boat all night to get any privacy myself," he said. "I'm shy about meddling with other people's."

"That's mature of you," Jacy said. "If you had rung my door-bell I'd probably have been rude."

She seemed about to kick off for the muddy south shore, but then noticed the open jar of pickles he held in his hand. She reached in, took a pickle and ate it.

"An old girlfriend's privilege," she said, smiling. Then she lowered her goggles.

"I hope the Mediterranean don't stink as bad as this frog pond," Duane said. In the slight morning breeze the water smelled particularly froggy.

"Oh, the Mediterranean's filthy," Jacy said. "But it's open water."

She looked up at him through her goggles.

"Don't you have a large family?" she asked.

"Yep," Duane said. "It's what's driven me to spending my nights in a motorboat."

Jacy kicked off and backstroked lazily a time or two.

"Was it you that I went skinny-dipping with?" she asked.

"No, that was Lester," he said.

"But I was your Esther Williams anyway, wasn't I?" she said. She straightened in the water, raised her arms to a point over her head and did an Esther Williams back somersault, her long white legs pointing straight toward the sky for a moment.

When she came up she was close to the boat again.

"Ring the doorbell sometime, Duane," Jacy said. "I'd like to hear about your family."

Then she turned and swam smoothly away.

CHAPTER 25

WHEN DUANE DROVE HOME, FISHLESS, AT SIX-thirty A.M., it was to find the house in an uproar. Karla was walking around the kitchen, a phone in each hand, trying to keep up with fast-breaking events.

Minerva had installed herself at the kitchen table and was reading the want ads with painstaking care.

Nellie sat across from her, sobbing, Barbette in her lap. Barbette was crying too.

A sound of screaming and banging came from the pantry—it could only be Little Mike. Duane picked up Barbette, who immediately hushed, and walked over to the pantry to liberate Little Mike, who had been banging on the closed door with a can of soup. The minute Duane released him he ran outside into the grass burs, sat down in them, and resumed his screaming. He was naked.

"Dickie didn't go to Ruidoso," Karla said, covering the receiver of one phone for a moment.

Duane had assumed that much, since the pickup he had loaned his son was parked in the driveway, looking as if it had just returned from a trip across Mongolia. Dickie was the only person Duane knew who could take a perfectly new pickup and reduce it to rent-a-wreck status in only a few hours.

"Is he in jail, dead or what?" Duane asked, rocking Barbette in his arms.

"No, he's married," Karla said. "He and Billie Anne have been secretly married for three weeks and didn't even tell us. Billie Anne's mother is having a nervous breakdown at the news."

"She won't be the only one," Duane said, thinking of Suzie and Jenny. "Psychiatrists will make plenty off this one."

"You have to go get the twins," Karla said. "I'm talking to the camp director now. They got kicked out, just like you predicted."

"What are *you* crying about?" Duane asked Nellie. It was almost a relief to think of Dickie married, however briefly, and he had never in his wildest dreams imagined the twins lasting a full term at church camp.

"Her fiancé disappointed her," Minerva said. "I'm looking for a new job. A household like this is no place for an old lady with stomach cancer."

"I thought you had a brain tumor," Duane said. "It was last year that you had stomach cancer."

"Anyway, it's no place for a lady as sick as I am, whatever I got," Minerva said testily. She took her illnesses with dead seriousness and did not like to be twitted about them just because she hadn't died of any of them yet.

Karla hung up both phones and immediately disconnected them.

"Will you hush that crying?" she said to Nellie. "Joe Coombs never meant to be unfaithful to you. It's just that after the twenty-fifth beer he goes blind and can't tell one woman from another."

"What'd he do?" Duane inquired.

"He tried to kiss Billie Anne, my own sister-in-law," Nellie wailed.

"He's told you a million times he thought it was you," Karla said. "He's real contrite, but if you want to break off the engagement, that's your business."

Little Mike came waddling back in, a picture of misery, seven or eight grass burs stuck to each fat little leg. He tried to climb up on his mother's lap, but Nellie stiff-armed him and he went reeling over to Minerva, who caught him by the arm and swiftly extracted the grass burs before going back to her scrutiny of the want ads.

"What'd the twins do?" Duane asked.

"Julie posed for naked Polaroids and Jack climbed up into the rafters of the shithouse and dropped a brick into one of the toilets," Karla said. "I guess the toilet broke and pretty much flooded things. They said they'd appreciate it if you'd come and get them before lunch."

"Who took the Polaroids?" Duane asked.

"A sixth-grader from Nocona," Karla said. "Where were you all night while I was going crazy?"

"I told Minerva to tell you I was going fishing," Duane said.

Karla turned a stern eye on Minerva, who ignored it.

"When people interrupt my movies I'm apt to forget their alibis," Minerva said.

"Joe could have told it was Billie Anne if he'd looked 'cause she's a lot taller than me," Nellie sobbed.

"What became of Junior?" Duane asked. "Did he ever calm down?"

"He's asleep in one of the guest rooms," Karla said. "He got so calm his legs stopped working. We had to carry him in the house."

"He wasn't so much calm as glassy-eyed drunk," Minerva observed.

"I think he wants to room here for a while until he can straighten things out at home," Karla said.

"Where's the newlyweds?" Duane asked.

"They went to Bowie on a honeymoon," Nellie said, still morose. "I'll never get a honeymoon."

"Bowie?" Duane said. It was a small town of no distinction about fifty miles away. As a honeymoon spot it seemed an unlikely choice.

"You've had plenty of honeymoons," Karla reminded Nellie. "You have one every time you meet a boy."

"I caught TB on my honeymoon," Minerva said. That surprised everyone. It was the first indication they had had that Minerva had ever been married.

Having revealed that much, Minerva clammed up and refused to provide any more details.

"Just tell us what color eyes he had," Karla asked, as Duane left the room.

He put Barbette in her crib and looked in on Junior Nolan, who was lying with his head hanging off the bed in one of the many guest rooms. Karla had thoughtfully put a bucket under his head, in case he woke up feeling puky.

Duane shaved and went out to the garden to have a word with Karla, who was now hard at work on her tomatoes. Just as he walked outdoors Bobby Lee drove up—summoned, no doubt, by Nellie. Bobby Lee's was the shoulder of choice when she needed one to cry on.

"Poor little Nellie, she sounds distraught," Bobby Lee said, coming over for a minute. Duane and Karla maintained a hard-hearted front.

"Did you get that bit out of the hole?" Duane asked.

Bobby Lee looked blank, as if he had forgotten the meaning of words such as "bit" and "hole."

"Oh, that thing," he said, and went into the house without further explanation.

"Tomatoes are considered a fruit in some countries," Karla said in the tone she was likely to take when furious.

"What'd I do now?" Duane asked.

"You'll know when you get the divorce papers," Karla said —a favorite line. She threw a green tomato at him. It missed and rolled toward Shorty, who regarded it with grave attention.

"Let's take a trip before you get in worse trouble than you're in," Karla said.

"Okay, as long as it ain't to Bowie," Duane said agreeably.

"They just went to Bowie because there's a café there that makes gravy Dickie likes," Karla said.

Duane decided Karla was operating solely on intuition, with no real knowledge to back it up. In any case he was in a mood to live dangerously.

"Guess who came swimming across Lake Kickapoo this morning, while I was fishing," he said.

"Probably Priscilla Presley, with your luck," Karla said.

"No, Jacy," he said. "She's kind of a long-distance swimmer. She was swimming across the lake."

"They say she's aged a lot," Karla said. "I'd like to meet her. I think she's interesting."

They saw another pickup approaching. This one belonged to Joe Coombs, who was coming to try and make up with Nellie.

"Oh, no," Karla said. "What if Joe and Bobby Lee get in a fight?"

"Joe will win," Duane said. "Bobby Lee couldn't whip Little Mike, unless he surprised him."

Joe, scrubbed to an unusual state of cleanliness, parked his pickup, waved stiffly at them and hurried into the house. He had had the forethought to provide himself with a box of chocolate-covered cherries, Nellie's favorite candy.

"Maybe we oughta start going to church again," Karla said.

"Again?" Duane said. "I can't remember that we ever went to church."

"We didn't, but we made the kids go to Sunday school a few times," Karla said.

"I thought you said religion was just for cowards," Duane said.

Karla looked thoughtful. "It is for cowards," she said. "Maybe I'm feeling cowardly. I'm about ready to resort to magic."

"I'm not," Duane said.

"Just make them give you all those dirty Polaroids when you get down to that camp," Karla said. "And I want you to lecture the twins all the way home."

"I've been lecturing them since the minute they were born," Duane reminded her, but Karla, obviously dying to know what Bobby Lee and Joe Coombs were finding to say to one another, was already walking toward the house.

CHAPTER 26

DUANE WHISTLED FOR SHORTY AND TWENTY MINutes later was lying in bed with Suzie Nolan, feeling only slightly let down. It had taken at least fifteen of the twenty minutes to drive to Suzie's house. She had been in the laundry room doing a washing when Duane walked in. The washing machine made a sound that seemed sexual as it thumped the clothes inside it.

What occurred between him and Suzie was in the nature of a gulp, and didn't seem quite as thrilling as it might have if they had got to gulp it in the car outside the hospital. The gulp had been far from boring, but when it was over Duane found that he could not entirely banish from his mind thoughts of consequences.

Suzie liked to play with her own nipples, and continued to play with them while he contemplated the various possible consequences of their action.

"It's all over town that Dickie married Billie Anne," Suzie said, the blush of pleasure still coloring her cheeks. "The little rat, he told me he was going to break up with that girl."

Then she rolled into his arms, a sad droop to her mouth, and began to sob. In his rush to her bed Duane had briefly forgotten that she was in love with his son.

While she cried herself out he thought of Jacy. Instead of coming to Suzie's he could have just driven down to Los Dolores and rung the doorbell. It wouldn't have resulted in an instant gulp of sex, but he would have at least had the chance to look at and talk to the woman he had wondered about for so long.

Bad timing, he thought, remembering the hungry way Suzie had uttered the phrase the night before, when he was trying to wiggle out of the car. Suzie had awakened his need only a few hours before Jacy swam back into his life.

It had seemed an imperative need, too. The fact that its consummation had been slightly anticlimactic didn't mean much. He and Suzie were not through.

In his minute or two with Jacy, no real need had been awakened—just sympathy and a certain curiosity. The image of her that he had nourished through the years had been the image of a girl—a girl of whom little trace remained. Flirtation had been a way of life with Jacy—he had caught an echo of it that morning when she had asked if she had been his Esther Williams. But it had been a faint echo—a habit from which the force had gone.

"I don't know why I do a single thing that I do," Suzie said, sitting up. She dried her eyes on the sheet.

"Junior could walk in and shoot us," she added.

"No, Junior's sleeping off a big drunk in one of my guest rooms," Duane said.

Suzie watched him solemnly while he put his socks on. It made him feel silly. Women all seemed to feel that they needed to study him closely while he put his socks on after lovemaking—it had happened so many times that he had often resolved just to leave his socks on—after all, they were no impediment—but he always forgot.

"I have to go to Bridgeport to get the twins," he said. "They got kicked out of church camp."

Suzie settled back against the pillows. She had become cheerful again—watching him put on his socks seemed to have revived her hopes for life. Her fingers drifted back to her nipples.

"I guess I'll just have to stay here in bed and think sweet thoughts about you, Duane," she said.

"Think a few about the centennial, too," he said. "We got to ram that liquor provision through the City Council tonight before G.G. gets organized."

"It's nice to have it to look forward to that I'll see you tonight," Suzie said. "I've spent the last five years without a single thing to look forward to. Jenny's got softball but I never was a bit good at games."

"You're good at some games," Duane said.

Suzie gave him a glowing smile and idly touched herself. When he bent to kiss her goodbye she caught his hand and bit it sharply.

"Drive careful, sweetie," she said.

CHAPTER 27

BEFORE SETTING OFF FOR BRIDGEPORT, DUANE stopped by his office a minute to see if any checks had drifted in.

"Yes, twenty-two thousand," Ruth said. "That won't hold 'em off long. When you go bankrupt, what happens to my pension?"

"I'll dig ditches twenty-four hours a day for the rest of my life rather than see you lose a penny, Ruth," Duane said.

Eddie Belt was in the office, high as a kite. Duane could tell he was high by the way he laughed.

"I'm glad you're that noble," Eddie said.

"If you fired all the drug addicts who work for you, you might not even go bankrupt," Ruth said.

She sustained a hard line on Eddie and Bobby Lee, although both did their best to get on her good side.

Ruth had the irritated look she often got when people stood around the office. She kept both hands poised above the typewriter keys as an indication that she hoped they'd leave so she could get back to her letters.

Duane put the twenty-two-thousand-dollar check in his shirt pocket.

"If these were normal times I'd be doing all right," he said.

"Times aren't normal or abnormal," Ruth said. "Times are neutral."

"I'm neuter too," Eddie Belt said. "It's because I've went too long without sex."

"Aren't you still married to Jerri?" Duane asked.

"I guess so, but we wasn't talking about slavery," Eddie said.

"The things you joke about reveal a lot about you," Ruth said. "Any psychiatrist will tell you that."

"None of the motherfuckers will tell *me* that because I ain't going near them," Eddie Belt said. He was known for his violent mood swings, and one swung before their eyes, dropping him from manic heights to deep depression.

"He's falling," Ruth said. "Make him go to work, Duane."

Duane took Eddie out in the bright sunlight, thinking that might help. Watching Eddie go through a mood swing was as unnerving as seeing someone fall out of an airplane. There was little bystanders could do to help.

Eddie stood in the sun, staring hopelessly at his feet.

"Why do you stare at your feet when you're depressed?" Duane asked.

"When you're depressed it don't really matter what you stare at," Eddie said.

"At least you've got a good job," Duane said, trying to think of something cheerful to tell the man.

"Just until you go bankrupt, then I'll probably starve," Eddie said.

Duane left him standing in the sun. He took the check to the bank and gave it to Lester, whose hair looked as if an electric current had recently been passed through it.

"I may go back to the hospital this afternoon," Lester said. "I'm feeling very fragile."

"Eat a healthy lunch," Duane suggested.

"I think the Federal investigators are coming today," Lester said. "They may want the bank to merge with someplace like Chase Manhattan."

"Those Federal investigators are probably in Newport

Beach, California," Duane said, once again dispensing what he took to be a cheerful remark.

He drove to the Dairy Queen, thinking to get himself a milk shake for the road, and happened to stop in the drive-in line behind Jenny Marlow, who immediately got out of her car and came back to his, licking an ice-cream cone.

"Where are you on your way to?" she asked. She still wore the vivid eye shadow.

Duane wondered why it had to be Jenny ahead of him in the drive-in line.

"Bridgeport, to get the twins," he said. Either her eyes or her eye shadow mesmerized him because he couldn't think of a lie.

"I'll park and go with you," Jenny said. "I need to get out of this miserable town."

"Bad news for you, Shorty," Duane said, while waiting for his milk shake. Jenny was parking. Shorty looked guilty.

"It's nothing personal," Duane said, dragging Shorty out and depositing him in the back. Shorty looked abject and tried to express his shame by crawling under the spare tire.

Though Shorty was gone, something of him lingered in the cab—namely hair, a thin blue mantle of which covered much of the pickup seat.

"I'm so unhappy I'll even sit in dog hairs," Jenny said, getting in and sitting in them.

"I guess if there was an unhappiest-town-on-earth contest we could enter Thalia in it," Duane said, in an effort to make conversation.

"We wouldn't win," Jenny said. "That place in Colombia that got covered by a mud slide would probably win it."

Jenny stuck her hand out the window and let the air slip through her fingers. She didn't look at all miserable. In fact, she looked perky.

"Your son's a little stinker," she said. "Wanta hear how he seduced me and ruined my life?"

"I don't know if I do," Duane admitted. "I've got a lot of bad news today already."

"A little more won't hurt you," Jenny said.

"I think one straw has been known to break a camel's back," Duane remarked.

Jenny let her hand trail out the window for several miles. She was smiling mysteriously, perhaps at the memory of her own ruin.

"You certainly hit the nail on the head when you named that kid Dickie," Jenny said. "He just walked up to me one night after a ball game and stuck my hand in his pocket. Did you know he cuts the bottoms out of his pockets so he can play with himself?"

"Yes," Duane admitted. That peculiarity of Dickie's was known to everyone in the family. Minerva commented on it often, though she pretended to be mystified as to its purpose.

A preference for pocketless Levi's had also caused Dickie to lose roughly a hundred sets of car keys during his adolescence. Though he liked to be able to reach in and grasp himself he was always forgetting that pocketless pants had less convenient aspects.

"He just stuck my hand right in his pocket," Jenny said. "It was like holding a hot little piece of pipe."

"I don't really want to hear this," Duane said.

He began to wonder what the twins would think of him showing up at their camp with Jenny, and what Karla would think about it once it was reported to her. He also wondered what they would all talk about on the ride home.

It seemed to him that he was hearing talk he should not be having to hear from the lips of respectable married small-town women. He decided Ruth Popper was crazy for not realizing how abnormal the times were. Ruth herself was abnormal, and it was certainly not normal for one of the best lady softball players in Texas to be talking about holding his son's penis.

"I personally think this sexual-liberation business has gone too far," Duane said.

"Dickie did that three or four times before I slept with him," Jenny said. "He'd just walk up to me anywhere and stick my hand in his pocket. I finally got curious and in no time it ruined my life."

"I doubt Lester was too happy about it, either," Duane said. "Maybe I should have made Dickie join the army or something."

"Lester's naive," Jenny said. "He's not a quick learner. It

took him nearly ten years to find my clitoris and by then I didn't care whether he found it or not. He's a good father, though. Everybody has their good points, don't they?"

"No, G.G. don't," Duane said. "He's gonna make trouble over the beer."

"I might be pregnant," Jenny said. "On the other hand it could just be worry and stress."

They were in the post oak country, and they passed a little roadside park. An elderly couple were eating their lunch at one of the little concrete tables, in the shade of a large post oak. An old pickup with an Airstream trailer hitched to it was parked nearby. The old couple were having a frugal repast of cheese and crackers, but they waved in a friendly way when Duane looked over. They were neatly dressed and looked cheerful. It was clear that they were enjoying their declining years, peacefully driving around America eating cheese and crackers at nice little roadside parks. Duane envied them so much that he felt, for a moment, that he might cry. It seemed likely that he himself would have to spend his declining years trying to locate all the grandchildren that his offspring had strewn around the country, one of whom might even be growing in the belly of the woman who sat beside him.

For all he knew, his declining years had already started, too.

"Would it be Dickie's or Lester's?" he asked, remembering that Lester had said he and Jenny never made love.

"Oh, Dickie's," Jenny said. "I told Lester I couldn't be his outlet anymore. He is a good father, though.

"I don't think he even has an outlet," she added, a few minutes later. "Sometimes I feel guilty but mostly I feel it's every person for themselves. Do you know what I mean?"

"Yep, I sure do," Duane said.

CHAPTER 28

THE CHURCH CAMP WAS SITUATED ON THE WEST side of a large brown lake not unlike the one where earlier that day Jacy Farrow had swum past his boat.

Riding for an hour and a half with Jenny made Duane remember Jacy with growing fondness. She might be sad, but she carried her sorrow with a certain dignity, whereas Jenny's conversation had not been rich in dignity. She made it clear that she was an unrepentant sinner who meant to go on sinning, but she still seemed to feel sorry for herself now that she was faced with the consequences of her behavior.

The twins were also unrepentant sinners. Locating them was not difficult, because they were sitting just outside the gate to the church camp with all their belongings piled around them. Two large teenage boys stood just inside the gate, apparently to make sure one of the twins didn't try to dart back in.

Just as he was about to get out and confront his offspring, Jenny grasped his hand. She wore a subdued look, for the first time on the trip.

"I'm not as wild as I sound, Duane," she said. "I talk a good game but I don't know if I play a good game. What if I'm pregnant by Dickie?"

In a matter of minutes, all the perk seemed to have drained out of her.

"I guess if you are we'll just have to deal with it," he said. The word "abortion" was on his lips, but he didn't say it. Jenny looked as abject as Shorty had looked when he tried to crawl under the tire.

"Karla and I could adopt it and mix it in with Nellie's," he said.

"Of course I might want to raise it if it's a boy," Jenny said. "I've always wanted a little curlyheaded boy. I wonder if I'll get kicked off the softball team."

Duane left her to muse about her future and walked over to the twins. Julie wore a sullen expression, but Jack was smiling his brilliant smile, as if he had just been awarded a prize of some kind.

"I'm starving," he said. "They feed you slop at this camp. Can we stop and get a hamburger?"

"You're gonna be eating bread and water for a few months," Duane said. "Why'd you drop that brick in the toilet?"

"Oh, that was a total accident," Jack said. "I was trying to drop it on the little kid who was taking a shit, but he moved too quick."

"Thank God he moved," Duane said. "Otherwise you'd have broken a skull instead of a toilet."

"I don't see why you sent us here in the first place," Julie said. "These people are all Jesus freaks."

In fact, Duane had been against sending them to the church camp—that had been Karla's idea.

"Your mother thought it would be a good idea for you to learn something about the Bible," he said, smiling at the absurdity of such a wish as applied to the twins.

When Julie saw that he was not really mad, she gave him a smile of such pure beauty that his heart melted. It always melted when Julie smiled at him. He thought she was the most beautiful little girl he had ever seen, and the knowledge that she was his child made up for many of the ills of existence.

"All I did was let a little boy from Nocona take a few pictures of my pee-pee," Julie said, a cheerful lilt to her young voice. "What's wrong with that?

"You and Momma go naked in the hot tub," she added, while he was trying to decide how to answer her question.

"We got revenge for being kicked out," Jack said, annoyed that his sister had managed to soften Duane up so easily. "You wanta know what we did?"

"You probably spent the whole night crawling through the rafters dropping bricks on people's heads," Duane said.

"Nope, we put LSD in the preachers' oatmeal," Jack said. "Now all the preachers are wandering around having hallucinations and seeing the devil and stuff."

"Who gave you the LSD?" Duane asked.

"Nobody," Jack said proudly. "I stole it from Dickie."

"Are you and Mrs. Marlow going to get married?" Julie asked.

"Of course not," Duane said. "She just felt like taking a little ride.

"We're just friends," he added, but he could tell from the look the twins exchanged that neither of them believed him.

"You oughta drive up and see the preachers," Jack said. "It's real funny. Some of them are rolling around on the ground."

"It's because we started laughing that they stuck us out in the road," Julie said. "I don't think that's very nice. Some hairy old man could come along and try to molest us."

"You've got sex on the brain," Jack said. "You think everybody in the world wants to molest you."

"I wish somebody would molest you," Julie said. "I wish they'd beat you black and blue till you vomit."

"Let's go home," Duane said. "Your mother might want to say a few words to you."

"I wanta ride in the back with Shorty," Julie said.

"Me too," Jack said.

"It's a long way home," Duane said. "You'll get dust in your eyes."

"I don't care," Julie said. "It's better than having to ride up front with you and your girlfriend."

"Mrs. Marlow is not my girlfriend," Duane said, but he let them ride in the back anyway.

CHAPTER 29

LATER THAT AFTERNOON, WHILE THE HOUSE WAS deserted, Duane went out by the hot tub and shot thirty or forty shots at the doghouse with his .44 Magnum. Karla, Minerva, Nellie and the kids had gone to Wichita Falls to inspect a duplex where Billie Anne and Dickie hoped to start their married life.

Earlier in the day Karla tried to persuade the twins that their behavior at the church camp had been disgraceful, but the twins flatly refused to buy her line of reasoning.

"I think it's a disgrace that our own parents try to get rid of us by sending us to a dumb camp full of Jesus freaks," Julie said.

"We're gonna run off for a few days anyway," Jack informed his mother. "How would you like it if we became child prostitutes?"

"You don't even know what a child prostitute does," Karla said. "At least you better not know, if you happen to know what's good for you."

Duane had once seen a television program about Zen. He

159

often remembered the program when he was shooting at the doghouse. What seemed impressive about Zen was the level of concentration the Zen masters were able to command. This remarkable concentration enabled them to see things that a normal eye, linked to a normal brain, could not see: the flight of bullets, for example.

Since no one was around to make him feel silly, Duane tried to attain the concentration of a Zen master and follow the flight of the bullets he was shooting. The doghouse was only fifty feet away, so he had to watch close. Once or twice he thought he glimpsed a bullet, just as it was about to hit the log he was aiming at.

The big gun made his hand sore, but it was worth it to try and concentrate, unobserved. He didn't know much about Eastern religions, but he knew that raising his powers of concentration would have many advantages. If he had started concentrating sooner he probably wouldn't be in half the trouble, financial or otherwise, that he was in. Better concentration would have enabled him to avoid such mistakes as borrowing millions of dollars just because the price of oil happened to be rising when the dollars were offered to him.

Another common mistake a little increased concentration might help him avoid was his habit of sleeping with women he had no business sleeping with, just because they happened to lie in his path.

When he got tired of shooting he put the gun away and drove to Janine's house. He was not eager to see her, but he didn't want to sit through a whole City Council meeting thinking guilty thoughts about Janine in her negligee. He knew he was going to have to break up with her, and he rehearsed several speeches as he drove into town.

The speeches were aimed at casting both of them in a noble light. He hoped to convince her that breaking up would only be the civic-minded thing to do. Having worked for the county all her adult life, Janine considered herself nothing if not civic-minded.

Still, Duane doubted that the argument would work, and if it didn't he was prepared to lie and tell her that the doctors had told him he would probably have a heart attack if he didn't lead a less stressful life. He had not actually been to a doctor in something like fifteen years, but people did often have heart attacks and die.

To his surprise, Janine was not home. The only sign of her was a can of sauerkraut which was sitting, unopened, by a saucepan on the stove. Evidently she had been planning to have sauerkraut for supper.

Her absence was a little annoying. He felt he had worked up enough resolution to break with her, and now it would only go to waste.

Also, it left him with nothing to do for forty-five minutes, the time he had allotted for presenting his arguments and hearing Janine's responses, which would undoubtedly be heated. Janine was not likely to let him, or anyone else, escape unscathed.

The fact that she wasn't home left him feeling sort of silly. He drove over to his office to see if Ruth had left any important messages, and was startled to see Janine on the tennis courts playing tennis with Lester Marlow.

Like virtually everyone else in town, Janine had taken a few tennis lessons during the height of the boom. Lester had taken a few, too, but neither could be said to have mastered the game. Lester had never been able to play anything, while Janine had spent most of her life being the kind of girl who could never get anyone to play anything with her, or at least nothing except sex.

Duane recognized that her inability to get anyone to play anything with her had had something to do with his decision to play at romance with her. He had never been able to ignore certain forms of hopelessness—and despite a proud disposition and quite a few boyfriends Janine had seemed quietly hopeless.

The sight of her on the tennis court amazed him, for she seemed far from hopeless there. She was wearing a saucy new tennis outfit that he had not even known she owned, and was chewing gum and whacking balls merrily over Lester's head as if she were playing softball and scoring hits.

Lester, looking livelier than he had looked in months, cheerfully retrieved them from the dusty tumbleweeds.

Duane was so surprised that he just waved and drove on by. The messages could wait for morning.

He drove to the Dairy Queen only to be smacked in the face by an even greater surprise: Jacy's black Mercedes was parked right between Karla's white BMW and Dickie's new Super-jeep. Through the big window of the DQ he could see the unaccustomed sight of his whole family eating together in apparent harmony.

More startling still, Jacy sat beside Karla, holding little Barbette in her lap. Jacy and Karla seemed to be chatting happily.

The sight of them all sitting together was such a shock that it made Duane feel lonely and strange. He would have liked to just drive past and wave, as he had at the tennis court, but he had parked and got out, visible to all. Shorty had his paws on the dashboard and was looking at the strange sight. Jack was giving Shorty the finger. Then he held up a nacho, dripping with cheese and jalapeño, to induce Shorty to try and jump through the windshield. Shorty had never quite grasped the principles of glass, and Jack was often able to tempt him to race into glass doors and bonk himself.

Duane walked on in, stopping at the counter long enough to order himself a cheeseburger. Jacy and Karla paid his arrival no mind—they seemed absorbed in their conversation. In fact, no one paid his arrival any mind except Nellie, who smiled at him charmingly, as Julie had that morning.

Nellie wore a white dress and looked absolutely beautiful, and nice as well. It interested Duane that at any given moment each of his children was capable of looking like the nicest kid on earth, as well as the best-looking. Ten minutes later the same child might seem a monster of self-indulgence. Nellie was momentarily at her best. She was feeding Little Mike a banana split as quietly and efficiently as any young mother could.

Dickie and Billie Anne were necking and giggling. To amuse themselves they were passing jalapeños from mouth to mouth on their tongues. The twins were slurping malts and foraging at will from a heap of cheeseburgers, French fries, nachos, steak fingers, tacos and other delicacies. Jack occasionally pelted Little Mike with pieces of taco shell.

It was the slack time between lunch and dinner, and they had the DQ to themselves, except for John Cecil, who sat in a back booth. Fired from his teaching position years before for alleged homosexuality, John had stubbornly refused to leave town. Instead he bought one of the town's two grocery stores, hung on and eventually prospered. He kept a tidy store, extended indefinite credit to those down on their luck, and finally came to be well liked in the town. A believer in exercise, he ran every day, and had done so long before the craze struck. Duane would sometimes see him cruising Ohio Street, Wichita Falls's grim little two-block tenderloin. He looked very lonely at such times, peering in the bars, hoping to meet an equally lonely recruit from the nearby air base.

The staff of the Dairy Queen, having done its duty, peeked out at Jacy from behind stacks of malt cups. They stared at her avidly—a legend who had suddenly walked into their midst.

She had combed out her long hair—longer but no blonder than the hair Duane remembered from high school. She wore a T-shirt and running shorts. He saw her lay her hand on Karla's arm while making a point. Karla laughed and Jacy laughed, too, and they both looked at him.

He got a chair from one of the empty tables and carried it over. Jacy gave Barbette several sucking kisses on the neck, and Barbette chortled.

"I just stole all your sweetest sugar, Grandpa," Jacy said, when Duane sat down.

Duane held out a finger to Barbette, who chortled some more but ignored the finger.

"It's mighty good sugar," he said.

"Guess what I did, Duane," Karla said. It seemed to him she had a gloating look in her eye.

"Every time I've guessed in my whole life I've been wrong," Duane said.

"See?" Karla said to Jacy. "He's got that dour personality, just like you said. Duane just plods along. He's real reluctant to take a chance."

Minerva stopped eating a T-bone steak long enough to come to his defense.

"A man that ends up with a bunch like this has taken a chance or two," she said.

"Good point," Jacy said, surveying the table. She held Barbette in her lap and ate a bite or two of her taco salad.

"He takes them, but he don't notice that he's taking them, or he wouldn't, if he could help it," Karla said.

"Momma bought us a house," Dickie said. He and Billie Anne had stopped necking.

"Yeah, I went on and bought that duplex," Karla said. "Dickie and Billie Anne can move in one side, and when Joe and Nellie get married they can move in the other. It'll save a lot on rent."

"How much did this money-saving duplex cost?" Duane asked.

"Just sixty thousand," Karla said.

"Momma's real good at finding bargains," Dickie said.

"I know, I just wish I was as good at finding money," Duane said. He felt very watched. Once he glanced at Jacy and saw that she was watching him. Her look was not unfriendly, nor was it amused. It was matter-of-fact. Meanwhile, Karla was watching him look at Jacy and she did seem to be amused. He wondered how the two of them had met but didn't feel he should ask.

He found it rather difficult to adjust to the fact that he was sitting by Jacy after so many years. She wore no makeup and seemed indifferent to her looks, a thing he wouldn't have thought possible in her high school years.

"Is it fun to be a movie star?" Julie asked.

"Not much," Jacy said. "Not unless you're more of one than I was."

"I think I'll be one," Jack said. "I don't want to be an oil millionaire."

"All you kids could be movie stars," Jacy said. "I've never seen a better-looking bunch of kids, and I have beautiful kids myself."

"You should bring your girls home sometime," Karla said. "They could stay at our house if they get on your nerves."

Jacy looked at Duane again in the same matter-of-fact way.

"It's the other way around," she said. "I get on *their* nerves."

She picked up a paper napkin and wiped her mouth. "They're very critical, my girls," she said.

"How many girls do you have?" Julie asked. It was clear that Jacy intrigued her.

"Two," Jacy said. "One your age and one Nellie's age."

"Girls can be real picky," Karla said. "I don't think they understand what their mothers go through."

"I'm not picky," Julie said.

Nellie gave them all a radiant smile. When she entered her nice phase she was so beautiful that it caused men to choke up. Duane only had to look at her, as she was at that moment, to understand why men fell in love with her on sight and proposed within fifteen minutes.

She had always been an affectionate girl, too. He remembered how wonderful it had been to have her run out of the house and jump in his arms and kiss him when she had been a little girl. She would sit in their backyard on a rocking horse and wait for him to spray her with a hose on hot days, shivering when the cold water hit her. When Karla washed Nellie's hair she would wrap the child in one of her big terry-cloth bathrobes and plop her, a tiny, wet-haired thing, in Duane's lap. Nellie would sit, quiet as a bird, swaddled in the robe. Duane could still remember how her hair smelled when it was wet. She had seemed the very definition of innocence then, and at times she still seemed so. It was just that she had unexpectedly acquired the habit of sleeping with all the men who proposed after fifteen minutes, and of marrying a fair percentage of them.

"My girls are such little Europeans," Jacy said. "I don't know what they'd think of Thalia. I can barely get them to go to New York."

Barbette looked at Jacy and made little welcoming sounds. She wanted Jacy to steal more sugar. Jacy held her high above her head and wiggled her around, lowering her slowly until she could cover her neck with kisses. Barbette laughed happily.

"Well, that's all the sugar supply for today, you'll have to wait for tomorrow, Grandpa," Jacy said, handing the baby to him.

She stood up, opened her purse and began to peel crumpled dollar bills out of a little change purse.

"That's all right, I'll pay for it," Karla said. "I had this crowd to feed."

"Thanks," Jacy said. "Come on out in the morning, Karla. I'll show you the house and we'll compare notes some more."

"Compare notes on what?" Duane asked. The sudden blooming of friendship between Jacy and Karla unnerved him a little.

"On you, honey pie, what else?" Jacy said, ruffling his hair lightly as she passed behind him on her way out.

"I want to know how you were in high school and Jacy wants to know how you turned out," Karla said.

"Don't tell her how I turned out, it'll just depress her," Duane said.

" 'Bye, kids," Jacy said. "I hope I see you again pretty soon."

Minerva had been meticulously cutting the last niblet of fat off her T-bone. She looked up just in time to see Jacy drive away.

"They eat too much spaghetti over there in Italy," she said. "That girl's put on weight. She was skinny as a rail when she was in high school, wasn't she, Duane?"

"Yep, kinda skinny," Duane said nervously.

CHAPTER 30

WITHIN A WEEK, KARLA AND JACY HAD BECOME BEST friends. Duane was bewildered, and so was Junior Nolan, who had taken up residence in one of the guest rooms at the Moores'.

"Where's Karla?" Junior would ask sadly, wandering from room to room with a glass of vodka into which he had squirted a little V-8 juice to try and fool people.

Junior's behavior rapidly became more erratic. He found one of Duane's old coyote calls and would sit for hours in the rocks below the house, trying to call coyotes. Once a skunk came, but no coyotes appeared. Junior had lost his hat the day he planned to shoot Dickie—the blazing sun turned him a strawberry red, but he kept his vigil with the coyote call five or six hours a day. He only returned to the house to get more vodka, or to inquire about Karla.

By seven every morning Karla was in her car and off to Los Dolores. The big shipment of centennial buttons, T-shirts, ashtrays and dozer caps almost got sent back to the sender because Karla was too busy visiting Jacy to drive to Wichita Falls and sign for it.

Her forgetfulness in this regard upset Duane a good deal, since it was clear to him that without a substantial sale of souvenirs the centennial would probably lose thousands of dollars. So would Buster Lickle, who had made a deal with the county for 50 percent of the concessions.

"You could take Jacy with you to Wichita," Duane suggested, one night when he and Karla actually happened to be home at the same time.

"No, she's too sensitive, going places reminds her of things."

"What could going to Wichita Falls remind her of?" Duane asked. "I doubt Wichita is much like Italy."

"It could remind her of bad things that happened at SMU," Karla said. "She's real sensitive. Her mind goes back and forth real quick."

"SMU's in Dallas," Duane said, turning the temperature dial on the waterbed down a little.

"Duane, stop turning down the waterbed," Karla said. She was lying on it, reading an old issue of *Playgirl*. She kept a stack by the bed in case she woke up in the night and felt bored.

"It's nearly summer," he said. "We don't even need it this hot in February. I think the reason I don't have any energy is because this bed boils it out of me at night."

"If a waterbed cools off in the night it can suck all the heat out of your body and you'll be dead by morning," Karla said. "Hypothermia."

"If you're so paranoid about hypothermia, why do we have to have waterbeds at all?" Duane asked.

Karla didn't answer immediately. She had taken to wearing panties that were almost skimpier than Nellie's bikinis—just a string with a patch of green silk at the crotch.

"Waterbeds are good for your posture," she reminded him.

"I'd rather have bad posture than wake up feeling boiled," Duane said.

The next day he came home to find Karla and Jacy drinking and weeping by the pool. Tears were streaming down both their faces. Four wet eyes looked at him for a moment. Neither woman spoke. Duane had been meaning to have a little swim, but he decided to go back in the house.

Frequently in the afternoon he would drive over to Aunt Jimmie's Lounge, only to discover the black Mercedes and the white BMW parked outside. At such times he just drove on.

He began to feel that there was almost no place he could go where there was any possibility that he might enjoy himself. If he went to his office Ruth Popper made him feel like an intruder. If he went home Junior would come out from the rocks and beg for instruction in the art of coyote calling. If he went to a bar in Wichita Falls, Luthie Sawyer, whose failure to get OPEC bombed had caused him to turn to drink, would corner him and talk about how terrible it was to go broke. If he went to the tennis courts Lester and Janine—now officially in love —would show up and want him to teach them how to hit backhands. If he went to Suzie's her kids would pop in and he would have to sit around pretending he had just come to pay a social call. If he went to his rigs either Bobby Lee or Eddie Belt would complain or ask for raises or start telling him gross stories about their love life.

Often even driving around in the pickup wouldn't work, because Bobby Lee or Eddie would call him on the CB and tell him the same gross stories about their love life.

And if he went to the Dairy Queen Jenny Marlow would find him. She seemed to spend her day circling around in the car, watching to see if anyone she wanted to talk to showed up at the Dairy Queen. If she did catch him she would invariably remind him that his older son had some very bad habits.

About all he could do when he felt hard-pressed was to go to the lake and drift around in his boat—but it was a very hot spring, and drifting around in an unshaded boat in ninety-five-to-one-hundred-degree weather was not much fun. He did it occasionally, though. Sometimes he would slip over the side fully clothed, except for his shoes, and then lie in the boat with his cap over his eyes while the sun dried his sopping clothes.

At such times he wondered what Karla and Jacy found to talk about all day. Certainly they would have long since finished comparing notes about him. He had always thought of his courtship of Jacy as one of the high points of his life, but when he tried to reexamine it, to recall what had made it special, he found he really didn't have many memories. He had a fairly clear memory of standing with her on the fifty-yard line the night he, as captain of the football team, had crowned her Homecoming Queen. They had kissed, and the band had played the school song. Some of the band members and a few of the football players wept with emotion, but he hadn't wept, nor had Jacy. They thought it was corny. That had occurred in their junior year, and they had already considered themselves about ten times more sophisticated than the rest of the kids in high school.

He couldn't quite remember when he had fallen in love with Jacy, but he must have, because they had gone steady all their senior year, and he had smashed one of Sonny Crawford's eyes out for daring even to date her during a period the following summer when he had been in Odessa, roughnecking. He remembered crying about her as he was riding the bus out of Thalia to go to boot camp, and he had a hazy memory of trying to call her one night from Korea. She had then been in a sorority house at SMU. The call had been unsuccessful, and he had never been sure whether he just got the wrong sorority house or whether Jacy just hadn't wanted to talk to him.

But of the actual romance he could remember nothing, a fact which made him feel slightly guilty and strangely restless. He couldn't remember their kisses or lovemaking or talk or dates or anything, though he thought he remembered that they had gone to bed together on their senior trip. He had always considered that it was an important romance—after all, it had cost Sonny an eye—and it was troubling not to be able to remember anything about it except a corny moment on a football field that they had both scorned at the time.

One night when Karla had taken pity on Junior Nolan and was cooking him a steak out on the patio, Duane fished around in a storage room until he found a couple of his high school yearbooks. He took them to the bedroom and looked through them, hoping they would make it all vivid again. There he was in his football uniform, and again in a sports coat he had bought when he was voted Most Handsome Boy.

And there Jacy was, as Most Beautiful Girl. There were even pictures of them at the homecoming game: one of her riding around the field in a white convertible, and one of him waiting for her on the fifty-yard line, his helmet in one hand and a huge bouquet in the other, and a third one of their kiss. That one was mostly obscured, though, because Jacy had chosen it to write on when she signed his yearbook. "To the sweetest man in the world, I'll love ya' forever!!!" she had written.

The yearbooks failed to meet whatever need had caused him to dig them out, and after browsing in them for about three minutes he dropped them on the bed and lay watching the sports channel. Connors and McEnroe were hitting long slashing forehands at one another, Connors grunting audibly every time he hit the ball. The grunts reminded Duane of Janine, who, despite her efforts to be ladylike in everything, issued a series of similar grunts when she was about to come. Hearing Janine's grunts always gave him a certain sense of relief, if not of release. The grunts meant it had worked again, at least from Janine's point of view. He had begun to doubt that anything of that sort was really going to work from his point of view, but the margin of failure was ambiguous and didn't trouble him much.

Janine had scarcely spoken to him since the night he had called her from the emergency room. She could be seen any day cheerfully doing her job at the courthouse or playing tennis with Lester, who had calmed noticeably under her ministrations.

Duane had had two discussions on the subject of Lester and Janine with Jenny Marlow, who took a tolerant—indeed, almost ecstatic—view of their romance.

"I just hope it lasts until I can divorce him," she said. "You can't imagine how hard it is to get a husband out of love with you if one wants to stay in love with you.

"I don't know how many times I've had to break Lester's heart in the last five years," she added. "If hearts were made of pottery his would just be little ground-up pieces of glass by now."

While he was watching Connors and McEnroe, Karla walked back into the bedroom. She was fully dressed but dripping wet.

"I don't know if it's gonna work out too well having Junior living here," she said. "It all started out platonic but I don't know if Junior's gonna be able to keep it that way."

"What makes you think he can't?" Duane asked.

"He just threw me in the swimming pool," Karla said. "He said he'd always wanted to try and do it underwater. I told him I thought we ought to keep it platonic but he misunderstood me."

"How could he misunderstand that?" Duane asked, as Karla peeled off her dripping T-shirt.

"Junior thinks a platonic is one of them little Japanese pick-ups," Karla said. "He thought I meant we oughta run away together."

"Where is he now?"

"Swimming around," Karla said. "He's so drunk he thinks I'm still in the pool."

She stepped into the bathroom and emerged a minute later wearing a purple bathrobe.

"I wonder what Suzie Nolan does all day?" she asked.

Duane pretended he was concentrating on the tennis match.

"Duane, are you mad at me?" Karla asked.

"No," he said.

"It looks like Suzie would get curious about why Junior lives out here now," Karla said.

"Not everybody's got curiosity," Duane said. So far as he could tell, Suzie had no interest in Junior's whereabouts.

"Wives usually have curiosity about their husbands, though," Karla said. "Or even about their ex-husbands."

"We could call her and tell her he's swimming around in our pool, hoping you'll run away with him in a Japanese pickup," Duane suggested.

"I heard it on the grapevine that you're in love with her," Karla said.

"The grapevine's misinformed you again, honey," Duane said lightly.

"Every time you call me honey there's a lie involved," Karla said.

Duane went outside to check on Junior. He didn't want him to drown, and fortunately Junior hadn't. He was sitting on the diving board with his coyote call. Despite much practice, he wasn't expert with the call. All he was producing at the moment was a kind of splutter, so weak that Shorty, who slept a few feet away, hadn't even raised his head.

"I called a toad," Junior said. "See him?"

In fact there was a fair-sized toad sitting by the pool. While Duane watched, it managed a lethargic hop into the thin grass.

"There he goes," Junior said. "Where's Karla?"

"She told me she had a headache," Duane said.

"I don't doubt that," Junior said. "Women all get headaches the minute I fall in love with them."

"I wouldn't take it personally," Duane said. "Quite a few have headaches around me too."

"I'll never really be in love with anybody but Suzie," Junior said. "Suzie's meant the world to me. I keep thinking she'll call up and tell me to come home, but I guess that's just wishful thinking."

The look on Junior's face made Duane feel sad. He had visited Suzie that very morning for a passionate twenty minutes. What he had told Karla was true. He wasn't in love with Suzie. The two of them were just having an interlude of good luck involving a high level of sexual compatibility. There was no reason to suppose it would last. The day might come when Suzie would wake up missing Junior and simply call him home. It was something Duane would like to see happen, even if it meant the end of an exciting interlude.

Junior crawled off the diving board and fell asleep in a lawn chair.

Duane went back in to find Karla looking at his yearbook. She had it open to the page with the homecoming photographs and was reading what Jacy had written across their picture.

"Well, she didn't love you forever, did she, Duane?" Karla said.

"Nope," he said.

Karla closed the book. "Duane, are you sad?" she asked.

"I guess," he said.

"Why? You can tell me. I'm your wife," Karla said.

Duane felt the beginnings of a headache. He went in the bathroom and splashed cold water on his forehead for a while. Sometimes that stopped headaches. He wet a washrag with cold water and when he lay back down put the washrag across his forehead.

"It's a lot better if a husband and wife communicate and tell one another the reasons when they're happy or sad," Karla said.

"Well," Duane said, and got no farther. He was thinking of Junior. From feeling sorry for him he had begun to envy him. Junior had taken less than a minute to fall asleep in the lawn chair. Perhaps he was already in the midst of a nice dream. He could be dreaming of his years of wealth, when two thirds of the wells he drilled turned out to be producers. Or he might be dreaming of even earlier years, when his passionate young wife had still wanted him. The moment he had fallen asleep the sadness had left his face, to be replaced by a look of peace.

Duane wished he could gain peace so easily. His own dreams were of bank meetings or of obscure but total breakdowns at one of the rigs. His dreams only left him the more tired.

"You don't look too happy yourself," he said to Karla.

"No, because I was brought up to believe it's a wife's duty to make her husband happy and you're laying there with a rag on your head looking as sad as a hound dog," Karla said.

"I'm not *that* sad," Duane said. "I'm just a little miserable."

"Is it because I spent sixty thousand on a duplex we can't afford?" she asked. "I was just thinking it would be nice if the children had a decent place to be married in."

"It would be even nicer if the children would stay married a decent length of time," Duane said.

"Do you think we raised them wrong?" Karla asked.

Duane tried to think back over the years when they had been raising Dickie and Nellie, before the twins were born. It seemed to him they had done all the things parents were supposed to do. They had taken the children to Sunday school, made them do chores, spanked them for particularly gross behavior, given them lavish praise when they were good. Obviously their attention had slipped at some point, but he was too tired to try and pick out the point, and so far his headache wasn't letting up.

"It makes me nervous when you don't answer me, Duane," Karla said.

"I've got a headache," Duane said. "I can't think of too many answers when I've got a headache."

"It makes me feel guilty when you get those headaches," Karla said. "It's probably because of me that you're so stressed."

"Blame it on OPEC," Duane said. "It's simpler, and we can both go to sleep."

Karla got out of bed, put on her gown and came back to bed. She picked up the remote TV control and roved through the channels for a minute before switching it off.

"Every night there's less and less on TV," she said.

"Karla, stop worrying," Duane said. "It's not much of a headache, and it's not your fault."

"I didn't really mean to spend all that money today," Karla said. "I guess it would have been better if we'd never got rich. I started spending money and now I can't stop. Every time I go to Dallas I think I'll buy one dress and then I buy ten."

"It's not the dresses, it's the oil rigs," he said. "A thousand dresses doesn't cost as much as one of those fuckers."

"Jacy's real curious about you," Karla said. "I think sometimes she wishes she had just stayed here and married you."

Duane didn't believe for a minute that Jacy wished anything of the kind. His curiosity was piqued, but he could tell from Karla's wide eyes that one question from him would set loose a manic flow of talk, which might flow for hours. He decided against setting it loose.

"You never did tell me why you were sad," Karla reminded him.

Duane couldn't remember, if he had ever known. His memory of the evening didn't want to go back farther than the time he spent splashing cold water on his forehead. The washrag wasn't cool anymore. He wished he had more cold water, but didn't feel like getting up to get it.

"I wasn't as sad as a hound dog," he said, hoping to reassure his wife.

"No, but your face gets kind of long when you're real depressed," Karla said.

She got up, unbidden, went to the kitchen, and returned with a large bowl filled with ice and water. She wet the washrag in the icy water, squeezed it out and returned it to him. It was very cold.

"Thanks," Duane said.

"I guess I'd just like to lead a sensible life," he added, thinking about the question of his sadness. "Do you think this is a sensible life?"

Karla had turned on a tiny reading light and was leafing through a *Playgirl*.

"It may not be too sensible but at least we know the difference between a platonic relationship and a Japanese pickup," she said.

CHAPTER 31

DUANE SOON FOUND IT ALMOST IMPOSSIBLE TO leave Thalia without Jenny Marlow catching him and demanding to ride wherever he was going. There were four roads out of town and his attempted exits became a game of tic-tac-toe, which Jenny almost always won. She seemed to have nothing to do but lay ambushes.

If he went north, toward Rising Star, she usually flagged him down at Aunt Jimmie's Lounge. If he tried to make a break to the south, she headed him off at Sonny's carwash. If he went west, she caught him at the Dairy Queen. And if he attempted a dash toward Wichita Falls, she would zip out of the alley behind the grocery store and honk until he pulled over.

It was true that he could have sneaked out along the little paved road that ran behind the cemetery, rejoining one of the major arteries a few miles out, but for years he had been accustomed to merely driving out of town at will, and he always forgot about Jenny until she roared up behind him and began to honk.

The sound of honking would catapult Shorty into a madden-

ing sequence of loud yips, which only a forceful beating with
the work glove would silence. Duane decided travel was
hardly worth it.

It was not that Jenny was seeking romance—apparently romance was the farthest thing from her mind. The thing closest
to her mind was her new job as director of the centennial pageant, a job that had fallen to her by default.

The gentleman from Brooklyn who had been a tentative candidate to direct the pageant had not exactly worked out, a fact
that was really no fault of his own. His name was Sally Balducci. Duane had finally persuaded the committee to bring
him down for an interview, although the committee was not
without qualms.

"I never heard of a man named Sally," Jenny said. "I hope
he isn't a transvestite."

"Or if he is, I hope he's good enough to fool G.G.," Duane
said.

Sally Balducci was definitely not a transvestite. He was a
short, fat gentleman with bushy gray curls who arrived wearing
a green sports coat and a wide white tie, casually knotted. He
got off the commuter plane that had brought him from Dallas
groaning and holding his hands over his ears. Apparently the
little plane had not been pressurized adequately.

While waiting for his luggage, Sally Balducci reeled around
the little airport, weeping. He muttered in a strange dialect,
frightening the few elderly matrons who had flown in with
him. Occasionally he groaned loudly and kicked the wall of the
airport.

To Duane's dismay, the flight seemed to have rendered Sally
stone deaf. As he drove into Thalia he kept whacking his head
with the heel of his hand in hopes of getting his hearing started
again. It didn't work. He looked with an expression of profound
sadness at the few dusty buildings that made up the town.

Duane took him home and gave him two or three of Karla's
quart-sized vodka tonics, which unfortunately put him to sleep.
Efforts to awaken him were unsuccessful. He slept most of the
night in a lawn chair by the pool, just as Junior Nolan had a
few nights before Sally's arrival.

He missed the committee meeting at which he was supposed

to be interviewed, giving G. G. Rawley the opportunity to lecture everyone for fifteen minutes on the unreliability of papists.

Sally awoke in the wee small hours and watched a sumo wrestling match with Minerva. His deafness did not abate, though Minerva, ever the skeptic, claimed he could hear perfectly well.

"That man can hear a worm crawl," she claimed. "He don't want to hear. If he could, he might have to stay around here all summer putting on that stupid pageant."

That was not likely, for the committee had hardened its heart against the man. That afternoon, in a twenty-minute rump session held in Sonny's laundrymat, the committee voted to make Jenny director of the pageant. Meanwhile Sally sulked in Duane's pickup, growing hotter and hotter. Out of sympathy Duane drove him to Dallas so he wouldn't have to ride the commuter plane again. Jenny rode along. She had the script of the pageant with her, but Sally was in such a foul mood that he refused to look at it. The minute they arrived at the airport he headed for the bar.

On the way home Jenny hauled out the script and began to brood about casting. It was not lost on anyone that the centennial was thundering down on them. Beards were sprouting on male faces all over the county, including Duane's.

"Please say you'll play Adam," Jenny said. "If you'll just play Adam it might give me some confidence. It's one of the best parts."

Duane had already agreed to play George Washington. The thought of playing Adam didn't excite him. "I've already grown a beard," he pointed out. "I don't think Adam had a beard."

He was rather vain about his beard, which was thicker and glossier than many of the beards under cultivation. Both Bobby Lee and Eddie Belt sported scraggly growths that made them look like depraved fugitives from a chain-saw movie.

In general the beard ordinance was creating anxiety. A water tank had been hauled onto the courthouse lawn but nobody had been ducked yet. Duane's son-in-law-to-be, Joe Coombs, was a likely candidate for ducking because he kept stumbling up every morning or two and shaving off his new beard before he was fully awake.

"Why don't you get Dickie to play Adam?" Duane suggested. "He thinks he *is* Adam."

"What makes you think I'd ever speak to him again, the little rat!" Jenny said.

Duane recalled that Suzie Nolan had also called Dickie a little rat. He himself had not seen the little rat lately. Evidently he and Billie Anne were in a phase of wedded bliss. Karla kept Billie Anne on the phone at least an hour a day making sure her baby boy was being cared for properly. When Duane attempted to lecture her about interfering mother-in-laws he was met with stony looks.

"He's my own child, I don't guess I have to stop being interested in him just because he married some girl we barely know," Karla said. "She might not know about botulism and things."

"Botulism?" Duane said. "After all the drugs that kid's taken, a little spot of botulism wouldn't stand a chance."

Meanwhile it seemed a long ride home. Duane wondered if there was anyone else in town Jenny might enjoy going on rides with.

He didn't dislike her. He was even rather interested in her —he was getting on quite well with one of his son's former girlfriends; perhaps he would get along well with another. But Jenny, like Karla, contained a manic stream of talk, and in her case he didn't have to say a word to unleash the flood. The minute she sat down in the car seat, the stream flowed out over a somnolent Shorty, who had gotten so used to Jenny that he went to sleep the moment she began to talk.

"It sure is a good thing Lester fell in love," Jenny said. "I'd never have the energy to direct this pageant if I had to keep breaking his heart three times a day."

"It's kind of lucky for Lester too," Duane observed.

Jenny looked startled for a second, as if it had not really occurred to her that Lester might not enjoy having his heart broken three times a day.

"Do you think Jacy would ever agree to be in the pageant?" she asked. "She'd be a good Eve."

Duane said nothing, but Shorty opened one red eye for a moment.

"Maybe Karla wouldn't mind asking her," Jenny said. "I'd never have the nerve to ask her myself."

"I guess you could try asking Karla," he said. He had no idea what protocol prevailed in Karla's friendship with Jacy. Karla gave out no details about their activities. When she mentioned Jacy at all her references were apt to be cryptic.

"Jacy's only been married to Frenchmen," she said one day. "All her husbands were Frenchmen."

Duane waited hopefully, but further details were not forthcoming.

"Her children speak perfect English," she said, at another time. "They teach kids to speak a bunch of languages over there."

Nellie, fallen from perfection, was sprawled on a couch, watching a game show and listening to Joe Coombs breathe into the telephone. Duane tried to remember when he'd even heard Nellie speak a complete sentence in any language, but decided he would only get depressed if he started comparing his children to Jacy's. Maybe hers weren't really as brilliant as Karla made them sound.

Jenny Marlow was rereading the Texasville skit, lead pencil in hand.

"I think I'm getting an anxiety attack," she said. "I never expected to be made director of the whole pageant."

"Duane, if I let you out of playing George Washington, will you play one of the Mr. Browns in the Texasville skit?" she asked, a little later.

"Which would I be, the one who drank himself to death, or the one who lived with rattlesnakes?" he asked.

"Ed Brown, the rattlesnake one," Jenny said. "There's a legend that he used to carry the snakes around at night. He'd have them wrapped around his arms and even around his neck. He'd sing and the snakes would rattle and hiss. They say they made a rhythm sort of like a cha-cha."

"I never heard that one," Duane said. "A cha-cha?"

"A cha-cha," Jenny said. "I think I'll write that in. A skit like that could be real effective, even if we just use little harmless snakes."

CHAPTER 32

A FEW DAYS LATER DUANE FOUND HIMSELF DRIVING the road to Dallas again. It was a two-hour drive and not among his favorites. This time he was accompanied by Karla and Sonny. Karla had come along to keep their spirits up, but in fact none of their spirits were up. Sonny had had his most disturbing lapse to date, and they were taking him to Dallas to see a neurologist.

The previous Sunday night he had walked out of the Kwik-Sack and disappeared. Customers came in and stood around, thinking he was in the bathroom or had just stepped over to his hotel to get something he forgot.

But an hour passed, and Sonny didn't show up. Roughnecks made themselves hot dogs or barbecue sandwiches, used the little microwave, left piles of bills and change by the cash register and went back to their rigs. The Kwik-Sack did a good business in the early-morning hours: soon there was so much change on the counter that the roughnecks had to get a sack to put it in.

Bobby Lee wandered in and became immediately paranoid.

Anything out of the ordinary always made him paranoid. He immediately hit the CB in his pickup and woke Duane.

"I think Libyan terrorists have kidnapped Sonny Crawford," he said.

Duane leaped out of bed. Bobby Lee had a way of issuing his most paranoid conjectures in a slow, reasonable voice that made them seem totally plausible, if only for a few seconds. Duane had most of his clothes on before he realized that it was unlikely Libyan terrorists had chosen the Kwik-Sack as a target.

"It said on TV they sent in a bunch of hit squads," Bobby Lee reminded him, when Duane got back on the radio to voice doubts.

"It didn't say they sent them to Thalia," Duane said.

"We *was* the top oil-producing county in Texas one year," Bobby Lee reminded him. "It could be they see us as a threat to the Persian glut."

"The Persian Gulf," Duane corrected, wishing he hadn't put his clothes on so quickly.

Karla turned her tiny bed light on and began to read *Playgirl.*

"The Persian Gulf is where the glut comes from," Duane said. Sometimes he had a compulsion to try and make Bobby Lee be reasonable.

"Anyway, they got him," Bobby Lee said. "Maybe they're hiding in the schoolhouse."

Duane turned off the CB.

"Bobby Lee thinks Libyan terrorists got Sonny," he informed Karla.

"I wonder where they find so many models with big dicks," Karla said. "There aren't that many big ones around here."

"Didn't you hear what I said?" Duane asked.

"Bobby Lee deserves to have his head bit off for waking me up," Karla said. "Now I'll just have to lay here all night and have fantasies."

"Come to town with me and bite it off," Duane suggested. "I might even help you."

Karla decided to take him up on the offer, which made Shorty so apprehensive that it took Duane five minutes to catch him.

Shorty wasn't used to having Karla along on middle-of-the-night trips. In Shorty's view, Karla was bad medicine. He slunk under Minerva's Buick and stayed there until Duane poked him out with a broom.

"You could just leave the little son-of-a-bitch," Karla said, once Duane caught Shorty and flung him in the back of the pickup.

"You're more loyal to that dog than you are to me," she added.

"I am not," he said.

Just as he said it seven coyotes crossed the road in front of them. Shorty leaped out of the speeding pickup to pursue them. Duane braked, horrified.

"Eat him, coyotes!" Karla said, leaning out the window.

Shorty soon came trotting back, out of breath.

"See, coyotes won't even eat him," Karla said.

"That was a lot of coyotes," she observed, a mile or two later. "I guess we're surrounded by coyotes out here.

"It makes me anxious, Duane," she added, as they topped a hill. Thalia was only a mile away, a tiny, peaceful cluster of lights under the deep black sky.

"Coyotes won't hurt you," he said.

"They might carry off Little Mike and raise him like Mowgli," Karla said.

"Who?" Duane asked. More and more frequently his wife's statements were incomprehensible.

"Mowgli, in the *Jungle Book* movie," Karla said. "We took the twins to see it."

"I didn't," Duane said. "You must have gone with one of your boyfriends."

Karla looked at the peaceful lights of Thalia.

"It's a nice little town at night, isn't it?" she said.

"I still don't understand about the movie you took your boy-friend to," Duane said.

"It was about a little boy who got raised by coyotes," Karla said. "Walt Disney."

"I didn't know Walt Disney got raised by coyotes," he said. He drove past the pipeyard with the towering, expensive rigs sitting in it. A pipeyard wouldn't make a bad place for a terrorist to hide somebody, but all he saw in his was a big jack rabbit nibbling a blade of grass beside some two-inch pipe.

They arrived at the Kwik-Sack to find half the roughnecks in the county standing around with their deer rifles or their .44 Magnums. A few of the deer rifles had starlight scopes—their owners were sighting them in on distant telephone poles. It was clear that if there were any terrorists around they had picked the wrong town.

Bobby Lee sat on the tailgate of his pickup, discussing the Persian glut in maddeningly reasonable tones.

Toots Burns, the sheriff, drove up just as Duane and Karla did. He looked horrified.

"What happened, did some war start?" he asked.

"Libyan terrorists," Bobby Lee replied calmly.

"No war started—Bobby Lee's brain went boing-boing," Karla said, making her fingers into a propeller. Bobby Lee looked hurt. Karla went into the Kwik-Sack and got herself some coffee. Duane followed her in, hoping to find that Sonny had left a note explaining his absence. Considering the mood everyone was in, even a lengthy note could have been overlooked.

But no note was found. He got himself some coffee and went back outside. It was a warm, beautiful spring night, with dawn not far off. Toots Burns was nervously trying to get the crowd to sheath their weapons.

"One of them guns could go off and we wouldn't want to be waking people up at this hour," he said. Toots had never been a particularly forceful sheriff. He liked to park his police car in front of the courthouse and drink beer until he fell asleep. Once asleep, an army could have marched past without awakening him.

Somehow the quietly unreasonable Bobby Lee had managed to impose his fantasy on the restless crowd.

"There could be greasy little fuckers crawling all around," one roughneck said.

Duane, unpersuaded, took a walk over to the courthouse. Shorty went with him. Karla sat in the pickup drinking coffee. Duane walked around the square and sauntered back to the Kwik-Sack, having seen no sign of Libyans.

"It's just the same old town," he said.

The roughnecks got in their pickups and drove off in ones and twos, looking annoyed. Some had clearly hoped for an opportunity to hone their paramilitary skills.

"It's depressing to just have to go to work and not even shoot," one said.

"We could shoot Bobby Lee," another suggested. "He's the one got our hopes up."

"It was just a theory," Bobby Lee admitted. He abruptly decided he was late for breakfast.

"I wish your beard would grow faster," Karla said, before he left.

"Why?" Bobby Lee inquired. He wore a pained expression.

"Because it makes you look like a crazed idiot," Karla said.

"You ain't never nice to me," Bobby Lee said as he left.

Karla and Duane went down to the old hotel that Sonny used as his home. He lived in a small apartment in it—just a room, really. They thought he might have taken a long walk for some reason. He had once liked to walk—people would come upon him far out on some little country road and stop and offer him rides, thinking his car must have broken down. Sonny would just smile and decline. Some people commented at the time that he must be mildly touched—why else would anyone take walks?

He was not in his room at the hotel, though. It didn't contain much, just a bed, chair and card table. The card table was covered with brochures and stock offerings for the little companies that Sonny invested in. Duane leafed through some of them. They seemed like odd companies. One made earmuffs and another a machine that graded eggs according to size. He glanced through a third—it described how chicken shit could be turned into methane and used to fuel the world of the future. There were piles of checks on the card table and an old adding machine, all rather dusty. The sun was well up by then.

"Duane, come here," Karla called, from somewhere upstairs.

He found her at the window of a tiny room on the top floor. She was looking across the roofs of the laundrymat and a hardware store, toward the jail.

The view allowed her to look into the ruined shell of the old picture show. The theater had closed in the early fifties, a victim of dwindling business. Several years later, during a violent storm, it burned down. Only the marquee, a fragment of the balcony, the ticket booth, and the stone outer wall were left standing. The old woman who owned the show died before she could even collect insurance on the building. For a few years, her children tried without success to sell the shell. Then Sonny finally bought it for two thousand dollars. At first he talked of rebuilding it and reopening it as a movie theater, but he never did. The stone wall, the marquee and the little ticket booth continued to stand, each getting shakier by the year. The City Council eventually persuaded Sonny to knock down the wall—it was so unstable that it might have blown over in a windstorm, smashing someone. He knocked it down and tried to sell the stones, but without success, though Karla bought a few of them just to be friendly. Now only the marquee, ticket booth and a small fragment of balcony remained.

Duane was surprised to find Karla crying. He looked out the window and saw Sonny, sitting in the fragment of balcony in one of the two seats that had not burned. There was nothing below him but the charred remains of the original floor, and nothing above him but the blue morning sky.

"I could cry forever, looking at him sitting there," Karla said. "It just makes me want to cry forever."

They left the hotel and went around to the theater. The door beside the little ticket booth had stood open for at least twenty years.

"Hey, Luke, let's go have breakfast," Duane said, stepping inside. Sometimes he adopted Karla's nickname for Sonny.

In a minute Sonny came down, looking very embarrassed.

"Oh, no," he said. "Is anybody watching the Kwik-Sack?"

"I think Toots is there," Duane said.

After a moment of awkwardness, Karla went over and gave Sonny a big hug.

"You worry me so much I'm even losing my gift of gab," she said in a teary voice.

Then she broke free, sat on the curb and burst into tears.

"And I've been too hard on Bobby Lee, too, and now I feel terrible," she said. "What were you doing up there?"

"I was watching movies," Sonny said. "I mean, I was imagining I was watching movies. I don't remember leaving the Kwik-Sack though. Maybe I'm kind of like a sleepwalker."

"Let's go eat some breakfast, we'll all feel better," Duane said. He waited until Karla stopped crying, and helped her up.

"Bobby Lee thought Libyan terrorists got you," he said, to make conversation.

Sonny looked depressed.

"It'll be all over town," he said sadly. "People will think I'm crazy. I guess the Kwik-Sack will lose business."

"It didn't lose any last night," Duane assured him. "You made a good seventy-five dollars while you were watching that movie."

"I told Bobby Lee he looked like a crazed idiot," Karla said. "I've got terrible guilt feelings."

"We can take him to breakfast and maybe he'll forgive you," Duane said. "I doubt it, though. Bobby Lee likes to think he's good-looking."

Fortunately Genevieve Morgan, who worked the morning shift for Sonny at the Kwik-Sack, had already arrived and was mopping the store. Genevieve had run the local café for many years, but had gone broke in the seventies, just before the boom started. Her husband drowned in a boating accident on Lake Kickapoo. Sonny had given her work in several of his little enterprises over the years. She had managed his laundry-mat and supervised his video parlor. Some thought Sonny had opened the Kwik-Sack mainly in order to have a way to hire Genevieve.

"I wonder if she heard I was missing?" Sonny said as they drove by.

They found Bobby Lee gloomily drinking beer in front of the TV. His wife, Carolyn, worked as a dispatcher for a trucking company in Wichita Falls, and was already gone.

"I'm sorry I said you looked like a crazed idiot," Karla said, when Bobby Lee crawled into the pickup. "I was outa my head with worry."

"You was not," Bobby Lee said, his vanity deeply wounded. "If a Libyan terrorist got me you wouldn't pay my ransom, even if it was only thirty cents."

"Of course I would, sweetie," Karla said, giving him a few kisses on the neck.

"I don't think anybody would pay my ransom," Bobby Lee said. "Nobody ever liked me in this town."

"Shut up about terrorists," Duane said. "There's not a terrorist within five thousand miles of here."

"There's one right in this pickup, and you're married to her," Bobby Lee informed him. "Karla Moore's a terrorist. She's a big-mouth terrorist. She terrorizes me every time I get near her."

"It could just mean I'm attracted to you," Karla said, continuing to give Bobby Lee hugs and kisses.

"No, it means you're mean and I'm a victim," Bobby Lee said. "I've always been a victim."

"I guess it was because it wasn't daylight that you looked crazed," Karla said. "Now you just look like a normal idiot."

"I wished I'd been born with a silver spoon in my mouth," Bobby Lee said. "If I had been I wouldn't have to work for the husband of a big-mouth terrorist."

"Forget it," Karla said. "You was born with one of those little plastic spoons like they give you to stir coffee with on an airplane."

Duane saw that the conversation was making Sonny nervous, though Karla and Bobby Lee talked that way to one another all the time. Bobby Lee's little sinking spells always made Karla's spirits rise.

It wasn't a long trip from Bobby Lee's house to the Dairy Queen, but Karla and Bobby wouldn't stop badgering one another, and Sonny looked more and more nervous. The more nervous he got, the more irritated Duane became with the conversation.

"You two are driving me crazy," he said.

"The movie I was watching was called *The Burning Hills*," Sonny said. "It had Natalie Wood and Tab Hunter in it."

"Natalie Wood, it's sad that she drowned," Karla said.

That afternoon Sonny got a crowbar and pried the little fragment of balcony off the frame of the picture show. The balcony had been so flimsily attached that it only took him an hour to complete the job.

CHAPTER 33

THE APPOINTMENT WITH THE NEUROLOGIST HAD
been made at Karla's insistence. Duane backed her up, and
Sonny didn't fight them. He was reluctant to talk about what
happened, though. He refused two dinner invitations to avoid
having to talk about it. They got the name of a neurologist and
made the appointment. When they showed up on the appointed morning he got in the BMW, but he didn't really look
willing.

"Just because you tore down the balcony don't mean you're
well," Duane said.

"Do you see whole movies in your head, or what?" Karla
asked.

Sonny considered the question—it seemed to interest him.

"I saw a lot of *The Burning Hills*," he said.

"It's like I have a VCR in my brain," he said, a few miles
later. Then he chuckled sadly.

"Was it a good movie?" Karla asked. Since the morning they
had seen Sonny in the balcony, her spirits had been volatile.
She had had several crying jags, and spent more and more time
with Jacy.

She had also stopped wearing T-shirts with mottoes on them, dropping them in favor of blank black T-shirts.

Sonny had no opinion on *The Burning Hills.* He said nothing. The road to Dallas seemed interminable. The three of them fell silent and rode along submerged in gloom. Once they hit the Dallas traffic the trip seemed even more interminable.

"Turn on the radio, Duane," Karla said. "Get the traffic reports. We don't want to run into any traffic jams."

"What do you call this?" Duane asked. They were inching along in bumper-to-bumper traffic, a mile or two inbound from the Dallas airport. The skyline of Dallas was clearly visible fifteen miles away. Like the mountains of Colorado, the skyline seemed near and yet far. Twenty minutes later it looked just as distant.

The impenetrability of the traffic made Sonny nervous.

"I wish I weren't causing this trouble," he said. "I hate to cause people trouble."

"Everybody causes somebody trouble," Karla said. "If you don't cause anybody trouble then you might as well be dead. Think of it that way."

"Don't think of it that way," Duane said. He didn't want Sonny thinking he might as well be dead. "Just think of it as a slow trip to Dallas with two old friends," he advised.

"I cause Duane trouble every day of his life," Karla pointed out.

"It's not fair, either," Duane said. "It's unilateral."

"I don't even know what that means," Karla said.

"It means I never cause you any back," Duane said.

"You cause me plenty," Karla said. "I have mental anxiety because you never tell me what you're doing with your girlfriends."

"There's little to tell," Duane said, grinning. "I just do simple things."

That was certainly true where relations with Suzie Nolan were concerned. Suzie seemed to be a great deal more relaxed than most people in Thalia—or perhaps than most people anywhere. For that reason, what they did seemed simpler than it had with other girlfriends. Their desire, though urgent, left no overhang and produced no complications, which seemed too good to be true, or at least, too good to stay true. Yet, so far, it had stayed true.

"Wipe that cocky grin off your face or I might jump out of this car," Karla said.

Sonny looked horrified at the prospect of Karla jumping out on a crowded freeway.

"Just kidding, just kidding," she said quickly. "I'm not going to jump out of the car."

Sonny's examination took four hours, during most of which time Duane and Karla sat in the BMW and listened to Willie Nelson tapes. Karla had a major collection of Willie Nelson tapes. Duane liked Willie Nelson's singing a good deal, but after a couple of hours he began to wish for the sound of another voice. Even Karla's. Even Jenny Marlow's.

"Don't you have any other tapes?" he asked.

"I don't like to hear anybody but Willie when I'm depressed," Karla said.

"Why are you depressed?" Duane asked. "It's Sonny who's sick."

"He doesn't understand us very well," Karla said. "He thought I was gonna jump out of the car just because you're in love with Suzie Nolan."

"I'm not in love with Suzie Nolan," he said.

"She's a step up from Janine, I'll admit that," Karla said.

Duane didn't say anything.

"You could just admit it," Karla said. "I wouldn't hold it against you."

Duane laughed.

"Are you calling me a liar?" Karla asked. "I solemnly promise I won't hold it against you. Curiosity can drive a person crazy."

"What are you so curious about?" he asked.

"What kind of sex things you do with your girlfriends," Karla said. "I'll get insecure if you don't tell me."

"Just listen to Willie," Duane said. "I don't believe in talking about my private life."

"You probably do a lot more things than you ever do with me," Karla said. "She's a younger woman, too. It makes me insecure for you to sleep with younger women."

"Arthur's about fifteen years younger than I am," Duane pointed out. "He went to Yale, too. He probably knows how to do things I never even heard of."

"He does, but he don't wanta do them with me," Karla said, looking glum.

"Why not?" Duane asked.

"Because he wants to do them with boys," Karla said. "Arthur was a big disappointment. It seemed like he was normal for a while, and then it turned out not to be true."

Duane immediately began to feel more cheerful.

"Win a few, lose a few," he said, not unkindly.

"I don't even win one twice a year," Karla said. "And now you've got a younger woman and who knows where that'll stop?"

"Suzie Nolan's not two years younger than you," he pointed out.

Karla looked pretty depressed. "I knew I'd get a confession out of you," she said. "I can't blame her for wanting you. Junior's a total dud. He claims he took a headache pill two years ago and has been impotent ever since."

"What do you and Jacy talk about all day?" Duane asked, hoping to change the subject.

"I wouldn't tell you if you were the last person on earth," Karla said. "Two years younger is a lot younger when you're staring forty-seven in the face."

"You've always been the best-looking woman in town, and you still are," Duane said truthfully.

"I wouldn't have been if Jacy had stayed around," Karla said. "I've got better skin but she's got those good cheekbones. But Nellie and Julie are both going to be more beautiful than me. At least I'm the mother of beautiful daughters."

"What do you mean, at least?" Duane said. "There's nothing wrong with your life."

"Nothing except my boyfriends and my husband," Karla said. "Every trouble I've had, a man was the cause of it. I might try being a feminist, only it's probably too late for me to learn it."

"Don't get depressed thinking I do a lot of weird things," Duane said. "I've never done a weird thing in my life."

"I know, you're just straight vanilla," Karla said. "That's why I took up boyfriends. You only live once. I thought somebody must know something you didn't know, but the truth is there's people who know even less than you do, Duane."

"Hard to believe," he said.

"Men are jerks," Karla added, turning up the tape.

The last hour seemed to go on for a week. Duane wondered if Willie Nelson ever sat around outside doctors' offices for four hours. He wondered what tapes he listened to, if he did.

Twice, feeling that the day would never end, he offered to take Karla shopping. She shrugged off the offer.

"I hate shopping," she said. "Just because I spend about a million a year don't mean I like doing it."

"Why do you do it then?" he asked, surprised. She didn't seem to be joking.

"I don't know," Karla said. "Do you think we ought to see a marriage counselor? It's not a good idea to let things slide too long."

"I didn't know things were sliding," Duane said. "They seem to be going along pretty level. Now and then there's a bump, I guess."

"No, it broke my heart seeing Sonny sitting in the balcony," Karla said. "Then I realized that was not what broke it. It was already broken. You broke it. Seeing him just made me realize I didn't have a whole heart anymore."

Duane looked at her. Her eyes, usually devilish, were blank, a sign of real depression. He decided the situation might be more serious than he had thought.

"You might be listening to too much Willie Nelson," he said.

Karla took the tape out of the tape player and threw it out the window. She took the shoebox containing her seventy-eight Willie Nelson tapes and threw it out the window too. She opened the glove compartment and found five or six more tapes. They immediately went out the window.

Duane didn't say anything. Neither did Karla. Two carpenters from a construction site just down the street came walking along. The sidewalk in front of the doctor's office was littered with tapes. The carpenters were drinking coffee out of Styrofoam cups. They looked curiously at the tapes. Both were thin kids with a rather hangdog look. They squatted down and began to give the tapes a leisurely once-over. They seemed to be connoisseurs, like Karla. They examined the list of songs on each tape carefully. They discussed one or two of the tapes quietly between themselves. Once or twice they glanced at the BMW to see if there could be any connection between it and the tapes. Karla had put on her darkest dark glasses. They rendered her totally inscrutable as she watched the two young carpenters picking among her tapes. They continued their leisurely examination. One of them began to make a tentative keep pile.

"Are you going to sit there and let them take eighty-five Willie Nelson tapes?" Duane asked. He was beginning to feel annoyed.

"Why not?" Karla asked.

"I think you should see a neurologist yourself," Duane said.

He got out of the car and began to gather up the tapes. The young carpenters looked startled, but immediately relinquished their find. One of them gave Karla a youthful, dubious smile as they left.

Duane filled the shoebox with tapes and brought them back to the car. Ten or fifteen tapes had to be piled on top, in a kind of pyramid.

As he was sliding under the wheel Karla threw the box of tapes back out the window. Then she got out herself and walked off in the direction the carpenters had gone.

Before she reached the construction site Sonny came out of the doctor's office. He got in the back seat. Then he noticed all the Willie Nelson tapes on the sidewalk.

"Are those Karla's tapes?" he asked.

"They were," Duane said. "I guess she doesn't want them anymore."

"It's a lot of tapes," Sonny said, with some anxiety in his voice.

"Well, I picked them up once, I'm not picking them up again," Duane said.

"I don't think I could have been married," Sonny said. "Tension upsets me."

"You're in for a rough trip then," Duane said.

He saw Karla coming back down the sidewalk with the young carpenter who had smiled at her. He started the BMW, backed up a little, jumped the low curb, and began to go forward and then backward in the area where the tapes were scattered. The tapes crunched like shells. When he felt he had crunched the majority of them he drove off the sidewalk and parked.

Karla and the young carpenter had stopped to watch. The young carpenter turned back. Karla strolled on toward the car.

"What will she do?" Sonny asked, apprehensively.

Duane didn't answer.

"I should never have caused you all this trouble," Sonny said. "I thought you were happy."

Karla squatted down amid the crushed tapes. She examined them in the same leisurely manner that the carpenters had displayed. She picked up three tapes, got in the car, and smiled at Duane.

"That was real childish of you, Duane," she said. "Besides, you missed the best three."

Duane immediately drove off. They passed the hangdog young carpenter, who had a frightened look on his face.

"I doubt he could put in a garbage disposal either," Duane said.

"If Richie bothered you that much you should have said something at the time," Karla said, with another vivid smile.

They were passing the airport before Duane remembered that Sonny had been to a neurologist. To the north, like silver steps in the sky, eight or ten jetliners were lined up in their landing pattern.

"Go a little faster, Duane," Karla said.

"Why?"

"One of those airplanes could land right on top of us," she said. "I never liked roads that go right under airplanes."

She continued to talk, but a DC-10 lumbered down just above them and the roar drowned out her words. The plane reminded Duane of an elephant. Air waves rocked the BMW. Karla shut her eyes and hid her head in her arms.

"That was another childish thing you did, Duane," she said, once they were past the airport.

"No, that was a coincidence," Duane said. "I don't think Sonny's ever gonna want to ride with us again, though."

"I don't want to ride with us either," Karla said. "If there is an us."

She looked back at Sonny, who was white with tension.

"What was wrong with your head, Luke?" she asked.

"The doctor did a lot of tests," Sonny said. "We won't know until the results are in. There's a lot of things I could have."

"There's a lot of things Duane's already got," Karla said.

CHAPTER 34

THE NEXT MORNING DUANE WOKE UP FEELING UN-expectedly optimistic. Normally, of late, depression had been just a part of his daily routine, like shaving. But this morning it didn't come.

He took the .44 out to the hot tub, but he didn't shoot at the doghouse. He didn't even get in the hot tub. He sat in a deck chair and watched the sunrise. The flats below his house became briefly beautiful as the sunlight filtered like a golden fog through the brown weeds and low mesquites.

He felt so good that he decided he must have been somewhat insane for the past several months. Only an insane man would take good ammunition and shoot it at a doghouse, even if the doghouse did look like a frontier fort.

Shorty lay on the eastern edge of the deck. The sunlight made him look like a spot of golden light with a dog's tongue hanging out of it.

Duane had half an hour of peace, by which time the flats below the hill looked as ugly as they usually looked. Minerva walked out and handed him a cup of coffee. She had a disapproving look on her face.

"What's the matter with you?" Duane asked.

"I don't approve of that Junior Nolan living here," Minerva said. "It's one more mouth to cook for."

"Nellie's getting married in three weeks," Duane reminded her. "That'll even things up."

"If she gets married," Minerva said.

"We rented the church and hired the preacher," Duane reminded her.

"I think that Junior Nolan's got designs," Minerva said.

"Karla thinks he's mainly just depressed," Duane said.

"It ain't Karla he's got designs on," Minerva informed him. "It's Nellie. She's a sweet-tempered girl and I love her. I've met worse mothers, too. She's just got one problem."

"Which is?"

"Laziness," Minerva said. "She'd rather lie down than stand up. She spends half the day flat on her back, and that does draw the men."

On that cheery note she went back in the house, to be replaced after only a minute or two by Karla, who picked up the phone that lay on the deck and carried it over to Duane.

"It's your next girlfriend," she said, handing him the phone.

"Who's my next girlfriend?" he asked.

"Just lift the receiver," Karla said.

He lifted it and listened to Jenny Marlow babble for ten minutes. Occasionally he held the phone out into space so Karla could listen too. Jenny was in a panic about the pageant. Rehearsals started in less than a week. She needed to see him badly. There were a million things to discuss. They were still hoping that Jacy would play Eve, but no one had asked her. Did he think Karla would ask her? Or Sonny? Or himself?

"Are you going anywhere today?" Jenny asked. "I thought I might ride along with you if you were going anywhere. I've done the pregnancy test of myself and it was positive."

"Little Mike's got a real high fever," Duane said. "We're waiting for a call from his doctor now. I'll try to catch up on the pageant planning tomorrow."

Abashed at the thought of a sick child, Jenny hung up.

"You're a smooth liar, Duane," Karla said.

"I try to be good at whatever I do," Duane said, grinning.

"Besides, his fever might be up, for all you know." Little Mike was prone to stratospheric fevers.

"It always cheers you up to know I hate your guts, doesn't it?" Karla said. She herself looked quite cheerful.

"Do you want to ask Jacy if she'll play Eve in the pageant?" he asked.

"No," Karla said.

Shorty came over, wanting love, and tried to poke his nose between her thighs.

"Minerva says Junior is after Nellie and not you," Duane said.

"That's true," Karla said. "It's a wonder I haven't blown my brains out. I've got a husband who's a smooth liar, a house guest who wants to fuck my daughter, and a dog so dumb it don't even know it's not supposed to stick its nose up ladies' snatches."

She poured a little coffee on Shorty to distract him. It dripped onto the deck and Shorty happily licked it up.

"Where *are* you going today?" Karla asked.

"Odessa," Duane said. "I had an idea just now. I'm going to sell the rigs."

"We should have all seen the neurologist, if that's what you're thinking," Karla said. "Nobody's gonna buy those rigs. This is the bust, not the boom."

"Twelve million's just two digits and a bunch of zeros," Duane said. "I'm tired of being paralyzed by a bunch of zeros. I'm gonna cut down the interest any way I can."

"Going bankrupt would cut it down," Karla said.

"Yes, but I don't want to go bankrupt," Duane said. "I didn't do all this just to go bankrupt."

"I don't think I'll spend much money for a while," Karla said, looking off across the pastures. "Now that I realize it was just a broken heart that was bothering me I probably won't need to."

"Why'd you start wearing blank T-shirts?" he asked.

"Because my heart's broken and I got no more to say," Karla said.

"See if you can ease Junior out," Duane said. "Messy situations just tend to get messier, particularly if they involve Nellie."

"If I send him back home you'll never get to see your new girlfriend," Karla reminded him.

"Send him back anyway," Duane said.

He called Shorty and raced to town, hoping to get a little cash and be on the road before Jenny Marlow began her rounds.

He found Ruth in the office. She had just put on her running clothes and was doing stretching exercises behind the desk.

"There's three messages on the machine from Janine," Ruth said.

"I'm in a big hurry," Duane said. "If she calls again tell her I had to go to Houston."

"Where are you really going?"

"Odessa," Duane admitted.

"She sounds desperate," Ruth said. "I don't know if she'll last the day."

"She'll last the day," Duane said.

"I didn't think you was the kind to leave a desperate woman in the lurch," Ruth said, looking at him sternly.

Duane went into his office and called Janine, who did indeed sound desperate.

"I think I'm pregnant by Lester," she said, in a tiny, trembling voice.

Duane sighed.

"Somebody must be making a fortune off fertility drugs in this country," he said, reflecting that a worst-case scenario would have Jenny pregnant by Dickie, Janine pregnant by Lester, Nellie pregnant by either Joe, Junior, or Bobby Lee, and Suzie Nolan pregnant either by Dickie or himself. The fact that the last two hadn't been suggested or confirmed offered only slim grounds for hope.

"I wish it had been by you," Janine said.

"I wish it had been by nobody," Duane said.

"Now that stupid Jenny doesn't even want to give him a divorce," Janine said. "She says she's pregnant too, but Lester says that's impossible. When can you come and see me?"

"It'll have to be tonight, after the meeting," Duane said. "I have to go to Odessa right now. You just hang in there. This is not the end of the world."

"Are you sure you'll come?" Janine asked.

"I'm sure I'll come," Duane said.

Ruth was outside, jogging in place. She had already worked up a good sweat.

"Looks like you'd leave that stupid dog at home sometime," Ruth said.

"That dog's the only person who really loves me," Duane said.

CHAPTER 35

DUANE SET OFF TO RACE OUT OF TOWN, THE MEN-
ace of Jenny Marlow much on his mind, but as he was passing
the Dairy Queen he saw Jacy's black Mercedes parked there.
She was probably waiting to meet Karla. They met almost
every morning.

On impulse he stopped and went in.

Jacy was sitting in a back booth with a cup of coffee and a
newspaper. She had been for her swim in the lake—her hair
was wet. She had a towel over her shoulders and occasionally
fingered the wet ends of her hair.

"Howdy," Duane said.

Jacy looked up without friendliness. Her swim goggles had
left faint marks on her face.

"Run along, Duane," she said. "I don't like you anymore."

"Why not?" he asked, startled.

"Because I think you're behaving like a horse's ass," she
said, her blue eyes cold.

"I might not be quite as black as I've been painted, if it was
Karla doing the painting," he said.

"You're probably blacker," Jacy said. "Karla still loves you. She doesn't even think you're a horse's ass. I figured that out for myself."

"Do you want to play Eve in the centennial pageant?" he asked.

"Eve?" she said, caught by surprise.

"The director asked me to ask you," he said.

Jacy stood up and scattered a little change on the table. She wore a T-shirt and running shorts, plus the towel.

"I suppose you're playing Adam, right?" she asked.

"Not necessarily," he said. "Adam hasn't been cast."

Jacy walked past him and Duane followed her outside. She went to her car.

"Well, at least I asked," he said. "Call Jenny Marlow if you're interested. She's the pageant director."

Jacy looked amused. "That poor frantic thing who's married to Lester?" she said. "She's a director?"

"It's just a pageant in a rodeo arena," he reminded her.

He got in his pickup, feeling depressed. To his surprise she strolled over and looked in. Shorty, who normally would have attacked, put his head between his paws and made a submissive little squirming motion.

"Hello, puppy," Jacy said. "Where are you going, Duane?"

"I have to go to Odessa," he said. "It's the worst town on earth."

Jacy reached in and scratched Shorty between the ears. She no longer looked hostile. It seemed to Duane that she looked rather lonely.

"I might like to see the worst town on earth," Jacy said. "I've certainly seen several of the runners-up."

"Come with me," Duane said.

Jacy leaned her elbows on the pickup window. She seemed in no hurry to make her decision. Duane didn't feel quite so relaxed. He had the feeling that either Karla or Jenny Marlow would drive up any minute.

"Hop in," he said. "The scenery's not much, but we could catch up on one another."

Jacy gave the inside of the pickup a calm scrutiny. The whitish carpet of dog hair on the seat did not escape her attention.

"Let's go in mine," she said. "You can bring the puppy if you want to. My car's just as messy, but it's more comfortable."

Duane considered the ramifications of leaving his pickup parked at the Dairy Queen all day, where it would be noticed in turn by Karla, Jenny, Suzie and Janine, not to mention Bobby Lee, Eddie Belt, Lester Marlow and various others.

"I'll tell you what," he said. "Follow me down to Olney. It's just fifteen miles. I'll leave my pickup there. I've got this paranoid man who works for me. If he sees my pickup and can't find me he'll start the rumor that I got kidnapped by Libyan terrorists or something. By the time we get back they'll have called out the National Guard."

Jacy scratched Shorty between the ears again. "I don't think that's the reason you want to hide your pickup, Duane," she said, giving him a skeptical, almost angry look.

She walked back to the Mercedes and got in. He thought he had driven her away, and for a moment was not sure whether he was glad or sorry.

When he pulled out onto the highway, the Mercedes was still parked at the Dairy Queen. But before he had gone five miles he saw a black car in his rearview mirror. His spirits immediately rose—he knew he was glad he hadn't driven her away.

"You better be on your best behavior, Shorty," he said sternly.

Shorty whined guiltily at the thought of all the bad things he might do.

CHAPTER 36

"YOU DRIVE," JACY SAID. "I THINK I MIGHT WANT A nap."

They had parked side by side in the parking lot of a grocery store in Olney.

"You sure you don't mind if I take this dog?" Duane asked. He saw that the inside of the Mercedes was quite messy. The floorboards were strewn with old fashion magazines, empty yogurt cartons and little yellow boxes that had once contained film.

"Bring the puppy," Jacy said. "I like to study people and their animals."

She evidently felt no need to begin her study at once, though, because she settled herself in the back seat, made her towel into a pillow and slept soundly for almost three hours. Occasionally Duane heard her stir, but only to shift her position. He was in the sandy hills east of Big Spring before she sat up, her face still blank with sleep.

"Find a town, Duane," she said. "I need to pee."

He stopped for gas in Big Spring. When Jacy came out of the

restroom she stood for a moment looking at the bleak, scrubby hills. Then she opened both doors and snapped her fingers at Shorty, who quietly got out of the front seat and crawled in the back. The sand was blowing a little.

"Odessa's uglier than this, huh?" Jacy said. "I'm not sure I believe that. Why are you going there?"

"I'm in debt," Duane said.

"I know, twelve million," Jacy said. "Karla told me."

"There's a man in Odessa who might help me out, if he's there," Duane said. "I'm sure your father knew him."

Jacy slumped against the door. Her hair was a blond tangle and she seemed without energy. The countryside was dotted with oil pumps. In places the thin grass itself looked as if it had been smeared with oil.

"You're right, it's getting uglier," Jacy said. "Maybe you're more truthful than I think you are."

"Not really," Duane said.

On the way into Odessa they passed a large motel. It was called the Oilpatch Inn and had a neon rig as a sign.

"Are you gonna be a while with this man my daddy knew?" Jacy asked.

"I could be an hour or two, if he's there," Duane said.

"I think I'd like a motel room, then," Jacy said. "I didn't bargain on a sandstorm."

"Oh, this isn't a sandstorm," Duane said. "This is just a breeze."

"I don't have any money on me but if you'll get me a motel room I'll pay you back," Jacy said. "I don't think I need to see any more of this town."

Duane got her a motel room at the Oilpatch Inn. She insisted on keeping Shorty.

"He might bother you," Duane warned. "He gets kind of frantic when I'm gone too long."

Jacy smiled, for the first time on the trip. "Are you afraid I'll woo your dog away from you, honey pie?" she asked.

"Well, it's a big risk," Duane said. He smiled and Jacy smiled back. She kicked him lightly with a sandaled foot.

"If you could get me back in love with you you wouldn't need to spend so much time making deals in ugly towns, would you?" Jacy said. "I might put my daddy's fortune at your disposal."

"But I never had you in love with me," Duane said. "You had me in love with you, and that was in high school."

Jacy looked thoughtful. "That's a good point, Duane," she said. "Did I have you madly in love?"

"Madly," he said.

"Would you have given me twelve million in a second, if you'd had it at the time?" she asked.

"In a second," Duane said.

Jacy seemed to feel tired, despite her long nap.

"I guess I once could summon some pretty mad love," she said, frowning at the blowing sand. "I hope you won't be too long. This looks like the kind of place where I could get real depressed."

"I won't be over two hours," Duane said.

Jacy selected two or three magazines from those strewn on the floor of the Mercedes, took her room key from him and grimaced again at the sand.

"Come on, puppy," she said. "We're in this together."

Shorty jumped out of the car and trotted right at her heels, though he did turn once to look guiltily at Duane before following Jacy into the motel.

CHAPTER 37

THE MAN DUANE HAD COME TO ODESSA TO SEE WAS named C. L. Sime. C.L. was a legendary wildcatter. Unlike most such men he exhibited no interest in his own legend. He had rubbed elbows with all the greats: with Doc Joiner, H. L. Hunt, Getty, Glenn McCarthy. Hundreds of reporters had pursued him and all had been disappointed. C. L. Sime liked to wildcat; he didn't like to talk.

"Yeah, I knew Hunt," he said. "Yeah, I knew Sid Richardson."

The reporters waited hopefully, but C.L. never amplified his remarks. He spent his days smoking and sipping coffee in a small café in downtown Odessa, conducting his business from a pay phone in the bus depot across the street. He dressed like an out-of-work cowboy, coughed a lot, and drove a rusty GMC pickup with a couple of pipe wrenches in the front seat.

Occasionally he would disappear for a few months. Only by a careful reading of the Railroad Commission reports—the monitor of the Texas oil business—could his movements be followed. He had been a partner in the first offshore lease ever

209

developed. He had been in Alberta five years before the boom. Major oil companies employed men just to scout his movements—two scouts were killed trying to follow his bush plane through a blizzard on his first trip to the North Slope.

No one knew how much money he had, but he had a lot. Billions, some said. A Houston reporter had once established that he had more than two thousand bank accounts, mainly in small-town banks scattered through Texas from Laredo to Dalhart.

Duane had known him for fifteen years, and had been in with him on a few small deals. Though their meetings had all been strictly confined to business, he had the feeling that C. L. Sime liked him. Fortunately their little deals had all been profitable. He might have helped C.L. increase his net worth by a few hundred thousand dollars, over the years.

Mr. Sime was in the bus depot talking on the pay phone. Duane waited on the sidewalk until he finished and came out.

"Howdy, Mr. Sime," he said.

"Hello, son," C.L. said. He did not sound enthusiastic, but then he never had. They walked across the street together, ignoring the blowing sand.

"Son, have you got your own teeth?" the old man asked, once they were inside the café.

"All but two," Duane said.

"Take care of your teeth," C.L. said. "I didn't and now I've got these goddamn bridges and they're a misery. This goddamn grit gets under them. I've stopped talking unless I'm inside a building. It's the only way to keep the grit out of my teeth.

"It pays to spend a little more on dentists," he added, as a decrepit and depressed-looking old waitress brought their coffee.

"I'll keep that in mind," Duane said.

The old man took off his weathered cowboy hat and hung it on a wooden hatrack. His thin gray hair was combed flat against his scalp, which was freckled in places his hair didn't cover.

"The reason he's so rich is because he ain't tipped a soul in this restaurant since 1941, and that includes me," the old waitress said.

"Who asked you to butt in?" C.L. asked, without looking at

either the waitress or the coffee. He was looking out the window at the gritty street.

"Nobody, but it's a free country," the waitress said.

"The reason I don't tip is because I don't like the coffee," C.L. said. "Anyway, I didn't hire you, it ain't my job to pay your salary."

"If you don't like this coffee why don't you take your business somewhere else?" the waitress asked. She was skinny as a plank. Her stockings sagged down her legs.

"I don't because the phone's right across the street," C.L. said. "Besides, I like the atmosphere."

He grinned faintly, as if he felt his last remark was a clincher, but the old woman was halfway to the kitchen and might not have heard.

"I've had more arguments with that old hussy than I would have had if I'd married her," C.L. said.

He extracted a toothpick from his shirt pocket and began to pick his teeth. He looked at Duane. His eyes were a watery gray and did not seem shrewd.

"Mr. Sime, I want to sell you a half interest in my deep rigs," Duane said. "I believe the way to get through this recession is to concentrate on shallow oil."

The old man directed his gaze out the window, as if he could not get enough of the sight of downtown Odessa, though he had had some seventy years in which to scrutinize it.

"Oh, I ain't interested in hardware, son," C.L. said. "I'm just interested in production."

"Quite a bit of production would go with the deal," Duane said.

The old man thought a minute.

"It's a funny time to be peddling rigs," he said. "This town's nothing but a parking lot for rigs, right now. Pretty soon they'll have to start parking them over in Midland, I guess. Odessa's about got all the parked rigs it can hold."

He paused for a moment, evidently thinking of Midland, twenty-six miles to the east.

"Midland was once a nice town," he said with a hint of apology for the neighboring community's decline. "It filt up with them necktie people, though. I never understood the point of neckties, except that it would make it easier for somebody to hang you. I don't know why a feller would want to make it easier for somebody to hang him."

"It sure puzzles me," Duane said.

The old man was silent for several minutes. He took a sip of his coffee and made a face.

"Worst coffee in West Texas, this right here," he said.

"It's not too good," Duane admitted.

"I been thinking of going to Norway," Mr. Sime said. "They're getting quite a bit of production up in Norway, but I don't know if I'll go. They've got some socialism up there."

Duane sipped the horrible coffee, which tasted as if it had been made from linoleum chips. He waited. There was absolutely no reason why C. L. Sime should help him, when probably at least a thousand other people had just as much claim on his concern—and his concern, in any case, was clearly sparse. Yet he continued to feel hopeful. He didn't feel that things were going badly.

"You must not know me very well or you wouldn't drive all the way out here in a sandstorm, hoping I'd do something stupid," C.L. said.

"When this thing bottoms out some people will still be in the oil business and a lot of people won't," Duane said. "I'd like to be one of the ones who are still in it. I think we'll live to see oil go up again, and when it does, a cut of my production wouldn't be a bad thing to have."

"I've got a fair amount of money," C.L. remarked.

"I know you do, but there's no such thing as too much," Duane said.

"You ain't a necktie person, at least," the old man remarked. "I doubt you'll end up in Midland. It was once a nice little town.

"Have you got anything written up?" he asked.

Duane had written a proposition several days before. He had the proposition plus his production records for the last five years in an envelope.

"It ain't true that I've wrote deals on napkins," the old man said with sudden heat. "I've never wrote nothing on no napkin in my life. You couldn't write much on a napkin, even if you wanted to. They soak up ink too quick. Then you couldn't read what you wrote even if you wrote it."

"My proposition isn't written on a napkin," Duane assured him.

"Well, give it to me then," C.L. said. "I'm sick of this napkin talk."

Duane handed him the envelope. The old man opened it carefully and looked inside.

"I see you typed it up," he said. "That's good. They say I write deals on the backs of envelopes, and that's another black lie. This napkin and envelope talk gets irritating. That would be no way to run an oil business."

"I agree," Duane said.

"I think I'm going up to Norway and see how I make out with that socialism," the old man said. "They're making good production up there. I like the way you typed this up. I'll look it over and ring you on the phone when I get back."

"Thanks, Mr. Sime," Duane said.

CHAPTER 38

J ACY CAME TO THE DOOR OF THE MOTEL ROOM wrapped in a towel. Her hair was pinned on top of her head and the TV was on. The room contained two beds—Shorty was stretched out on one of them, warily watching a game show. Jacy walked back to the TV and turned the sound down.

"I had it turned up to drown out the wind," she said.

A room-service tray containing a grilled cheese sandwich and a glass of milk sat on the floor by her bed.

Jacy got back in the bed and put the tray on her lap.

"I figure a grilled cheese sandwich is safe even in Odessa," she said. "Did you make your deal?"

"I didn't get turned down," Duane said. "I can think hopeful thoughts for two or three weeks, at least. That's something."

"Yes," Jacy said, her voice dropping. She looked at the sandwich in her hand and put it back on the tray. She stared at the television, frowning a little, as if trying to force herself to concentrate on something.

Duane felt awkward. He felt he had said something wrong. Jacy picked up her sandwich and took a listless bite. She chewed it slowly, as if even that small effort took more energy than she had to spare. But then her appetite appeared to revive and she ate half the sandwich and drank all the milk.

"Want the other half?" she asked.

Duane shook his head.

"Here, puppy," Jacy said, tossing the other half to Shorty. Never shy in the face of food, Shorty ate it in a gulp. Jacy offered Duane the slice of pickle on her plate.

"I could pay you back that pickle I stole from your boat," she said. "Who would have thought an opportunity to do that would come so soon?"

"Not me," Duane said.

Jacy switched her attention to the TV. A plump young couple had just won a motorboat, a new station wagon, a dishwasher and a dining-room set. They beamed with happiness. The young wife was wearing very bright red lipstick.

"Do you think they're happy?" Jacy asked.

Duane glanced at the TV. The young couple seemed ecstatic. The plump young wife kept saying "Oh, I can't believe it, I can't believe it." The host, a dapper man in his sixties, offered them a chance to say hello to their families, which they did rather timidly.

"They just won a pile of stuff," Duane said. "They might be happy."

"That's a junky dining-room set, but do you think they know that?" Jacy asked.

Duane looked again.

"It sort of looks like our dining-room set," he said. "Or our breakfast-room set. I keep forgetting we have a dining room. We only use it twice a year."

"Christmas and Thanksgiving?" Jacy asked.

Duane nodded.

"Do you think they have a nice home life?" Jacy asked.

Duane's mind was back in the coffee shop with C. L. Sime. He wondered if the old man was sitting reading his proposition and pausing occasionally to bicker with the waitress. He found himself hoping that C.L. would like what he read so much that he would call and make him the loan before he even went to Norway. After all, Duane had offered him a quarter of his production for five years. It might strike a billionaire as a very fair offer.

Attempts to read C. L. Sime's mind from halfway across Odessa made it difficult for him to analyze the home life of the beaming young couple who had just won the motorboat.

"She might be a good cook," he ventured.

"You're not trying," Jacy said. "You don't even care about them. I don't think she's a good cook. I bet they eat frozen pizzas half the time. They look like big pizza eaters to me."

"I'm too far in debt to care about anything but getting out," Duane admitted.

"That's not what Karla thinks," Jacy said. "Karla thinks you get fucked about every five minutes. Do you?"

"No," Duane said.

Jacy was still intent on the game show. "I wonder about little couples like that," she said. "They look silly but maybe they're great in the sack. I've had silly-looking men who were great in the sack."

Shorty stood up and began to lick the crumbs of the grilled cheese sandwich off the bedspread.

"Do you think she goes down on him?" Jacy asked, still looking at the TV.

Duane found that it was a strain to get his imagination even to undress the young couple who had just won all the goodies. His imagination was reluctant to take them as far as oral sex, or any sex. They were dressed in their Sunday finery—in the case of the young man, a green suit—and the jump from their Sunday finery to oral sex was a bigger jump than his mind was willing to make.

"I don't have any idea what they do," he admitted.

Jacy looked amused. "You certainly have a dull attitude toward television," she said. "What's the point of it, if you're not going to speculate about the sex lives of people on game shows?"

"I hardly ever watch game shows," Duane said.

"I can see that," Jacy said. She got out of bed, picked up her T-shirt and running shorts and went into the bathroom. She shut the door and came out a minute later, dressed. She reached around the TV and turned it off without looking at it.

"If I see another couple I'll just get interested and you'll have to sit here and be bored," she said. "Come on, puppy, I guess we're leaving our little home away from home."

Once in the Mercedes she carefully buckled her seat belt, carefully locked the door and then leaned back against the door she had just locked and kicked off her sandals.

"Are you so far in debt that it would bother you to rub my feet?" she asked.

"Nope," Duane said. He massaged one foot and then the other. Soon they passed Midland with its little cluster of skyscrapers. The skyscrapers, shrouded in a haze of dust, seemed as forlorn as the occasional hitchhikers they passed.

"You oughta watch more game shows," Jacy said. "You see some lucky people on game shows."

"It's one thing I haven't tried, getting on a game show," Duane said.

"You'd just lose," Jacy said. "You don't have an open mind. A lot of people think soap operas are successful because they're like life, but that's horseshit. Soap operas are successful because they *aren't* very much like life. Game shows are what's really like life. You win things that look great at the time but turn out to be junk, and you lose things you might want to keep forever, just because you're unlucky."

She reached into the back seat, got her towel, wadded it into a pillow and was soon asleep.

From time to time, back through Big Spring and across the gray range country west of Abilene, Duane looked over at Jacy. In sleep some people became peaceful and looked younger. Karla did. No matter how hard her day, how filled with shouting, tears and trauma, sleep returned her beauty to her, and also her youth. Asleep, Karla could be taken for a woman in her late twenties.

With Jacy the opposite occurred. The deeper she sank into slumber, the more her unhappiness seeped into her face. She did not sleep silently, either. Occasionally she jerked and made sounds that were like grunts. The composure with which she carried herself soon vanished. Her body sagged; her mouth fell open.

Duane soon stopped looking at her—it seemed inconsiderate. He felt depressed, not so much by the change in Jacy as by the change in everything.

He didn't notice when she woke, but happened to glance over and catch her looking at him, her eyes big. The mere fact of waking had restored her dignity—she had not bothered to correct the sag of her body, but her look was tranquil, even a little amused.

"Well, you're pretty good at foot rubs, but I don't believe you get fucked every five minutes," she said. "I guess married people always believe their mates are doing better than they are."

"You've been married, I hear," Duane said. "How'd you do?"

Jacy smiled. "I did fine," she said.

CHAPTER 39

"ARE YOU REALLY ATTACHED TO THAT DOG?" JACY asked, when they drove up beside his pickup in the supermarket parking lot.

The question took Duane by surprise.

"He's my dog," he said. "Or else I'm his person, however you want to look at it." Shorty, in the back seat, was looking particularly drunken. He was not the sort of creature one easily confessed an attachment to.

"I hate to tell you, but I think I've won him away from you, despite my vow not to," Jacy said. "I think he'd go with me in a minute."

"Well, he might," Duane said, though previous to that moment infidelity was the last thing he would have accused Shorty of.

"Maybe it's time you two tried a trial separation," Jacy said. She was brushing her hair, but without much energy.

"You mean you want him?" Duane asked. "You want Shorty?"

"Well, kind of," Jacy said, grinning.

"He's probably the single most hated animal in Hardtop County," Duane said. "He's more hated than any living thing in these parts, people included."

"He might just be misunderstood," Jacy said. "Maybe he just needs a good woman's love."

Duane realized that she really wanted Shorty. He had assumed at first that she was only joking. He looked so puzzled that Jacy laughed.

"Come on, he's not Hitler, he's just a dog," she said. "I'm too alone, Duane. I have to start trying to let some living creature back in my life, even if it's just your scroungy old dog. Just tell me what to feed him—I wouldn't want to hurt his digestion."

"Shorty's digestion?" Duane said, his amazement growing. Shorty had eaten parts of several human elbows, along with a great variety of dog food, road kill and scraps. It had never occurred to anyone that his digestion need be considered.

"Feed him dead skunks," he said. "Feed him ground-up rocks or nearly anything else."

"Can I have him, then?" Jacy asked.

"Yeah, if you really want him," Duane said, though he realized it was all happening too fast for him to believe.

"Thanks," Jacy said. "I just want to try a companion and see how it works out. Otherwise there's a big chance I'll spend the rest of my life totally alone."

"But you wouldn't want to try a human companion?" Duane asked.

Duane got out. He felt the conversation was unfinished in some way, but he didn't know how to finish it.

"Thanks for letting me have the dog," Jacy said. "And for showing me the ugliest town in the world."

"I'm glad you could come," he said. "We didn't really catch up, though."

Jacy scooted under the wheel.

"Let's not bother catching up," she said. "I hate talking about the past, and not just because Benny got killed. And if there's one person I really don't want to talk about the past with it's my first boyfriend."

She looked at him with sudden hostility, a spot of color in her pale cheeks.

"I'm sorry," Duane said. "It's just one of those things you say. I guess it was stupid to say it."

Jacy was squeezing the steering wheel of the Mercedes. He could see her hands tightening on it.

Duane was not quite sure what he had said wrong, or what he might say to correct it. He felt very awkward.

"I'm real glad you went with me," he said finally.

Jacy gave him an irritated look and then relaxed and leaned back in the seat.

"Yeah," she said. "I liked that motel room. The longer I lived in Europe the more American I felt. Staying in a motel room like that was perfect. That motel room was pretty American."

She started the car. Shorty was wide-awake—Duane thought there was a good chance that he would try to jump out of the window as soon as he realized that a momentous change was about to take place in his life.

To make Shorty aware of just how momentous, he walked over to his pickup and opened the door.

"Hey, tell that woman I'll be Eve," Jacy said. "I've gotta stop being so reclusive. Causing the fall of humanity might be just the kind of challenge I need."

"She'll be thrilled to hear that you want to do it," Duane said.

Jacy looked at him for a moment and then drove slowly off. Duane was not sure what the look meant. The Mercedes turned toward the street and then made a slow circle and came back toward him. Obviously she had had second thoughts about Shorty, Duane thought.

But Jacy completed her circle and drove slowly up to where he stood, his pickup door open.

"Hey, I'm not mad at you, honey pie," she said, smiling.

Then she drove on and turned up the highway. Duane waited for Shorty to come flying out of the car. Soon he would be racing back on his little short legs. But in a minute the Mercedes was no more that a dot, and the racing Shorty did not appear.

"Shorty, you're too damn dumb even to know what's happening," Duane said, though all the way to Thalia he expected to see his dog running back to him.

CHAPTER 40

UNDER THE CIRCUMSTANCES DUANE FOUND THE centennial meeting hard to focus on. He spent much of it wondering what Jacy and Shorty were doing. Several times he lost track of the agenda, causing Suzie and Jenny to look at him anxiously. He was as absent on this occasion as Sonny was during his lapses.

Sonny, fortunately, showed no trace of his problem and conducted much of the meeting himself. Few of the issues to be settled were large. Jenny, the universal den mother, was in charge of getting people to take tickets, run concessions, print programs, pick up trash, etc., and she delivered a brisk report on her efforts to line up volunteers.

Meanwhile Suzie Nolan smiled her mysterious, unusually fetching smile. Duane decided she smiled that way because for some reason she looked at life happily, unlike almost everyone else he knew. Suzie didn't tax herself with knowledge of the world and was not even particularly interested in what was going on in Thalia. She took the committee work, like almost everything else, lightly. The burning issues over which the committee raged did not burn for Suzie. She took her days slow, watching a little television, reading a fat paperback romance, doing a little washing, delivering her kids to the athletic events in which they always triumphed. She might wash a window if one seemed particularly dirty, she might do a spot of yard work; but she was always happy to lay aside her modest chores or her fat paperbacks if Duane showed up. Adultery interested her more than dirty windows, but neither blemished her serenity.

"It's funny," she reflected. "I was totally faithful to Junior for fifteen years. Then we got rich and that loosened me up. Then we went broke and I was all loosened up and started sleeping with Dickie. Now Junior's gone and all I can think of is that there's lots more room in the house.

"A six-foot-five man takes up a lot of room," she added.

Duane found that he had to grit his teeth when Suzie talked about Dickie, as she did frequently. Just as Duane would conclude that he was beginning to be in love with Suzie, a conclusion based on what seemed to him an unusually good sexual relationship, she would drift casually into a conversation about what a prize Dickie was. Duane found himself becoming more and more passionate about her. Suzie seemed richly responsive, and yet it became increasingly clear that she regarded him as someone sweet and cuddly. It was Dickie who elicited more lip-smacking remarks.

"That Billie Anne probably don't know what a prize she's got," Suzie said. "She's not old enough to know. You should be proud of yourself, Duane, for having a son like that."

The remark came while Duane was putting on his socks—he continued to fail in his resolve to keep them on.

"I guess I am proud," he said, though in fact he felt a little chagrined. Several times he wanted to ask what Dickie did that was so special, but he always changed his mind and choked off the question. If he himself hadn't done it yet, or done it as well, then it was probably better not to know.

Had he asked, though, he had no doubt that Suzie would have told him. She was quiet, but not reticent, and would describe her own sexual responses as casually as if she were reporting on a high school basketball game. She regarded her body complacently and took attentive, though not compulsive, care of it. She considered it a handy plaything and frequently played with it. She loved to take little naps—her "yawny" periods, she called them—and upon awakening would always let her hand stray downward to give herself a little touch. It seemed to Duane that she spent much of the day in light masturbation, frequently interrupted but just as frequently resumed. Her mysterious smile contained a large component of laziness—Suzie was always willing just to lay back and rest, and usually willing to let someone do to her what she had just been doing to herself.

"That Dickie," she said often. "That little rat, he's just a treasure."

Duane spent much of the meeting wondering what his son had to offer that caused women to talk about him with such appetite.

The Reverend G. G. Rawley had been sullenly silent throughout the last two meetings. Duane knew it was a tactical silence. G.G. was just waiting. He had taken to bringing his Bible to the meetings. When a proposal came up that seemed to him to be in patent violation of the Scriptures, he would tap the Bible with a heavy forefinger. Now and then he would open it, purse his lips and pretend that he was reading the rule that had just been violated. He became a kind of silent umpire, calling moral balls and strikes in his head—mainly strikes. His attitude became patiently condescending. When the time came, the Lord's team would annihilate the sinners' team with a few towering home runs.

The last item on the agenda that evening was the selection of a carpenter to build the replica of Texasville on the courthouse lawn. It was to be called Old Texasville, to help people get the point.

"That which the heathen raises up can always be struck by lightning," G.G. pointed out. "And if it ain't rainy it can be struck with crowbars and a sledgehammer or two."

Duane awoke from his revery about what Jacy and Shorty might be doing to discover that the committee was about to award the plum assignment of building Old Texasville to none other than Richie Hill, the one carpenter in town that he couldn't stand.

"I don't think much of Richie's work," he said. "He can't even put in a garbage disposal right."

The committee looked embarrassed.

"But Duane," Jenny said, "we just voted to give it to him. We thought you were abstaining."

Duane felt silly. He had not even noticed the vote. Now if he tried to wrest the job away from Richie everyone would know the carpenter had once had an affair with his wife.

"Well, it's hard to have confidence in a man who can't put in a garbage disposal," he said lightly, and let the matter drop.

He was halfway home before he remembered that Janine thought she was pregnant. He had promised her he would come by. He swung around in the road and drove back to Thalia. Without Shorty in the front seat the pickup seemed strangely light—even a little unbalanced, although Shorty only weighed thirty pounds.

He realized he would soon have to explain Shorty's absence to Karla and the kids. He had no idea what he would say. A few hours earlier he would have assumed it would take the Budweiser Clydesdales to drag Shorty away from him. Shorty's obsession with him was a staple of conversation in Thalia, and had been for years.

His defection would no doubt become a staple too. Duane felt stunned by it. On the whole it was more surprising than the oil bust. Rational men knew that oil could always go down, if only because there was always the possibility that somewhere, in some country where no one had thought to look, a strange old man like C. L. Sime might find a trillion barrels of it.

But Shorty had been at his side since his days as a short, fat puppy. He had seemed like a dog born to worship, and Duane happened to be the one person he worshipped. And yet, he had just trotted away. Jacy hadn't even had to beg, plead or cajole. Shorty had just switched.

It was profoundly puzzling.

"It's stupid to get involved with dogs," Duane remarked, as he pulled up in front of Janine's house.

A few minutes later he felt he could expand his remarks considerably. It was also stupid to get involved with someone who would get pregnant by Lester at a time when Lester was not only still married but indicted on seventy-two counts of bank fraud.

Janine, so confident in the Dairy Queen, so saucy on the tennis court, had had the wind taken out of her sails, the light out of her eyes, and the appetite out of her stomach. She existed primarily as a lack, too weak even to open the door for him. He found her lying on her bed, covered by a wreath of wet Kleenex. The cartons from a couple of drugstore pregnancy tests were in the wastebasket. The person who invented pregnancy tests must be at least as rich as the person who invented fertility drugs, Duane decided.

"There's no hope and there never will be none again," Janine said, in her dullest, most broken voice.

"Yes there is hope," Duane said. "People survive lots worse messes than being pregnant by Lester. Your family could have been killed by a tornado."

"But mine was already killed in a car wreck," Janine pointed out.

Duane felt like an idiot for not remembering that fact before he spoke. The sight of a woman plunged into total despair always unnerved him and caused him to say stupid things. It was a common problem, since every woman he knew, however merry they might look, stood only a step or two from total despair.

"I'll never have a family," Janine went on, seeming to gain strength from the very blackness of her own plight. "I'll never have a single thing I want, especially not you."

"I thought you were in love with Lester now," Duane said.

"No, we're just dating," Janine said. "I hate his tall ugly guts for getting me and his wife pregnant both."

"I don't think he got his wife pregnant," Duane said. "He might be telling the truth about that."

"Who got her pregnant then, a stork?" Janine snapped, brushing the wet Kleenex off her lap and sitting up.

"I think Dickie might have gotten her pregnant," Duane said.

Janine thought that one over carefully.

"Yeah, he probably did, I forgot they was even dating," Janine said.

"I think it was a little more than dating," he said.

"No, it's just dating, unless there's a commitment," Janine said dogmatically. "I will admit Dickie's cute—he just don't have no morals. I'm surprised you didn't raise your kids better, Duane."

"I'm surprised I didn't either," Duane said. "Do you want to have an abortion?"

"I certainly don't," Janine snapped. "I'd eat grass off the lawns and be disgraced before I'd give up this little curly-headed baby I'm gonna have."

"Curlyheaded?" Duane inquired. Neither Lester nor Janine could be described as curlyheaded.

"Well, that's the way it is in my dreams of happiness," Janine said.

"What does Lester think about this development?" Duane asked.

"He thinks I'll make a real good mother," Janine reported proudly. "He thinks we might want to hire a PR person to explain things to the county so I won't lose the next election."

Duane wondered if he himself had developed a brain sickness of some kind. For the past several months it had seemed to him that the citizens of Thalia were talking utter nonsense. Each wildly aberrant remark, many of them miles beyond the boundaries of rationality, would be followed by one even more aberrant. Who had ever heard of hiring a PR firm to protect a county clerk's job?

"Lester says everything's just images, these days," Jenny said. "He says a good PR person can show things in a positive light. My psychiatrist thinks it's good to be positive too."

She opened a package of gum, of which she kept a plentiful supply close at hand, and popped two sticks into her mouth.

"Lester thinks he might get a reduced sentence if he can show that he has lots of responsibilities here at home," she said.

"Could be," Duane said.

To his surprise Janine came over and curled up in his lap.

"I feel like we're just best friends now, so you behave," she said, poking him sternly in the crotch to emphasize her point.

"I'm behaving," Duane assured her.

She put her head back against his chest and lay still for several minutes, the working of her jaws and the popping of gum the only sound. Duane thought for a moment she might be asleep, but when he looked he saw that her eyes were not only open, they were glowing. The despairing creature blanketed in Kleenex had vanished, and a young woman in the bloom of early pregnancy had taken her place. Total despair might be only two steps away, but it was also, in some cases, only two steps wide, as well.

"My tits already feel bigger," Janine said, in a soft happy voice. "I'm glad you're here—it's nice when there's a man that behaves."

Duane held her for a while, marveling at the changeability of women. It seemed to him he had been the same forever—it would require a decade for him to change as much as a woman could change in a few minutes.

"You don't really hate Lester's tall ugly guts, do you?" Duane ventured.

"Naw," Janine said cheerfully. "I just said that. Don't you ever say things like that?"

Duane didn't answer. Now that she had risen like a bubble from total despair to cheerful equanimity his own thoughts had drifted back to Shorty, who was spending his first night in his new home. Duane wondered if he was homesick.

Janine poked Duane's crotch again—more gently this time—to see if he was still behaving.

"I guess I can trust you," she said, evidently a little surprised by his impeccable behavior. "Do you think I'll get fired?"

"I doubt it," Duane said. With things as they were, it seemed unlikely anyone would get too outraged over the fact that the county clerk was pregnant out of wedlock.

"Will you loan me the money to build a fence around my house?" Janine asked. "If it's a boy it'll be out in the streets in no time."

"I can probably manage that," Duane said. "What will it be doing if it's a girl?"

"Little girly things, of course," Janine said, unpeeling another stick of gum. It was obvious that she was no longer depressed about being pregnant. In fact, he had never seen her look so happy or so appealing.

"It'll be something that's mine," she said wonderingly. "I've always wanted something that's mine."

Duane tried to weigh that statement against his twenty erratic years of parenthood. Only rarely, and then for fleeting moments, did he have any sense that his children were his, in the way Janine seemed to mean. Of course he had produced the seed that met the egg which formed them, but otherwise, from birth on, they had mainly seemed like little strangers, belonging to themselves, not to him or Karla. Of course at times they swept close to him and he found himself loving them keenly; at other times their orbits swung apart and he was mainly conscious of the distance between himself and them, as they raced around Texas like human comets, trailing crises in their wake.

But why tell such things to Janine? It might be different for her. It might be very different.

"Duane, are you upset because we're just gonna be friends now?" Janine asked, feeling, for a third time, between his legs. She seemed to have a new confidence in her appeal and felt the need to keep checking.

"Oh, well, I'll live," Duane said, trying to walk the fine line between cheerfulness and depression which the question seemed to require.

"We'll still do lots of things together," she assured him. "You have to help me think of names, for one thing. Names of boys, particularly. If it's a girl I've already got the name picked out."

"What?" Duane asked.

"Danielle," Janine said. "Don't you think that's a great name?"

"Pretty great," Duane said.

CHAPTER 41

ALL DUANE COULD THINK OF, DRIVING HOME, WAS how nice it would be just to go to bed. He was so tired he felt it would even be nice to go to bed in a vast waterbed. But he arrived to find his house a blaze of lights and confusion. Even his backyard was a blaze of lights and confusion.

Only Minerva, reading the *National Enquirer* at the kitchen table, seemed unconfused.

"Little Mike climbed up the satellite dish," she said. "I never knew a kid his age who could climb like he can. I guess he'll climb Mount Rushmore before he's through."

"Isn't that the one with the Presidents' faces?" Duane asked. "Why would he want to climb that?"

"Why would he want to climb a satellite dish?" Minerva said.

Sure enough, Little Mike was perched on the very top of the dish, crooning his favorite word, "Ball."

Karla, looking grim, stood on a kitchen chair a few feet below him, promising amnesty from all punishment if he would just climb down.

"You try," Karla said to Duane. "I've stood on this chair so long I'm getting dizzy."

Duane got up on the chair but found Little Mike well beyond his reach.

"Where's Julie?" Duane asked. "He'd come down for her."

Little Mike worshipped Julie and would immediately do anything she commanded. He was also apt to do things she didn't command, such as spitting on her. Little Mike regarded spitting as an act of love, and was always shocked when Julie kicked him into the furniture for spraying her with saliva.

"I have no idea where the twins are," Karla said. "I think they left. They said it was getting too crazy around here, which is right."

"I'm gonna whip your little butt if you don't get down here right now," she yelled at Little Mike, abandoning the amnesty tactic.

"Where's Nellie?" Duane asked. "She's his mother, let her get him down."

"No, Nellie's over at Joe Coombs's explaining why she don't want to be engaged to him anymore," Karla said.

Duane heard sobbing from the swimming pool and saw the long skinny figure of Billie Anne paddling on a blue floatie in the middle of the pool. She was sobbing loudly.

"What's wrong with her?" he asked.

"Dickie smashed all their new furniture with a tire iron," Karla said. "You oughtn't to leave me alone on days like this, Duane. I can't even get drunk. The faster I drink vodka the faster things happen that sober me up."

"Little things like a broken engagement and a broken marriage?" Duane said.

"Yeah, and broken furniture," Karla said. "Plus I'm real worried about Junior. The bank called his notes today."

"They called his notes?" Duane said.

That was a real shocker. Everyone knew Junior was deeply in debt, but no one expected the bank to actually call his notes. Even he hadn't expected matters to go that far, and he considered himself a skeptic where banks were concerned. He had expected Junior to muddle through, perhaps losing his ranch or his drilling company but not everything.

"How many notes did they call?" he asked.

"All of them," Karla said. "Junior just went down the tubes."

Duane walked over and sat down in a lawn chair. He felt weak in the legs all of a sudden.

"If they could call his, they can call mine," he said. "Where is Junior?"

"He took a lariat rope out of his pickup and went walking off down the hill," Karla said. "He's probably hung himself by now."

"Why didn't you stop him?"

Karla dropped into the lawn chair beside him. She looked a little wobbly in the legs herself.

"I can't do everything, Duane," she said. "I meant to call the stress hot line, but then Billie Anne came in screaming and yelling and I forgot all about Junior until it was too late."

As if on cue, Billie Anne began to scream and yell again. She paddled around the pool on her blue floatie, flailing her arms rapidly.

"Maybe the world's coming to an end," Karla said. "Do you think Jesus would help us if we went and rededicated our lives?"

"No," Duane said. "Anyway, I never dedicated mine in the first place."

"That's right, you never even tried to be religious," Karla said. "No wonder bad things are happening to us."

"Most of them are happening because there's too much oil on the market," Duane pointed out. "It's got nothing to do with religion."

"Do you think oil really comes from squashed dinosaurs?" Karla asked.

"It's fossil fuel," Duane said. "More things got squashed than dinosaurs. Ferns and plants."

"Who would have thought there was that many squashed dinosaurs under Saudi Arabia that they could just make the market drop like this," Karla said. She seemed in a ruminative, even philosophical mood.

"Why did Dickie smash the furniture?" Duane asked.

"He caught Billie Anne talking on the phone to a man," Karla said. "She claims it was the dishwasher repairman but I've got my doubts because it was a brand-new dishwasher."

Little Mike came walking up, having climbed off the dish unassisted.

"Ball," he said cheerfully.

Karla caught him by the arm and gave his bottom a couple of hearty smacks. Little Mike's cheerful look changed to one of shock and heartbreak. He began to wail. Before he could run off Duane caught him and put him on his lap. He felt sorry for his grandson, for once. He had only been seeking conversation and had been punished.

"Let him alone," Duane said. "He doesn't realize he's done anything wrong."

"He deserves about a hundred spankings," Karla said, though she herself seemed to regret having dispensed one.

Little Mike buried his face in Duane's shirt and sobbed. Then Karla began to sob, out of guilt. Billie Anne was still sobbing in the pool, and no doubt Junior Nolan was sobbing somewhere in the dark pastures below, if he wasn't already hanging dead from a mesquite tree. Duane wanted to cry himself, but felt too tired. The emotion was there, but such muscle as it took to cry seemed to have atrophied.

Little Mike recovered first. The sight of his grandmother crying astonished him so that he forgot his grievances and pointed a finger at her.

"Ball?" he said inquiringly.

Duane passed him over to Karla so the two could make up.

"I talked to Jacy," Karla said. "She says Shorty's a wonderful companion. I guess she was really lonely and didn't know it."

"I guess so," Duane said.

"Duane, it was sweet of you to let her have your dog," Karla said, drying her eyes.

Touched by the way she said it, and lonesome for Shorty, Duane began to cry.

CHAPTER 42

Neither Duane nor Karla could sleep for worrying about Junior.

"I ought to go look for him," Duane said several times, as they bobbed, wide-awake, on the waterbed.

"He's probably just asleep under a tree," Karla said. "I bet he shows up at breakfast. He likes Minerva's biscuits."

"Why doesn't Nellie want to marry Joe?" he asked.

"She might have met somebody she likes better," Karla said. "That's the only reason Nellie ever has for not marrying somebody."

After staring sleepless at the ceiling for an hour Duane got up and dressed.

"I'm going to go look for him," he said. "It won't hurt to look."

Karla got up too.

"You don't have to go," he said.

"I'm going, though," Karla said. "I don't want to be alone with my thoughts."

They got in his pickup and drove through the pasture below

the house. Numerous small pumpers' roads wound through the mesquite. Neither of them felt the least bit hopeful about finding Junior. The pasture contained three thousand acres. Unless Junior happened to be sleeping in one of the roads, their venture had little chance of success.

"What thoughts didn't you want to be alone with?" Duane asked.

"I haven't got a thought left in my head that I'd care to be alone with for five minutes," Karla said.

"Nobody's dead yet, that we know of," Duane said. "Where there's life there's hope."

"No, things are too fucked up now," Karla said. "I doubt my life will ever be unfucked again.

"It takes longer for things to straighten out than it does for them to get tangled," she added.

"Maybe the twins will grow up perfect," he said.

Karla laughed. "You've finally gone round the bend, Duane," she said.

"They might make respectable marriages and become lawyers and do fine," he said. "If they'll just do that we'll be batting five hundred as parents, which ain't bad."

"They won't though," Karla said. "They'll become criminals and we'll be batting zero. We don't know where either one of them are right now. We should be looking for them instead of Junior. He's a grown man."

Duane could not convince himself that the twins were in any danger, wherever they were.

"I have to do something about Dickie," he said. "He can't be allowed to smash furniture and stuff."

"He's got a jealous temperament, like me," Karla said.

"You don't smash furniture," Duane said, looking at his wife. Since seeing Sonny Crawford in the balcony she had seemed far too subdued.

"The big smash might be coming, any day," Karla said, but the remark was made without energy.

After two fruitless tours of the pasture, they gave up. Junior was not in the road. On the way back to the house they had to stop while two possums ambled across the road. The sight seemed to cheer Karla up.

"I like the way their rear ends wobble," she said. "Now that Shorty's gone, could we have a possum for a pet?"

"Let's give it a few days," Duane said. "Jacy might not like some of Shorty's bad habits."

Karla laughed. "You can't believe he just walked off and left you, can you?" she said. "You better face it, Duane. Your faithful dog wasn't faithful at all."

They crawled back in bed and Duane had a terrible dream in which Shorty was found hanging from the goal posts at the football field. He staggered up, to discover that it was dawn. He decided to go nap for a bit in the hot tub, but smelled biscuits and went to the kitchen first.

"Did Junior ever come in?" he asked.

"No, and I hope he don't," Minerva said. "He's just another mouth to feed."

"You ought to show a little sympathy," Duane chided. "The man's just lost everything he's worked forty-five years to get."

Minerva curled a scornful lip.

"He's down the hill trying to rope an oil well right now," she said. "There's nothing to stop him from making another fortune. Nothing to stop you, either. My own daddy went bankrupt three times. Junior's not going to get nowhere sitting around whistling at coyotes all day."

Duane went outside and saw Junior staggering around the nearest oil pump, which he did appear to be trying to rope.

Taking four or five biscuits, in case Junior was starving, Duane walked down the hill. Junior had managed to rope the top of the pump. He dug his heels in the earth as if he had roped a steer, but the pump was stronger than a steer. It promptly jerked him off his feet.

"I used to be a pretty good team roper," he said, when Duane handed him the biscuits. "I might hit a few rodeos. Make a new start."

"Now don't do that," Duane said. "You're too old to rodeo. You'll just get all busted up."

Junior thought it over. His face looked terrible. Various levels of sunburn were peeling at different speeds. He looked as if he were molting.

"I guess I ought to go home," he said. "I can't mooch off you and Karla forever. Besides, Minerva don't like me. She says I'm just another mouth to feed."

"Minerva's not too tolerant," Duane said.

"Did you ever know a tolerant woman?" Junior asked. "If you did you're luckier than me. I ain't met one yet."

Duane thought Junior's wife, Suzie, was tolerant, but he didn't mention it. They started climbing the hill. Junior gave out halfway up and sat down on a rock.

"This is a cruel place to live," he said. "Cruel and ugly. I was in the Navy. I should have gone AWOL in the South Pacific and not come back."

Junior looked to be at the end of his tether. Duane thought there was cause to be alarmed about him. When they got to the house he took Karla aside and made her promise to keep a watch on the man.

"I think I can talk Suzie into taking him back," he said. "I think I better try—otherwise we might lose Junior."

"They're having a longhorn sale in Fort Worth," Karla said. "I might take him to that."

"Take him but don't let him start bidding," Duane said. "He don't have anything to bid with."

He drove to his office and sat by himself for an hour. Ruth was off on her run. When she returned she noticed him sitting in the dark office. She stuck her head in the door and gave him a sharp look. Sometimes she reminded him of Briscoe, a roadrunner that lived around the office—thin and irascible. In fact, Briscoe had been there earlier, pecking at the glass window. He was like a determined transient. He wasn't going to be satisfied until he broke in and stole something.

"It's not like you to brood," Ruth said.

"I haven't done anything but brood for the last six months," he pointed out. "There isn't anything to do around here but brood."

"You're not equipped to brood," Ruth said. "Go run one of the rigs. Make yourself useful to the company. That fourth rig's just sitting there."

"Why?" Duane asked. "What happened to Abilene?"

Abilene was the old driller in charge of the fourth rig. He had once worked for Jacy's father and been in love with her mother—Duane had even roughnecked on his crew when he was in high school. Abilene had always been hard to get along with. He was vain, humorless and quick to quarrel.

"Abilene didn't show up," Ruth said. "He's probably found a new girlfriend. You better stop brooding and go to work or this business will sink like a stone."

"It can't sink, it's resting on the bottom now," Duane said.

"Where's Shorty?" Ruth asked.

"He went to live with Jacy," Duane said, not eager to talk about it.

"I wouldn't have a dog, they're too much like humans," Ruth said. "How's Jacy doing?"

"I think she's doing pretty well," Duane said.

"You might not be the best judge," Ruth said. "You've lived with Karla most of your life. Karla's buoyant. Not too many are that buoyant.

"I like Karla," she added. "You're lucky she married you."

"It must be the one thing I've done that you approve of," Duane said.

"No, I think it's nice of you to let Jacy have your dog," she said.

She walked over and raised the blinds. The sunlight that flooded the office was so bright that Duane put on his dark glasses.

"You keep this office too dark," Ruth said. "No wonder you brood. Sunlight helps you to keep a cheerful disposition."

"Then how come there's so many sad people around here?" Duane asked. "There's certainly no shortage of sunlight."

Ruth looked out the window at the dusty tennis courts.

"Sometimes sadness is just in people," she said. "Look at Sonny. He was sad when he was a teenager, and he just never got rid of it."

"I don't know what he found out at the head doctor," Duane said. "Sonny avoids me. I only see him at meetings."

"I'd avoid you too, if I were Sonny," Ruth said. "You're successful and he isn't."

"What do you mean? I'm stone broke and he owns four or five solvent businesses," Duane said. "They may not be Exxon or Mobil, but they're solvent. I'm the one who ought to be sad."

"Some people can only see defeat," Ruth said. "You're not that way, Duane."

They were silent for a while. It sometimes annoyed Duane that no one seemed to perceive the slightest change in his own circumstances. They calmly continued to regard him as the most successful man in town, although his personal life was bizarre, his children uncontrollable and his business on the verge of ruin.

"I might be looking right at defeat myself," he said, in an effort to force Ruth to recognize that he wasn't indestructible.

Ruth ignored his effort. She went to shower, and he soon heard her typing away at her mysterious letters.

Duane got a sheet of yellow paper out of his desk, meaning to make a list of all the things he ought to do that day. Karla had read somewhere that it was good to make lists of things one needed to accomplish in the course of a day. She herself constantly made lists on little pieces of yellow paper. Some she stuck on the deck of the hot tub. The sun quickly melted the little piece of adhesive the note paper had on it—those lists blew off into the yard, to become prizes for ants and beetles. Others she stuck on the icebox, and still others on the dashboard of the BMW. It was not apparent to Duane that she ever did any of the things on the lists, but it created an impression of efficiency that he envied.

He studied his piece of paper and wrote: (1) Check on Abilene's rig. (2) Suzie Nolan. (3) Dickie.

After scrutinizing that promising list of responsibilities for a while, he crossed off "Dickie" and wrote in "Jacy." He couldn't think of anything to add to the list, and it seemed silly to be carrying around a list of only three things to do, so he wadded it up and threw it in the wastebasket. He got up and started to leave—in fact, got all the way to his pickup before the existence of the list began to bother him. Ruth and Karla were both pesky. It would be just like either or both of them to discover a wadded-up piece of paper in the wastebasket and unwad it. Of course, both of them already knew that he was becoming friendly with Jacy, and both seemed to approve. What they knew about his relations with Suzie Nolan was more ambiguous—he had not exactly admitted to anything, but neither had he been precise in his denials. He had left it shadowy, or at least liked to suppose that he had. But if either Karla or Ruth fished the piece of paper out of the wastebasket and saw the names of the two women they might jump to conclusions. They would probably be the right conclusions, too.

After hesitating at his pickup for a minute, he went back in and retrieved the list. "Forgot something," he said awkwardly, to explain his sudden reappearance to Ruth.

"That's all right, Duane," Ruth said. "Nobody's gonna be mad at you if you want to play safe."

When he went back outside, he noticed Briscoe, the roadrunner, on the tennis courts. Briscoe sailed over the net, raced around the far court and then sailed back over. It was as if he had served himself into one court and then returned himself to the other. Then he began to peck irritably at the bottom of the net. When he noticed that Duane was watching him he raced to the service line, cocked his head and looked annoyed.

Duane felt better just watching him. A roadrunner capable of being his own tennis ball had possibilities. Perhaps he could be trained to sit in a pickup and peck people who tried to steal tools. He was taciturn and wouldn't always be yipping like a Queensland blue heeler.

"Briscoe, you can have Shorty's job any time you want it," he said, as he drove off.

CHAPTER 43

DRIVING THROUGH TOWN, HE NOTICED TWO FAMIL-
iar-looking bicycles outside the Kwik-Sack. He stopped and
went in. Genevieve was mopping the floor.

"You haven't seen any twins around here, have you?" he
asked.

Genevieve grinned. She had always had a capacity for seeing
the funny side of life, which was fortunate, since hers had
largely been grim.

"I just now saw a pair, watching videos in the storeroom,"
she said. "They're having Fudgsicles for breakfast."

Duane looked in the storeroom. The twins were there all
right, sitting on their sleeping bags watching rock videos on a
small TV which sat on some cartons of canned chili. Before
leaving home they had given themselves punk hairdos. They
both wore dark glasses. They had managed to turn the storeroom into a small but well-equipped apartment. Among the
modern conveniences it contained was their mother's brand-
new compact-disk player and a tote bag full of compact disks.

"Hello," Duane said.

The twins stared at him from behind their dark glasses. Although their hair had become different colors, they had never seemed more twinlike. They were totally expressionless.

"I hope Bobby Lee don't wander in here," Duane said. "If he was to, he'd probably have a heart attack. He'd think you were Libyan terrorists."

"We won't hurt Bobby Lee," Jack said. "He's not on our list."

"Well, who is on your list?" Duane asked.

"They'll find out when we strike," Julie said.

Duane took a seat on some crates of dishwashing liquid.

"You look kinda settled in," he said.

"We're gonna live here," Julie said. "It's more interesting than living at home. Uncle Sonny says we can shower in the hotel when we get dirty."

"I don't see how anything could be more interesting than living at our house," Duane said. "Seems to me life at our house is a thrill a minute. Just last night we had three people lost, for example."

The twins didn't regard that remark as worth answering. They turned their attention back to the video.

Duane saw no point in attempting to drag them back home. The storeroom seemed like a peaceful environment; if anything he felt rather envious of them for finding it first.

"It wouldn't hurt you to give your mother a call," he said.

"She'd just try to browbeat us into giving back the CDs," Jack said.

"I think she's more worried about your safety than she is about the CDs," Duane said.

"She can find us if she really looks," Julie said. "Our bicycles are right outside."

"Okay," Duane said. "Don't get in Genevieve's way, though. Or Sonny's."

"We're going to help him at night," Jack said. "He forgets how to do the cash register, but don't worry, we won't let him get robbed."

"Maybe I'll stop in once in a while," Duane said.

He drove out to Suzie Nolan's. Suzie was in the backyard in a hammock Junior had strung for her. She was still in her blue nightgown and was leafing through a fat paperback called *Isle of Passion.*

"Dickie came by last night," she said, yawning cheerfully. "I told him it was about time he came by, the little rat."

Duane hadn't been sure what tack to try and take with Suzie. The news of Dickie made him even less sure. He pulled up a lawn chair.

"I ought to get dressed and go to Wichita," Suzie said. "The kids are both in the finals of the tennis tournament. But they're always in the finals of something, and they always win. Do you think I'm a bad mother for not wanting to go?"

"Yes," Duane said. He felt rather annoyed with Suzie in general.

Suzie seemed undismayed by his disapproval. She marked her place in the fat paperback with a nail file and idly touched herself here and there.

"I sorta wish you'd let Junior come home," he said. "He's in pretty bad shape, and having those loans called didn't help."

"I'm a bad everything," Suzie said. "Bad wife and bad mother too."

Duane didn't comment.

"After a night with Dickie there's nothing nicer than just lying in a hammock," Suzie said.

The recognition that she was a bad wife and mother was clearly not causing her much mental anguish. Duane knew his own position was weak, since he had helped make certain negative contributions to her record as a wife.

"I'm really worried about Junior," he said. "I don't think Junior's gonna make it unless he gets a little more support."

"He could get a girlfriend if he'd just start wearing his hat more so his sunburn wouldn't always be peeling," Suzie said.

"I guess if worst comes to worst I can get a job," she said. "I can clerk in a drugstore or something. But I don't want Junior to come home."

"Don't you like him at all?" Duane asked. He himself liked Junior. Suzie seemed to like almost everyone else in her life. It struck him as sad that she had hardened her heart against her own unfortunate husband, of all people. It made him wonder if he really understood anything about women.

"I been married to him twenty-one years," Suzie said. "He's only been happy five times that I can remember. You know what I'm like, Duane. I'm a happy person. It's not good for a happy person to constantly get their spirits brought down by an unhappy person. I'm a lot happier now that I just see Dickie and you than I ever was when I was living with Junior. I don't think I can go back to being the other way."

Duane had no answer to that. It was becoming clear to him, after only a few weeks, that Junior's unhappiness could become oppressive. It was not hard to imagine that twenty-one years of it would produce enough oppressiveness that a person might not want to see Junior ever again.

Suzie took his hand and held it to her breast in a way that seemed friendly, not passionate.

"He don't want to just hold hands," she said. "He don't like to just sit and touch."

Duane knew she was referring to Junior. He was at an awkward distance from the hammock, and moved a little closer, so as to be more comfortable.

In a few moments he noticed that Suzie was asleep, his hand folded against her breast. He sat beside her for a while. The yard was shaded by a nice sycamore tree. Suzie liked birds, and a mockingbird and a blue jay were quarreling at one of her feeders. The mockingbird flew over and sat on the clothesline.

Duane bethought himself of his idle rig, and Abilene, his missing driller. He gently disengaged his hand. As he stood up Suzie opened her eyes and mouthed him a little kiss before settling back into her nap.

CHAPTER 44

He had hardly backed out of Suzie's driveway before Jenny Marlow raced up behind him, horn blaring. She parked and was in the pickup in a flash.

"You've been neglecting me," she said, chewing gum a mile a minute. "You better not neglect me."

"Why can't I?" Duane asked. He felt oppressed himself. It seemed to him that his life had become a bewildering melange of responsibilities. There were people who welcomed neglect, such as the twins, and people he wasn't allowed to neglect, such as Jenny, and people in between who sometimes demanded attention and at other times welcomed neglect. Karla was a good example of the in-between category, whereas his drilling business was an even more clear-cut example of something that needed attention but received neglect.

"If you neglect me in my time of need I'll go crazy and you won't have anyone to direct this pageant," Jenny said.

Duane took her to the Dairy Queen and bought her coffee. He had decided that long solitary rides with Jenny were a kind of ride he wanted to avoid.

"Lester's told everybody in town my baby isn't his," Jenny said. "Do you think he really knocked up Janine?"

"I hope he did," Duane said honestly. "I hope it wasn't anybody else I know."

At that point a white Lincoln roared up to the Dairy Queen and Abilene got out from under the wheel. He still dressed as he had when he was thirty years old: very dark glasses, well-pressed gabardine pants and a cowboy shirt with pearl buttons. His hair had thinned quite a bit and the unforgiving sun had given him several skin cancers, but Abilene confidently ignored his own blemishes.

The girl who got out of the other side of the Lincoln looked a year or two younger than Nellie. Abilene had recently concentrated his attentions on farm girls a week or two into their first secretarial jobs in Wichita Falls or Lawton. He found them in obscure discos all over Texhoma—a region of North Texas and southern Oklahoma overlapping the Red River. The farm girls tended to be breasty, and wore a painful abundance of makeup.

The one with him at the moment was tall and looked frightened. She clutched Abilene's hand tightly when they came in. She stood nervously with him at the cash register, looking at the menu for the day, which was scrawled on a blackboard. She seemed to be as unnerved by having to choose between a cheeseburger, a Mexican plate and a chicken-fried steak as some might be if faced with a menu written in French in an elegant establishment in Dallas.

Duane felt sorry for the girl and didn't look around when they passed behind his chair, though he was very much in the mood to fire Abilene on the spot for taking an unauthorized leave.

Seconds later Janine, Charlene and Lavelle walked in, taking an early coffee break. Duane heartily wished he hadn't come to the Dairy Queen. He didn't want to confront Abilene in front of his frightened date, nor did he want to gossip with the ladies from the courthouse. Janine's year in psychotherapy had given her a strong belief in eye contact. Whenever she and Duane happened to find themselves in the same public place she expected a virtual orgy of eye contact and would be bitterly critical if she didn't get it. She wasn't far away, either. The room had filled up so quickly that the courthouse crew was forced to sit at the next table.

He wasn't too eager to look at Jenny, for that matter. She had given up blue eye shadow in favor of a color that she claimed was champagne—it matched her new lipstick.

"Now they'll eavesdrop," Jenny said, meaning the courthouse crew. "Every word we say will be all over town."

"Every word anybody says is always all over town no matter where they say it," Duane pointed out.

"Hi, girls," he said, feeling that he could not well ignore the women of the courthouse any longer.

"I hear a human fly is going to climb our courthouse during the centennial," Charlene Duggs said. Charlene would often take it upon herself to relieve awkward silences, an attribute for which Duane felt grateful. Almost everyone else in town made awkward silences yet more awkward.

"Oh, yes, he's a nice little human fly," Jenny said. "He lives in Megargel."

"Does he climb people or just buildings?" Lavelle said with a bold grin. "If he's so nice I might get him to try and climb me."

Janine meanwhile was staring fixedly at Duane, determined to have a least a flicker or two of eye contact. Duane obliged. He knew from the way she was frowning that Janine was trying to communicate something to him, though he had no idea what.

A boothful of wheat harvesters had just finished a vast meal and were headed for the door.

"I wonder where those wheat harvesters are headed?" Duane said, aware that it was the stupidest imaginable comment. Wheat harvesters always headed north, toward Saskatchewan and Alberta.

"Isn't this hot weather we've been having?" Janine said, as if to show that she could match him inane remark for inane remark. The thermometer had hit one hundred and seven the day before.

To Duane's relief, Bobby Lee's pickup came flying off the highway and braked to a stop in a cloud of dust, inches from the plate-glass windows of the Dairy Queen. Bobby Lee drove as if he were a horseman in an old cowboy movie. He flung his pickup back on its heels right at the hitch rail outside the saloon.

"Someday that little dumbbell's foot is going to slip off the brake pedal and he'll go right through this Dairy Queen as if it was tarpaper," Lavelle said. "And I'll probably be the person that gets turned into a grease spot."

In a moment the little dumbbell sauntered in, with his usual elan. He had recently gone to a Western-wear store meaning to buy himself a new cowboy hat to wear during the centennial festivities—but in a moment of frivolity he had bought a huge, drooping Mexican sombrero instead. His beard was still not much more than an advanced stubble. The sombrero and the stubble made him look so funny that Duane burst out laughing every time he saw him.

He burst out laughing immediately. One of the reasons he treasured Bobby Lee was that he had only to look at him to be reminded that life had its comic aspects.

"If they hold a contest for the ugliest beard, you'll win without even trying," Lavelle told Bobby Lee bluntly. None of the women were as charmed by him as Duane was.

"If you keep talking like that I won't let you be the president of my fan club," Bobby Lee said amiably, straddling a chair.

Duane knew that if Bobby Lee had arrived, Eddie Belt could not be far behind, and he wasn't. Before Bobby Lee's coffee had even grown cool enough to sip, Eddie came in. He had given up on a beard and was trying to grow a handlebar mustache.

"They can't duck you if you've got a big handlebar mustache, can they?" he asked Duane several times.

Duane promised to refer the matter to the committee on ducking, a nonexistent body. In any case, Eddie was a redhead, not the perfect hair color for a prominent handlebar mustache. At the moment he looked as if he had a few flecks of cinnamon toast stuck to his upper lip.

Eddie was somewhat affronted by Bobby Lee's sombrero. As a serious oilman, he disdained cowboy trappings, and Mexican trappings as well. New cowboy hats were blossoming all over the county, but Eddie still wore his oily dozer cap.

"Seeing you in that sombrero makes me want to puke," he informed Bobby Lee.

"It's a free country—puke," Bobby Lee replied. He seemed to be in an unusually good mood.

"If you was in a Pancho Villa movie you'd be the peon that has to hold the horses while the *jefe* goes into the saloon and gets drunk on tequila," Eddie said.

Even this insult failed to stir the placid Bobby Lee. He had a beatific smile on his face.

"Has Abilene quit, or what?" he asked, glancing at the couple in the rear booth.

"He better hope that girl's rich and wants to marry him," Duane said. "He's not gonna have a job after today."

At that point, to everyone's surprise, conversation died. Duane thought he might try to reopen the entertaining question of whether women want sex more or less than men—after all, most of the original panel had assembled—but he didn't reopen it. He remembered that it had been Junior Nolan who had asked the original question about women and sex, and where was Junior now? A bankrupt man whose wife didn't want to put up with his glooms anymore, and whose perfectly nice children had to keep winning athletic tournaments unobserved by either parent. It seemed like a sad time, or a sad place, or both.

Also, whenever he raised his eyes, he noticed that everyone at his table, as well as the three women at the courthouse table, were looking at him. They instantly looked away when he looked up—all except Charlene Duggs, who didn't try to pretend she hadn't been looking at him. Charlene continued to look at him, with what seemed like sympathy. The others, before they glanced away, all seemed expectant. They wanted him to start a sexy conversation. They wanted him to make a joke about Bobby Lee's hat, or Eddie Belt's little cinnamon-toast mustache.

Mainly, as he read it, they wanted him to initiate something that might relieve the boredom or anxiety they each lived with. They weren't picky. They'd follow any move he wanted to make, but they wanted him to be the one to make the move.

Duane felt a sullen impulse to deny them what they wanted.

Why should he always have to be the starter-upper? Let someone else start something up, for once. Let Janine do something
besides practice eye contact. Let Jenny do something besides
dump insecurities at people's feet.

He kept resolutely silent, nursing his sense of unfairness. He
was more deeply in debt than anyone in town. His kids caused
more trouble than anyone else's kids. His wife spent more
money than anyone else's wife. His employees were at least as
lazy and incompetent as anyone else's employees. Why, with
those things to worry about and more, did he also have to provide lively conversation for anyone who happened to straggle
into the Dairy Queen? He wasn't the president of the town, or
the master of ceremonies of the Dairy Queen.

He determined not to say a word, to force one of the others
to show at least a whisper of initiative. It was bad enough that
he was president of the Centennial Committee and would be
held responsible if the glorious celebration was a fiasco—as
there was every reason to suspect it would be. Just once, he
didn't intend to be the one who came up with the first move.

Silence lengthened. Bobby Lee and Eddie Belt, who would
instantly begin an argument if they happened to arrive in the
office at the same time, seemed to have become mutes. Bobby
Lee grinned idiotically from beneath his sombrero. Duane remembered that Nellie had broken up with Joe Coombs. He
tried to push dark thoughts from his mind. Surely Nellie
couldn't have succumbed to Bobby Lee, after resisting him
almost daily since she was fourteen.

Silence spread like a winter cloud across the Dairy Queen.
Jenny took out a mirror and cautiously studied her new
makeup. The women from the courthouse had the stoic look of
people who were about to attend the funeral of someone they
had scarcely known.

Only Abilene, secure in his vanity, was unfazed by Duane's
refusal to bring life to the party. Soon he finished his meal and
sauntered out, his sunglasses in place and his toothpick held at
a jaunty angle. He was followed by the big, unhappy-looking
girl. Abilene didn't so much as glance at Duane. He and his
date got in the Lincoln and left.

"He didn't even hold the door open for her," Lavelle observed, but the remark failed to ignite much feminist rage. No one expected Abilene to be nice.

"I don't doubt he made her pay for her own cheeseburger, too," Lavelle added. "I hate to think there's men that won't even pay for a stupid cheeseburger."

"He's always been loose with his mouth and tight with his money," Duane said, feeling that Lavelle deserved at least a little help.

Out the window he saw a large blue pickup bounce off the highway, and immediately felt a sense of relief. Karla was on the prowl in her Supernova. He felt a rush of admiration for his wife—perhaps even love. Karla might have her flaws, but when she showed up something would happen. She was not loath to initiate conversations, or fights either.

The Supernova slowly circled the Dairy Queen, observed by all. Everyone perked up a little. Karla was just sizing up the crowd, seeing if there was anyone there she was feeling particularly friendly—or perhaps particularly unfriendly—toward. In a minute she would walk in, ready to rev up on coffee and get things crackling. The ladies from the courthouse took out their mirrors and looked at themselves.

To everyone's surprise, Karla didn't come in. After circling the building she drove off a little distance and then backed up, rapidly and expertly, braking to a stop a few inches from the rear bumper of Bobby Lee's pickup. In a flash she jumped out of the Supernova and disappeared from view.

Duane glanced at the happy Bobby Lee and noticed that he had stopped looking happy. In fact, he had turned pale beneath his stubble.

"What's she doing to your pickup?" he asked Bobby Lee.

"I'm just hoping for the best from all this," Bobby Lee said weakly. "I'm just hoping it will all work out for the best."

Karla reappeared and reached into Bobby Lee's pickup, to take it out of gear. Then she tapped on the window of the Dairy Queen. Everyone looked. Karla gave Bobby Lee the finger. There were gasps from a few wheat harvesters who hadn't left for Saskatchewan yet—they were unaccustomed to local ways.

Then Karla jumped in her Supernova and raced away, dragging Bobby Lee's greasy little pickup like a puppy on a leash.

When Karla whipped onto the pavement the little Datsun bounced a foot or two in the air and landed on its side. Karla kept accelerating. Showers of sparks flew everywhere as she dragged the small pickup up the highway.

Duane decided the dark thoughts he had had regarding Bobby Lee and Nellie were almost certainly accurate thoughts.

Of all the spectators, Eddie Belt seemed most unnerved by the sight of a pickup being dragged up a highway.

"Oh, shit, look at what that woman's doing now," he gasped.

To everyone's astonishment, he grabbed the sugar jar, tilted his head back, and poured a thick stream of sugar directly into his mouth.

Duane burst out laughing. He decided he loved his wife, after all. Who else could scare Eddie Belt so badly that he would start drinking sugar straight from the jar?

CHAPTER 45

JENNY MARLOW WAS THE FIRST TO SPEAK.

"What'd you do that for?" she asked Eddie.

Eddie wiped sugar off his lips and took a sip of water.

"I thought I was gonna black out," he said. "The sight of that poor little pickup made me feel real weak. She drug that little thing off like a calf to the branding fire."

He began to be embarrassed by what he had done. Everyone who had been looking at Duane was now looking at him.

"It was like I went into shock, you know," he said. "My insides just felt real mushy, all of a sudden. Sugar's the best thing for shock, they say. It just goes right into the bloodstream."

Bobby Lee seemed to be in shock himself, but not so far in that he enjoyed seeing Eddie seize all the attention.

"It wasn't even your pickup," he said. "It was my damn pickup. I guess if she'd have drug off your pickup you'd have died on the spot."

"I might have," Eddie admitted, too weakened to take offense.

Duane got up and looked out the window. Karla was dragging the pickup straight through town. Cars and trucks were whipping to the side of the road, their drivers unnerved by the strange spectacle.

"It's the only pickup I got, too," Bobby Lee said, his spirits falling even lower.

"I wonder why she's so mad at you," Duane said.

"I have no idea," Bobby Lee said. "She's just one of those kind of women that can always find something to be mad at."

"You mean like your wife, Carolyn?" Duane asked. Carolyn was known to be a woman of temperament, and the same people who knew her to be a woman of temperament knew Bobby Lee to be a man of easy virtue. Most people thought Carolyn had done a good job of keeping him cuffed more or less into line for the last twelve years.

"Yeah, Carolyn's another of them kind of women," Bobby Lee said. "Ever' woman in this stupid town is the kind that can always find things to be mad about."

Beneath his sombrero he was looking more and more depressed.

"They just mow you down like you was grass," he added.

"It's true," Eddie Belt said, agreeing with his colleague for the first time in years.

"This doesn't have anything to do with Nellie, does it?" Duane asked.

"Yeah, 'cause we're getting married," Bobby Lee said in a toneless voice.

Duane laughed. It was exactly what he had expected to hear.

"I think what this town needs is one of those boards like they have in stock exchanges," he said. "Only instead of telling stock prices it would just keep up with divorces and pregnancies and who's married to who, or expecting to be. We could put it on the courthouse lawn and give some kid a nice summer job, changing the names around every day."

"Summer job?" Charlene said. "Year-round job, you mean."

"That's right," Duane agreed. "It would have to be kept current. Otherwise, after a month of two, quite a few women wouldn't even know what their last names was."

"Duane, you get some silly ideas," Janine said, standing up.

"I'll always know what my last name is because I wouldn't change it if I got married fifty times."

"Don't worry, there ain't fifty men in the universe crazy enough to marry you," Eddie said, his old bitterness flaring up.

Janine seemed amused. "Too much sugar causes irreversible brain damage," she said as she walked past him.

"I was under the impression you and Nellie both are already married," Duane said to Bobby Lee.

"We are but nothing's forever," Bobby Lee said.

"It's good you've got that attitude if you're marrying Nellie," Duane said. "Nothing's for much more than a month with Nellie."

"He's wrong anyway," Lavelle said. "Dead is forever."

She made a little gun of her finger and pointed it right between Bobby Lee's eyes.

"Bang," she said.

Charlene Duggs gave them all a pleasant smile before following her friends outside.

CHAPTER 46

DUANE TOOK BOBBY LEE TO THE OFFICE AND LEFT
him with Ruth.

"Why are you leaving him with me?" Ruth asked. "I've got
better things to do than look after men who wear sombreros."

"I know, but Karla stole his pickup," Duane said. "I don't
have anything else to do with him."

"Go in Duane's office and go to sleep," Ruth commanded.
"It's dark in there."

Bobby Lee, who seemed numb, docilely went in the office
and shut the door.

"Could I impose on you to figure up Abilene's hours and
give me a check for what we owe him?" Duane asked. "I can't
tolerate him any longer."

"Who's gonna run that rig?" Ruth asked.

"I am," Duane said. "It beats brooding."

He found some overalls in a closet and put them on. Ruth
looked at him as if he were a wayward boy, but held her
tongue.

On his way to the rig he passed Los Dolores. He had been

toying with the idea of stopping to pay his respects to Shorty, but he saw Dickie's pickup parked out front and decided not to stop. He didn't feel much shock or surprise at seeing Dickie's pickup there.

Shortly after passing the house he noticed a tiny dust cloud in his rearview mirror. A small blue blur was racing down the road after him. Duane stopped and opened the door. In a moment Shorty raced up and jumped in his lap. He seemed ecstatic to be back.

"Nobody told you to leave in the first place," Duane said, but Shorty wasn't listening. He lay on his back and wiggled, adding a few hundred hairs to the substantial blanket that was already there. Then he looked at Duane guiltily, as if expecting to be beaten with the work glove.

"Forget it, Shorty," Duane said. "Worse things can happen than losing you."

As he approached the rig he heard the familiar sound of gunshots. The roughnecks, happy to be collecting eight fifty an hour for loafing around, were shooting at beer cans with their .22s. Their faces fell when Duane drove up.

He worked them steadily all day. About six, Abilene drove up. Shorty hated Abilene and began to snarl. Duane stepped off the rig floor long enough to hand Abilene his check.

"Your services are terminated," he said.

Abilene looked contemptuous. "You'll be a bankrupt son-of-a-bitch before the summer's over, anyway," he said.

Duane went back to work. He felt rather good. He had not forgotten how to work, and being at the rig was a nice change from sitting around the office trying not to irritate Ruth.

As he was driving back past Los Dolores, toward town, Shorty began to whimper and look unhappy. He even went so far as to scratch at Duane's leg. Duane stopped the pickup and held the door open. In a second Shorty was out. He trotted off toward the house.

"She might go back to Europe, and then where would you be?" Duane said, but Shorty didn't look around.

Going through town, Duane stopped at the Kwik-Sack to buy a six-pack. He thought he might look in on the twins, too. He expected to see one of them handling the cash register, but instead Sonny was in his old place, watching TV. Duane looked in the storeroom but neither the twins nor their effects were there.

"Did Karla come and get them?" he asked.

"Jacy came and got them," Sonny said.

Duane thought that one over for a minute.

"She's in for some fun and games, then," he said.

"They're very nice kids," Sonny said. "They're just full of mischief."

"Mischief, plus homicidal tendencies," Duane said, though it always made him feel good when someone complimented his children.

"We sold about four hundred dollars' worth of centennial souvenirs today," Sonny said. "Maybe this thing's going to be a success after all."

He spoke in a cheerful tone, but he had a downcast look. Duane had been studiously not asking him how he felt, but it occurred to him that everyone else was probably tiptoeing around the issue of Sonny's illness, and that perhaps Sonny found that depressing.

"How's your brain problem?" he asked.

"Well, I got some pills," Sonny said.

"Do they work?"

"Oh, well," Sonny said, "I don't see movies in the sky and I haven't lost my car lately. I guess that's an improvement."

"You don't seem very convinced," Duane commented.

"No," Sonny said. "The pills make me feel like I have fuzz in my head. Sort of warm fuzz. It's not a great feeling."

"What's supposed to be wrong with your head, anyway?" Duane asked.

Sonny chuckled. "I guess it's just degenerating," he said. "The neurologist wanted to try the fuzz pills before he did anything more drastic.

"I'd rather see movies in the sky," he added.

"Seen any good ones lately?" Duane asked.

Sonny grinned. "I saw *To Kill a Mockingbird* last week," he said. "Pretty good movie. I haven't seen one since I started taking the fuzz pills."

"Maybe you oughta lay off the pills until we get through the centennial," Duane said. "Once that starts we're all gonna need our wits about us."

"I think my wits live somewhere else now," Sonny said.

Duane drove on home. Talking to Sonny was depressing. Once he thought about it, he realized it always had been. Even in high school, Sonny had been depressing. He seemed to have convinced himself at an early age that he would never really have what he wanted, though it seemed to Duane he could have most of the things he wanted if he had just made a little effort. Not Jacy, perhaps—but a world of other things to want did exist, including many other desirable and interesting women.

Yet Sonny had settled for a carwash, a Kwik-Sack, a laundry and a hotel that only operated three weeks a year. As for women, once Ruth left him, he had settled for nothing. He hadn't even allowed himself to be tempted by Karla, and Karla tempted most men to distraction.

Sometimes Duane and Karla talked of trying to fix Sonny up with someone who would make him a good wife, or at least a friendly date, but they never quite got around to it.

"Luke's not easy to help," Karla said. "Maybe we better just mind our own business. If I can't get him to fall in love with me I don't see how I could get him to fall in love with anybody else."

"You aren't the only kind of woman there is to fall in love with," Duane informed her.

"No, but I'm the best kind," Karla said, laughing.

Duane secretly agreed. He himself had stayed fairly madly in love with her for at least fifteen years. Her energy alone was a constant marvel. He had rarely seen Karla tire. Until Ruth came to work for him she ran his office, was a substitute teacher in the high school, coached several Little League teams, was secretary of the Rodeo Association, and still danced all night whenever she could get him or anyone else to go with her to a dance hall.

Remembering the efficient way she had hitched up Bobby Lee's pickup that morning, he suddenly felt an urge to see her, and stepped on the gas. There was no one quite like Karla.

When he got home he saw Bobby Lee's pickup, still hitched

to the Supernova and still on its side. Karla had apparently been content just to drag it home. She hadn't set it on fire, or rolled it down the hill with their little lawn tractor, or anything that drastic.

He didn't see the BMW, though—only the Supernova, and Minerva's Buick.

He let himself into the kitchen, where fortunately he found some smothered steak in the oven and a pot of pinto beans. Maybe everyone had gone to a dance hall. He sat at the kitchen table, idly leafing through a huge stack of bills, while he ate the steak and a large bowl of beans laced with jalapeño.

While he was eating, Minerva came in.

"Who told you to put on overalls and go to work?" she asked.

"I thought of it myself," he said.

"You've been an executive too long," Minerva said. "You just look silly wearing them overalls."

"Is that what I am? An executive?" he said. "No wonder I'm so far in debt."

Minerva studied the liquor stock for a minute or two, before choosing Cuervo Gold. She poured an iced-tea glassful.

"Some people put ice in tequila, but I don't," Minerva said. "Ice has them little amebas in it."

"Where's the gang?" Duane asked.

"They're spending the night down at Jacy's," Minerva said.

Duane nearly choked on a bite of beans.

"All of them?" he asked.

"All of them but me," Minerva said. "I thought I'd stay around because Karla wasn't sure if Jacy gets the good cable."

"Are they just gonna stay overnight?" he asked.

"I wouldn't know," Minerva said. "You can look on the calendar and see if it says anything about them coming back."

Karla kept a massive calendar hanging on one wall of the kitchen. The spaces for each day were the size of post cards. She believed in writing down her plans, as well as things that were not exactly plans.

"Sometimes I think it's things that are more like hopes," she said.

At that time, a year or two back, Duane had been staring apprehensively at an entry that read "Chew Duane's ass out."

"Why would chewing my ass out be a hope?" he asked.

"It might perk you up," Karla said. "You used to get a hard-on every time I chewed you out. Remember?"

Duane did remember. Karla on the attack had once seemed incredibly sexy to him. He liked the way her eyes flashed and the way her mouth moved when she was delivering a rapid-fire rundown of all his shortcomings. He still liked it, but the years had passed and some of the better effects were wearing off.

Karla also encouraged the kids to scribble their plans on the calendar, on the theory that it might make it easier to find them in case of emergency. She had tried to start calendar training when Dickie and Nellie were teenagers, but it hadn't worked well.

Dickie liked the idea of a calendar, but his entries had often alarmed his mother. His very first entry read "Go fuck girls." Many of his plans seemed to involve criminal violence. Once he wrote "Go start a fire." Or he might write "Go beat the shit out of Pinky." Pinky had briefly been a friend. Karla was always having to tear pages off calendars and buy new ones for fear that Dickie's entries might be used against him in criminal proceedings.

Nellie's entries were safer but also duller. Her favorite entry was "Go to the dance," but "Take a nap" ran it a close second.

Duane walked over to the calendar to see if it would tell him how long his family planned to stay at Jacy's. He already missed little Barbette.

The entry for the present day was short. In the morning Karla had written in: "Make Bobby Lee wish he was dead."

Later in the day, switching from blue Magic Marker to dark red lipstick, she had written "Adiós, sayonara, goodbye!"

Duane decided not to take it too seriously. "Adiós, sayonara, goodbye!" was a line from a hillbilly song, which might mean that Karla was getting in a good humor again.

"You'll have to take them clothes off or I can't wash them," Minerva said.

"Were you planning to wash them right now?" he asked.

"Once that grease sets it's hard to get out," she said.

Duane found a piece of custard pie in the icebox.

"Could I just have time to eat this piece of pie before I have to undress?" he asked.

"Executives that go out and try to work are just fooling themselves," Minerva said. "It won't do you no good to pretend you're still young. You ain't young."

Duane sat down and ate the pie. He was aware that he didn't quite have Minerva's blessings, but then if he waited to eat until he had a woman's blessings, he would rapidly starve. When he finished he left his dirty clothes by the washer and went out to the hot tub. It was a beautiful night, the dark sky richly speckled with brilliant stars.

To his surprise, he found Bobby Lee stretched out on his back on the deck. A ring of empty beer cans had been meticulously placed around the rim of the hot tub. Duane had to step over them to get in. Bobby Lee's eyes were open, but he gave no sign of being aware of Duane's presence.

"Bobby, are you pretty drunk?" he asked.

"I'm nine sheets to the wind," Bobby Lee said. "Hell, I might even be more sheets than that. I might be a hunnert sheets to the wind."

Duane soaked for a while. Far off toward town, he saw the flicker of a headlight. Five minutes later a car turned onto the hill and drove up to the house.

"Karla's trying to destroy our love, Nellie's and mine, but she ain't gonna make it," Bobby Lee informed him. "I'm a hard dog to get out from under the porch."

"I'll say that for you," Duane said, getting out of the tub.

"Don't you roll off into one of these pools and drown," he cautioned, before going into the house. "You're so drunk you might not even realize you were swimming."

"Nine sheets to the wind," Bobby Lee said happily.

Duane checked Barbette's baby bed, but she wasn't in it.

He found Karla in bed. She had an old *Playgirl* in her lap, but she wasn't reading it.

"Well, I guess now Jacy's got my dog and our kids both," he said. He smiled.

"Yeah, she just loves those kids," Karla said. "I think it's good for her to have some kids around."

"What brought you back?" he asked.

Karla looked at him a little sadly. She seemed subdued again.
"I was gonna stay but I missed my husband," she said.
Duane lay down beside her and took her in his arms.
"I missed you too, honey," he said.

CHAPTER 47

THE NEXT MORNING DUANE DECIDED TO HAVE A talk with Dickie. He sat on the deck and discussed it with Karla. Bobby Lee had disappeared into one of the many guest rooms and nobody had the energy to look for him.

"If he finds his way out, talk him out of leaving Carolyn," Duane said. "I like Carolyn."

"I like her too," Karla said. "All the more reason she shouldn't have to live her whole life with Bobby Lee."

"Somebody has to stay with somebody they're married to," Duane said.

"Why?" Karla asked.

"I don't know why," Duane admitted. "It just seems like it would be appropriate."

"Okay, you can stay your whole life with me," Karla said, blowing on her coffee.

"Jacy says Dickie is one of the sweetest boys she's ever met," she added.

"How'd she happen to meet him?"

"He sells her marijuana," Karla said. "He started the week

264

she got back and never said a word to us about knowing her, the little rat."

Karla wore an unhappy little frown. Duane felt sad. Last night they had been happy for an hour—back in love, almost. They had both awakened feeling cheerful. Yet already cheerfulness was proving hard to sustain.

"How come you're depressed?" he asked.

Karla shrugged. "Because I just figured out the bottom line," she said.

"What is the bottom line?"

"Men are scared of me," Karla said. "That's the bottom line. They don't like it that I'm smart."

She paused, still frowning.

"Shit, they don't even like it that I'm pretty," she said. "They think they do but it scares them. I don't know which scares them most, that I'm pretty or that I'm smart."

"Well, you're both," he said.

"I know, but so the bottom line is that men act like they want me but then they run," Karla said.

Duane reached over and began to massage the back of her neck. The muscles were as tight as a drum.

"I'm not scared that you're smart and pretty," he said. "I like it that you're smart and pretty."

Karla tilted her head back against his hand.

"That's right, Duane," she said. "You're the only one who isn't. That's why I married you and that's why I'm still around."

He massaged her neck until the muscles loosened a little and then got dressed and drove to Wichita Falls to see Dickie.

Dickie was lying on the couch with his shirt off, reading a volume of the *World Book Encyclopedia*.

"What are you reading about?" Duane asked.

"I'm reading about Italy," Dickie said. "I might move there."

"Why, ain't there enough dope around here to suit you?" Duane asked. He felt his anger rise. It was unreasonable and he tried to control himself. It was not a crime to read about Italy, or even to move there, and yet he felt an urge to grab the boy and shake him.

"It has nothing to do with dope, I just need to get away from Billie Anne," Dickie said, without looking up.

"You just married her," Duane reminded him.

"Stupidest thing I ever did, too," Dickie said.

Duane felt his anger rise more rapidly. It was as if he had poured beer in a glass too quickly. Unless he acted instantly it was going to overflow the glass. He had to suck it off quick.

A second later he knocked the book out of Dickie's hand and yanked him off the couch. The boy looked surprised, but he rose quickly, so quickly it caught Duane off balance. He threw a punch but then found himself on the floor. Dickie had thrown one first. When Duane got up, Dickie grappled with him and managed to shove him out the screen door. In the yard Duane realized that he was in a fight with his son—and not only that, he was losing. He threw two punches and they both missed. Dickie was too quick. Duane felt tired, although the fight had not been happening for more than a minute. He looked at Dickie and saw that the boy was crying, although he still had his fists clenched.

"Stop it, Daddy," Dickie said. "Please stop it."

"I think that's a good idea," Duane said, breathing hard. "I think I better stop it."

His anger had passed and he felt a deep, crushing sense of shame. He had attacked his own son, and for no reason—or at least for no reason that was clear.

"Dickie, I'm sorry," he said. "There was absolutely no reason for me to behave that way. I'm real sorry."

He went back in the house and sat down on the couch. Apologizing had not helped much. He felt that he could no longer trust himself. Never in his life had he done anything so troubling. He had never before attacked one of his own children. He was trembling, and felt that he might be sick at his stomach.

"You're white as a sheet, Daddy," Dickie said. "Are you sick or something?"

Duane couldn't think of what to say. What *was* the matter with him?

"I didn't hurt you, did I?" Dickie asked.

"No, I just feel a little queasy," Duane said.

"I'll bring you a Dr. Pepper," Dickie said. "It'll help settle your stomach."

While Dickie was getting the drink Duane looked around the room and noticed that the furniture didn't seem to be smashed. In fact the house looked rather orderly. Dickie, looking nervous and worried, came in and handed him the Dr. Pepper.

"I thought you smashed all the furniture with a tire iron," Duane said.

"Who told you that?" Dickie asked.

"Billie Anne told your mother," Duane said.

Dickie shook his head. "She lies every minute of the day," Dickie said. "If I'd even tried to come in the house with a tire iron she'd have shot me five or six times before I could move. All I did was kick a lawn chair and break my toenail."

Duane felt silly on top of guilty. Besides attacking his own child, he had also assumed the worst about him. That Billie Anne might be lying had never crossed his mind.

"Well, I owe you another apology," he said. "I should have known you wouldn't do anything like that."

"She's a good liar," Dickie said. "She can fool anybody. She fooled me or I wouldn't be sitting here. I'm even afraid to sleep in the same bed with her. She keeps a loaded gun in her hand all night."

"Mrs. d'Olonne thinks I should just leave," the boy added. "She says that's the only thing to do if you're living with somebody you're scared of. She's had to run from a couple of men herself."

"Mrs. who?" Duane asked.

"Mrs. d'Olonne," Dickie said. "I think that's how you pronounce it. She's a real nice lady.

"You know, Jacy," he said, seeing that his father still looked puzzled. "She says I can go live in her house in Italy if I want to."

Dickie grinned shyly.

"I think she wants to fix me up with one of her daughters," he said.

Duane had stopped trembling, but he felt weak.

"Did you and Mrs. d'Olonne really go together once?"

Dickie asked. It was obviously something he was deeply curious about.

"We sure did," Duane said. "We went steady in high school."

"She's shown me pictures of her daughters," Dickie said. "The oldest one is just my age."

"Pretty?" Duane asked.

"Better than pretty," he said. "She's just flat beautiful."

Duane got up and retrieved the *World Book* that he had knocked across the room.

"Italy sounds like a fine idea," he said. "You're young. You oughta get out and see the world. You don't have to make the oil patch your whole life."

"It's been your whole life, though," Dickie pointed out.

"That's my limitation, it don't have to be yours," Duane said. "Besides, I got sent away to war when I was your age. That's different. I wasn't offered any choice, and all I wanted to do was get back here alive."

They sat for a while, not speaking.

"Why does Billie Anne lie?" Duane asked.

"She just likes to," Dickie said. "She believes her own lies, too. She's gonna have a shit fit when she finds out I got Mrs. Marlow pregnant."

"Have you been seeing Mrs. Marlow again?" Duane asked.

"No, just Mrs. Nolan," Dickie said. "Mrs. Nolan's more relaxing."

"It's not real smart to get too many women in love with you at the same time," Duane pointed out.

"That's what Mrs. d'Olonne says," Dickie said. "I'm gonna try to stick to Mrs. Nolan for a while."

"Does Jacy know about Mrs. Marlow being pregnant?" Duane asked.

"Sure, I tell her everything," Dickie said. "She gives real good advice."

Duane found it astonishing that his wildest child, whom both Karla and he regarded as totally beyond their control, had been eagerly getting his advice from Jacy for several months.

"What does she think you ought to do about the baby?" he asked.

"Wait and see if it looks like me or Mr. Marlow," Dickie said. "She says you can't trust married people to tell the truth about their sex lives. She says even if they claim they never do it they probably do it once in a while."

Duane finished his Dr. Pepper. He tried to sort out the complexities that he faced, plus the ones his son faced, plus a variety that people he liked or cared about faced. The more he thought, the more the complexities seemed to form intricate knots. Finally he just went blank. It was as if he had added one too many appliances to an electrical circuit. The circuit blew. He sat on the couch, sucking on an ice cube, aware only that it was pleasant to be with Dickie. That in itself was a surprise. Since Dickie was Jack's age, when they had often gone hunting or fishing together, it had rarely been pleasant to be with him.

"When would you be going to Italy?" he asked.

"I don't know yet," Dickie said. "Mrs. d'Olonne says I can live at Los Dolores while I make up my mind. She don't want me to stay around here and get shot by Billie Anne."

"Would that girl really shoot somebody?" Duane asked.

"She shot two different people in Arizona in one fight," Dickie said. "Her boyfriend and his new girlfriend. They didn't die, it was just flesh wounds, but then they were in a moving car when she started shooting."

"Did you tell your mother about that?"

"No, Billie Anne never showed me the newspaper clippings until yesterday," Dickie said. "No charges were filed. I guess it's wild over there in Arizona."

"Why don't you put a shirt on and get your shaving stuff," Duane said.

"Where am I going?"

"You're going home until we sort a little more of this out," Duane said. "Then if you want to go to Italy or move into Los Dolores, that's fine."

Five minutes later they were on their way to Thalia.

CHAPTER 48

AT HOME THEY FOUND BOBBY LEE MOROSELY scrambling some eggs.

"You burned the bacon," Duane observed.

"That's because Karla's damn stove is so complicated it could take an engineer just to cook bacon on it," Bobby Lee said. "Hi, Dickie."

It was true that the stove was complicated. The cockpit of a jetliner had only a few less dials. Nonetheless, Minerva had mastered it in a few seconds.

"Where's Minerva?" Duane asked.

"She went down to live with Jacy," Bobby Lee said. "Everybody else did, too. I wish she'd invite me."

Bobby Lee seemed to have been crying. His scraggly beard had tears shining in it.

"Did Nellie already break your heart?" Duane asked.

"Yes," Bobby Lee said. "Now she don't wanta run away with me this week."

"Why not?" Duane asked.

"Jacy's teaching her to cook pesto," Bobby Lee said.

"What's that?"

Bobby Lee shrugged. "Spaghetti," he said.

"It's not spaghetti, it's pasta," Dickie said.

"Since when did you become an I-talian?" Bobby Lee asked, looking annoyed.

In seconds the scrambled eggs had turned as black as the bacon. Bobby Lee, embarrassed, snatched the frying pan off the stove and rushed to the door. He flung the black, smoking eggs out on the deck.

"We got a perfectly good garbage disposal," Duane pointed out. Richie hadn't put it in, either. He had seen to that.

"I thought Shorty could eat them," Bobby Lee said sheepishly.

"Shorty lives with Jacy," Duane informed him.

"Hell, everybody does, it looks like," Bobby Lee said. "We'll all starve to death if we don't get somebody around here who can work this goddamn stove."

"I can work it," Dickie said. "Sit down and I'll cook you some breakfast."

Bobby Lee browsed in the fridge until he found a raspberry Popsicle; he sucked unhappily on it while Dickie quickly fried more bacon and scrambled more eggs.

Duane found a note on the cabinet from Karla saying she had gone down to Jacy's and would see him at the pageant rehearsal. It all seemed odd to him: within the space of two days his whole family, including his maid and his dog, had vanished into Los Dolores. He didn't feel alarmed. It might well be for the best. It was just unexpected.

The heartbroken Bobby Lee was soon eating a hearty breakfast.

"Nellie said she was gonna learn to cook and become a chef in a restaurant," Bobby Lee said.

That news was also unexpected. So far in life Nellie had rarely been able to make herself a bowl of dry cereal without something going wrong.

"Mrs. d'Olonne likes to teach people to cook," Dickie informed them.

"I hope she teaches Carolyn then," Bobby Lee said. "A pig would get indigestion if it had to eat Carolyn's cooking very long, and I've been eating it for twelve years."

"What made you think Nellie would run off with you anyway?" Duane asked.

"It's always been my dream," Bobby Lee said, his eyes reddening.

"Don't cry, don't cry," Dickie said, looking alarmed.

"Why not, my life's ruint," Bobby Lee said.

However, instead of crying, he had another raspberry Popsicle for dessert.

"If Little Mike comes back and finds you ate all his Popsicles, I don't know what we'll do with him," Duane said.

Dickie left the room for a minute and returned with two pistols, a .357 Magnum and a small .22 automatic. He sat at the kitchen table and loaded them. Bobby Lee seemed alarmed.

"Why are you loading guns, is a dope war coming down?" he asked.

"No, but Billie Anne could be coming down anytime," Dickie said. "I want to be ready."

"If you're so scared of her, why in hell did you marry her?" Duane asked.

"I was just bored," Dickie said. "It gets too boring around here. Half the people in Thalia probably got married because they were bored."

"Or else horny," Bobby Lee said.

"All I do when I get bored is buy two-story doghouses," Duane pointed out.

Nobody had an answer to that. Dickie idly rotated the chamber of the .357 Magnum. Bobby Lee regarded the weapon with some apprehension.

"If that gun went off accidentally it could make a big hole in somebody," he said.

He noticed a tiny speck of green on his plate and pushed it around with his fork.

"What'd you put in them eggs?" he asked. "They tasted different. Good, but different."

"Just some herbs," Dickie said.

"Herbs!" Bobby Lee said, with a look of alarm. "Why'd you put herbs in my eggs? I like plain old eggs."

"I guess you liked those," Dickie said. "You ate every bite."

"Yeah, but I don't like foods from other states," Bobby Lee said. "I just like plain old Texas food."

"Herbs grow in Texas," Dickie said.

"I never seen one growing around here," Bobby Lee said. He seemed near panic.

"I have bad dreams when I eat things that ain't from Texas," he said. "I bet I have terrible dreams tonight. You drug dealers are all alike. You don't care what you put in people's food."

"Calm down," Dickie said. "You'll be fine."

"Better yet, go to work," Duane said. "If you work all day you'll be too tired to have a dream, good or bad."

He looked at Dickie, who looked very young. The boy promoted his own macho image so successfully that it had even fooled Duane. Sitting at the table, he looked like a nice, shy teenager.

"What's a herb anyway?" Bobby Lee asked. "You shouldn't trick me like that, Dickie. You know I get the dry heaves real easy."

"You can't have the dry heaves with eggs and bacon in your stomach," Dickie pointed out.

"I've read about herbs but I can't remember much about them," Bobby Lee said. "Don't they give you visions of God and stuff?"

"That's mushrooms" Dickie said. "Certain mushrooms."

"We can sit here and talk about herbs all day or we could go do an honest day's work," Duane said.

"Let's go, I'm ready," Dickie said. "If Billie Anne comes after me at the rig at least there'll be witnesses."

"Why would Nellie want to be a chef in a restaurant?" Bobby Lee asked. "She never had no ambition at all. It's taken me all these years to get her in the mood to run away with me."

"Go to work and don't brood," Duane advised.

"I like to brood," Bobby Lee said. "What else is there to do around here except brood and feel sorry for yourself?"

"Well, there's a centennial to put on, for one thing," Duane said. "And rehearsals start tonight."

CHAPTER 49

AT 6 P.M., THE HOUR WHEN PAGEANT REHEARSALS
were supposed to get underway in the rodeo arena, the summer sun was at its most vicious angle. A high of 108 had been
registered that afternoon, and the thermometer had not
dropped much off the high.

Only one car was parked in the huge gravelly parking
lot behind the arena when Duane arrived. It belonged to
Lester Marlow, who sat in it dressed in a suit and tie. He
had parked facing the sun. Duane drove up beside him
but did not park facing the sun. He got out and walked
around to have a word with Lester, who was sweating as a
man might who wore a suit and had a hundred and eight
degrees of sunlight pouring directly in on him. He looked
very hot.

"If I open my mouth to say hi, I might drown in my own
sweat," he said.

"Turn your car around," Duane suggested. "You won't be as
hot. Better yet, get out and let's go sit in the shade."

It occurred to him that if Lester had enough common sense

not to park facing the sun, or even to take his coat and tie off, he might well not be indicted on seventy-two counts of fraud.

Lester got out, as drenched with sweat as if he had been underwater for several minutes. Even his shoes seemed soaked. He was a little wobbly, but managed to make it across the road to the shade of the grandstand.

"I came early hoping to catch Jenny alone," Lester said. "My mother claims Jenny's pregnant."

Lester's mother was an elderly terrorist who habitually abused everyone she knew, particularly Lester. Fortunately she spent most of her time traveling the world, but the moment she arrived back in Wichita Falls she resumed her terrorist habits.

"I didn't know your mother was back," Duane said.

"She got back late this afternoon," Lester said. "She went to the pyramids, this time."

"Did she like 'em?" Duane asked. Karla sometimes agitated for a trip to the pyramids.

"Didn't say," Lester said. "Momma works quick. She had only been home twenty minutes when she called to tell me Jenny was pregnant."

"Well, you're married to her," Duane said. "Maybe she's pregnant by you."

"Not likely," Lester said.

Duane waited. Even that statement was an improvement on Jenny's many comments on the subject.

"It's very unlikely," Lester said. "It would be almost a miracle if it's mine."

"Why would it be a miracle if you slept with your own wife?" Duane asked, glimpsing an unlooked-for ray of hope.

"We rarely find the time," Lester said, craning his neck to watch the highway. He seemed to expect hundreds of cars to arrive at any minute.

"You don't have to make excuses, my wife usually won't sleep with me either," Duane said, feeling slightly guilty for saying it. In the case of himself and Karla, nothing was so clear-cut. Hesitancies arose on both sides and then vanished and then reappeared again.

"I think we had sex once or twice a few months back," Lester said. "Sundays are interminable around here.

"Millions of women probably get knocked up on Sunday afternoon," he added. "Does Dickie want to marry Jenny or what?"

"Dickie's just trying to survive his own marriage," Duane said.

Lester kept wiping his face with his handkerchief although the handkerchief was wet as a dishrag.

"Nobody cares who anybody's pregnant by anymore," he said. "All people think about is ways to get out of paying their banker."

"Don't get cynical," Duane said.

"Cynical's not the word," Lester said. "Desperate is the word."

At that point Jenny raced up and parked. She was out of the car in a flash. The sight of the two men sitting in the shade seemed to annoy her tremendously.

"Don't you two talk about me," she said, dragging a shoulder bag containing her script out of the car. Virtually everyone in the county had contributed a pet scene or two to the script, which had swollen enormously.

"You should have helped me cut this script," Jenny said to Duane. "It's a hundred times too long. This pageant is going to be a disaster."

Duane had made one or two stabs at reading the scripts, but had quickly been defeated each time. He never managed to get past the Gettysburg Address, which had somehow found its way into the historic story of Hardtop County. Sonny Crawford was playing Lincoln.

To his dismay and Lester's, Jenny suddenly burst into tears. She stood under the grandstand and sobbed.

"It might not be a disaster," Duane said soothingly.

Lester seemed touched by the sight of his wife's tears. He quickly got up and put his arm around her.

"Don't touch me, you're sweaty as a pig," Jenny said, but when Lester started to move away she clutched him tightly and sobbed more loudly.

Thirty seconds later she stopped sobbing and began to look cheerful.

"I'm very vulnerable right now," she said. "You two should remember that."

"We'll remember, honey," Lester said. "Let's go. Are you okay?"

"Let's go hook up the P.A. system," Jenny said. A tear dripped off her lip but she was all business again.

As Duane stood in front of the microphone on the arena floor, feeling silly and saying "Testing, testing" over and over again, raising or lowering the volume dials in response to hand signals waved to him by Jenny and Lester, who were in opposite bleachers, cars began to pour into the parking lot. The cars were soon emptied of about half the citizenry of the county. In no time a couple of hundred people were milling around in the arena, eager to begin their acting careers. They stood in clumps in the bright late-afternoon sunlight, waiting for someone to tell them what to do.

Duane was soon engulfed and forgotten, though he still stood manfully at the microphone and even occasionally said "Testing," in order to convince himself he was doing something useful.

While he was saying "Testing" he saw Jacy's Mercedes and Karla's BMW pull up together and disgorge his entire family, all the way down to Little Mike, Barbette and Shorty. Dickie made a beeline for a group of young married women who were only in the pageant to take part in a frontier dance sequence. Their husbands were all cowboys, there for the cowboys-and-Indians sequence. The cowboys were shy in crowds. They hung back by the bucking chutes, coiling and uncoiling their ropes.

Karla and Jacy looked as if they had just been shopping. They both wore cool-looking white slacks and black sleeveless T-shirts. Jacy, who was carrying Barbette, also wore a large white visor. She strolled over and handed the baby to Duane.

"You can stop saying 'Testing' now, Duane," she said. "The mike is obviously working fine."

"Hi, Duane," Karla said. "How's life without a single soul to come home to?"

"I had two souls to come home to, Bobby Lee and Dickie," Duane said.

278 / Larry McMurtry

Karla laughed. "I don't think Bobby Lee has a whole soul," she said.

"Dickie didn't smash up any furniture," he informed her.

"I know, he just married a lying slut," Karla said.

"One that's shot two people, too," Duane said.

Before they could discuss that situation, Jenny hurried over. Her nervousness was gone. The sight of people to be organized had activated some sense of command—the same sense that had led her to organize thousands of concession stands, bake sales, charity drives, softball tournaments, overnight hikes, half-time shows, senior trips and community picnics, over the years.

"Hi, Jacy, I'm Jenny," she said, giving Jacy a quick handshake. "We're real glad you decided to play Eve, and I even thought how nice it would be if we could persuade you to sing a hymn at the end of the show."

"Why not?" Jacy said tolerantly. "A hymn never hurt anybody."

Duane sat down with his back against the fence and let Barbette amuse herself by dipping her bare feet into the tickly grass. She giggled, pleased to see her grandfather. Jacy and Karla sat on either side of him. Both were in excellent spirits. They all watched in amazement as Jenny, with easy efficiency, organized the ever-growing crowd of roughnecks, farmers, cowboys, merchants, wives, retirees and kids. She had acquired a blue megaphone and she didn't hesitate to use it. She only had to glance at a person to decide which skits or groups the person would fit into.

"Okay, now you boys are the redcoats," she said, splitting a lounging group of high school boys down the middle. "You stand over by the bucking chutes. The rest of you are revolutionary patriots, get over by the calf pens."

She quickly carved the cowboys into a group of cowboys and a group of Indians. A little clique of roughnecks were assigned to be Mexicans, led by Bobby Lee, whereas another group, led by Eddie Belt, were cast as the heroic defenders of the Alamo.

A bunch of senior citizens were sent to the shady side of the arena to practice being a wagon train. G. G. Rawley was a member of that group. He was not happy to be taking orders from Jenny Marlow, a stray from his own flock.

"How are we supposed to be a wagon train when there ain't no wagons?" he asked.

"Oh, G.G., just use a pickup, or pretend you're building a campfire or looking for a water hole or something," Jenny said.

"Duane, are you playing Adam?" Karla asked.

Duane had finally agreed to play Adam under Jenny's relentless pleading, but now he was having second thoughts.

"I don't think I should," he said.

"Why not?" Jacy asked.

Duane didn't have a reason. He just felt reluctant to play Adam.

"I'd look silly in a bathing suit," he said.

"Who said you get a bathing suit?" Jacy asked. "Adam just had a fig leaf."

"A bathing suit is the least I'd have to have," Duane said.

"He probably wants to wear his bathrobe," Karla said. "He's such an old prude he even undresses behind the door."

Jacy laughed. "He wasn't a prude when I knew him," she said.

Karla laughed too. "I guess you got his best years," she said.

Duane felt slightly uncomfortable. He knew the women were just teasing him. He didn't usually mind being teased, but it felt different when Karla and Jacy did it. They were both wearing shades—he could tell they were watching him, from behind their shades. They were enigmas, the two women. Powerful enigmas. It was hard to sit between them and feel very relaxed. Too many currents surged through him when they were both around.

Meanwhile Jenny Marlow was yelling through her megaphone, repositioning various groups.

"That way! That way!" she yelled at the wagon train of senior citizens. "You were born in Missouri and Kentucky, you wouldn't be coming from the west."

Bobby Lee straggled over and squatted in the shade of his sombrero.

"Get over there where you belong, you're Santa Anna," Karla said.

"It's too hot where I belong," Bobby Lee said.

"Jacy, this is General Santa Anna," Duane said.

"Hi, General," Jacy said. "You're kinda cute."

The compliment cheered Bobby Lee immediately.

"I didn't wanta be Santa Anna," he assured her. "I'm already unpopular enough. I wanted to be Daniel Boone."

He cast envious looks at Dickie, who was still flirting with the cowboys' wives.

"I wish I was lucky like Dickie," Bobby Lee said. "That kid can get away with anything, and I never got away with nothing in my life."

"If you was as lucky as Dickie you'd be so pussy-whipped you'd die," Karla informed him.

It was the night of the full moon. It rose in the east, where the band of wagoneers were moping about listlessly, pretending to build campfires. The moon was orange as it rose, but soon became golden, then white. Duane pointed it out to Barbette—he could not remember that he had ever shown the child the moon before. Barbette was transfixed. She watched the moon in silence, lying in Duane's lap.

To start the rehearsal, Willis Ray, the smartest kid in high school, demonstrated the light show that was going to represent Creation. Whirling disco lights flashed rainbow colors into the darkening sky.

A brisk walk-through followed. Duane rose reluctantly when Jenny called for Adam and Eve. He still felt reluctant, but didn't want to make a scene. Karla and Jacy pushed him over to the spot Jenny had chosen to be the Garden of Eden.

"Okay, we'll put the tree with the forbidden fruit on it right between you," Jenny said. "When you wake up, Duane, hold your side, so everybody will know you're missing a rib."

"I'm missing a brain or I wouldn't be doing this," Duane said, but Jenny had already hurried off to start positioning the revolutionary patriots.

"Don't you put this down, this is going to be great," Jacy said. She looked happier and more beautiful than he had seen her look since her return. Duane was a little startled by how lovely she looked. He had thought her beauty was gone, something to be recalled only in his deep-held memories; and yet, before his eyes, it was returning, fitting itself once again to the contours of his fantasy.

She linked her arm in his.

"Remember when I was homecoming queen, Duane?" she asked, in a softened voice.

"I sure do," he said.

"I bet you never thought we'd be standing here thirty years later as Adam and Eve," she said.

"I never would have thought it, Jacy," he said.

"I feel like we are, in a way," Jacy said. "I feel like we're the Adam and Eve of this town."

Before they could say more, Jenny came back. He had no further chance to talk to Jacy. He watched most of the proceedings from his spot by the fence, Barbette asleep in his arms.

Janine, Charlene Duggs and Lavelle had been chosen to sing the national anthem. As they were clearing their throats and trying a few high notes, Karla collared Jenny.

"Why don't all the women sing it?" Karla asked. "All the women in the whole pageant."

"It might be too feminist," Jenny said. "The men might start throwing rocks at us, or something."

"I'm sick of the national anthem," Ruth Popper said. She had arrived in her running clothes.

"I'm sick of it too," Jacy said. "Let's sing the 'Battle Hymn of the Republic.' That's patriotic, and it's a better song."

"Okay, okay, as long as it's patriotic," Jenny said, grabbing her megaphone. "All the women and girls get over here. Let's have all the women and girls."

The women straggled toward the microphone. Some plodded, a few young girls ran. The cowboys' wives tore themselves away from Dickie. Nellie, who had been receiving the homage of several young roughnecks, drifted over. Even Minerva, who had been sitting skeptically in the bleachers, wandered into the arena, liberating Little Mike in the process. He raced over and began to climb the gate to one of the bucking chutes.

Jenny strung the women all across the arena, with Jacy, Karla and the three women from the courthouse in the center. The high school band, which hadn't been taking the proceedings

very seriously, swung into the "Battle Hymn of the Republic."
The women of the county, short and tall, young and old, weak
and strong, pretty and plain, began to sing.

Duane had felt surprisingly emotional all evening. When
Jacy linked her arm in his, he had felt a swelling of feeling,
and he had felt it also while showing Barbette the new moon.

As he sat on the ground listening to the women sing, the
emotion that had been moving through him in a light current
suddenly surged into his chest. Something dripped onto his
hand and he realized he was crying. It was the second time in
two days that he had cried. It embarrassed him, though Barbette was asleep and no one was watching. Despite all the
problems, past, present and to come, he felt deeply happy to
be where he was.

The singing of the women touched him. He wanted them to
sing on and on. Their singing brought him a rare feeling of
peace, and he wanted it to last.

Then, while lost to emotion, he felt something cold touch his
hand. It proved to be Shorty's nose. Shorty thrust his head
under Duane's arm, trying to get as close to him as possible.
Duane scratched his head.

The singing ended, and the lengthy rehearsal dragged on.
Sonny, as Abraham Lincoln, read the Gettysburg Address. The
rival armies of the Alamo mimicked an exchange of shots. The
make-believe Indians raced after buffalo, in this case Shorty,
who could never stay out of any race. The wagon train of senior
citizens plodded across the arena. Doughboys marched off to
World War I, oil boomers drilled holes, cowboys swung ropes,
and, finally, the class of '65 reenacted its great victory in the
Class A state finals, the last significant event to occur in the
county except the oil glut, which it had been decided to ignore.
Then it only remained for Jacy to sing the closing hymn, but
the hymn had not been selected, and was not rehearsed. People began to wander off to their cars, though many stood
around chatting in the arena, enjoying the coolness of the evening.

Through it all, Duane floated quietly in a world of emotion
and memory. People smiled and let him alone, not because
they realized the singing had moved him so deeply, but because they saw a sleeping child in his arms and didn't want to

risk waking her. Though the tide of emotion was ebbing, he enjoyed sitting quietly with his granddaughter, enjoying the receding waves.

Then a hand waved back and forth in front of his eyes. It was Karla's.

"Have you sat there and gone crazy?" she asked.

"You're always trying to get me to say I'm crazy," Duane said. "I don't think I'm crazy."

"Then give Nellie the baby and let's go home," Karla said.

"Hey you, let's go," Jacy said loudly.

For a second Duane thought she meant him, but then saw that she was talking to Little Mike, who was wandering in circles on the twenty-yard line. He instantly made a dash for the corner of the arena. Jacy just as instantly ran in pursuit. Little Mike was on the top rail of the fence, about to drop over into the calf pens, when Jacy caught him. She snatched him casually from the top rail as if she had planned it that way all along.

Minerva cackled. "He's finally met his match," she said.

Little Mike seemed to feel that he was in the hands of a power who would brook no resistance. When Jacy sat him down he toddled along after her as docilely as Shorty had.

Shorty, who had been dozing with his head on Duane's leg, suddenly awoke, looked around in his usual bleary way and immediately trotted after Jacy and Little Mike.

Nellie, who was back in a phase of serene beauty, came over and took her baby.

Soon Karla was the only one left with Duane. She waved her hand in front of his eyes again.

"What are your thoughts, if you're not crazy?" Karla asked.

"You're supposed to offer at least a penny for a person's thoughts," he said.

"Too much, Duane, just tell 'em to me free," Karla said.

"I was thinking it might be nice to have a square meal," he said. "Do you want to go to the Howlers?"

"Okay, but I'm gonna ask Sonny," Karla said. "If he ate better he might not lose his mind."

"Leave him alone," Duane said. "Life might be easier for Sonny if he had a different mind."

CHAPTER 50

KARLA DID ASK SONNY, BUT SONNY REFUSED TO GO to the Howlers or anywhere. He pointed out politely that it was nearly time for him to do his shift at the Kwik-Sack.

"Genevieve wouldn't mind if you were late," Karla said. "She probably needs the overtime."

But Sonny wouldn't go with them, a fact that plunged Karla into depression.

"He won't do anything I ask him to," she said, on the gloomy ride to Wichita Falls. "He's stubborn."

"He's not married to you like I am," Duane said. "He don't owe you total obedience."

"Fuck you," Karla said.

"I was just trying to joke," Duane said.

"You couldn't be funny if you tried, Duane," Karla said.

Duane shut up and they rode in silence. The Howlers was a place where people tended to get rowdy, and then get loud. In order to be heard it was often necessary to be rowdy oneself. Karla was often rowdy enough to be heard all over the restaurant, but not that night. Duane ate his steak and she ignored hers. She stared into space.

Luthie Sawyer weaved past the table, towed by his tall, stringy wife. He was very drunk.

"Luthie, if you're gonna bomb OPEC, I wish you'd hurry," Duane said. "This glut's gettin' serious."

Luthie was too glazed to respond. As he and his wife went out, Bobby Lee and Carolyn came in. They went briskly to a table, looking tense. Though Duane and Karla were only using half of a table for four, Bobby Lee and Carolyn did not offer to join them. Carolyn had coal-black hair and, for the moment at least, a demeanor to match.

"I guess they're negotiating," Duane offered.

Karla exhibited no interest in the domestic life of Carolyn and Bobby Lee, though in other moods she had been known to speculate about it for hours.

"I should have made Sonny have a love affair with me years ago," Karla said.

"What stopped you?" Duane asked.

Karla's eyes were more icy than the ice in her iced tea.

"You probably won't believe it, Duane, but I'm not the kind of woman that just goes up and grabs somebody by the dick," she said.

Duane gave up on conversation. The customers of the Howlers got rowdier and louder. By the time they finished eating, Duane could not remember why he had thought he wanted a square meal. He had just eaten one, but Karla's silence was so unnerving that he felt as if he might throw it up. Only an hour before, at the rodeo arena, she had been in a fine humor, too.

They walked out into the parking lot in time to see old Turkey Clay, the cocaine-happy swamper, have a fistfight. Turkey was squared off against a younger man Duane didn't know, a tall, brawny roughneck. Before he could move to stop it, the two flew at one another and exchanged a flurry of blows, none of which really struck home. Then the fighters glared at one another for a second, breathing heavily, and walked off in opposite directions.

The fight had the happy effect of distracting Karla briefly from her depression. She walked after Turkey, whose truck was parked at the far end of the lot. Duane followed.

"What was that all about?" she asked Turkey.

"It was a fistfight," Turkey replied in an unfriendly tone. It was not clear that he realized who he was talking to, or that he cared, one way or the other. He was getting a beer out of the front seat of his truck and didn't look around.

"Turkey, this is Karla," she said cautiously. "I know it was a fistfight. I just wondered why you two were fighting."

"I told him he was nothing but a walking sack of snot, that's why we were fighting," Turkey said.

"Turkey, you've got to quit jumping these younger men," Duane said mildly.

Turkey looked at him coldly. "I guess if I see a sack of snot walking around on two legs I can hit it a time or two," he said. He got in his truck, drained the beer, dropped the can out the window and left.

"You shouldn't tease him about his age, Duane," Karla said, becoming depressed again.

"Well, hell, I can't open my mouth anymore without somebody jumping down my throat," Duane said.

As they were walking back to the BMW the phenomenon occurred which had given the restaurant its name: the howling began.

The howling could be started by any patron who happened to be feeling good—or bad—enough to howl like a hound. But once one happy or unhappy diner howled, the tradition was that everyone in the restaurant must howl too. The waitresses stopped with plates in their hands and howled. The cooks howled from the kitchen, the dishwashers from the sink. Children too young to produce a proper howl cried or screamed. Couples in the parking lot often rushed back inside to howl with the group.

The howling might last only three or four minutes, or it might go on for half an hour, depending on the spirits of the group. Since the restaurant stood three miles out of town, on the edge of the weedy prairie, the howling disturbed no neighbors—although travelers, unfamiliar with the tradition, approaching Wichita Falls on the lonely road that led from the Staked Plains, were sometimes unnerved by it, particularly if it was summer and they happened to have their car windows down.

Just as they approached the glimmering lights of the city, buoyed up by the sense that they might be about to reach civilization again, they heard the howling. From a distance it sounded as if a pack of starving dogs waited only a turn or two down the highway in the darkness. People immediately rolled up their windows. Some stopped and sat in terrified indecision. One gentle couple from Seattle lost all hope, turned around, and drove in panic all the way back to Lubbock. Their story made the headlines; the Howlers magnanimously offered to pay their way to Wichita Falls and give them a free steak dinner, but the couple did not accept.

Karla and Duane had heard the howling countless times. The restaurant offered a Howler-of-the-Year award, and only last year Karla had made news by winning the award two years in a row, an unheard-of honor.

"You wanta go back in and howl a little?" Duane asked. "I guess your title's on the line."

Karla got in the BMW. "I don't, for your information," she said. "I'm surprised my own husband don't think I've got anything better to do than sit around with a bunch of drunks and howl like a dog."

Then she lapsed back into silence.

"God!" Duane said. "What'd I do now?"

As Duane was about to get in the car the door of the restaurant flew open and a man staggered out. Duane looked around and recognized him—he was a driller from Duncan, Oklahoma. Duane assumed he was just drunk, but as he started to get in the BMW he saw the man's legs go out from under him. He folded like a shot bird, not ten feet away. Thinking he might have had a heart attack, Duane stepped over to him. The driller, whose name was Buddy, straightened up, looked around a time or two, curled himself into a fetal position and went to sleep in the gravel. Duane caught him under his arms and dragged him over near the building, where at least he wouldn't get run over.

He heard a car start, turned and saw that it was the BMW.

"Adiós, sayonara, goodbye, Duane!" Karla said.

"You already used that line!" he yelled. "Come back here."

For an answer Karla delivered the long soprano howl that

had made her a two-time winner of the Howler-of-the-Year award. She was soon out of sight.

Duane sat in Bobby Lee's pickup until he and Carolyn came out. Carolyn was in no better mood than Karla, but they gave him a ride home. Karla was nowhere to be seen.

CHAPTER 51

THE NEXT MORNING DUANE WOKE TO A HOUSE THAT seemed very empty. Dickie, who had only moved back in yesterday, had not spent the night there. Karla was gone. It appeared that he had twelve thousand square feet of unpaid-for house entirely to himself.

Then, while he was cooking eggs, he remembered Junior Nolan, who had been living there when last seen. He went in search of Junior and found him in a remote guest room, sitting on the floor with a box of Cheerios at his side. He had a handful of Cheerios and was eating them dry, as if they were popcorn, meanwhile watching *Sesame Street*.

"Junior, how about some eggs?" Duane asked. "I've got some pretty good sausage, too."

"No, thanks, Duane," Junior said. "I'm on a diet."

"Why?" Duane asked, reflecting that the man already looked like the survivor of an around-the-world walkathon.

"Actually it's not a diet, it's a fast," Junior said. "You know, when you starve yourself for a cause."

"What cause are you starving yourself for?" Duane asked.

"The oil cause," Junior said. "I'm fasting for an embargo on foreign oil. And if that don't work I'm gonna call up some of these rock singers and get 'em to give an Oil Aid concert, to help out starving oilmen.

"Gandhi did fasts," Junior added. "I think I could do one."

Junior's impressive familiarity with world history startled Duane a little.

"Junior, we barely even know you're in the house," he said. "We don't see you for days. You could sit here and starve to death and not a soul would know it. You wouldn't get an oil embargo. You'd just be dead."

"Yeah, but I ain't on the real fast yet," Junior said. "I'm just practicing with Cheerios. Once the centennial opens I plan to set up a tent on the courthouse lawn and do my fast there. I might even get statewide coverage on TV."

"I don't know if your starving away on the courthouse lawn in going to mix too good with the centennial activities," Duane said. "Tourists might look at you and get so depressed they wouldn't stay around to buy T-shirts."

The T-shirt-and-souvenir shop had started off promisingly, but after a day or two sales had slipped to a discouraging level. The initial flurry had been caused by local buyers snapping up cheap birthday presents. A few people who found themselves passing through Thalia—mainly because of a too-casual attitude toward map reading—stopped and visited the souvenir shop, but most of them just wanted to ask directions. One or two soreheads, unhappy at finding themselves in a place they didn't want to be, even criticized the souvenirs. One blunt old customer from Nevada offended the saleswomen by volunteering the opinion that towns with nothing to offer shouldn't be celebrating their own existence.

"Oh, yeah, what's Nevada got to offer except crooked slot machines?" Lavelle asked him.

"If you're so ignorant you ain't even heard of Boulder Dam you ought to put a sack over your head and drown yourself," the old man said. "Besides, ever' damn inch of Nevada is prettier than this hellhole."

"We didn't ask you to come here and we'll all be glad when you go," Lavelle said.

The man left, in a Winnebago so ancient it was hardly larger than a Volkswagen. Lavelle's bold stand made her a heroine for a day, but did not produce a rush of suitors.

Junior followed Duane back to the kitchen and moodily consumed several eggs and some sausage. Duane felt relieved. The man had a hearty appetite and might soon forget the notion of a fast.

"Hell, ain't there anybody here but us?" Junior asked, becoming aware of the ringing emptiness.

"Nope, they're all gone doing errands," Duane said. He didn't want to have to try and explain why his whole family had moved in with Jacy.

He went outside and tried to set the expensive sprinkler system, which was not much less intricate than the stove. He had agreed to the system reluctantly, but his interest in it had increased.

He tried to tell himself that the absence of his family was just some temporary joke, but part of him suspected that it wasn't a joke. He wanted his family back, and studied the dials of the sprinkler system a little desperately. If it could just be made to work properly, a soft green lawn might flower almost overnight—given adequate moisture the lawns of Thalia grew so rapidly in the summer that most people spent most of their time doing nothing but cutting them.

He felt sure that Karla, for one, would not be able to resist a nice green lawn, and if he could just get Karla back, on a more or less regular basis, the others would eventually follow.

He finally got the sprinkler going and drove into town, wishing he had Shorty to talk to, or at least look at. He was supposed to help Eddie Belt and some other volunteers string centennial banners across the main street, but no volunteers were in evidence so he went to his office and sat in silence for a while.

A glance at the oil news was not reassuring. So little drilling was in progress that a glance allowed him to grasp not only the main developments, but all the developments. He found himself wondering if the legendary C. L. Sime had returned from Norway yet, or if he had even gone. He had the nervous feeling that the old man's enthusiasm for his well-typed proposal might have waned, and that no millions would be forthcoming from Odessa.

The nervous feeling made him feel restless, so he got in his pickup and drove out to Suzie Nolan's house, but well before he got there he saw Dickie's pickup parked in front. Duane made a U-turn and drove back into Thalia, feeling disappointed. There was no getting around the fact that Suzie Nolan was very pleasant to be in bed with. Though he was feeling well disposed toward Dickie, it seemed a little unfair that a twenty-one-year-old should be getting such a high percentage of what pleasure was available around Thalia.

The Dairy Queen was deserted, but the main intersection in front of the courthouse was packed with people. As Duane parked, he saw a body lying on the sidewalk. Bobby Lee was standing over the body, fanning it with his sombrero. Meanwhile Ruth and Jenny, evidently indifferent to the body, were up on tall stepladders, trying to string a centennial banner between two light poles.

Duane walked over and saw that the body was Lester Marlow's. Janine sat beside him on the pavement, chewing gum and holding his hand. Toots Burns, the sheriff, was also there.

Toots, a lifelong bachelor, had recently startled the electorate by marrying the runaway girl who had strayed into Thalia thinking she was in Georgia.

Lester had his eyes open, but he wasn't moving.

"Lester tried to commit suicide," Bobby Lee said, in the same reasonable tones with which he had announced the arrival of Libyan terrorists.

"He did not, you can't prove it, shut up," Janine said.

Bobby Lee, who was sporting a promising black eye, looked unhappy. Any challenge to his statements always caused his confidence to slide.

"Well, he dove off the stepladder," he said.

"He *fell* off the stepladder," Janine insisted.

Lester's wife, Jenny, tying a banner right over her husband's head, sided with Janine.

"He probably fell," she said. "I don't think he knows how to dive."

Duane squatted down by Lester, who was politely staying out of the controversy about his own recent fall.

"Howdy," Duane said. "How do you feel?"

"I'd like to go to the quiet room," Lester said. "Sonny's gone to get the ambulance."

"How come you to fall off the ladder?" Duane asked.

"I was thinking about having to sit on that board with the water underneath me and the next thing I knew I fell," Lester said.

With true civic spirit, Lester had agreed to take the least popular job in the whole centennial. He was going to sit in a cage over a tank of water all day. For a quarter people could throw baseballs at a trip-board, and if they hit it Lester would be plunged into the water. Since he was the bank president he was thought to be the victim most likely to produce an unending flow of quarters. All the people nearing bankruptcy could take out their frustrations by trying to duck the bank president.

"I only like to swim in heated pools," Lester said.

"That ambulance probably won't even start," Janine said cheerfully. She seemed to be enjoying the crisis.

"I could just walk to the quiet room," Lester said. "It's only three blocks."

"No, no," Bobby Lee said. "Your neck might be broken."

Duane asked Lester to move his fingers and lift his leg. Lester not only moved his fingers, he pretended he was typing on an invisible word processor. He typed rapidly.

"His neck isn't broken," Duane said. "Let him walk if he wants to."

Lester got up and he and Janine ambled down the street hand in hand.

Jenny Marlow was having trouble pulling the banner tight. She climbed down the ladder and Duane climbed up to finish the job. Ruth watched his efforts critically from her perch on the other ladder, across the street. Despite Duane's efforts, the banner continued to droop. The crowd watched and offered advice. The consensus was that it was a very droopy banner and would not encourage travelers to stop, buy souvenirs and enjoy the centennial.

"If I saw a banner hanging down like that I'd stomp on the gas pedal and keep on going," one old man said.

"It won't be there long, anyway," another old-timer allowed. "The first truck that comes through with a rig on it will tear it right down. It's too low."

Duane stopped and looked down at the crowd. It was, it seemed to him, a typical, thankless Thalia crowd.

"Anybody who thinks they can do better is welcome to my job," he said.

Eddie Belt, whose job it was supposed to have been anyway, drove up and parked.

"Haven't you two got that banner up yet?" he asked nonchalantly.

Duane stopped working. He climbed up a step or two and sat on the top of the ladder, gesturing to Ruth to do the same. Ruth climbed up and sat on the top of her ladder, too.

"If we ain't appreciated, why should we work?" he asked, looking over at Ruth, who sat inscrutably on her ladder. She gave no indication that she was in sympathy with his sentiment. She might simply have been resting.

From the top of the ladder Duane could see to the far ends of the town. No cars were in sight, no tourists turning back in annoyance. Across the street, Richie Hill was putting the finishing touches on the replica of Old Texasville. He was painting the brand-new shack with a paint called Antique Gray. Buster Lickle had selected the color, which he said was very close to that of the authentic Texasville boards he had kicked up.

"This is a hell of a way to spend a day," Eddie Belt remarked, though he seemed quite happy to be spending his so pleasantly.

"Duane's getting touchy," Jenny remarked to the crowd. "I can't open my mouth anymore without hurting his feelings."

"It serves him right, he's hurt my feelings a million times," Bobby Lee said.

Duane thought he saw a familiar car approaching at a high speed from the east. Scarcely a minute later Karla edged her BMW through the crowd and stopped right under the banner. Her spirits seemed to have improved.

"Momma's on a tear," she said, looking up at Duane. "I guess I better go out there for a few days and see if I can quiet her down."

Karla's mother lived in Pecos, Texas, far to the west.

"She's been on a tear ever since I've known the family," Duane said. "What'd she do now? Murder, arson, rape or what?"

"Very funny, Duane," Karla said, taking off her sunglasses. "If you stop to wonder why I'm not around the house anymore, just remind yourself of jokes like that.

"What are you doing up there, anyway?" she asked.

"Right now I'm just sitting," he said. "I might become a stepladder sitter. What'd your momma really do?"

The crowd, indifferent to their domestic discussion, began to drift off. Only Bobby Lee, Eddie and Jenny hung around.

"She ran Casey off," Karla said. Casey was her mother's long-suffering boyfriend.

"Uh-oh," Duane said.

"That's right," Karla said. "If I don't get out there and patch things up she might decide she wants to move in with us. I don't think we want that to happen."

"You're not there, why would you care?" Duane asked.

Karla laughed. "You miss having a slave around, don't you?" she said.

Duane laughed too.

"If I ever had a slave I'm sure I'd miss it if it left," he said. "I just wouldn't know what a slave looked like."

"Men don't understand the slavery issue," Jenny said. It was clear to Duane that she had been dying to chime in.

"They don't realize how much they get out of us in a normal day," she added. "Just casually. They don't even need to ask. We do things for them as if it was their right."

"Yeah, things like slipping poison in the iced tea, things like spending all the money we work our asses off to make," Bobby Lee said. "Things like leaving hairs in the bathtub."

Karla looked at him and grinned.

"My goodness, you're a sensitive little thing," she said. "Do hairs in the bathtub upset you?"

"They sure do, it makes me want to puke to see a bunch of wet hairs in the bathtub," Bobby Lee said.

"Is it just pussy hairs that bother you or any kind of hair?" Karla asked. "This is Karla asking."

"It's just hairs," Bobby Lee said. "Ugly old hairs."

"Where'd you get the black eye?" she asked.

Bobby Lee, who had seemed on the verge of having a fit, calmed down and resumed his reasonable tone of voice.

"You probably won't believe this, but a big slimy bullfrog jumped out of a tree and landed right in my eye," he said.

Karla laughed.

"You're quick on your feet, aren't you?" she said.

"Survival of the fittest," Bobby Lee said.

Eddie Belt laughed caustically at the notion that Bobby Lee was the fittest.

Ruth began to jerk the banner up and down.

"Let's finish this job and go make ourselves useful elsewhere," she said.

"It really just needs to be a little higher," Jenny Marlow said, surveying the banner's droop.

Karla looked up at Duane. " 'Bye, Duane," she said.

" 'Bye, Karla, have a nice trip," Duane said.

"Don't you get in a lot of trouble that won't be good for you while I'm gone," Karla said.

"I may just sit here on this stepladder the whole time," Duane said. "It's peaceful up here and I can watch the drought spread."

Karla blew him a little kiss with her fingers. Duane made a smooching sound. A minute later the BMW was out of sight to the west.

CHAPTER 52

SONNY HAD RUSHED TO THE HOSPITAL TO GET THE ambulance but on the way had forgotten why he needed the ambulance. He was sitting in the waiting room of the hospital, looking embarrassed, when Lester and Janine walked in. As soon as she got Lester settled in the quiet room, Janine came back and reported this fact to Duane, who had exerted himself in the meanwhile, pulling the banner so tight that it showed not the slightest sign of droop.

"He's just not the same old Sonny," Janine said.

"What if he forgets the Gettysburg Address?" Jenny said. "It could ruin the whole pageant."

Duane knew he ought to go do something about Sonny, but he felt resistant. He didn't know what to do about Sonny, and he didn't want to be the one who had to do anything about him.

To his surprise, Ruth Popper came to his aid.

"Never mind, Duane," she said. "There's no reason you should have to do everything in this town. Go on and have a nice day."

Just at that point they all noticed a struggle on the courthouse lawn. The beardless Joe Coombs had stopped to make a call from the pay phone on the corner. Bobby Lee and Eddie Belt, who exhibited no interest in going to work, decided to put the new ducking law into effect on the spot. They rushed Joe and attempted to throw him in the horse trough where beardless males were to be ducked.

But Joe Coombs proved to be a scrapper. Though beardless, he was far from muscleless. It soon became clear that Bobby and Eddie would be lucky to get him ducked.

A few roughnecks, passing through town, stopped to watch.

"See, the banner's up," Duane said to the roughnecks. He was proud of his handiwork, but the roughnecks ignored the banner and sat watching the fight.

"Help us, Duane," Bobby Lee yelled. "This man don't want to obey the law."

Joe Coombs held Eddie Belt down with his foot and pitched Bobby Lee into the horse trough. Then he picked Eddie up and threw him in as well. The roughnecks applauded and honked their horns. Joe walked over and made his call.

"That little Joe Coombs is a strong one," Janine said, a cheerful light in her eye.

Bobby and Eddie crawled out of the horse trough looking thoroughly mortified.

"He don't obey the rules," Bobby Lee said. "He was supposed to be the duckee, not the ducker."

"Whose idea was it to make a law that you had to duck people?" Eddie said. "We'll never live this down. We might as well move to Lubbock."

"I *am* moving to Lubbock," Bobby Lee said. "I'm gonna start packing right now."

"If it's not asking too big a favor, check by the rig on your way west," Duane said.

The two men drove off without making any promises.

Duane went to his rig and worked all day. It was hot, but he found that he preferred being out of town to being in town.

The pageant rehearsal that night was listless compared to the first rehearsal. The new had worn off so quickly that only about half as many people showed up.

Jenny had made a few script changes. Duane, in his role as

George Washington, no longer had to throw a silver dollar across the arena. That had been scratched because of the danger that the silver dollar might hit somebody. Instead, Duane was to cross the icy Delaware in a boat.

Duane pointed out that the dusty rodeo arena did not look much like an icy river.

"And if it did, how would I get across it?" he asked.

"Oh, Duane, you can just be in a motorboat," Jenny said. "Somebody can pull it around the arena behind a pickup. Don't be literal. Use your imagination a little."

"I am using it," Duane assured her. "I'm using it to imagine how damn silly I'll look being pulled around the arena in a motorboat."

"Stop complaining, Duane," Jacy said. "I've had to do sillier things than that in a movie."

She had come in right on time, bringing his dog and his children. She sat on the grass studying a hymnal. Barbette wiggled and kicked on a blanket at her feet. Little Mike indulged in an orgy of climbing, going over the fence and then climbing right back over.

"You don't look too cheerful, honey pie," Jacy said, when Duane sat down beside her. "Come to supper after the rehearsal. Nellie's making pasta. We'll watch a movie or something."

Duane felt grateful for the invitation. Going home to an empty house and listening to Junior Nolan practice his coyote calls was not enticing. Still, thinking about going to Jacy's house made him feel hesitant. He didn't answer right away. Jacy continued to leaf through the hymnbook, occasionally humming to herself. When she looked at him again she seemed amused.

"Don't strain your brain, sweetie," she said. "If you're not up to social life tonight, just forget it."

"No, I want to come," he said quickly.

"I guess I make you nervous, don't I?" she said.

"Well, I got in the habit of feeling I shouldn't intrude," he said.

"A person who's invited isn't intruding," Jacy pointed out. "Besides, it's mostly your own family you'd be intruding on.

You're being a touch too sensitive. We're just gonna eat pasta and watch a movie."

"I didn't think it was possible to be too sensitive," Duane said. "When's dinner, then?"

"I don't know, Duane, now I feel like I've pressured you," Jacy said. "If you'd just said yes right away it would have been fine, but now *I'm* getting nervous. Maybe you would be intruding."

Duane felt annoyed with himself. He had finicked around, for no reason, and complicated a simple invitation. Or at least it should have been simple, but in fact it involved Jacy and he didn't have a simple feeling about her. He wasn't in love with her, but not being in love and having a simple feeling were different things.

"I guess we'll have to work up to this a little longer," Jacy said, looking a little depressed.

"No, we don't really," he said. "When you asked me it just made me feel shy for a minute. It's silly. I'd like to come and eat.

"I guess it's partly that you're doing better with my family than I've ever done," he added. "I feel like I should keep my fingers crossed and stay out of the way."

"It's easy to do things with other people's children," Jacy said. "You aren't responsible for them, so you can relax."

She looked at him quizzically for a moment.

"I've got an idea," she said. "Let's pretend this conversation was just a rehearsal. We've just been rehearsing getting to know one another again, after thirty years."

She looked at him and shut the hymnal.

"Take two," she said. "You don't look too cheerful, honey pie. Come to dinner. Nellie's making pasta. We'll watch a movie or something."

"Fine," Duane said. "I'll help you set the table."

CHAPTER 53

SHORTY RODE TO LOS DOLORES WITH HIM FOR OLD times' sake. But instead of lolling in the seat, licking himself, Shorty stood up with his paws on the dashboard. He watched the Mercedes just ahead. Part of the road to Los Dolores was dirt, and when they turned off the pavement the Mercedes disappeared into the dust. Shorty immediately began to whimper.

Julie had ridden with him too. When Shorty began to whimper she pounded him on the head.

"Shut up, you slop dog," she said. She pounded him some more, but Shorty continued to whimper.

"Honk, so I can ride with them," Julie said. "I hate riding with a slop dog."

"Don't be so impatient," Duane said, relieved to see that Julie had not become a total angel under Jacy's tutelage.

"I suppose you're a big-time chef now, like your sister," he said.

"I am not," Julie said. "Jack and I are cutting a record."

"Cutting a record?" Duane said. "Where?"

"Right in the house," Julie said. "There's all sorts of equipment."

"What song is it you're recording?" Duane asked, intrigued.

"Just a song," Julie said.

"Punk or country-and-western?" he asked.

Julie snickered. "Punk," she said. "Jack and I wrote it."

"That's great news," Duane said. "Maybe you two will become rich songwriters pretty soon. You can take care of me in my old age."

Julie managed to push Shorty into the floorboards. She held him down with her feet.

"Sing me the song," Duane suggested.

"No, it might shock you," Julie said.

"Up until a few days ago I lived with you and Jack and Nellie and your mother," he said. "Nothing could possibly shock me."

"The song's called 'Vaseline,' " Julie said. "It's about getting off."

"Julie, you found the one combination that could shock me," Duane said.

"I warned you," Julie said.

"Who have you been getting off with?" Duane asked. "That's the aspect that shocks me."

"Oh, Daddy, it's just about masturbation," Julie said. "It's not a big deal."

"That's a relief," Duane said.

By the time they reached Los Dolores Duane's sense of hesitancy had returned. He felt strangely reluctant to go into the house. It felt as if he were entering a world where he didn't belong.

He was obviously the only one who felt that way, though. Dickie's pickup was there, and Dickie himself was in the large kitchen, rolling a joint. Little Mike wandered around, crooning in his own language. Jacy put Barbette on the kitchen table. She kicked her feet and looked solemnly at her uncle.

"Look around, Duane," Jacy said. "I'll help Nellie get dinner started."

Duane wandered through the house, amazed at the number of books it contained. Room after room had bookshelves filled with books from floor to ceiling. The halls were also lined with books—thousands of them. Duane had never supposed that any one person would want, or own, so many books.

He found Minerva in a den with a large TV and thousands more books. Minerva was watching a baseball game. A picture of a youthful Steve McQueen sat on the TV—perhaps the rumor about him passing through Thalia had been true after all. Several other framed photographs sat on a desk. They were all of beautiful women who looked vaguely familiar.

"This is quite a house," he said.

"Yeah, you get real good reception down here," Minerva said.

"And when you get tired of TV you could always find something to read," Duane said.

"I'd hate to have to read all these books," Minerva said. "That much reading could put your eyes out."

Duane wandered down a long book-lined hall. He heard music, partially muffled, coming from behind a door. He knocked, and Jack opened the door. Jack wore dark glasses with rhinestone frames, and very heavy headphones of a sort once associated with test pilots. Now that the door was opened, the music was no longer muffled. The room was full of expensive-looking sound equipment, plus several guitars and a small piano.

Julie was dancing around with a singer's mike in one hand.

"What's up? We're working," Jack said.

"I don't think anything is up, unless dinner's ready," Duane said.

"I hope it's ready, I'm starving," Jack said, and shut the door in his face.

Duane wandered outside. There was a nice patio and a large pool. He had not lost his sense of awkwardness. He was there, but he felt left out. He started to go back into the kitchen but happened to pass the kitchen window. Jacy and Dickie were sitting at the table, finishing the joint. Dickie was talking with some animation, and Jacy seemed to be listening. Nellie worked at the stove, and Minerva was slicing tomatoes.

Such a scene would have been unimaginable to him a few weeks, even a few days, earlier. Now it was both imaginable and visible. What he wasn't able to imagine was himself in the midst of it.

After a while, Nellie came out and set the table.

"Mrs. d'Olonne wants to eat out here," she said. "Is that okay?"

"Sure," Duane said.

Nellie came back with the pasta, and Minerva brought the tomatoes before going back to her ball game. The twins appeared and immediately filled their plates. Dickie came out, filled a plate and disappeared into the house with it. Then Jacy came out, bringing a bottle of wine. She stopped behind Duane's chair, put a hand on his shoulder and filled his wineglass.

"Have a little vino," she said. "Maybe you won't be so nervous."

"He's always nervous," Jack remarked, expertly twirling pasta around his fork.

"Who can blame him with a child like you under his roof," Jacy said. "A child who steals vaseline."

Jack flashed her a brilliant grin, as if proud to be labeled a vaseline thief.

"He steals vaseline?" Duane asked. "Why?"

"As an aid to autoerotic practices, one assumes," Jacy said.

"Oh," Duane said.

"You knew that," Julie said. "I told you about our song."

"I guess I was hoping you were kidding," Duane said, looking at Jacy.

"Eat your fettucine, Duane," Jacy said. "Let Aunt Jacy worry about these kids."

She reached over and ruffled Jack's hair.

"What's a little vaseline between friends?" she said.

"I'll pay you back if our song gets on the charts," Jack said.

"I'm thinking of taking these kids to Italy with me when I go back," Jacy said. "I might make them into little Romans. They don't have far to go as it is. I'll get them Hondas and turn them loose in a piazza."

"I hope you're not going back before the centennial," Duane said.

"Why, would Adam miss his Eve?" Jacy asked.

"Yes, and besides that the whole centennial would collapse," he said.

Little Mike wandered out. Jacy offered him a bite of pasta. Little Mike shook his head. "No," he said.

"Okay," Jacy said. "Be that way." She ate the bite herself.

Little Mike, regretting his decision, reached supplicatingly toward the pasta. Jacy gave him a bite. After savoring it, he turned and sat astraddle of Shorty, who was sleeping nearby. Shorty promptly dumped him on his back. Little Mike began to squall. Jack picked him up by his feet and dangled him over the swimming pool.

"Stop squalling," Jack said. "If you don't I'll drop you."

Little Mike stopped.

"He knows I mean business," Jack said.

"You're a bully," Julie said. "He's just a baby. He could develop a fear of water and never learn to swim because of you."

"Who cares if he learns to swim?" Jack said.

"What if he fell out of a motorboat?" Julie asked.

"What if you fell in a tub of shit," Jack said.

"What if you drowned in a bucket of puke," Julie said.

Jacy poured Duane some more wine.

"You're looking a little less nervous," she said. "Lulled by the familiar sound of your own children's invective, I guess."

"I guess," Duane said.

"Go work on your getting-off song, kids," Jacy said. "Leave your father and me in peace. And take your nephew back to his mother, please."

Jack carried Little Mike into the house by his heels. Nellie soon came out and got the plates.

"That was good, honey," Duane said.

Nellie smiled at the compliment, but seemed a little downcast.

"I think you've got problems with that one," Jacy said.

"I thought I had problems with all of them," Duane said.

"Come and meet my girls sometime," Jacy said. "I'll show you problems."

Her remark seemed to depress her.

"How'd you teach Nellie to cook so quick?" Duane asked.

"I haven't taught her to cook, I just taught her how to make fettucine," Jacy said in a flat voice. "Let's go in and watch a movie."

They went into the house and down a hall, passing the den. Both Minerva and Dickie were now absorbed in the ball game.

"This is the master bedroom," Jacy said, leading him into a large room. She pulled back some curtains on the south wall, revealing long sliding glass doors, which she opened. The edge of the bluff was only a few feet away from the doors. Below it the plains stretched far to the south. Duane stepped outside a moment. To the southwest he could see one of his own rigs, the lights twinkling on it.

"Is that yours?" Jacy asked.

"Mine today," Duane said. "I don't know about next week."

Jacy turned on a light and began to look through a stack of cassettes by her bed. The house in general had seemed very neat, but the bedroom wasn't. The bed was piled with magazines and tapes, and there were several wineglasses beside it.

"Don't look at this mess," Jacy said. "Do you want to see *Paris, Texas*?"

"Whatever you'd like," Duane said.

"Whatever I'd like," Jacy repeated. "I guess I'll have to reflect on my preferences. Excuse me while I do that."

She disappeared into the bathroom and came back a minute later, wearing a kimono and carrying a hairbrush. She put the cassette into the VCR, came back to the bed and sat down, arranging a variety of pillows.

Duane stood awkwardly in the doorway.

Jacy looked at him in a way that seemed rather unfriendly.

"Are you going to watch the movie standing up?" she asked.

"I'd rather not," he said.

"Then take your boots off and get comfortable."

He did as commanded and sat on the bed. Jacy offered him some wine. Somewhat later, when they were into the movie, she offered him her foot to rub.

"My preference is for a foot rub," she said.

Other than that, she didn't speak during the film. She left the room once and returned with another bottle of wine. From time to time she put her feet in Duane's lap to be rubbed. Parts of the movie interested him, parts of it didn't. He had stopped feeling nervous and began to feel tired. Once or twice he dozed. Though silent, Jacy seemed wide-awake. Duane tried to stay alert but it became harder and harder. He was sinking into fatigue. When the movie was over Jacy removed her feet from his lap. She picked up a remote-control gadget and clicked the TV off.

"They should have called it 'Houston, Germany,' " she said.

Duane yawned. He felt so tired he thought he might have to drive home in his stocking feet. He thought he might make it to his pickup, and once in the pickup could make it home, but the amount of energy it would take to pull his boots on was an amount he didn't believe he could summon. They were new boots, and it was a tussle to get them on.

"Are you as tired as you look?" Jacy asked. She no longer seemed unfriendly.

"I'm tired," he said.

"There's an empty bedroom right across the hall," Jacy said. "Do you think you can make it that far?"

"If I don't have to put my boots on I can probably make it," he said.

The bedroom seemed vast to him. It was vast, though no more so than the master bedroom in his new home.

"It's stupid to build bedrooms this big," he said. "When you're really tired you don't want to have to walk ten minutes just to get to bed."

He stood up, though.

"That's a good point," Jacy said. "I wouldn't want a bedroom this large, personally."

He stooped and picked up his boots. Jacy was looking through her stock of movie cassettes.

"Are you going to watch another movie?" he asked. He felt so tired that it was momentarily hard to imagine anyone in the world who was not tired.

"Sure," Jacy said.

Duane hobbled over to the door. A swinging pipe had brushed his hip that afternoon. He had considered it a light blow at the time, but now it felt sore.

"I could probably drive home," he said. "I might get a second wind."

"Duane, just go across the hall and go to bed," Jacy said.

"You don't need a second wind. I normally wouldn't have even made you get off the bed, but there's the kids to consider."

"The kids?"

"Your kids, remember?" she said. "Dickie, Nellie and the twins."

"Oh," he said. "The ones who steal vaseline and write songs about getting off."

"That's perfectly normal," Jacy said. "Nothing wrong with that. But they wouldn't think it was normal if Daddy spent the night in bed with Aunt Jacy just because he was too tired to get to his feet."

"I don't know how those kids would know what normal is, anymore," Duane said. "I don't know myself."

"You may not but they do," Jacy said. "They're young. To them, normal is simple."

He nodded and opened the door. Jacy got up, stepped past him, and opened a door across the hall.

"This one," she said. "Come on now. It's only a few steps."

He walked across the hall, carrying his boots, into the empty bedroom.

"Goodnight, honey pie," Jacy said, shutting the door behind him.

CHAPTER 54

DUANE WOKE EARLY, FEELING DISORIENTED. THE bedroom, like every other room in Los Dolores, contained wall-to-wall bookshelves filled with books. Out his window he could see the patio and the pool. Shorty was asleep on the diving board. The sun was up, how high he couldn't tell, but he had the feeling that he had overslept by hours.

However, when he went to the kitchen, the only person around was Minerva.

"Who won the ball game?" he asked.

"What do you care, you don't follow baseball," Minerva snapped.

"I was just seeing if my voice would work, Minerva," he said. "I wasn't really trying to make sense. I know I don't make sense."

"You do sometimes," she said. She seemed a little sorry that she had snapped at him—even chastened, perhaps. In his experience of Minerva, such moments were rare.

"You better have some coffee," she said. "You look shaky."

Duane felt shaky. In the night he had had several dreams in

which he ran into Karla in unlikely places. One of the places had been the Oklahoma City airport, where he had only been once in his life.

"Jacy's up and gone," Minerva said. "Why anybody would go swim in a lake when it's still dark is beyond me. I wouldn't swim in that lake in broad daylight.

"How's Junior?" she inquired.

"He's thinking of going on a fast," Duane said.

"I guess he's caught anorexia," Minerva said.

"You can't catch anorexia," Duane said.

"You'd argue with a stump," Minerva replied. "Of course you can catch it. Horses and cattle give it to you. If Junior had stayed an oilman he'd have been fine."

Duane thought of drawing a distinction between anorexia and anthrax, but decided not to bother. Minerva seemed almost friendly for the first time in years, but she was not likely to stay that way if her judgments were questioned.

It proved to be only six-thirty in the morning, a respectable hour. He pulled on his boots and drove to town.

Jacy was breakfasting at the Dairy Queen, as he had hoped she would be.

"Well, you popped right out of bed, didn't you?" she said.

"You bet," Duane said. "I didn't wanta give those kids the wrong idea."

Jacy looked at him solemnly. She didn't look happy.

"I don't want to joke about love, Duane," she said. "I don't feel like it today."

"I'm sorry," he said at once.

Jacy shrugged. "I know I flirted a little but that's just my nature."

She thought a moment, blowing on her coffee.

"Actually, it's just the vestige of my nature," she said. "The ghost of my nature."

Once again, her vivacity had left her. At the rehearsal the night before, and during the meal, she had seemed full of color and spirit. Even resting on the bed she seemed possessed of energies that made him feel embarrassed by his own listlessness.

But now she herself had become listless and toneless. She

pressed her long fingers against her temples as if trying to relieve a pressure.

"Headache?" Duane asked.

Jacy ignored the question. "When's Karla coming back?" she asked.

"I don't know," Duane said. "Today, probably. She don't usually stay around her mother long."

"Good," Jacy said. "I hope it's today."

Her eyes reddened suddenly and she stood up, quickly gathering her purse and comb.

"I need her," she said.

She hurried out of the restaurant, fighting back tears. Duane quickly followed. She stood by the Mercedes, crying and trying to find her keys in the small purse.

"This is a small purse," she said. "Why can I never find my keys in it when I just want to go away in a hurry?"

She found them and quickly got in the car.

"Is there anything I can do to help?" Duane asked.

"No," Jacy said angrily. "I don't need you, I need Karla."

Not knowing what else to do, Duane stepped away from the car.

Jacy started to back up and then stopped. She looked out the window at him.

"I don't think I paid for my breakfast," she said. "That's something you could do if you would."

"I sure will," Duane said.

CHAPTER 55

AFTER PAYING FOR THE TWO BREAKFASTS, DUANE started for his office, but stopped before he got there. He sat in his pickup, a hundred yards from the tennis courts. People driving down the road waved at him. After three or four waved at him Duane realized he hadn't been waving back. Embarrassed, he drove quickly to the lake and got in his boat. He wanted to be somewhere where no one would wave at him.

He felt anxious, drifting in the boat. It seemed that life was becoming very abnormal. His family life had begun to swell and bulge in disturbing ways. Through the unexpected intervention of Jacy, his family seemed to be shaping up in certain areas—but he had the sense that he was becoming irrelevant to them. Somehow, in only a week or two, Jacy had forged a union with Karla and his family which more or less left him out.

It made him feel ineffectual. His wife and his old girlfriend needed one another, but neither of them seemed to need him.

In Jacy's vivid moments she outshone the woman of his fantasy. A time or two he had felt himself slipping into loving her again. When she herself sank back into her pale, lonely unhappiness, he felt a great urge to hold her and comfort her.

But, as she had made clear, she wanted Karla, not him, to be her comforter.

He didn't know what to make of it, but he felt disquieted. Drifting on the muddy lake, he tried to imagine Karla and Jacy together. His imagination didn't take him far. Karla had lots of women friends. Duane realized he had never given much thought to what they said and or did when they were together. He assumed they ran around and bought clothes, or drank beer, or flirted with whatever were around. Probably they talked about children or traded complaints about men.

The thought kept nudging at his mind that maybe Karla and Jacy had a physical relationship. He didn't know why the thought arose. The surface of the lake was dotted with the heads of mud turtles, with here and there a snapper. The thought that Jacy and Karla might be lovers kept bobbing up, turtlelike, in his mind.

What if they were falling in love?

He told himself he was probably being extremely foolish to think such a thing. Probably nothing of the sort was happening between Jacy and Karla. Not three weeks ago, when they were in the hot tub, Karla had specifically warned him not to imagine things about her life.

"Why can't I?" he asked.

"Because you don't know a thing about women and you never will," Karla told him bluntly. "If you go around imagining things you'll just cause trouble for everybody."

"I guess I know a few things about you," he said. "I've been married to you twenty-two years."

"Yes, you know a few things," Karla said. "About six or seven. Ten at the outside."

She spoke in a flat tone.

"How many things are there to know about anybody?" he asked, wishing, almost before the words were out, that he hadn't said them.

Karla laughed. "There's only three or four things to know about you but there's a million things to know about me," she said. "There's new things to know about me every day."

"Name a few," he challenged.

"They don't have names, Duane," she said. "They can just be feelings. They're like those little plants I read about in the *Smithsonian* magazine that only bloom for one hour in twenty years. I've got little feelings that bloom like that. One might only bloom once in our whole marriage, and you'd be sitting right there, two feet away, and never notice it."

She had said it rather unhappily. Duane had not taken the remark too seriously at the time. A feeling wasn't a plant. There was no reason one could only bloom once in a marriage.

But now, as unhappy feelings of a sort he had never known before bloomed inside him, he realized Karla had not necessarily been exaggerating. He was not fool enough to suppose he knew everything about Karla. In the awkward years when their sexual relationship had ebbed, he had sometimes looked at her in bed, after a none-too-thrilling bit of lovemaking, and felt that a strange woman lay beside him, one he didn't know at all.

Her remarks in the hot tub came back to him as he drifted amid the turtles, and he realized she might have been describing the situation accurately. He might only know a few simple things about her. Thousands of complicated things might largely have escaped him.

He felt he had almost lost his basis for judgment in the last few weeks or months. Whatever Karla and Jacy were doing, he could hardly criticize, since he himself was occasionally to be found in bed with a woman who was in love with his son.

He had never supposed that people really lived as they ought to live, but he had gone through much of his life at least believing that there was a way they ought to live. And Thalia of all places—a modest small town—ought to be a place where people lived as they ought to live, allowing for a normal margin of human error. Surely, in Thalia, far removed from big-city temptations, people ought to be living on the old model—putting their families and neighbors first, leading more or less orderly, more or less responsible lives.

But he knew almost everyone in Thalia—indeed, knew more than he wanted to know about most of them—and it was clear from what he knew that the old model had been shattered. The arrival of money had cracked the model; its departure shattered it. Irrationality now flowered as prolifically as broom weeds in a wet year.

Worse, people had stopped even expecting themselves to behave rationally. They no longer cared—though some, who behaved little better than certifiable lunatics, for some reason expected him to remain sane and even expected him to be an arbiter of their behavior.

If he tried to hint that he could no longer rely on his own experience, people not only refused to believe him, they simply refused to hear him.

Duane stayed on the lake for two hours, turning things over in his head, worrying about Karla and Jacy without really being able to decide what it was he was worrying about. He remembered how awkward he had felt at Jacy's. He didn't know how to be with Jacy. Probably Karla would soon become more like Jacy, and he wouldn't know how to be with her either.

Finally he started his motor and went ashore. It was getting very hot. There had hardly been a cloud in the sky for the past three weeks.

Genevieve Morgan was fishing near the dock when he pulled his boat up. It was her day off. She had backed her old Plymouth station wagon as close to the water as possible and was fishing from the tailgate of the car. Like Karla, Genevieve had a fondness for vodka tonics. She liked to spend her day off fishing and getting sloshed. She wore an old cowboy hat to keep the sun out of her eyes.

"I don't see no fish," she said, when Duane tied up his boat.

"I wasn't fishing," Duane said. "I was just boating."

Genevieve looked at him a little disapprovingly, it seemed to him. He didn't dislike her, but they had never been friends. She had doted on Sonny from as far back as he could remember, and perhaps had never forgiven him for the fight that cost Sonny his eye. She had never said so in so many words, but Duane felt she would have liked for Sonny to be a big success, and somehow held it against him that Sonny wasn't.

"I wish I could boat," she said. "I never could afford one. Dan and I were saving up to buy a boat when he was killed. I guess his coffin was our boat."

Duane felt a little ashamed of himself. So many people in

the county had boats that it had slipped his mind that there might be those who wanted them but couldn't have them.

"You can borrow this one any time, Genevieve," he said. "I rarely use it. Just stick the key under the seat."

"Oh, I couldn't run a boat," she said. "I've fished off this bank all these years."

She looked across the long brown lake.

"I guess it's like anything else," she said. "You think there might be greener pastures. I've looked across this lake a million times and wondered if I'd be catching the big ones if I just had a boat and could get out in the middle, or across to the other side."

"Well, you might," Duane said. "Some fishermen think the west side's better."

Genevieve slugged down a swallow of vodka and grapefruit juice.

"If I caught a big fish I'd be so excited I'd probably fall in and drown," she said. "I'm better off just sticking to little ones."

"You're still welcome to the boat," Duane said.

"That's nice of you, Duane," she said.

"Want me to show you how to run it?"

"No, thanks, honey," Genevieve said. "I'd rather keep my dreams."

"How's Sonny?" he asked. "Do you think that medicine's working?"

Genevieve shook her head. She didn't say anything more. Duane started to get in his pickup.

"Duane," Genevieve said, "see if you can get them just to let him alone. I think Ruth and I can take care of him unless he gets a lot worse. He's just forgetful. He's not going to hurt anybody. It would be terrible if somebody decided to send him to a hospital."

Duane had not given such a possibility any thought. It startled him that Genevieve supposed Sonny might get that bad. Certainly no one in Thalia had raised the possibility. Sonny was still mayor, for that matter.

"It don't really matter if he forgets how to work the cash register," Genevieve said. "Just let him stay in town. He'd die in a hospital."

"I doubt it will come to anything like that," Duane said.

He waited a moment, in case she knew something else about Sonny that she needed to tell him. Probably she was as close to Sonny as anyone could get.

But Genevieve had no more to say. She just sat looking at him.

"What dreams do you want to keep, Genevieve?" he asked, finally, feeling awkward. It was the most personal conversation he had ever had with the woman.

"Just the dream that there's a big fish out there in the lake somewhere that I could catch," she said. "I'd drag it up into the station wagon and haul it to town and park. All the men would stop standing around the filling station and come over and look at it."

Duane drove back toward town. On the way five pickups passed him. All were traveling at such high speeds that they made him feel like he wasn't moving, and all had HARDTOP COUNTY CENTENNIAL bumper stickers.

It seemed to him that it had only taken the county one hundred years to become completely crazy and also completely sad.

CHAPTER 56

WHEN HE WALKED IN THE HOUSE HE WAS IMMEDIately confronted with an unwelcome sight: Jeanette Burr, his mother-in-law. She was sitting at the kitchen table glaring at Casey, her elderly boyfriend. Jeanette, in her mid-seventies, was only less elderly by a few months, but she referred to Casey as elderly and spoke of herself as being in late middle age.

Casey, a retired postmaster, was glaring back. He and Jeanette gave one another little quarter. A .22 pistol and a deck of cards lay on the table in front of them.

"Hello, folks," Duane said, trying to bring a note of enthusiasm to his voice.

Jeanette didn't turn her head to look at him.

"You don't sound very glad to see us," she remarked.

"Well, you're armed and I'm not," Duane said. "I don't know if I'm glad to see you or not."

"You must be laying down on the job," Jeanette informed him. "If you aren't, how come my daughter and all my grandkids have moved off somewhere else?"

"They've got a restless nature," Duane said.

Junior Nolan straddled a kitchen chair, watching the action with a bemused expression.

"What's the pistol for?" Duane inquired.

"We're gonna cut the cards," Jeanette said. "The person that draws the high card gets to shoot the other one."

"Why?" Duane asked.

"Because we hate one another's guts," Jeanette said.

"I don't hate her guts," Casey said. "I just despise her."

Duane took the pistol, stepped outside, and threw it as far as he could, which was far enough that it disappeared over the edge of the bluff.

"If you wanted to shoot Casey you should have stayed home," he informed Jeanette. "I won't have shooting in this house."

"That was my Saturday night special," Jeanette said. She was clearly shocked by his action. "Now somebody can just walk in and rape me any time they want to."

"If they do they'll wish they hadn't," Casey said.

"Shut your ugly mouth," Jeanette said.

Duane felt a bad headache coming on. He heard the sound of a pickup and looked around hopefully, thinking Bobby Lee might be coming. Jeanette had an inexplicable soft spot for Bobby Lee.

Instead he saw Billie Anne wheel up. The sight made his temper flare, and his headache worse. He went out the door, walked around the pickup, and without formality yanked Billie Anne out of the car.

Billie Anne looked startled.

"I came to apologize for all my lies and stuff," she said.

"Good, we all need to do the right thing once in a while," Duane said. There were three pistols in the seat and another in the glove compartment. He took them all to the edge of the bluff and threw them over.

Billie Anne started to weep.

"That's over a thousand dollars' worth of collectible guns you threw away, and I said I was going to apologize," she said.

"You might have changed your mind," Duane said. "You might shoot first and apologize later. I've already had to break up one gunfight here this morning and I'm not in the mood to take chances."

He took the clip out of the rifle in Billie Anne's gun rack and threw it off the cliff too. Then he went in, shaved, and lay in the bathtub for an hour, holding an ice pack to his temples. His head felt as if it were full of sand, with the sand packed so tightly that his heart could barely pump blood through it. When the hot water in the tub cooled he ran in more hot water, vaguely listening for gunshots. Billie Anne could have had another clip, or Jeanette could have bullied Junior out of his Winchester, which was still around the house somewhere.

His head finally got a little better, so he dressed and went to the kitchen to have a bowl of cereal. Jeanette, Casey, Junior and Billie Anne were playing poker for toothpicks. They were laughing and joking, happy as larks. Duane felt almost as irritated with them as he had when they were about to shoot one another. Couldn't they even stay mad for an hour? Their jollity almost revived his headache. He felt like going out and shooting at the doghouse awhile, but even that pleasure was denied him because, having thrown away five guns, he couldn't afford to be caught enjoying himself with one.

Jeanette, a deadly poker player, was winning all the toothpicks, but Junior, Casey and Billie Anne didn't seem to mind.

"Who's that girl my daughter and all my grandkids have gone to live with?" Jeanette asked. "Is she some old girlfriend of yours, or what?"

"It's none of your cheesy business," Duane said. He was not in the mood for Jeanette and felt very annoyed with Karla for having hauled her in and dumped her on him.

"Bite my head off, I just asked," Jeanette said. "No wonder none of your family can stand to live with you."

"Now hush, be nice to Duane," Casey said, looking nervous.

"You hush, it wasn't you he insulted," Jeanette said.

"No, but it's his house," Casey pointed out. "He'll deport us if we don't behave."

"I don't take orders from an elderly senior citizen," Jeanette informed him. "Do you want a card or not?"

"Four cards," Casey said, looking resigned.

Duane munched his cereal. He watched Billie Anne, who was behaving circumspectly. She didn't look like a girl who would just drive up and start shooting, yet she was the only person he knew whom Dickie would admit being afraid of. This morning she merely looked mousy and depressed. Duane felt he might have overreacted in throwing all four guns off the bluff. On the other hand, the presence of four handguns and an automatic rifle in one pickup certainly suggested a penchant for violence.

"Tell Dickie I really am sorry I told all those lies about him smashing furniture and stuff," Billie Anne said, when she came to the counter to replenish her coffee.

"I wish he'd just move on back in," she added.

The phone rang. Duane was hoping it was Karla, for whom he had been rehearsing a few choice words. But it proved to be Bobby Lee.

"Duane?" Bobby Lee asked. He moved into phone calls cautiously.

"Yes, I'm Duane," Duane said. "Who might you be?"

He instantly regretted his mild attempt at wit, because Bobby Lee took it as a rebuff and fell silent. Bobby Lee was prone to drastic losses of confidence, at which times he required careful handling.

"I'm sorry," Duane said. "I know who you are. What's going on?"

"I think we hit that Mississippi," Bobby Lee said.

"We did?" Duane said.

"I think we hit that sucker," Bobby Lee said.

The news, if true, was electrifying. A Mississippi was a rich oil sand. Even better, the well Bobby Lee had been sent to drill was on a lease Duane owned. He had drilled four wells on it over the years, hoping to hit the Mississippi. All had been dry. Once in a while, when he had a rig idle, he tried again. If they actually had hit the Mississippi it might affect his survival. A good well in such a sand might produce a hundred barrels a day, perhaps even more.

"I hope you aren't having one of your little fantasies," he said. "I'm not in the mood for anybody's fantasies today."

"I think we hit that sucker," Bobby Lee repeated, in the same confident tone with which he had announced the likelihood of Libyan terrorists' having hit Thalia.

"I'll be right there," Duane said.

CHAPTER 57

BOBBY LEE HAD NOT LIED. BY MID-AFTERNOON Duane was convinced he had hit one of the best wells of his life. All he could think about was setting pipe and getting the well on pump. Although Bobby Lee remained his usual melancholy self, Duane felt almost giddy.

He was the one who began to have fantasies—fantasies of not having to go bankrupt, of being out of debt, even affluent again. What if the well pumped two hundred barrels a day, as it seemed it might? What if he could quickly punch two or three more wells into the Mississippi, now that he knew where it was? His brain spun out figures like a cash register all afternoon, multiplying two hundred, four hundred, six hundred by the current price of a barrel of oil. Then he multiplied that by three hundred sixty-five, the number of days in a year, to convince himself he had a rough estimate of when he might be out of danger.

He completely forgot about the pageant rehearsal, about Jacy and Karla, Jeanette and Casey, everyone. He sent Bobby Lee to pull part of the crew off another well, so they could work faster.

All the while he told himself to calm down. He reminded himself of all the good wells he had brought in which had looked like millionaire-makers for a week or two, only to dry up within a month. He told himself that the pessimistic attitude was the only realistic attitude. Oil was unpredictable. The new well looked great, but it might yet disappoint him. Many wells had.

His efforts to restrain his own hopes didn't help at all. His months of idleness, depression, hopelessness just made the new well more seductive. He couldn't help believing that it would solve all his problems, although he knew that hope was wildly unrealistic.

He was still at the well at midnight, waiting for the midnight crew to arrive, when he saw a set of headlights flickering through the brushy mesquite. Bobby Lee was sitting around. Though he could claim credit for having brought in the wonderful new well, he seemed more morose than usual.

"Here comes your wife, to drag you home by the ears," Bobby Lee said.

"Or it could be *your* wife," Duane said. "You've been known to get your ear pulled once in a while, haven't you?"

"It's a wonder I've even got an ear left," Bobby said.

"If this well gets me out of debt I'll give you such a big bonus you can buy an airplane and fly off to Louisiana to the race track ever' Friday," Duane promised.

"I'd crash," Bobby Lee said. "I'd crash and that'd be that. Then everybody'd be sorry they was so mean to me all my life —especially Karla and Carolyn."

A minute later Karla drove up, with Jacy in the car. Duane walked off the rig floor and over to the ladies. Bobby Lee shuffled along behind him, unable to stay away from any drama.

"From the way you're strutting around it must be a good well," Karla said. "Momma didn't like the way you bawled her out today. She'll hold a grudge for the rest of her life, you know."

"I didn't bawl her out," Duane said. "I just told her to mind her own cheesy business."

"This is my momma you're talking about," Karla said. "She said you treated her like a war criminal."

"Well, she was about to shoot Casey when I walked in," Duane said.

"Momma's real sensitive," Karla said, in the relentless manner she adopted when she intended to extract an apology.

"All girls are sensitive, old and young," Bobby Lee said in a tone of quiet sagacity.

Jacy had one leg cocked up against the dashboard. She was listening to a Walkman, but after a moment got out of the car and dropped the Walkman in the seat. She was wearing a T-shirt, running shorts and flip-flops. She wandered over and climbed up on the rig floor. The roughnecks all stopped as if turned to stone.

"Hey, put on a hard hat," Duane said.

Jacy walked into the toolshed and found one.

"I knew to do that," she said. "I was raised in the oil business."

"Momma's not going to go away until you apologize, Duane," Karla said.

"*I'll* go away then," Duane said.

"Tell her you were stressed out from being bankrupt," Karla said. "That might do it."

"I'm not going to tell her a fucking thing," he said. "I'm not going to apologize to Jeanette for keeping her from shooting her own boyfriend."

"I think she just planned to scare him," Karla said.

Jacy was sitting on the edge of the rig platform, dangling her feet. Though she had her back to them, the roughnecks were still frozen in place. Rather than continue the argument with Karla, Duane walked over and looked up at Jacy.

"Pretty night," Jacy said. "My daddy used to take me out to his rigs sometimes. He was a nice man."

"I know, I worked for him," Duane said. "He didn't want me to marry you, though."

"That's right, and I didn't," Jacy said. "I was an obedient daughter in some respects. Anyway, I was far too big a snob to marry you."

Duane felt Karla looking at him. She was directing a steady wave of pressure at the back of his neck. He decided to ignore it.

"You didn't show up at the pageant rehearsal," Jacy said. "I didn't have my Adam to practice with, and all your women decided you'd found a new girl and run off with her. They're pretty dependent on you."

"I guess," Duane said.

"Did you find a new girl?" Jacy asked.

"Nope," he said.

"Are you looking?" she asked.

"No," Duane said.

Jacy got up, returned the hard hat to the toolshed, waved at the roughnecks and strolled down the steps.

"You're cute with one of those hats on," Duane said.

Jacy stopped and looked at him a moment.

"I haven't been cute in a long time, Duane," she said. "I'm something but I'm not cute. Don't let your new oil well warp your judgment."

She strolled past him and got back in the BMW.

Duane was a little deflated. He felt that he had said a silly thing and been immediately slapped down for it. Karla slapped him down for similar remarks all the time, but it felt worse when Jacy did it.

He walked over and stood by Bobby Lee, who was looking distrustfully at the women in the car. The women had fallen silent, each of them thinking her own thoughts.

"What am I gonna tell Momma?" Karla asked, looking at him pointedly.

"If you're afraid of your own momma, why'd you bring her home?" Duane asked.

"I don't want to have an argument in front of all these people," Karla said. "Why can't we just have a civil discussion for once?"

"We are having a civil discussion," he said. "I haven't yelled. I haven't raised my voice."

"Did you know he was this stubborn when you married him?" Jacy asked.

Karla didn't answer. She stared at Duane in silence. Bobby Lee found her silence unnerving. He began to fidget.

"I been working sixteen hours a day, I think I'll go home," he said.

"You better come to rehearsals tomorrow," Jacy said to Duane. "Jenny will crack up if you don't. Hardly anybody showed up today."

"I'm gonna try to come," Duane said. He wanted to apologize to Jacy for having called her cute, but he couldn't very well do it in front of Karla.

"I been working sixteen hours a day, it's time for me to get in my pickup and go home," Bobby Lee said again, but he made no move toward his pickup, which was only ten steps away.

"Why don't you keep out of this, Bobby Lee?" Karla suggested.

"Keep out of what?" Bobby Lee asked. "I'm just standing here trying to draw a little overtime."

"You might draw something you don't want if you provoke me," Karla said.

"By the way, your dog's fine, in case you're worried," Jacy said.

"What dog?" Duane said. "I don't have a dog. If I had one he'd be living with me, helping me live a normal life."

Jacy grinned. She seemed to have forgiven him his unfortunate remark.

"If I were you I'd try to forget about a normal life," she said.

"I can't," Duane said. "I wasn't meant to live any other kind."

"Too bad for you, honey pie," Jacy said, as Karla began to drive away.

"You know some scary women," Bobby Lee said, watching the taillight vanish into the mesquite.

Duane didn't immediately answer. The adrenaline that had kept him working all day and most of the night began to drain away. He felt a little flat.

"Why did they come out here?" Bobby Lee asked. "Why do they always pick on me?"

"I thought you were going home," Duane said.

CHAPTER 58

THE MINUTE DUANE WALKED INTO THE FINAL
meeting of the Hardtop County Centennial Committee he
sensed trouble. Locating the source was not difficult, either.
G. G. Rawley and four of his deacons were seated along one
wall. All the deacons were wheat farmers from the northern part
of the county. Duane knew a couple of them well enough to say
hello to. Drought had pretty much got their most recent wheat
crop, and what little wheat had come up was destroyed by a
series of freak hailstorms that had peppered the county during
May and June. On the whole they formed a somber group.

G.G. was not somber, however. He looked scrubbed, healthy
and ready for a fight.

"Hello, folks," Duane said. The whole committee was present, including Old Man Balt, who had acquired an empty
Crisco can in which to spit his tobacco juice, an improvement
over the small tomato-juice can he had used before falling out
of the car.

The committee as a whole seemed indifferent to the presence of the wheat farmers. Sonny looked tense, as he had ever

since his head started failing him. Suzie Nolan yawned several times—she was obviously ready to go home and take a nap. Jenny scribbled last-minute changes into her pageant script. Ralph Rolfe was studying a brochure about Nubian goats.

Despite his efforts not to let the new oil well make him unrealistically optimistic, Duane felt very optimistic. A good oil well always had a tonic effect on his spirits. If there had to be confrontation, he was up for it.

"G.G., this is an official committee meeting," he said. "We don't usually allow visitors."

"Duane, you're headed for hell," G.G. said. "You ought to think about your immortal soul, which will be frying over a spit if you don't change your tune."

Sensing battle, everyone looked up from whatever they had been looking down at.

"You don't fry things on a spit," Suzie remarked. "You fry things in a frying pan."

G.G. ignored that technicality.

"The devil can fry a soul as quick as you or me could fry a piece of bacon," he informed them cheerfully.

"Be that as it may," Duane said, "we have to keep these meetings private or pretty soon we'll have the whole town in here."

"Look at it this way, son," G.G. said. "You got your committee and I've got mine and the Lord's. We're the committee for the Byelo-Baptist boycott, and we're gonna boycott everything in sight unless you back off on these liquor sales."

"The City Council voted unanimously to approve the sale of beer during the centennial," Duane said. "The City Council speaks for the people of this town."

"No, it just speaks for the sots," G.G. said. "My committee speaks for the decent people, and we suggest you cease and desist from this immorality."

Duane laughed. In his unrealistically optimistic mood the situation struck him as comic.

"We can't cease and desist because we haven't started yet," he said.

"I'm not going to sit here and listen to a lot of verbal wordplay," G.G. said. "Our position is simple. If you sell liquor on that courthouse lawn we're gonna form a Broom Brigade."

"A what?" Buster Lickle asked. Buster had been following the discussion closely.

"We mean to arm ourselves against vice and sin with brooms," G.G. explained. "Any time we see a drinker about to drink we'll swat the poison out of his hands with a broom. Those that get unruly will be arrested. The Liquor Control Board has promised to send us a number of well-trained agents to make the arrests."

"Can we call the meeting to order?" Sonny asked. "It hasn't been called to order."

"Why bother?" Duane asked. "We can call till we're hoarse and there won't be any order."

Sonny looked pained. He was a stickler for correct parliamentary procedure.

"The meeting is now called to order," Duane said. He didn't want to do anything that might trigger one of Sonny's lapses.

"I move that all nonmembers be expelled from this meeting forthwith," Suzie Nolan said with astonishing crispness. Everyone looked at her in surprise. Suzie had risen from her naplike condition to a state of blazing indignation. Her eyes shone and there was high color in her cheeks. Duane was not too surprised—he knew she was capable of amazing transformations, and so, apparently, did G. G. Rawley, who was glaring at her with bitter intensity.

"You're another one whose soul will be sizzling like bacon one of these days," he said.

From the looks they exchanged, Duane found himself wondering if Suzie and G.G. had ever been lovers. The mere fact that the latter had brought four solemn wheat farmers into the meeting could hardly have stirred the level of animosity they were exhibiting.

"I second that motion," Ralph Rolfe said. As a cattleman he had an ancestral dislike of all farmers, whatever their stamp.

"Now wait a minute," Duane said. "There's no reason to be discourteous and kick these gentlemen out."

Though he had been the first to question the right of the wheat farmers to be there, he had already come to feel a certain sympathy for the men, all of whom were going broke and none of whom were deriving anything but embarrassment from the controversy raging around them.

"You said yourself we don't allow visitors," Jenny said.

"We don't, generally, but these men are here and they've gone to some trouble," Duane said.

"G.G. put them to the trouble, not us," Suzie said. "I think we ought to expel him too."

"A motion has been made and seconded," Sonny said. "We have to vote on it."

"Now wait a minute," Duane said. He was beginning to get annoyed. "We're not the joint chiefs of staff or anything. Surely we can be courteous enough to let these men sit here for a few minutes."

"You just have one vote, Duane," Suzie said. She was looking at him angrily, the glow still in her eye. Duane found her very appealing and wondered what flaw in his character caused him to find angry women so attractive.

"Listen," Duane said. "This committee has been known to debate things for three or four months before actually voting. We don't have to do something rude just because you popped off and made a motion."

"But you wanted them out yourself," Jenny said. "Be consistent, Duane."

"I move we table the motion," Duane said. Jenny's passion for consistency annoyed him, too.

There was an awkward silence.

"I don't think you can table a motion that's been seconded," Sonny said.

"I just did," Duane said.

One of the wheat farmers smiled. Then another smiled. The twists and turns of civic affairs had begun to amuse them.

"I've made another decision," Duane said. "We're gonna give away the beer, not sell it. I'll buy a few thousand cases myself and contribute to the centennial. That way there won't be any question of illegality to deal with, and G.G. can go jump in the lake."

"What I'll do is go call the Texas Rangers," G.G. said. "If you lowlife politicians are planning to degrade the public with free liquor I think it's time the Rangers came in to bust some heads."

"This meeting is adjourned," Duane said. The statement

caught everybody by surprise. Duane was even a little surprised to hear himself say it, but he was not sorry. He meant it. The meeting was silly, he was getting no help from anyone, the whole centennial was silly, he missed his family and he had had enough.

"You can't adjourn us, we just got here," Jenny said. "We have a lot of important things to discuss."

"No we don't," Duane said. "None of this is important."

He got up and walked out, leaving a roomful of stunned people behind him. He went to his pickup, drove it around the block and parked behind the post office. Then he hurried back to the courthouse and peeked around a corner to watch the committee take its leave. Jenny Marlow led the pack. She was in her car and off in a flash, no doubt to spread the word of his defection. The others straggled behind. The wheat farmers plodded to their pickups and drove slowly off to their battered fields. Sonny headed for the Kwik-Sack and Ralph Rolfe for his ranch.

The last people out, as Duane had hoped, were Suzie Nolan and Old Man Balt, whose faithful daughter, Beulah, was waiting for him as usual. Suzie helped the old man down the sidewalk, waiting while he emptied his Crisco can onto the courthouse lawn. The minute he was in the car Beulah whisked him off to whatever TV show was about to come on.

Duane could not tell if Suzie was still angry, but she was obviously in no hurry. She slipped her shoes off before getting into her car. Driving in shoes, or even wearing them, didn't appeal to her.

Seeing her take her shoes off gave Duane an idea. He looked around and saw not a soul in sight except Suzie. The square and the town seemed deserted, the reason being that two crucial Little League games were being played that night on the local diamond. His son Jack was pitching in one of them, his daughter Julie playing shortstop in another. He meant to go, but had developed more immediate plans.

He quickly slipped off his boots and his pants. It generally took Suzie three or four minutes to find her car keys, comb her hair and get started. He watched her do all those things, his pants and boots in his hand. When she started the car he tiptoed over and hid behind a cedar tree on one corner of the lawn.

The traffic light had no traffic to stop, but it was still doing its job of turning red and then green anyway. Suzie had to pass through it. She had started the car, but hadn't backed away from the curb. She was lazily combing her hair. The light changed to red. Duane felt annoyed. If she had only stopped combing her hair and backed out, she would have immediately caught the light. But she was still combing. He waited, remembering how much he had wanted her that night in the hospital parking lot. The light turned to green and his heart sank, for Suzie had finally begun to back out. She would undoubtedly drive through it, leaving him with his old want and his new. Of course he could follow her home, but that was not exactly what he desired.

Then Suzie dropped something—her comb, an earring?— and bent over to retrieve it from the floorboard. She found it, and just as she did the light changed to red again. Suzie eased up to it. By the time she was fully stopped Duane was at the window on the driver's side. Suzie looked up. She didn't seem in the least surprised to see him standing under the traffic light in the very center of downtown Thalia with his boots and pants in his hand.

"Hi, you rat," she said, and put her car in park. Duane stuffed his boots and pants in the back seat and kissed her. Her kisses were as quick and eager as they had been at the hospital. He considered trying to go through the window, which would have made things perfect, but he decided to be mature and settle for 98 percent. The streets were totally empty. He opened the door, still not sure how things were going to work. He was every bit as aroused as he had been the first time, but felt a momentary faltering of confidence. Cars did pose logistical problems.

Suzie had lost none of her confidence, though—in such matters she seemed to experience no doubt.

"Sit in the seat, dummy," she said, with a grin. "We don't have to do it like we was married."

She slid as far from the steering wheel as she could. Duane got in, his legs stretched toward the far door. They were long legs, and the far door not really very far, but Suzie immediately straddled him. Passion, which rendered so many people awkward, brought her a heightened grace.

"This way I can watch the road," she said, easing him into place.

"We might have to hurry," Duane said. "We might have to set an all-time speed record." He felt as if he easily could, though he was also highly aware of what a bizarre thing they were doing. The town looked more brightly lit than it had when he was hiding in the darkness by the courthouse.

Suzie smiled. She opened his shirt. Then she leaned back and touched her breasts.

"We don't have to do any such thing," she said. "We can just take our time. There's not a soul in sight."

CHAPTER 59

EVENTS PROVED SUZIE RIGHT. TRAFFIC FLOW through downtown Thalia obligingly lapsed for five minutes, more time than Duane needed and then some. Suzie rose and sank with an authority that quickly proved irresistible.

Though, as she said, not a soul was in sight, the fact that he was involved in a deeply exciting sex act practically beneath the red light in the epicenter of Thalia may have hastened matters too. Seconds after enjoying a fine orgasm, Duane began to wonder why he hadn't asked her to pull around in the darkness behind the post office. That would have been an excellent site, he decided too late. Suzie soon came too, but that didn't mean she was through. The first orgasm often merely served to heighten her interest—if she paused at all it was merely to consider what kind of little game she might enjoy next. She liked to make a leisurely selection, to rummage through the possibilities for a while, perhaps choosing one game only to stop it after a bit in favor of another. Caution played no part in her choice, or her life—she seemed to feel that whatever time was needed was hers by right. She had no intention of hurrying from one pleasure to the next.

Duane found such leisure understandable when they were in bed, but less so when they were parked under bright street lights at a public intersection.

"Let's drive around behind the post office, where it's dark," he said.

"No," Suzie said. She was seated rather firmly on his legs, and gave him a squeeze with her inner muscles to emphasize her point.

"Why not?" he asked. "Then we don't have to worry about traffic."

"What traffic?" she asked. "There's not a car in sight."

"I know, but somebody'll come along sooner or later," he said.

"I like to see you," Suzie said. "The street lights make your body look different—sort of like a ghost. It's real interesting."

"Yeah, and it'll be real interesting to anybody who drives by," Duane said. "And I *will* be a ghost if Karla drives by."

Suzie was unimpressed. "It might just be strangers," she said. "People passing through. They won't even know us. Didn't you ever want to know how it would feel if people were looking?"

"No," Duane said truthfully. "It wouldn't feel at all, if people were looking, because I'd be too embarrassed to do anything."

Then he saw lights, far behind them—truck lights, he guessed.

"Here comes somebody," he said. "We gotta move."

He attempted to squirm out from under her, but Suzie gripped him more firmly with her inner muscles. She smiled and teased her nipples.

"It feels sexy, just knowing they're coming, don't it?" she said.

"No," Duane insisted. "It feels embarrassing. I can't appreciate sexy feelings when I'm embarrassed."

"Maybe you could learn to," Suzie suggested.

"I don't think I can learn to before that truck gets here," he said.

"You could try," Suzie pointed out. "Men don't ever want to try anything different."

The truck, by that time, was only a quarter of a mile away.

Duane managed to reach under the steering wheel and turn on the hazard lights. If the truck rear-ended and killed them in the position they were in, the town would receive a rude shock. They themselves would be dead, and the credibility of the Centennial Committee destroyed forever.

Suzie continued to squeeze. The roar of the approaching truck aroused her even as it chilled Duane. His erection was shrinking so fast that even Suzie's squeezing failed to hold him in.

The truck, seeing the hazard lights, cut smoothly to the right of them. The driver tapped his brakes for a second at the light, glanced east and west, and roared on toward Wichita Falls. He didn't look at the occupants of the car at all, though one of the occupants came just as the other ceased to occupy her.

The fact that an orgasm occurred at a moment of exit didn't seem to diminish Suzie's pleasure at all. She grabbed his hand and stuffed it underneath her, leaning far back in ecstasy.

The streets were empty again. Duane relaxed a little. Suzie was an unusual woman, he had to admit. Though not entirely at ease in the situation, he wouldn't have wanted to miss her.

She straightened up, draping an arm across the seat. She scooted back down his legs, stroked his stomach lightly and fingered his equipment.

"Sorry," he said, assuming still more was expected.

"Why?" Suzie asked. "It's cute when it's floppy."

She scooted farther back down his legs, until her back was against the far door. Then she squatted on her haunches.

"Put your toe in me," she said.

"No," Duane said, horrified. He had just spotted another set of approaching headlights.

"I'm real wet," Suzie said. "Put your toe in."

"Another truck's coming," he said.

"I know," Suzie said. "I like that sound they make when they come roaring through town."

Duane decided she was interesting but crazy. He kept his feet to himself.

"I got my socks on," he said. "It won't work."

Suzie immediately reached down and peeled the sock off one foot.

"Now what's your excuse?" she said.

"Why would you want me to do that with my old smelly foot?" Duane asked, as the truck roared nearer.

"To see if it feels interesting," Suzie said. "Stop asking dumb questions."

"I don't think I can. My foot's gone to sleep," Duane said, grasping at straws.

"Dickie does it," Suzie said. "Dickie's not afraid. He's the only one in this town with any imagination."

"I'm glad to hear it," Duane said, "but I'd rather be hearing it on the back side of the post office. What if that trucker saw me with my toe in you and lost his mind? He might run right through the hardware store, and then what would we do for lawn-mower parts?"

Suzie was still squatting on her haunches, more or less over his feet, when the truck arrived. This time the truck driver braked carefully at the light. The big motor throbbed beside them for several seconds, then the truck went on. The second driver showed no more interest in the car or its occupants than the first one had.

"If I let you drive around behind the post office will you try it?" Suzie asked.

"I don't know," Duane said. "It's a possibility. I don't want to commit myself."

"What do you think I'll do, make your stupid toe rot off?" Suzie asked. She seemed to be becoming irritated.

"No, of course not," Duane said.

"You put your finger in me," Suzie said. "You put your dick in me. Why not your toe?"

"Let's see what life's like around behind the post office," Duane said. He got his feet free and slipped under the wheel. He waited for Suzie to sit down, but she didn't sit down. She continued to squat.

"It's not very far to the post office," she pointed out.

Duane started the car.

CHAPTER 60

IN THE COMFORTABLE DARKNESS BEHIND THE POST office Duane gingerly indulged in a number of games. Suzie made it clear that she regarded him as a coward, but she didn't let his cowardice prevent her from pursuing her interests.

When she was content, he asked her if G. G. Rawley had ever participated in any of her games.

"You bet," she said. "He was the first man I was ever unfaithful to Junior with. It happened in the Sunday-school room. He got me up there pretending he wanted me to help him tune that old piano they use in Sunday school."

"Is that why you're mad at him?" Duane asked.

"I'm mad at him because he wouldn't do it anywhere except in the Sunday-school room," Suzie said. "He could have come to my house, or we could have gone to a motel. I got tired of trying to get comfortable on a piano bench."

"There's the floor," Duane observed. Now that he was in the dark, he enjoyed talking to Suzie about sex.

"G.G.'s got arthritis," Suzie said. "It's all he can do to stoop over.

"It was good, though," she added. "I yelled so loud I scared him to death a couple of times. Doing it with a preacher's real exciting, I guess because they're not supposed to be doing it with you. It sure beats doing it with your husband."

"Couldn't get old Junior to play too many games, huh?" Duane said.

Suzie looked out the window. Her face changed—it looked for a moment as if she might cry.

"No," she said. "Junior gets scared if you even mention a game."

Duane saw that he had touched a raw nerve. He felt sorry he had asked.

"That was the sadness of our marriage," Suzie said. "I could have made him very happy if he'd let me. But he just never would let me."

She sighed and came back into his arms.

"We got nice kids," she said. "They win everything, everything. I think we would have had a real nice marriage if Junior hadn't been so scared. It seems such a waste. I don't think he wanted to be happy. Why would anybody not want to be happy, Duane?"

"I don't know," Duane said. He thought of Sonny, who had never been happy. Though he himself had often been sad, he had also been keenly happy. Sonny hadn't. He had concentrated on holding some middle space between victory and defeat. Now, despite a life of good planning, defeat was staring him in the face anyway.

"Junior's mother was never happy," Suzie said. "She had a real hard life. I guess it made Junior feel guilty to think of being happy when his mother never got to be.

"I'll tell you who's happy, and that's Dickie," she said. "You ought to be proud of yourself for raising such a nice kid. It just lifts my spirits the minute I see him coming. That's a great gift, to be able to lift people's spirits just by showing up."

Duane knew she had paid his son a fine compliment. But he was remembering Junior, her husband, nervously asking the question about whether women wanted sex more than men, at the Dairy Queen a few weeks earlier. It seemed sad. Junior had struggled hard and become wealthy. He had done all that he had been taught to do: work hard, save, get ahead. Then the economy had turned out from under him and he had lost his wealth. And all the while, for rich or for poor, he was being overmatched at home by a nice woman who just happened to have a much richer sexuality than he had.

"What are you thinking about?" Suzie asked.

"I just can't help feeling sorry for Junior," he said.

"Oh, well," Suzie said, "Junior enjoys feeling sorry for himself. Maybe all you men enjoy feeling sorry for yourselves. I'm hanging on to Dickie while I can. He don't feel sorry for himself. Dickie likes to live.

"I gotta go," she said. "The kids will be getting home from their swim meet any time."

Duane got into his pickup and followed her around the courthouse. They both caught the red light beneath which they had had such an interesting ten minutes. Duane felt a little sad. He —they—would never do that again, not in that place, that way. A short but exciting part of life was behind him.

Suzie had recovered her spirits. She wasn't sad at all. She grinned and blew him a kiss.

"I sure hope your toe don't rot off, Duane," she said, as the light changed.

CHAPTER 61

IT WAS STILL EARLY, SO DUANE DROVE TO THE BALL
park. He saw Julie hanging around the Sno-Cone stand with
two of her girlfriends. Jack was on the mound. Duane parked
and walked over to the small section of bleachers. There were
lots of spectators, but few of them bothered with the bleachers.
They pulled their cars and pickups up to the ball-park fence
and sat in their cars, drinking beer and chatting.

Jacy sat in one of the lower rows of the bleachers, Shorty
dozing beside her. That Shorty was asleep in the bleachers was
in itself a remarkable thing. He was never allowed out of the
pickup at ball games because he ran around biting people.
Sometimes he bit children; at other times, excited by the play,
he ran onto the field and bit the players.

Jacy not only had Shorty, she also had Little Mike, who was
walking barefoot in the dust behind the home-plate screen,
talking happily to himself. When he noticed his grandfather he
smiled and ran over. Duane hoisted him into the bleachers.

"It's about time you showed up," Jacy said. "Your son's got
a no-hitter going."

Jack was indeed an exceptional young pitcher. On the mound he assumed a deadly, cold, relentless manner and blazed fast ball after fast ball over the heart of the plate. He had no confidence in his fielders and preferred to strike out as many batters as possible.

"How many has he struck out so far?" Duane asked.

"Just about all of them," Jacy said. "A couple popped up, and one or two got on on errors."

"I wouldn't have wanted to be the one who made the errors," Duane said. "Jack never forgets."

Shorty opened his eyes and looked at Duane guiltily. Duane ignored him.

"Don't be so unyielding," Jacy said. "Pet your old dog."

Duane hammered Shorty between the eyes a few times with his fist. Shorty stopped looking guilty and looked pleased.

"I said pet him, not brain him," Jacy said.

"I'm not hurting him," Duane assured her. "Shorty don't operate off a brain."

Jacy seemed relaxed. She scooted closer to him, looked at him curiously, wrinkled her nose, sniffed.

"What have you been doing, Duane?" she asked. "You smell funny."

Duane immediately became rattled. He had not expected to find Jacy at the ball park. He told himself he should have gone on home, even if Jack was pitching. He could not tell that he smelled any particular way, but under Jacy's eye he felt very aware of what he had been doing just before he came to the ball park.

"I came from a meeting," he said. "I think they must have fumigated the courthouse today—getting it spiffed up for the crowds."

Jacy lifted an eyebrow. "Give me some credit," she said.

A fat kid swung at a fast ball and rapped a weak grounder to the left-field side of the pitcher's mound. Jack pounced on it and threw a dead strike to the first baseman. The ball popped out of the first baseman's glove and sailed like a low pop fly over toward the second baseman. He fumbled it, dropped it, and, in attempting to pick it up, kicked it toward home plate. The fat boy was lumbering down the base path. Jack dashed

over, grabbed the trickling ball barehanded, and raced the fat
boy toward first. The first baseman was begging for another
throw but Jack ignored him. It became clear that the fat boy
had too big a lead. He was going to be safe by half a step. At
the last second, instead of throwing the ball, Jack threw himself. He hit the fat boy with something between a tackle and a
clip, knocking him off the base path. Jack popped up first, the
ball still in his hand, and crossed the bag. Horns were honking,
people were yelling, the opposing manager came racing across
the infield in protest.

"That a-way, Jack!" Jacy yelled, forgetting the issue of
Duane's smell. She jumped up and clapped. Shorty jumped up
and yipped. Thanks to the pickup horns, all of which were
blaring, the small crowd made as much racket as a large crowd.

The umpire not only ruled the base runner safe, he awarded
him an extra base. Jack's manager protested. The crowd yelled.
Several indignant mothers who had seen Jack resort to similar
tactics many times rushed onto the playing field to demand his
ouster from the game. The umpire was unwilling to go that far,
but the mothers insisted.

"Boo, kill the ump," Jacy said.

"Shut up," Duane said. "Jack might hear you."

"I want him to hear me!" Jacy said. "Didn't you love the way
he tackled that kid?"

"This is baseball, not football," Duane pointed out.

"I never would have expected you to become such a wimp,
Duane," Jacy said.

Jack, who still had the ball, walked back to the pitcher's
mound calmly, as if accepting the call. Duane knew better.
Jack always seemed calm just before he did something unfor-
givable. He was watching the umpire, waiting for him to turn
his back.

"Don't do it, Jack!" Duane yelled, standing up. "You'll spoil
your no-hitter."

The umpire turned his back, trying to herd the mothers off
the field, and the second he did Jack hit him right between the
shoulder blades with the ball.

"That does it, you're out of the game," the umpire yelled.

Jack walked up to home plate and threw his glove as high as

he could. It came down on the backstop and stuck there. Then he walked off the field, climbed up in the bleachers and sat down by Jacy, who gave him a big hug and a kiss.

"You were just great," she said.

"That wasn't very smart, throwing your glove up on the screen," Duane said.

"I won't need it," Jack said. "I'm never pitching again."

"Don't be ridiculous," Duane said.

Jacy looked at him hostilely.

"I hope you're not one of those fathers who insist that their kids play athletics whether they want to or not," she said.

"No, that's up to him," Duane said.

"Well, he just said he wasn't ever pitching again," Jacy pointed out.

"I would pitch again if they hadn't spoiled my no-hitter," Jack said.

"It wasn't spoiled," Duane said.

"Sure it was, there was a runner on second," Jack said.

"But he didn't get a hit," Duane said. "He got on by an error. That doesn't count against your no-hitter."

"It's not a real no-hitter if somebody gets on base," Jack said. "That first baseman should have his throat cut."

"Hey," Duane said. "This is Little League baseball. An error doesn't mean you should have your throat cut."

"Not for that," Jack said. "He's squirrely. He jacks off for any girl that asks him to."

"And you don't?" Duane asked.

"Yuk, of course not," Jack said. "I just jack off for the top girls."

"Who would a top girl be?" Jacy asked.

"The prettiest," Jack said, as if that should be obvious.

"Would I be a top girl if I were still a girl?" Jacy asked.

"Sure," Jack said.

"That umpire should have his throat cut fifty different ways," he added.

"You need to learn to control your temper," Duane said. "What if your team loses because you got thrown out?"

"Be serious," Jack said. "We're ahead twenty-six to nothing."

He got up and strolled off.

"He's probably gone to look for some top girls," Jacy said.

Little Mike was attempting to climb out of the bleachers. Since the steps were each roughly his height, he was finding it slow going, but he was going, nonetheless.

"Where's Karla?" Duane asked.

"I think she went home to beat up her mother," Jacy said. "Are you getting lonesome without her?"

"Yeah, come to think of it," Duane said.

"Are you mad at me for kidnapping your family?" she asked.

"Oh, no," Duane said. "They all do exactly what they want to, anyway. If they all want to live with you, that's fine. There's no way I could stop them, anyway."

"But you do miss them a little, don't you?" she asked.

"A little," he admitted.

"I guess you'll just have to suffer," she said. "I'm taking Karla and the twins to Europe with me right after the centennial."

That was a shock—so much of a shock that he could only stare blankly at her.

"For good?" he asked. It didn't seem unlikely, considering the last few weeks.

"Of course not for good," Jacy said. "Just for a couple of weeks. It'll be good for them to see a little bit of Europe. Besides, I need them to help me ease back into a life there."

"You're a glutton for punishment," he said. "Traveling with the twins is the worst ordeal I've ever lived through."

"For you, maybe," Jacy said. "I'm not uptight, like you are."

"I'm not uptight," he protested.

"The hell you aren't," Jacy said. "You're like a wire."

Little Mike had reached the bottom. He clapped for himself briefly and then started climbing the screen behind home plate. He could get his toes through the wire.

"I might take Dickie to Europe," Jacy said. "I want him to meet my daughters."

"Take him," Duane said. "If he stays around here his wife will probably shoot him. Or if not his wife, then somebody else's husband."

"Maybe he'll fall in love with one of my daughters," Jacy

said. "Maybe they'll marry. You and I might have grandchildren in common."

Duane stepped out of the bleachers and pried Little Mike off the screen before he got too high to reach. Little Mike looked aggrieved but kept quiet.

"I don't think you understand Dickie," Jacy said. "Dickie has absolute charm. If I were in the mood for love I wouldn't let my daughters near him. I'd keep him for myself.

"He's one in a million, that boy," she added.

"That's what the cops think, too," Duane said. "They're glad he's one in a million."

"You're not very partisan about your own kids, are you?" Jacy said. "You're kind of stingy with your praise. You didn't even cheer for Jack when he tackled that kid."

"He wasn't supposed to tackle him," Duane said. "He can do all the tackling he wants to when football season starts."

"That's not the point," Jacy said. "Your kids are great. You should root for them no matter what."

"Why aren't you in the mood for love?" he asked.

Jacy looked amused.

"What does it matter to you?" she asked. "If I were, it'd be Dickie I wanted, not his old man. Dickie's got more bounce than any five men I know. Plus he has very sweet eyes."

"He may be totally perfect, for all I know," Duane said. "I just wondered why you aren't in the mood for love?"

Jacy looked thoughtful. On the field, Jack's team was struggling to end the inning. The fat boy had advanced to third on another infield error.

Jacy studied Duane a moment, and then reached over and picked up Little Mike.

"I'm not telling you why, Duane," she said. "If you want to catch a glimpse of your wife, you better run home and catch it while the catching is good."

"Are the twins going home with you?" he asked.

"Sure they're going home with me," Jacy said.

He stood in the bleachers and watched them go. Julie came over and hooked arms with Jacy. At first he couldn't spot Jack. Then he saw him. Jack was lying on top of a pickup. As Shorty passed underneath him, Jack bombed him with a strawberry

Sno-Cone. Shorty yipped and tried to get red ice out of his eyes. Jack jumped off the pickup and began to chase him.

Duane waited until the inning was over and persuaded various members of both teams to throw baseballs at the screen until they managed to dislodge Jack's glove. The fat boy, who had been stranded at third, caught it when it fell.

CHAPTER 62

DUANE CAME INTO HIS KITCHEN TO FIND MINERVA dealing blackjack to Jeanette and Casey.

"What a surprise," he said. "I thought you'd moved off with the rest of the bunch."

Minerva didn't look up from the cards. "When you've got terminal stomach cancer you want to be with people your own age," she said.

"I'm not your age but Casey is," Jeanette reminded her.

"I thought you had terminal brain cancer," Duane said.

"When I'm gone you'll be sorry you made fun of me," Minerva said.

"Is Karla here?" he asked.

"Yeah, she came with me," Minerva said. "That flimsy little car of hers fell apart."

Casey seemed to be pouting. He was a poor loser, and he was losing.

"I wish I was in Pecos, Texas," he said. "I've done nothing but lose at cards ever since I let you bring me here."

"You didn't let me bring you here," Jeanette said. "You let

Karla bring you here. I told her she should have left you to rot."

"I wish I could go back tonight," Casey said.

"Hit the trail," Jeanette said. "Hitchhike. We don't need a sourpuss around here."

Duane went in the bedroom. Karla, looking rather cheerful, was flopped on the bed watching a James Bond movie.

"What a surprise," Duane said.

"Duane, don't try to be witty, I'm watching a movie," Karla said.

"I didn't see Junior's pickup," he said. "Did he finally go home?"

"You sure don't keep up very well," Karla said. "He and Billie Anne ran off to Ruidoso. Dickie's happy as a lark. He's already filed divorce papers accusing her of desertion."

"She might come back, if things don't work out with Junior," Duane said.

"Why wouldn't they work out with Junior?" Karla asked. "Junior's sweet. Everybody don't have to be macho, like you."

"I don't think I'm macho," he said.

"I didn't used to think so, but Jacy explained all your problems to me," Karla said.

Duane felt annoyed.

"I wish she'd explained them to me, then," he said. "I just saw her at the ball game."

"Did Jack do anything awful?" Karla asked.

"Yes," he said, and waited, but Karla didn't ask what. She was watching Roger Moore look sophisticated. He was in a ski lodge somewhere in the Alps.

Karla seemed to have a new hairdo. Her hair was cut shorter. She seemed to look younger. Her beautiful skin seemed even more beautiful. The more Duane looked at her the more confused he felt. She had only been gone a few days, and yet she looked a great deal better than she had when she left—and she had looked fine when she left.

"You look great," he said.

Karla glanced at him, lifted an eyebrow and went on watching the movie.

"Why did Jacy have to explain my problems to you?" he

asked. "She hasn't seen me in thirty years. You've seen me every day for twenty-two years. Why didn't you explain my problems to her?"

"Duane, she's lived in Europe, don't get uptight," Karla said.

Not an hour before, Jacy had accused him of being uptight.

"I am uptight," he said. "I can't help it. I don't know what's going on. She says she's taking you and the twins to Europe. And maybe Dickie too. I don't know what's going on."

"Nellie wants to go too," Karla informed him.

"Why don't I get to go?" Duane asked. "I've never been to Europe. Maybe I'd like to go."

"And leave your oil well just when you finally got one?" Karla said.

She had a point. He didn't want to leave his Mississippi. He wanted to drill another one, in fact. But for the sake of argument it was a point he chose to ignore.

"If all you have to do to understand people's problems is live in Europe, then I want to move there," he said. "I don't understand anything. Everything around here is crazy. People run off with one another at the drop of a hat. One kiss and they're gone."

"Well, that's just the the way life is, Duane," Karla said. "Talk quieter or you'll wake the baby."

Duane didn't feel like talking quieter. He felt like yelling. The fact that Billie Anne had run off with Junior was the last straw. It might appear to solve Dickie's problem, and also Suzie's, but he still didn't care—it was still the last straw. Everybody was crazy. Nobody had any restraint. He himself had just had sex with a married woman in the middle of downtown Thalia.

It made him feel like throwing something. He looked around the room and noticed his leather hippo. Karla had bought it in Dallas to go with the new house. It sat in front of a fancy leather chair that was supposed to be his. The hippo was designed to be a footstool. He could sit in the leather chair, which had cost untold thousands, and put his feet on the hippo, which had only cost something like eighteen hundred. In fact, he had never sat in the chair, much less put his feet on the hippo.

He grabbed the hippo and flung it at the glass doors before

noticing that they were open. The hippo sailed harmlessly outside and landed on the deck.

Karla raised an eyebrow again.

"Duane, you worry me," she said. "There was no reason at all for you to throw your hippo outside."

"I know that," he said. "I just threw it outside for no reason at all."

"Nothing happens for no reason at all," Karla said. "Any psychiatrist will tell you that."

He went down the hall and looked in on his grandaughter. To his surprise, she was awake. She was lying in her crib, her eyes wide-open, babbling and chortling to herself. She was happy to see him too. She began to kick her legs and wave her arms, chortling strenuously. Duane picked her up and walked outside with her. Barbette stopped chortling and stared at the stars. Duane sat down by the pool and in the space of a minute or two she went to sleep. Duane soon felt much calmer. He heard some coyotes yipping. They were having a party under the bluff.

When he got up to take Barbette in, he noticed the hippo. Not wanting it to escape unscathed, he addressed it as if it were a football and kicked it into the pool.

"I don't understand what's going on between you and Jacy," he said, when he came back to the bedroom.

"That's all right because it's none of your business," Karla said, without belligerence.

"Let's go to a psychiatrist," she added.

"Why?" he asked.

"Something new," Karla said. "We don't ever do anything new. A marriage can get stagnant if the husband and wife don't ever do a single thing new."

"I'm going bankrupt," Duane said. "That's new. And you just moved in with one of my old girlfriends. Doesn't that count as new?"

"No, because it makes you uptight," Karla said, "and there's nothing new about you being uptight."

"Okay, okay," Duane said. "I'll do anything to convince you I'm willing to do something new."

"Duane, that's sweet that you agreed," Karla said.

CHAPTER 63

KARLA PROMPTLY MADE AN APPOINTMENT WITH A psychiatrist in Fort Worth. Unfortunately the appointment was on a Monday morning, the day the centennial was scheduled to officially begin. But the appointment was for 8 A.M. and the centennial didn't kick off until noon, so they could easily make it back in time. The first event was a mini-marathon which would start at Aunt Jimmie's Lounge and end at the red light. Duane was supposed to hand out ribbons to the winners.

During the night he had had a dream about Jacy. He had been ineffective in the dream. He and Jacy had been going somewhere and his pickup had run out of gas. Jacy hadn't been angry. She had smiled tolerantly. But he still woke up feeling inept. He decided not to tell either Karla or the psychiatrist about the dream. They would just try to convince him that he was falling back in love with Jacy, and he didn't think he was, although the dream left him feeling quite depressed.

"I wonder what he'll want to talk to us about?" Karla asked, as they parked in the gloomy underground parking garage beneath the building where the psychiatrist had his office.

"I hate underground garages," Duane said.

"Duane, don't always be a fault finder," Karla said.

"A lot of people get mugged in these big-city garages," Duane said.

"There's no law saying you couldn't park on the street," Karla said.

"Sure there is," Duane said. "Every sign in downtown Fort Worth says 'No parking.' "

"I hope you tell the psychiatrist how you can't stop exaggerating," Karla said.

"I will, if we don't get mugged going into his office," Duane said.

They didn't get mugged, or even noticed.

"I hope we don't have to describe our sex life," Karla said. "I don't like to describe mine."

"That's news," Duane said. "You used to describe it on T-shirts all the time."

"Duane, I did not," Karla said.

Their psychiatrist turned out to be a handsome, cheerful young Hispanic named Carillo. That he was Hispanic took Duane by surprise. He had been under the impression that most psychiatrists were Jewish. Karla seemed surprised too, though mostly by the man's youth.

"Have you been out of psychiatry school long?" she asked.

Dr. Carillo chuckled. "We're here to talk about you folks," he said. "We're not here to talk about me. Mr. Moore, I find it very interesting that you choose to wear a heavy beard."

"Well, that's because our county centennial starts today," he said. "We're all supposed to look like pioneers. Any man that don't grow a beard can be ducked in a horse trough, if the people who catch him are strong enough to duck him."

"Do you fear drowning?" Dr. Carillo asked, scribbling on a pad.

"No," Duane said. "I don't much fear being ducked. But I'm the head of the Centennial Committee, so I couldn't really refuse to grow a beard. Everybody would have said I wasn't patriotic."

"A beard can be a mask," Dr. Carillo said enigmatically.

"With a heavy beard like that it is harder for people to detect your feelings."

"I just grew it because of the centennial," Duane said. "I don't like beards. They itch too much."

"Your age is forty-eight?"

"That's right."

"Beards can be a symbol of virility," Dr. Carillo said. "Men sometimes grow them who aren't feeling too young anymore. If they have doubts about their potency they may grow a nice beard to reassure themselves. You know, a nice beard looks virile."

Duane said nothing. He had already stated plainly that he had grown the beard because of the centennial, and saw no reason to say it again.

"He's got one of the nicest beards in the whole county," Karla said, trying to be helpful. "A lot of the men just look scruffy."

Dr. Carillo seemed to be extremely cheerful. He stopped asking questions about the beard and merely sat and beamed at them. Silence grew. Dr. Carillo seemed in no hurry to ask questions. He just sat behind his desk and smiled.

Duane looked at Karla. She had been to psychiatrists before and should know what to do. Perhaps they were supposed to be talking, describing their problems, asking advice.

But Karla seemed uncertain. She didn't say a word. Minutes passed—perhaps four of five of them. Duane kept glancing at his watch. It seemed like hours were passing, but in fact the silence had only lasted a few minutes.

"You folks aren't very forthcoming," Dr. Carillo said. "I think we have to look more deeply into the matter of the beard. Often things appear to have simple causes. We think we do them for a simple reason. But underneath lurks the real reason. We may not want to admit to ourselves what the real reason is. We may want to mask this reason from ourselves because we feel uneasy about it."

"I think that's true," Karla said, grateful for any comment.

"That beard may help you mask your true feelings from your wife," Dr. Carillo said. "That's one use of a mask. But then you mention this centennial. You say you grew the beard because of the centennial. But stop and think, Mr. Moore. The centennial may only have provided you with an excuse. If you didn't want a beard, you didn't have to grow one just because of a little peer pressure. What's a little ducking, anyway? In this heat we all ought to jump in a horse trough. It's a cheap way of getting cool. So if the centennial was just an excuse, we ought to ask ourselves what was the real reason you grew the beard."

"The centennial was the real reason I grew the beard," Duane said. "The real reason and the only reason."

"I hear belligerence in your voice now," Dr. Carillo said. "Maybe we are making progress. You don't like me asking these questions. You don't want to discover the real reason you grew the beard."

"I told you the real reason," Duane insisted.

"Then why do you sound belligerent?"

"Because you won't believe me," Duane said. "I've told you several times but you won't believe me. I didn't grow the damn beard because I was impotent. I've been impotent off and on for years. I grew the beard because of the centennial."

Dr. Carillo kept beaming.

"I think you're lying about this impotence," Dr. Carillo said. "You look like a virile man to me. You have a fine beard and that in itself is a sign of virility. You are probably just trying to distract me. As a psychiatrist I have to deal with many patients who try to distract me. A patient might casually admit to impotence in order to keep me from questioning him about what is really disturbing him."

"His impotence really disturbs *me*," Karla said. She was getting tired of being left out of the discussion.

"I wouldn't mind it so much," she added, "except that I hear all over town that he has girlfriends and nobody ever claims he's impotent with them."

"One person at a time," Dr. Carillo said. "I'm just beginning to make some progress with Mr. Moore. The ladies will have to wait."

"What ladies?" Karla asked. "I'm the only woman here."

"Keep quiet, woman!" Dr. Carillo said. "It's very important that I discover your husband's true feelings. Don't interrupt when the doctor is talking."

"What about *my* true feelings?" Karla said. "You wouldn't have to poke around for an hour to discover mine. I could tell you my true feelings in about two minutes."

"Go on, Mr. Moore," Dr. Carillo said. "Ignore her. Aren't you lying about this impotence?"

"No," Duane said.

"He better not ignore me, either," Karla said. "I'm his wife. We came here to get healed together and all you've done is ask him stupid questions about his beard. You haven't even looked at me."

"Shut up, you hysterical bitch," Dr. Carillo said. He suddenly jumped up, seized his wastebasket and flung its contents willy-nilly about the room. He seemed to have eaten lots of oranges. Several carefully pared rolls of orange peel got scattered around.

"Hysterical? I'm just sitting here with my hands in my lap," Karla said.

"You don't obey!" Dr. Carillo said. "You should be put in a straitjacket and shot full of mood drugs. Those mood drugs would fix you."

He began to pull drawers out of his desk and fling their contents around the room. Papers and file cards mixed with orange peels on his carpet.

"If I had a straitjacket I'd put it on you myself," Dr. Carillo said. "I'd shoot you full of mood drugs. We'd see how you like being a vegetable."

Duane and Karla looked at one another.

"Win a few, lose a few," Karla said. "Let's go home."

Duane looked at his watch. They had only used up half their hour, but it was obviously no time to count pennies. Dr. Carillo ran over to a file cabinet and yanked open a drawer. He began to fling files in the air.

"I wonder if psychiatrists go to psychiatrists?" Karla asked, as they were driving out of Fort Worth. Dr. Carillo, busy flinging his files around the room, had not appeared to notice their departure. He seemed intent on flinging every single file.

"I don't know why, but I feel better," Duane said.

"I don't," Karla said. "It's unfair if you do. Why do you?"

"Because we got out of that garage without being mugged," he said.

"Oh, Duane, it's broad daylight," Karla said.

She was studying a questionnaire Dr. Carillo had handed them at the beginning of the interview. They were supposed to fill them out before the next visit.

"There's a question about frequency of sexual intercourse," Karla said.

"Don't answer it," Duane said. "We're not going back, anyway."

"I know, but just reading these questions makes me feel depressed," Karla said. "I was feeling real cheerful this morning, but now I feel like I don't know which way to turn."

"You don't have to turn anywhere," Duane said. "The centennial's about to start, and when that's over you're going to Europe with Jacy. By the time you get back things might look completely different."

"You won't be completely different," Karla said. "You don't know how to be completely different. You don't know how to be *any* different."

"Well, neither do you," Duane said. "Why do we have to be so different? I still love you."

He reached over and took her hand. Karla immediately began to cry.

"Why are you crying?" he asked. "What's happening that's so bad?"

"Reading this questionnaire's real depressing," she said in a choked voice. "I bet everybody we know could give more normal answers than we can. Even Bobby Lee's probably more normal. It makes me feel like we're freaks, but when we got married we were just as normal as anybody."

Duane grabbed the questionnaires and threw them out the window. There was a brisk south wind blowing. The papers blew high in the air.

"We're still as normal as anybody," Duane said, though he knew he had no way of judging just how normal other people were.

"Duane, you didn't have to litter," Karla said.

CHAPTER 64

EVEN BEFORE THEY ENTERED HARDTOP COUNTY, traffic began to pick up. The main artery through Thalia—little more than a farm-to-market road—was solid with pickups and cars. When they passed Aunt Jimmie's Lounge they saw several mini-marathoners warming up.

A big sign with an arrow had been erected beside the road. It read: ORIGINAL SITE OF TEXASVILLE, FIRST TOWN IN HARDTOP COUNTY, ONE HUNDRED AND FIFTY YARDS DUE NORTH. The arrow pointed to an empty pasture, but Buster Lickle was already there, showing two or three astonished farmers the authentic boards he had kicked up.

Ruth Popper stood by the side of the road, doing stretching exercises. She had equipped herself with goggles for the event, a wise move. The south wind had become brisker, moving a good deal of grit across the road.

Lester, an occasional runner, had also entered the mini-marathon. He was jogging around and around Aunt Jimmie's Lounge, watched by Janine, who sat in the car with the windows rolled up. Janine had never liked the dust.

John Cecil, who was likely to be Ruth's only serious competition, looked natty in a blue running suit. He was doing exercises. Karla waved and he gave her a quick smile.

"I feel sorry for John," she said. "I don't think Thalia's a good town to be gay in. I wish he could find a steady boyfriend."

"Maybe he doesn't want one," Duane suggested.

Karla thought it over. "Well, he might like a nice little person to come home to," she said. "Somebody to watch TV with at night."

"We could lend him Minerva," Duane said.

"Not unless we lent him the dish too," Karla said. "Minerva really would get a brain tumor if she had to watch normal TV."

They followed the line of cars and pickups into Thalia. The square was already packed with people.

"I guess they came to hear the Governor," Duane said. The Governor was due to arrive shortly after lunch to congratulate the county on its one hundredth birthday.

"No, they probably heard you were giving away beer," Karla said. "You shouldn't have let G.G. back you down, Duane. You should have sold the beer, and if he didn't like it, tough shit."

"He didn't back me down," Duane said. "I just got tired of arguing about it."

"Wore you down then," Karla said. "It makes me jealous. He can wear you down and I can't."

"What did you want to wear me down on now?" Duane asked.

"I don't want to talk about it," Karla said. "We drove all the way to Fort Worth to talk about it and all that happened was that a Mexican psychiatrist tore up his own office. I'll just give up and do exactly as I please from now on."

"I thought you were already doing exactly as you pleased," Duane said.

"Why did you grow that beard, Duane?" she asked. They were inching toward the crowd, hoping to spot a place to park.

"You know perfectly well why I grew it," he said. "I grew it because of this centennial that we're in a traffic jam in."

"Jacy says you're not very self-aware," Karla said. She was smiling and waving at various people they knew.

Duane waved too, but he had a sinking heart.

"I guess all you and Jacy have to do is talk about me," he said. He was hoping she would deny it and describe what the two of them did do, but Karla acted as if she hadn't heard him.

"I grew this goddamn beard because of the centennial," he said, but he no longer expected anyone, even Karla, to believe him.

They found a parking place three blocks from the square. Karla had her cowgirl clothes in the car. She was supposed to ride into town with the centennial wagon train, which had been straggling across the county for the past two days and was supposed to arrive in Thalia in time to lead the parade that afternoon. The wagon train consisted of five or six wagons and anyone with a horse who wanted to ride along.

The sight of all the people caused Karla's spirits to rise.

"I'm getting excited," she said. "This is a lot more people than show up for a rodeo. It's nice to see people all over the streets."

The minute he parked she grabbed her cowgirl clothes and walked into the nearest house to put them on. Duane was shocked. The nearest house happened to belong to a strange couple who took walks in the middle of the night with their fat dog. Karla didn't know them very well, nor did anyone else.

Three minutes later Karla popped out. She pitched her other clothes in the back seat.

"Those people might not want you just walking into their house," Duane said.

"I looked at their wedding pictures," Karla said.

"Why?" he asked. "How can you just walk into somebody's house and look at their wedding pictures?"

"It was my only chance," Karla said. "It looks like they had a real nice wedding."

Duane had bought a cowboy hat, which was all he intended to do in the way of costuming, but Karla had got him a velvet vest of the kind riverboat gamblers were supposed to wear. Duane thought he looked silly in it and had refused to bring it.

"You couldn't get a riverboat within a thousand miles of here," he had pointed out that morning, when Karla was badgering him to bring the vest.

As they were walking toward the courthouse she returned to the subject.

"It wouldn't hurt you to wear that nice vest I bought you, at least on the first day," she said. "You could have gone along with the centennial spirit at least that much."

"I'm not putting on any velvet vests," Duane said, more angrily than he meant to.

"Why not?" Karla asked.

"There's no reason," Duane said. "I'm just not putting on that vest. Do we have to argue about it?"

"Duane, there's a reason for every single thing you do," she said. "The reason in this case is that you just don't want to do anything I ask you to, or else you don't think you look macho enough in velvet."

"I don't think I look macho enough in velvet," Duane said. "That's the reason. Now are you happy?"

"I think Richie did a real nice job of building Old Texasville," Karla said.

CHAPTER 65

UNDER HEAVY PRESSURE FROM DUANE, BOBBY LEE and Eddie Belt had agreed to represent the founders of the county, Mr. Brown and Mr. Brown. The roles required them to sit in front of the replica of Texasville all day, dispensing the free beer Duane had ordered. If there was an assault from the Byelo-Baptists, they would be the ones to receive it.

Bobby and Eddie both had cups of beer in their hands, but no Byelo-Baptists were assaulting. The largest crowd was over in one corner of the square.

"Howdy," Duane said. "Had any trouble with G.G.?"

"Nope," Bobby Lee said. "He's got worse sinners than us to worry about."

"If you're the bartender, make me a red dog," Karla said.

"I can't unless you brought some tomato juice," Bobby Lee said. "They didn't carry tomato juice in the Texasville days."

Old Man Balt, in his honored position as the county's oldest citizen, sat under the best shade tree on the lawn. He wore a crisp white shirt and a ten-gallon hat. Several people with cameras were squatting to take his picture.

"What's the crowd in the corner doing?" Duane inquired.

"They're looking at Junior and Billie Anne," Bobby Lee said. "They're gonna starve themselves to death unless they get what they want."

"What do they want?" Karla asked.

"I don't know if they even know themselves," Bobby Lee said.

"Sure they do," Eddie Belt said. "He's fasting for an oil embargo and Billie Anne's fasting for no-fault divorce."

Duane edged through the crowd. Junior and Billie Anne had erected a small tent and were sitting outside it in lawn chairs, holding hands for all to see. G. G. Rawley was glaring at them.

"These sinners have a mattress in that tent," G.G. said, spotting Duane. "Who said they could put up a tent and put a mattress in it?"

"Not me," Duane said.

"We're on a fast," Junior said. "We just brought the mattress for when we get too weak to sit up."

Billie Anne was glaring at G.G. She didn't appear to be entirely sober.

"You old bully," she said. "Just leave us alone so we can starve in peace."

G.G. turned his glare on Duane.

"Make 'em take down this filthy tent," he said.

"Go away or I'll shoot you," Billie Anne said. "I've shot two people already and you'll make three."

Like many people, she was taking advantage of the historical nature of the celebration to wear holsters with pistols in them. They didn't look like cap pistols, either.

"In the old days people that behaved like you two would be stoned with rocks," G.G. said. He looked as if he would enjoy stoning them with rocks.

Duane stepped back. He decided he would pretend he was a simple visitor to the events. It might be fun to wander around, drink beer and strike up conversations with residents of remote areas of the county—people seldom seen in town.

On the south side of the square, several carnival workers, all of them sickly-looking, were putting up a small Ferris wheel and one or two other rides. The barbecue caterers were setting up long tables on which to serve the first of many barbecues. The wind had increased, and many men wearing new Stetsons had them suddenly blow off and sail through the air. Men who rarely chased anything were chasing new hats across the courthouse lawn.

Normally no one paid much attention to wind in Thalia. It was usually blowing and, like tap water, was either hot or cold depending on the season. But the present wind seemed unusually stiff. The tent Junior and Billie Anne had put up for their fast began to flap. It was not very securely pegged and the wind seemed capable of blowing it away. In fact, the wind was so strong that it threatened to blow the crowd away. People were beginning to drift to the north side of the courthouse seeking shelter from it.

Bobby Lee and Eddie Belt began to experience troubles, too. The wind suddenly blew several huge stacks of beer cups off the tables. Beer cups rolled everywhere. Stacks broke up and clumps of beer cups flew into the street. Bobby Lee and Eddie Belt, working frantically, caught a few of them, but many escaped.

Duane stooped to catch a stack of cups just blowing past him and happened to notice a large tumbleweed blowing down the main street. It was nearly the size of a Volkswagen and it tumbled at a good pace right through town.

Tumbleweeds were common enough. They blew off the cracked fields and parched pastures south of town. South winds were not uncommon, particularly in August—they were hot winds, and unwelcome. But this particular south wind seemed to be getting out of hand. Men were holding their hats, women their skirts. The wind was becoming a gale.

Duane looked to the sky, thinking perhaps they were in the path of a late-summer tornado. There was a dull coloring of dust in the lower reaches, but otherwise the sky was clear.

The big tumbleweed rumbled under the red light and rolled on toward Wichita Falls. Bobby Lee, his arms full of beer cups, stood watching it with a certain awe. The sight of the tumbleweed had raised his spirits.

"Where's Toots?" he yelled. "Where's the Highway Patrol?"

"Why do you want 'em?" Duane asked.

"I want them to give that tumbleweed a ticket," Bobby Lee said. "It's exceeding the speed limit and besides that it ran a red light."

Then his sombrero blew off. It soared over the crowd like a bird. Bobby still held the beer cups. At first he merely watched his sombrero go. Then he began to run after it, dropping beer cups as he ran. By then the hat had a big lead. It landed thirty yards down the street, but then the wind lifted it again and it sailed on in the wake of the tumbleweed. It flew about waist-high, reminding Duane of Briscoe the roadrunner. Duane's new hat blew off too. He grabbed for it but missed, and since he really didn't like cowboy hats, let it go.

He looked around in time to see the tent jerk loose from its pegs and slide into the street. It smacked up against the fire truck, which had been parked close by in case of emergencies. Junior and Billie Anne continued to sit in their lawn chairs, holding hands.

The wind, hot as the exhaust of a truck, was increasing in force. Eddie Belt struggled against it, trying to reach Duane's side. He had a happy look on his face—like many Texans he was cheered by extremes of weather.

"Oh, boy," he yelled. "It's really starting to blow now. Just feel this wind."

"I feel it but I wish it would stop," Duane said. "It's almost time for the Governor to show up."

CHAPTER 66

DUANE BEGAN TO LOOK FOR KARLA. HE ARRIVED AT the barbecue tables just in time to see all the paper plates blow away in a whoosh of wind. The caterers, trying to keep the barbecue itself secure, could only watch things go.

Virtually the whole crowd was now huddled on the north side of the courthouse, trying to keep from blowing away themselves. Karla wasn't there, nor was she in the courthouse—probably she had already left to join the wagon train. Duane had no real need to find her—he just wanted to. He felt that she was in a strange mood, and experience had taught him that it was better to try and keep her in sight at such times.

It wasn't a catastrophic mood, in his view, but it was not exactly a good mood either, and the knowledge that Karla was in it made him feel tense.

So it had been all through their marriage. In order to relax, himself, he had to know that Karla was no longer in a bad mood. Since he had to greet the Governor of the state in a few minutes, he needed to be as relaxed as possible, and it wasn't possible to be very relaxed in a towering gale when he didn't know what state Karla might be in.

In the courthouse he ran into Sonny. As mayor of the town, Sonny also had to greet the Governor. Sonny looked silly. He had bought a cowboy hat for the centennial, but, being frugal, had only spent twelve dollars on it. Duane didn't have the heart to tell him that a twelve-dollar cowboy hat looked worse than no cowboy hat at all. Sonny had also bought a cheap string tie with a piece of fake turquoise as a knot. It was the sort of tie sold in truck stops all over the west. The tie and hat made Sonny look like a tourist—in the town he had lived in all his life.

"We better go out," Sonny said. "The marathoners should be here in five or ten minutes. We're supposed to hold the finish line."

They looked out the door and saw several more tumbleweeds blowing across the lawn and down the street. They were not as big as the first tumbleweeds, but they were zipping along.

"Those marathoners won't be setting any world records today," Duane said. Unfortunately the route of the marathon led directly into the wind.

"I'm going up to the second floor," he said. There was a little balcony there. He could look up the road and see how far away the marathoners were.

Sonny followed him up. From the balcony they could see twenty miles to the north, and at least that far to the south. It took only a little height to reveal Thalia for what it was—a tiny spot of town in the midst of a vast, scrubby plain.

Duane easily spotted the marathoners. The road to the north was speckled with them.

Two runners were far ahead of the pack.

"I guess this wind's weeded out the men from the boys," Sonny said.

"No," Duane said, "it's weeded out the runners from the walkers, and one of the runners isn't a man or a boy. One of them's Ruth."

"It was just a figure of speech," Sonny said quickly.

Duane happened to glance to the south and immediately forgot all about figures of speech. The road to the south was also speckled with racers—and not just the road, either. These racers spread across the pastures and fields as well. Several hundred were already in the streets of Thalia, blowing across lawns and crashing into fences and parked automobiles.

The racers from the south were tumbleweeds, thousands and thousands of them. The extraordinary wind had broken them loose from the thin soil—they were rumbling into Thalia like a herd of migrating beasts. They bounced, they skidded, they rolled over cars, now and then soaring for a few yards like great thorny birds.

"My God," Duane said, "it's a tumbleweed stampede."

Sonny seemed dumbfounded, and Duane couldn't blame him. A spiky parade of tumbleweeds was bouncing down the main street, and tributary parades down all the other streets. They came tumbling across the courthouse lawn so rapidly that Junior and Billie Anne didn't have time to run for their pickup —all they could do was cower behind the mattress that had aroused G.G.'s ire.

"They'll wipe out the marathoners," Duane said. To the south, as far as he could see, more tumbleweeds were coming. From horizon to horizon they came, covering the whole plain solidly, as the herds of buffalo had once been said to cover it.

The tumbleweeds rolled in, bouncing and leaping like live things. A startled Bobby Lee, returning exhausted from the successful pursuit of his sombrero, took refuge behind the gas pumps in the filling station. The people on the north side of the courthouse watched in amazement as the tumbleweeds swept past. Weeds began to smash into parked cars, entangling themselves. Barricades of tumbleweeds began to grow— fences of weeds, stretching beyond the lines of cars. Small tumbleweeds the size of Shorty raced on through town. Larger ones, the size of cows, hit the barricades and stuck.

To the north the marathoners were still coming, jogging relentlessly, perhaps not yet aware of what was sweeping down on them. The two in the lead were almost to the city limits sign; they matched one another stride for stride.

"It might just be temporary," Sonny said. "The wind might die."

Duane looked south. The wind was not dying, and the tumbleweeds in their tens of thousands were still racing into Thalia. He heard a droning noise. A speck that could have been a bird but sounded more like a helicopter hovered over the marathoners.

"Here comes the Governor," Duane said. "We gotta get down there."

They raced down the stairs and out into the street. The marathon was to finish right under the red light. Duane remembered his moment of bliss in that spot but had no time for pleasant reminiscence—stretching a finish line with tumbleweeds the size of Volkswagens bearing down on one was no simple feat. The little scurrying tumbleweeds they could jump, but the larger ones presented problems.

Just as they were about to get the line stretched, a tumbleweed of modest size bounced right between them and yanked the line out of Sonny's hands. Duane hung on to his end, but the tumbleweed, unwilling to stop, bucked and cracked around like a roped animal. The line was soon hopelessly snarled. Sonny tried to get it loose but merely lost his twelve-dollar hat in the process. Duane, seeing that it was hopeless, turned his end loose. The tumbleweed immediately carried the finish line down the street toward the marathoners.

"Let's just line up," Duane said. "Whoever goes between us first is the winner."

"I don't think they're gonna make it," Sonny said. "They seem to be slowing down."

Indeed, both the marathoners and the helicopter were tiring. The adverse wind factors seemed to be holding them in suspended animation. The marathoners' legs still went up and down, the helicopter's blades went round and round, but neither were making more than minimal forward progress.

Duane glanced around and saw a phalanx of at least fifty tumbleweeds bearing down on them. Dodging one only brought one into the path of another. Sonny did just that, and a middle-sized tumbleweed smacked into him with such force that he was caught, his legs entangled, as if he had jumped into the weed. As Sonny tried to pull the weed off his legs, another struck and stuck. A barricade began to form around Sonny as more weeds quickly added themselves to the pile.

Duane started to run for the shelter of the bank but decided that would be cowardly—he concentrated on dodging. He felt like laughing at Sonny's plight. Sonny could be the victim of a horror movie—the man attacked by killer weeds. Soon the weeds would cover him completely, and when they were finally pulled off him he would be found to be a bloodless corpse. Or perhaps the weeds would incorporate him into their species, and he would stalk the town on windy days, the dread Tumbleweed Man, a huge hulk of weeds ensnaring beautiful women in his thorny clasp.

Sonny was trying to drag his heap of weeds over to the courthouse before so many piled on that he couldn't move.

Duane found that by facing the oncoming weeds he could dodge them if he stayed nimble. It reminded him of a football drill—sometimes he had to dart right, sometimes left.

Meanwhile the runners and the helicopter had inched a block closer to the intersection. They were only three blocks away. The runners, Ruth Popper and John Cecil, were tired but game. So many tumbleweeds rolled down the street that they too had to keep dodging left and right, making only lateral progress. Both looked determined, though.

The helicopter was only a few yards ahead of them. Duane could see three men in it, one of them undoubtedly the Governor. Trying to be hospitable, he waved. He felt a little awkward, being the sole welcomer of the Governor of the state. The helicopter inched closer and came lower. Duane, still dodging weeds, could not give it his full attention, but when the noise of its motors began to drown out the wind he glanced up again. The helicopter had come level with the hardware store. It was only thirty feet off the ground. Two men in suits seemd perplexed as they looked down upon the huddled crowd and the wilderness of tumbleweeds. Wherever cars were parked, walls of tumbleweeds had formed, and the walls were rising higher.

Duane recognized the helicopter pilot, too. It was Karla's old friend Randy, who had a knack for turning up just when no one wanted him. He looked as cocky as ever, but the Governor's aide, sitting beside him, didn't look cocky. The aide turned to the Governor and gestured hopelessly. The Governor looked dazed, and with some reason. From where he sat he must have been seeing a strange sight—a town buried by an eruption, not of lava, but of tumbleweeds.

Ruth and John were only fifty yards away. Duane tried to concentrate on his duties as an official finish line. He pretended he was holding up a tape. It looked as if John might win. He had a step on Ruth, but John had never been lucky, and the bad luck that had dogged him all his life smacked right into him in the form of four tumbleweeds that were traveling as a pack. Two veered slightly toward Ruth, but she managed to hurdle them. When her feet left the ground the wind blew her back a step. John Cecil tried to slip between the two that were headed for him, and miscalculated. A tumbleweed hit each leg. He didn't fall, but it was all he could do to lift his feet. Game to the end, he tried dragging the tumbleweeds over the finish line, but other tumbleweeds, as if sensing a victim, began to pile on. Ruth crossed the finish line and ran for shelter. Duane went to help John, who was making no forward progress at all. Together they reached the bank building. John was too winded to speak.

Above them, the helicopter hovered. Duane waved, trying to indicate to Randy that he could land in the shelter of the bank building. Randy, with his usual insolence, ignored him. The helicopter hung just over the red light. The Governor and his aide were whispering to one another. Tumbleweeds continued to bounce down the street. They were piling up against the front of every building that faced south. Some buildings were covered almost to their roofs. The gas pumps behind which Bobby Lee cowered were completely covered. He could barely be seen, crouched with his sombrero in an igloo of tumbleweeds.

The Governor looked down at Duane and made a gesture of helplessness. He waved vigorously at the people beside the courthouse. Then the helicopter banked sharply and headed back north. Soon it was just a speck in the distance.

Duane watched it go with mixed feelings. It was too bad to lose the Governor, but who could regret losing Randy? The wind had reached its height—they could scarcely see ten feet in the dust. John Cecil had stopped trying to get the tumbleweeds off his legs and stood quietly, catching his breath. Another Volkswagen-sized tumbleweed rumbled beneath the red light, followed by a host of little ones as a mother hen would be followed by her chicks.

Duane felt a sudden, inexplicable pride of place. The same land that had broken the two Mr. Browns had lost none of its power or its capacity for surprise. It had shown its strength once again, driving away a Governor and temporarily stopping the Hardtop County centennial dead in its tracks.

"I guess the Governor doesn't like our weather," he said.

"I didn't vote for him anyway," John Cecil said.

CHAPTER 67

IN ANOTHER FORTY-FIVE MINUTES THE WIND BLEW itself out and the tumbleweeds stopped tumbling. The people stepped out from behind the courthouse and looked in awe at their town. Walls of tumbleweeds covered every store front, every fence, every line of cars.

People with cameras took pictures. The tiny TV crew, sent from Wichita Falls to cover the Governor's visit, covered the tumbleweeds instead. The barbecue team went to John Cecil's grocery store and Sonny's Kwik-Sack and bought every paper plate in town. Pitchforks were secured from the feed store, tumbleweeds were raked off doorways, and the centennial was soon proceeding merrily. People wandered around with plates of barbecue, staring at the tumbleweeds with pride.

Everyone was in a remarkably good humor. Any county could have a centennial, but how many had had a tumbleweed stampede? Junior Nolan and Billie Anne, who had survived it with only a mattress for cover, felt that their fast for an oil embargo and no-fault divorce was off to a good start.

G. G. Rawley was equally cheered. In his view the Lord had

given the town a mild but unequivocal warning. Always a big eater, he consumed several plates of barbecue, assuring people, between bites, that unless they kept the celebration sober they were sure to reap the real whirlwind next time.

Almost everyone was outraged that the Governor had not cared to wait out the little storm. Bobby Lee, who had to be cut out of his igloo of tumbleweeds with a chain saw, was the most indignant. He favored taking a delegation to Austin to picket the Capitol with signs declaring the Governor a cowardly chicken-shit.

A report, relayed through Toots Burns, that the Governor had merely rushed back to Austin so he could immediately recommend the county for disaster aid, fooled no one.

"What disaster?" Eddie Belt asked. "The only bad thing that's happened is that a woman won the marathon."

Duane ate a little barbecue and then walked over to the bank. He had about twenty thousand dollars' worth of production checks to deposit. The sight of even modest deposits usually cheered Lester Marlow up, but this one didn't. He sat in his office staring blankly at some computer read-outs. His hair looked wilder than ever and he was still in his running clothes. He took the deposit listlessly and put it on his desk.

"That's twenty thousand dollars," Duane said. "Don't forget I gave it to you."

"Somebody will find it after I'm gone," Lester said.

"Gone where?"

"After I've committed suicide," Lester said. "The centennial's off to a good start now, I don't see any reason to wait."

"Ride out to the well with me," Duane suggested. "It might cheer you up."

Lester agreed, but decided to change clothes first. While he was changing, Duane reclaimed his deposit and gave it to a teller. The tellers were all wearing cowboy hats in honor of the centennial. Some wore cap pistols too. When Lester came back he wore a shirt and tie but also a cowboy hat and a cap pistol.

"You won't need a tie out at the well," Duane remarked.

"It makes me feel more confident that I've made the right choice," Lester said.

Over the last two years, Lester had often talked of suicide, but had never attempted it. The town had grown complacent, and Duane with it, but looking at Lester's wild hair, cap pistol and dull eyes, he decided complacency might be a mistake. Lester might really do it. He might just be taking slow aim at himself.

They drove past the square, Duane rehearsing antisuicide arguments. On the square they saw a struggling knot of men. For a moment Duane thought a fight had broken out between the Byelo-Baptists and the drinkers, but then he spotted Joe Coombs at the center of the knot and revised his opinion. It was just a group of celebrants trying to duck the beardless little Joe. There seemed to be about ten men trying to duck him, but so far little Joe Coombs was holding his own.

"That little Joe Coombs has got a low center of gravity," Duane remarked.

Lester observed the scene dully. He had grown a little fuzz on his big chin. It was not much, but so far it had kept him from being ducked.

"Janine's happy," he remarked. "I've made someone happy, at least."

"That's true," Duane said.

"I've lived nearly twenty-five years with Jenny and never made her happy a single day," Lester said. "I never thought I'd live to see the day when I could actually make someone happy."

"But now you have," Duane said.

"Maybe that's why I want to commit suicide right now," Lester said. "I think I ought to kill myself before I spoil it."

Duane started to point out to Lester that his death might well spoil Janine's new happiness. It might ruin his two nice daughters' lives. It might drive Jenny over the edge she seemed to live on. It might even have a ripple effect in Thalia itself. People who had never particularly liked Lester might blame themselves for his death. The whole town might slip into an emotional decline matching its economic decline. It might even be slipping into one anyway, with Lester still alive.

But he didn't make any of those points. The more he thought about Lester and suicide and emotional decline, the less talkative he felt. The two of them rode in silence along the hot dusty road. The heat had been so intense all summer that the juice had burned out of the mesquite beans within a week. They hung from the trees in brown clumps. From a distance it looked as if some madman had decorated the trees with lots of burned French fries.

Nonetheless, as they approached the well site, Duane felt his spirits rise. Somewhere, deep beneath the baking mesquites, was a lake of precious liquid, and he already had a pipe that reached into the center of that lake. As soon as storage tanks were in place he could turn the switch and liquid money would begin to flow upward—millions' worth, perhaps. If he could just sink a couple more pipes into the lake, his troubles, and at least some of Lester's, would be over.

"This might be the best well I've ever drilled," he said, his excitement growing as they bumped along the rutted road to the site. "It might solve all our troubles."

Lester looked at him with the same dull hopelessness.

"Didn't you read *The Wall Street Journal* this morning?" he asked.

"No, I went to a psychiatrist this morning," Duane said.

He never read *The Wall Street Journal*. Sonny brought his copy to the Dairy Queen each morning and read the assembled oilmen whatever it said about the international oil situation or the Texas oil situation. Sometimes there would even be something in the *Journal* about the local oil situation, but Duane never had to bother reading it for himself. The news, good or bad, would be on everyone's lips by the time he arrived at the Dairy Queen for coffee.

"What'd it say today?" he asked.

"It said the Saudis were going to open the pipes," Lester said. "Minister Yamani's tired of fucking around with the British. He says he'll make us all listen. He says he'll show us five-dollar oil, if that's what it takes to get our attention."

"Minister Yamani's probably bluffing," Duane said. "He don't really want to sell his oil that cheap."

"He might, though—just to make his point," Lester said. "What if he isn't bluffing? What if they open the pipes?"

Duane pulled up at the well site and stopped. There was no one there—just a new oil pump, waiting to be turned on. Like all such well sites, this place was ugly: the grass had been scraped off, the mesquites bulldozed. The slush pits stank, the soil was rutted, there was not a smidgin of shade, and the trash the roughnecks left had not been hauled away.

There was nothing about the site that offered the eye the slightest pleasure. It was just a half acre of ruined earth in the middle of a scrubby pasture. Only the liquid money that the new pump would bring from the ground could redeem the ugliness. The black flow from just such sites had built Karla her new home. It had paid their bills throughout their married lives—not to mention the town's bills, the state's bills, and the bills of almost everyone they knew.

But five-dollar oil? Duane tried to dismiss it from his mind. For years the Saudis and their threats had been a staple of Dairy Queen conversation. During all that time, no one had even seen a Saudi, and the pipes in Arabia had not been thrown open. To most locals OPEC was a shadowy entity, like communism—its threats were met with macho rhetoric, at least in the Dairy Queen. Some doubted that OPEC really had much muscle, but Duane was not among the doubters on that score. Billions of barrels of reserves added up to muscle, in his view. What seemed doubtful was that the matter would ever go beyond threats.

He still doubted it, but Lester's hopeless look made him uneasy. The sense of optimism that just being near the new well usually gave him had begun to slip away. If oil went to five dollars a barrel, the costly new pump he was looking at might never be turned on. It would sit there and rust, unused. No one could afford to bring up five-dollar oil. The black lake would remain where it was, deep in its limestone cavern, if that occurred. Dickie could bring it up, or Dickie's children.

On the drive back to town Lester kept idly pointing his cap pistol out the window and snapping it. Duane started to tell him he looked silly wearing a cap pistol, but he didn't say it. In Lester's present mood it wouldn't do for him to wear any other kind of pistol.

"I hear Karla's moving to Europe to live with Jacy," Lester said. "That's the rumor going around."

"She's just going on a vacation," Duane said. "She'll be back in a couple of weeks."

"That's not what I heard," Lester said. "I think you've lost her, this time."

"Now why do you think that?" Duane asked. "Here I take you on a ride to cheer you up and you tell me I'm losing my wife. You're a hell of a friend."

"The ride didn't cheer me up, though," Lester said. "Nothing can cheer me up now. My wife's about to bear you a grandchild, your old girlfriend's about to bear me a child, and unless I'm very lucky I'm headed for prison. What do you think the state of Texas will feed its felons if oil goes to five dollars a barrel? They'll make us eat our own toenails, if they don't make us eat one another."

The thought seemed to cheer him slightly.

"I can see the headlines now," Lester said. " 'Cannibalism Rife in Texas Prison System.' "

"Maybe you should stop reading *The Wall Street Journal*," Duane said. "It just puts gloomy ideas in your head."

Lester laughed. "Gloomy ideas," he said. "If oil hits five dollars a barrel you'll see some gloomy ideas, all right. When that happens I'll take my chances in prison, because this place will be a total madhouse. Some bankrupt who's lost everything he worked his whole life for will walk in and shoot me. People will start foaming at the mouth or having sex in the middle of the street. Every marriage in the town will break up. You should be glad your family's moving to Europe."

"My family's not moving to Europe," Duane said. "Karla and the twins are just going for a couple of weeks. Why would my family move to Europe? None of them has ever set foot in Europe."

Lester shrugged. "You must not have heard the story I heard," he said.

"What story did you hear?" Duane asked. He tried to sound casual, but in fact he was burning with curiosity. After all, it was quite possible that his family *was* moving to Europe. He might be the last to be informed.

"I heard Jacy and Karla were in love," Lester said. "It didn't particularly surprise me."

"It didn't?" Duane said.

"No," Lester said. "They're both advanced women. Any woman who's advanced is going to get bored with men sooner or later."

"I don't see why," Duane said. "We can be just as advanced as they can, I guess."

"No, we can't," Lester said. "We're not half as advanced as they are. It's only logical that they'd come to prefer their own company, sooner or later."

Lester sat up straighter and began to look more cheerful. The thought of how advanced women were seemed to cheer him a lot.

"It's a good thing you came by and got me," he said. "If you hadn't I might be dead by now. This ride was just what I needed. Once in a while I just seem to lose my perspective."

Duane was getting a bad headache. They were on a hardtop road and the sun glinted off it, sending arrows of pain straight into his head. The ride that had raised Lester's spirits had sent his own plummeting. It was blindingly hot and Thalia seemed very distant, although it was only two miles away. He felt like getting out and lying down under the nearest shade tree. Lester could have the pickup—for that matter, he could have the town.

"Who told you Karla and Jacy were in love?" he asked.

It sounded like something Bobby Lee would make up. In his more demented moods Bobby Lee liked to tell wild lies involving Karla. The more far-fetched they were, the more convincing he made them seem, as in the case of the Libyan terrorists.

"I don't know," Lester said. "It's been all over town for the last week or so now. I think Sonny told me."

Duane kept driving grimly.

CHAPTER 68

By the time they got back to the bank, Lester was in a manic mood. He rushed into the bank, snapping his cap pistol and pretending to be Jesse James. His spirits had clearly risen. Duane sat and watched the spectacle through the bank's huge plate-glass windows. The secretaries and tellers soon got into the frontier mood and began to snap their cap pistols back at Lester.

Duane's headache was no better, and his perplexity was worse. He decided to go home and get straight in the hot tub. He might shoot at the doghouse a few times to see if it did anything for his perplexity. He doubted that it would. The fun had largely gone out of shooting at the doghouse.

Before he could get through the red light his pickup was suddenly engulfed by a cluster of depressed citizens, led by Buster Lickle and Jenny Marlow. Duane had seen them coming, but, like a fool, he had waited in a law-abiding way for the light to change. He should have broken the law, run the light and escaped the crowd.

It struck him, just as he was being engulfed, that the trafffic light had become a nuisance, even a danger. He decided that at the very next City Council meeting, if he lived to attend another one, he would advocate removing the light. Let people who wanted to pass through Thalia take their chances in the town's second century. He knew it was not the light's fault that he had accidentally had sex beneath it. His own intention had been to have sex in the comfortable darkness behind the post office, but the apprehensiveness he had felt before, during and after the act had not left him. He felt that just stopping at the light had probably helped intensify his current throbbing headache.

The crowd was oblivious to the fact that he had a splitting headache, felt terrible and just wanted to go home. He was their trouble-shooter, and it was clear there had been some trouble.

"Duane, the wagon train's lost!" Jenny said. "It's terrible. They won't get here in time for the parade."

"How can they be lost?" he asked. "They were just going fifteen miles along a road."

"That was the plan," Buster Lickle said. "But then somebody had the bright idea of cutting across a pasture like wagon trains did in olden times. They got down in the brush along Onion Creek and couldn't find their way back to the highway. I think a wagon or two may have turned over. I don't know what we're gonna do."

"Maybe they'll find their way to town by tomorrow night," Duane said.

"But the parade's tonight!" Jenny said. "It'll ruin the whole parade if the wagon train isn't here to lead it."

She was at the point of tears.

"The first settlers came in wagons," Buster pointed out. "Wagons are a historical part of our county heritage."

"How come a bunch of cowboys can't find their way across a pasture?" Duane asked. He had a feeling he wasn't getting the whole story.

"Because they're sot drunk and your own wife hauled them the liquor," G.G. said. He was looking more and more cheerful.

"The way I heard it, all those wagons were upside down in Onion Creek and half the people have drowned," he added happily. "God's punishment is swift."

"Onion Creek is as dry as this pavement, G.G.," Duane said.

"They might have all broken their necks but I doubt anybody drowned."

"Sin carries a high tariff," G.G. said to the crowd at large.

"Do something, Duane!" Jenny pleaded. "A lot of these people have come a long way to see the wagon train be in the parade."

"It's four-thirty," Duane pointed out. "The parade starts in two hours. If the wagons are still out at Onion Creek they aren't going to make it in time. A wagon only travels so fast."

"One that was on a flatbed truck could travel faster, though," Buster Lickle said. "We was hoping you could haul the wagons to the city limits on some of your trucks. It might save the day."

"I thought this celebration was supposed to be sort of authentic," Duane said. "The pioneers didn't haul their wagons around on flatbed trucks."

He thought that argument might at least shame Buster Lickle. Buster was such an apostle of authenticity that he had wanted to have the old boards he found carbon-dated.

"Can't you just go get 'em, Duane?" Jenny said. "We don't have time to argue."

Duane drove through the light, which was red again, and pulled up at the curb in front of the courthouse. Bobby Lee and Eddie Belt, authentically drunk at least, were sitting in front of Old Texasville, surrounded by empty beer cups. They seemed to be doing a fine job of impersonating the founders of the county.

Duane poured four Excedrin tablets out of a bottle he kept in the glove compartment and got himself a beer to wash them down with.

"I guess we better go rescue the wagon train," he said. "They say it's lost."

"You know why, don't you?" Bobby Lee said.

"No, I don't know why," Duane said. "I thought those cowboys could at least find their way to town."

"Dickie traded some LSD for a quarter horse," Bobby Lee said. "It was just some old LSD he's had laying around for a year or two. I guess it hadn't lost its punch though."

"Those cowboys are higher than kites," Eddie said.

"They think they're in Colorado, having Rocky Mountain highs."

"Why would Dickie want a quarter horse?" Duane asked. That was the puzzling part of the news. Dickie had never had any interest in horses.

"Jacy wanted a horse so she and Karla could take rides together," Bobby Lee said. "Dickie thought the LSD was worthless so he traded and gave her the horse."

Shorty came trotting around the courthouse carrying a beer bottle in his mouth. He dropped it at Duane's feet and began to try and climb up his leg.

"The twins ran off and left him," Bobby Lee said.

Duane scratched Shorty between the ears. Despite himself, he was glad to see him.

"Let's go get the wagon train," he said.

CHAPTER 69

TO BE ON THE SAFE SIDE THEY TOOK TWO FLATBED trucks. Bobby Lee and Shorty rode with Duane. Normally Bobby Lee refused to ride in any vehicle containing Shorty, but centennial fervor plus around forty beers had rendered him less cautious.

They were scarcely out of town before a red Porsche whizzed by them. Dickie was at the wheel and Suzie Nolan was with him. The Porsche, going at least a hundred, was soon out of sight.

"Where'd he get a Porsche?" Bobby Lee asked.

"I don't know," Duane said. He felt a stab of jealousy, soon smothered by his headache, which was no better. He realized that he liked Suzie Nolan more than was likely to be convenient for either of them.

"I wanted to marry Suzie when I was in high school but I was two grades below her and she wouldn't even give me a date," Bobby Lee said.

"I think the whole county's waited till now to go crazy," Duane said.

"Speak for yourself," Bobby said. "I'm not a bit crazier than I was fifteen years ago."

"I admit you got an early start," Duane said. "Did you spread that lie about my family moving to Italy?"

"It ain't a lie," Bobby Lee said. "Karla says Jacy needs her worse than you do."

"Who told you that?" Duane asked.

"Karla," Bobby Lee said.

"Oh," Duane said.

"I didn't ask her to tell me," Bobby Lee said. "I know too much about your life already."

"I didn't say I blamed you, did I?" Duane said. In fact, he didn't blame him. Karla had always made a practice of confiding whatever she had to confide in anyone who happened to be handy when she felt like confiding. Bobby Lee had apparently just happened to be handy.

"How does she know how much I need her?" Duane asked. "She hasn't been home in a week."

"No, but she's been home for twenty-two years," Bobby Lee pointed out.

"I can't tell whose side you're on," Duane said.

"I'm not on Shorty's," Bobby Lee assured him. He clutched a heavy pair of pliers, in case Shorty tried anything, though Shorty had spent most of the trip trying to give Duane dog-kisses.

They found the wagon train by following a trail of beer cans and other debris a couple of hundred yards into a pasture. Sure enough, two wagons had turned over, though neither was anywhere near the creek. Two or three cowboys stood by, looking dejected, and the rest were wandering around looking stoned. A group of happy cowgirls sat under a post oak tree painting their fingernails. Karla sat on the wheel of one of the overturned wagons, talking to her Appaloosa, named Willie Nelson in honor of her favorite singer. She was drinking vodka and grapefruit juice from a Neiman Marcus thermos. Duane knew it was vodka and grapefruit juice because she offered him some and he took a swallow.

"Pretty slow wagon train, isn't it?" she said.

"I wish people would quit telling me you're moving to Italy because I don't need you anymore," Duane said.

"Don't believe everything you hear, Duane," Karla said, grinning. She seemed in high spirits, and was more beautiful than all the other cowgirls put together.

"I don't, but I'd like to believe something," Duane said.

"Duane, I think you better just wait till after the centennial to start believing things again," Karla said. "It's gonna take enough energy just getting through the centennial."

That was undeniable. No one was quite sure how the wagons happened to turn over. When questioned about the accident the cowboys who had driven the wagons turned sullen. One of them, a large cowboy named Mossy White, offered to whip Bobby Lee's ass on the spot.

"Why mine?" Bobby Lee asked.

"Why not yours?" Mossy said.

"Let's not scuffle, now," Duane said.

"Scuffle?" Mossy said. "I might pound this little son-of-a-bitch into a juicy pulp. You call that scuffling?"

Eddie Belt, who had just arrived with the second truck, grabbed Bobby Lee and persuaded him not to fling himself into battle.

"There's three of us and fifteen of them," he pointed out.

Duane ignored the potential hostilities and set about winching the wagons back upright. That took forty-five minutes. Then he winched two of them up on one truck and two more up on the other truck. He got little help from anyone. Bobby Lee considered that his honor had been besmirched. He puffed up like a toad and tried to get Eddie to stand aside so he could attack the cowboys. Eddie, not wanting to be beaten to a pulp for someone else's remark, held Bobby off. The two of them scuffled around in the underbrush, talking it over in loud whispers. The fact that Karla kept laughing at them didn't improve matters.

Finally the cowboys got on their horses and rode off toward town. The cowgirls finished their nails and prepared to leave too. Duane persuaded them to drive the horses that had once been hitched to the wagons, since without the horses the wagons would have to ride in the parade on the back of his trucks, a spectacle too unauthentic to contemplate.

Once the cowboys were gone, Bobby Lee and Eddie Belt

settled down and helped him chain the wagons securely to the truckbeds.

"Shoot, I didn't bring near enough vodka and grapefruit juice," Karla said, as she mounted her beloved Appaloosa, Willie Nelson.

"Duane, I hope you're not going to go around looking gloomy during the whole centennial," she added.

"I might," Duane said.

"If you do, it'll just make Italy look that much better," Karla said, before riding off.

CHAPTER 70

DRIVING BACK TO TOWN WITH THE WAGONS ON HIS truck, Duane's headache began to get worse. His headaches always got worse when he was nervous, and he felt extremely nervous. He had so many things to be nervous about that he had given up trying to separate them, but one major thing he was becoming more nervous about, as the time approached, was having to appear in his bathing suit in front of the whole county. He bitterly regretted having agreed to play Adam. The dress rehearsal hadn't been so bad, because he had kept his shirt on, but the real show was only hours away.

"Have you got butterflies in your stomach, or what?" Bobby Lee asked.

"What makes you ask?" Duane said.

"You drive funny when you're nervous," Bobby Lee said. "Kinda jerky."

Duane abruptly stopped the truck and got out.

"You drive," he said.

"I didn't mean to insult you," Bobby Lee said, once he was under the wheel and they were on their way to town.

"I'll give you five hundred dollars if you'll play Adam," Duane said.

"I don't look like Adam," Bobby Lee said.

"How in the hell do you know what he looked like?" Duane asked. "Did you ever meet him?"

"No, but I've seen pictures of him in Sunday school," Bobby Lee said. "Adam was taller than me. He was about your height."

"Five hundred quick dollars," Duane said, exasperated. "Just think of the money."

Bobby Lee refused to discuss it further. Duane thought of asking Dickie, who loved money and had no shame, but Dickie had just been seen going south in a new Porsche at a high rate of speed. He was not available to be asked.

They got the wagons off the trucks and the teams hitched up again just in time for the parade to start. The cowboys had become jumpy and paranoid. The ones who got to remain cowboys in the pageant stayed as far away as possible from the ones who were due to become Indians.

"Maybe that LSD was spoilt after all," Eddie Belt theorized. "Some of those old boys look like they're having bad trips."

Karla, who had the prettiest horse, and Old Man Balt, the oldest citizen, led the parade. Mr. Balt carried Old Glory, Karla the Lone Star flag. Riding clubs from many neighboring towns had come to assist Hardtop County in its centennial effort—the parade strung out down the Wichita highway for more than two miles. Riding clubs alternated with floats. Jenny and a team of volunteers had stayed up all night putting the finishing touches on the courthouse float. Janine, Charlene and Lavelle rode on the float dressed in crinolines and bonnets—they represented pioneer filing clerks, and waved merrily to the large crowd.

As soon as the covered wagons were off the flatbed trucks a second replica of Texasville, this one made of papier-mâché, was hoisted up on one of them. Bobby Lee and Eddie Belt continued to perform as the two Mr. Browns, assisted by Nellie as Belle Brown.

Nellie looked so beautiful that people all along the route clapped for her as the float went by. Several cowboys interrupted their bad trips long enough to pay her compliments from horseback. Bobby Lee gazed at Nellie with lovesick eyes and made threatening gestures at any cowboy who came too close to the float.

Duane decided to sit out the parade. He walked down to the Kwik-Sack and bought some more Excedrin from Genevieve, who was watching the parade from a lawn chair in front of the store.

"There's another chair in the back," Genevieve said. "Sit down and watch a minute, Duane. You look tired."

Duane got a chair and sat beside her. Karla and Old Man Balt had already passed, but he was in time to see his own company's float go by. It was a float of a drilling rig, on the back of yet another of his trucks. Turkey Clay and a little roustabout named Squirrel stood beside the papier-mâché rig, representing the career roustabouts of the area.

Then came the bank float, with Lester and his tellers and secretaries, in their cowboy hats and cap pistols, followed by the high school float. The high school float was decorated in the school colors, purple and green, and bore a huge crepe-paper replica of the school flower—a thistle—inside a heart.

By far the most striking feature of the high school float was Jacy, who had agreed to ride in it and represent the Homecoming Queen Through the Ages. She was flanked by four of the more recent homecoming queens, all of whom faded into insignificance in comparison to her. Jacy wore an evening dress and looked supremely glamorous. She had become again, at least for an evening, the woman of mythic beauty that everyone in town had supposed she must be in the years when she was away in Europe being a movie star.

Duane, who had forgotten that Jacy had agreed to be Homecoming Queen Through the Ages, was stunned. Most of the hundreds of parade watchers were also stunned. They had clapped and hooted for Nellie, who was familiar to them, but when the float carrying Jacy came by they merely stared in silence. There in the hot street, on the back of a truck that usually hauled oil rigs, was a movie goddess looking just the way a movie goddess should look. Amid the absurdities of crinolines and cap pistols one local legend had actually come alive.

Just as Duane was unfolding the second lawn chair so he could sit in it, Jacy spotted him and walked over to the edge of the truck. She might be a legend risen up, but she was not in the least inhibited by her own prominence.

"Hey, Duane, get up here!" she yelled.

Duane made a "Who, me?" gesture.

"Yeah, you, you!" Jacy yelled. "Come on!"

She marched up and banged on the roof of the cab until the driver looked back at her.

"Stop this float!" she said.

The driver stopped so abruptly that two of the younger homecoming queens nearly fell off.

Duane set the lawn chair down. Genevieve was looking at him with an amused expression.

"That girl never would let you alone," she said.

"She's not a girl anymore," Duane said.

"The older we get, the more dangerous," Genevieve said. "You better run along."

Duane realized again that Genevieve didn't like him very much. He walked over to the truck and climbed on the back of it.

"I don't know what you want me up here for," he said.

The crowd knew, though. They began to cheer and clap. Jacy led him over by the heart with the thistle in it, linked her arm in his, and waved at the crowd as the truck moved slowly down the street.

"What's a homecoming queen without the captain of the football team?" she asked. "She'd be like Eve without Adam."

"Don't remind me," Duane said. "We've still got that Adam and Eve skit to get through."

"What do you mean, get through?" Jacy said. She kept smiling but her look contained a hint of ice.

"I'm looking forward to that skit," she said. "Don't you think I'll make a good Eve?"

"You'll do fine," he said. "I'm the one I'm worried about. I'm so nervous I'm half sick."

"I believe that," Jacy said. "Just holding your arm is like holding a big wire of some kind. You better learn to relax, Duane. You're at the age when men have heart attacks if they stay too uptight."

"I've been trying to relax all day, but everything that's happened so far just makes me more nervous," he said.

"Including being up here with me?" she asked.

"Yep," he said.

Jacy put her arm around his waist and waved to the crowd with her free hand. People on both sides of the street were clapping and cheering.

"You should love this," Jacy said, her eyes gleaming. "I love it, and you should love it too. Put me up here alone and they don't know what to do with me, but put me up here with you and they love us both. We're kind of their royalty, Duane. To them we're a romance. They think we've been fucking all these years and that we'll probably be fucking tonight. We're more to them than we could ever be to one another. Doesn't that move you? It *should* move you."

"It confuses me," Duane said, looking down at the crowd, which had gone wild. People were honking horns and climbing on cars.

"You're an idiot!" Jacy said. "It's not confusing. It's wonderful."

He saw tears in her eyes, but she blinked them back and continued to smile at the crowd.

"Wave!" she said. "Wave at them."

Duane waved. He kept waving as the truck eased slowly along. The knot of tension in his chest gradually loosened. He felt that he too might cry, even as he smiled and waved. Jacy kept her arm around his waist, and he put an arm around hers. The crowd became wilder. The float was almost blocked by people who ran into the street with cameras. Duane kept waving. A swell of emotion drowned his confusion, and then his headache. He waved at friends, he waved at strangers. At one point, with a start, he realized he had just waved at his wife. Karla sat on her Appaloosa, Willie Nelson, the Lone Star flag stuck in her stirrup, watching them as they glided by. Then she waved her flag and cheered.

"Hey, that's more like it," Jacy said, smiling at him. "You're finally loosening up."

Duane stood beside her and kept waving all the way to the last car, parked almost a hundred yards past the city limits on the far south edge of town.

CHAPTER 71

BEFORE THE LONG PARADE HAD FINALLY TRICKLED through Thalia, Duane was miserably drunk. He sat in a lawn chair behind Karla's BMW, which had been preparked beneath a shade tree on Jenny Marlow's lawn.

Around him swirled the thirtieth reunion of the class of 1954. Jenny had not been a member of the class of 1954, but she was married to Lester, who had. They were hosting the reunion because their house was easy to get to, and the reunion had to be squeezed into the brief hour and a half between the parade and the pageant.

Karla and Duane had spent almost a year arguing about whether to host the reunion at their new mansion. Duane had argued against it, reasoning that no one would want to drive five miles out of town on a dirt road to see classmates they had long since forgotten anyway.

"Yeah, but you don't really like people, Duane," Karla said. "You wouldn't drive six feet out of your way to see Rita Hayworth. Other people *like* people. Besides, this is Texas. It only takes four minutes to drive five miles."

"I like people," Duane insisted. "I'd drive a long way to meet Rita Hayworth."

In the course of the year the argument grew more and more baroque. One element that affected it was that the thirtieth reunion was actually the thirty-second reunion. Plans had been made for a reunion in the true thirtieth year, but that turned out to be the year that about 75 percent of the class decided to get divorced. Adding a reunion to so many divorces would only have piled trauma on trauma. Nearly everyone would have had to decide whether to bring ex-husbands and ex-wives or current boyfriends and girlfriends.

"It doesn't matter to me who anybody brings," Duane said. "I don't remember but two or three of the people I graduated with anyway."

"It's because you don't really like people," Karla pointed out. "I remember almost every single person I graduated with. Just one or two of the boys are growing a little fuzzy."

Duane himself had begun to grow fuzzy immediately after the parade from drinking too much Stolichnaya and papaya juice, a concoction Karla often mixed up on festive occasions. It was profoundly intoxicating, as Duane knew, but he was both euphoric and very hot, and drank two or three cups of the punch hoping to cool off. Karla was drinking it, Jacy was drinking it, Jenny and Lester were drinking it, many old classmates whom he only dimly remembered were drinking it, along with a great many friendly strangers who could not have been members of the class of 1954.

Duane was not sure how so many nonclassmates had got invited to the class reunion, but before he could start wondering too much about it he found his hand being pumped by a legitimate classmate, Joe Bob Blanton, the preacher's son and first lover of Janine, who had removed himself university by university until no one was quite certain where he was.

Duane's impression, after looking into Joe Bob's face for the first time in at least a quarter of a century, was that his grip had certainly improved. He was pumping Duane's arm so vigorously that for a second Duane felt he had turned into an oil pump. He saw himself as a pump, pumping steadily night and day, bringing rich, expensive oil up from the earth.

It was at that moment that he realized he had been incautious in regard to the punch. He knew he was drunk. He had meant to put on the brakes, not drink too much of the punch. After all, he was president of the Centennial Committee; whatever went wrong would be blamed on him. Now he himself had gone wrong. He was drunk and that was that, although it was really Karla's fault. She didn't need to be so lavish with the Stolichnaya. She didn't even need to *use* Stolichnaya.

"Duane, it's just great to see you," Joe Bob said. "It really is great."

"Nice to see you too," Duane said. It seemed to him that Joe Bob had changed a great deal. As a youth he had been skinny —now he was plump. He had a thin little mustache that hung down at the corners, past his mouth. It was a Fu Manchu mustache, but instead of having a hard lean face, such as Fu Manchu had in the movies, Joe Bob had a round soft face. His hair was mostly gray and he wore a shiny blue coat and corduroy pants. His shoes seemed to be made of plastic.

"Where do you live now, Joe Bob?" Duane asked. The realization that he was drunk made asking even the simplest question a struggle. He had decided at once to ask Joe Bob where he lived, but getting the words out seemed to take several minutes.

"Oh, I'm still in Syracuse," Joe Bob said. "I've been there twenty-two years."

Karla wandered up. She had been slugging down Stolichnaya and papaya juice herself, but it seemed to have no effect on her.

"Hi, you must be Joe Bob," she said. "I've heard a lot about you."

"Probably the part about me molesting little girls," Joe Bob said, smiling a soft smile.

Duane remembered that he was mad at Karla for having caused his awkward drunkenness.

"I wish you'd quit buying that Russian vodka," he said. "I don't like making communists rich just in order to get drunk."

Karla waved her hand in front of his eyes, her new way of indicating that she thought he had gone crazy.

"Actually, more of a case can be made for pedophilia than you might think," Joe Bob said.

"Don't you have to have a lot of blood transfusions, though?" Karla said.

Joe Bob looked slightly taken aback. "That's hemophilia," he said. "That's different."

Minerva happen to overhear a snatch of the conversation. "I was told I'd die of nosebleeds by several doctors, but I beat the odds," she said.

She wore an ancient cowboy hat, inherited from her father. It stood a fair chance of winning the prize for the Most Authentic Cowboy Hat, one of several such prizes to be given.

"Gosh, I miss Texas," Joe Bob said, still smiling. "Lots of times I think of coming back."

"Shit, come on back," Bobby Lee said. He had wandered up.

"Yeah, pack up and come," Karla said. "Why live your life in agony?"

"Oh, the truth is the pedophilic community in Syracuse kind of needs me," Joe Bob said. "I'm sort of their spokesperson. We put out a little newsletter and I edit it. It's called *Child's Play*."

"Well, it's nice to be needed," Bobby Lee said amicably.

Duane walked off and sat down in a lawn chair. His head was whirling. If he closed his eyes for even a moment he became dizzy. Bright particles seemed to be swimming around behind his eyelids.

While he had his eyes closed, waiting for the particles to stop swirling, he smelled perfume at his elbow. It didn't smell like Karla's perfume, or Jacy's either. After thinking a bit he decided it was Janine's perfume. He opened his eyes to see Janine herself kneeling beside his chair.

"I found out the sex today," she said. "I'm gonna have a little curlyheaded boy, just like I always dreamed."

"Goodness," Duane said.

"You don't sound a bit impressed," Janine said, chewing gum. "It's the one thing I've wanted all my life."

"I'm drunk or I'd sound more impressed," Duane assured her. "I got hot and drank too much of the punch."

Janine leaned close to whisper—he felt her breath in his ear.

"I want you to be my boyfriend again," she whispered.

That was startling news. "Why?" he asked.

"Lester's afraid of germs," Janine said, giggling.

Duane decided to shut his eyes and think that over. The little particles swirled wildly for a while. He thought of them as brightly colored germs, irritating but nothing to be afraid of. While they were swirling he felt Janine's breath in his ear again. She was so close he could smell both her perfume and her chewing gum.

"You don't have to decide right now," she said.

Duane was grateful for that. He was thinking of opening his eyes when the perfume changed. He opened his eyes just in time to see Jenny Marlow bend down and give him a big kiss. Duane decided to pretend that he was unconscious. If he opened his eyes he might find out that Jenny, too, was soon going to have a curlyheaded boy.

"He's asleep," Jenny said to someone. Then her perfume gave way to Karla's perfume.

"If I ever find any more of that Russian vodka in our house I'm gonna pour every drop of it out," he said, his eyes still closed.

"Duane, you haven't introduced me to a single one of your old classmates," Karla said. "I think that's real tacky."

Duane opened his eyes and looked around at the classmates he hadn't introduced her to. A tall, gawky woman in a green dress stood nearby. She seemed familiar—he thought she had been a classmate. In high school she had also been tall and gawky—he seemed to remember that she had even then been partial to green. He tried hard to locate her in his memory, but his memory was drunk too. He thought he remembered a basketball trip long ago in which something had happened between himself and the tall, gawky girl who had become a tall, gawky woman. Hadn't they sat together in the back of the school bus, going to Crowell? Hadn't they necked, petted, done something? He thought he remembered kissing her once and being surprised when she kissed back.

But the memory was very vague, and he could not attach a name to the woman. Maybe it was Wilma—hadn't there been a Wilma somewhere in the class of 1954? But all he really remembered was how sexy the girls' basketball uniforms had seemed then. The uniforms were silky or satiny, as well as being loose. It was easy to get a hand inside them—though just stroking the silky uniforms was almost as exciting as stroking the bodies inside them.

"I think that's Wilma," he said, in response to his wife's accusation.

"Wilma who?" Karla asked.

"I don't know," he admitted. "I'm not even sure it's Wilma."

"You sure don't care much about your old classmates," Karla said. "You can't even remember their names for thirty years."

"Most of them moved away," Duane said, though he knew it was a poor excuse. Most of them had not moved all that far away. Only Joe Bob and one or two others had actually moved out of the state; the majority had gone no farther than the suburbs of Fort Worth, and many not even that far. He had gone straight through school with most of them—twelve years, first grade to senior trip. It seemed unthinkable that he could ever forget their names, and yet the unthinkable had happened. All but a few had become nameless. He watched them drink Stolichnaya and papaya juice and eat chicken gizzards. They were all trying hard to make merry, but none of them really looked very merry—in fact, none of them even looked modestly happy.

Jacy was chatting with Joe Bob, doing her best, but she no longer looked happy and excited, as she had on the homecoming queen float. She seemed listless, melancholy.

"This reunion was a terrible idea," he said. "Everybody looks disappointed. Nobody looks successful."

"They're trying, though," Karla said. "Everybody's trying real hard. You're the only one that's just sitting around sulking."

"I'm not sulking," he said. "I got drunk on that stupid communist vodka you're so fond of."

"Why was Janine Wells licking your ear right in front of everybody?" Karla asked. "She wasn't even in your class."

"Where'd Dickie get that Porsche?" Duane asked, deciding to counter a question with a question.

"Suzie Nolan bought it for him," Karla said. "They're real lovey-dovey now."

"Suzie bought it for him?" he said, astonished. "Her husband's had his notes called and is fasting to death on the courthouse lawn and she buys Dickie a Porsche?"

"I think it's nice that Dickie likes older women," Karla said. "He's not a snob about it like some men."

"This reunion depresses the shit out of me," Duane said. "I hate to see people pretending to be happy when they're miserable."

"It's nearly time for the pageant to start, anyway," Karla said. She drained her drink and left.

Duane felt a little less drunk, but he didn't get up. He sat and watched his classmates and their wives. In most cases he was unable to remember whether it had been a wife or a husband who was his classmate. Collectively, though they might be disappointed, they were far from quiet. Many had voices so loud that it made him feel like putting his hands over his ears. One woman he couldn't identify had a voice that reminded him of the screech of air brakes. Listening to it made him feel like he was starting his hangover before he could even stop being drunk.

Just as he was about to get up, someone walked up behind him and put a hand lightly on each of his shoulders. He looked up and saw Jacy. She seemed sad.

"Coming to this reunion was a terrible idea," she said. "*Having* it was a terrible idea."

"I agree," Duane said. "I can't remember a tenth of these people."

"That's not the point," Jacy said.

"Well, I'm drunk," Duane said. "I can't be expected to get the point."

"What we can't expect anymore *is* the point," Jacy said. "We can't expect most of the things we once could have had, if we'd just been smarter, or had more guts."

Duane didn't quite understand, but he liked it that Jacy was still resting her hands on his shoulder.

"Do you read poetry?" she asked.

He shook his head.

"Remember Keats?" she said. "John Cecil used to read him to us in class."

"I was too busy thinking about you in that class," Duane

said. "If I slumped down in my seat I could almost see up your skirt sometimes."

"It might have been better if you'd listened to the poems, instead of just trying to look at my cunt," Jacy said. "In the long run it might have got you more."

"I never gave a thought to the long run," Duane said.

"But now you've almost run it and you don't have the cunt, or the poem either," Jacy said. "When old age shall this generation waste."

"What?" he asked, puzzled.

"When old age shall this generation waste," Jacy said again. "It's a line from one of the poems you were too cunt-fixated to bother reading."

"It looks like middle age has pretty well wasted this one," Duane said, looking around at their classmates. The most disappointed-looking were also the most raucous. Many faces seemed lumpy, like the faces of aging prizefighters.

"We're not even fifty yet," he said.

"We might as well be," Jacy said.

She took her hands off his shoulders and walked away.

CHAPTER 72

"IT WAS BLOWING A GALE THIS MORNING, WHY couldn't there at least be a breeze tonight?" Jenny Marlow asked. She was wearing a red satin cowgirl shirt and looked sweaty and apprehensive. The first performance of the pageant was about to begin.

"It doesn't work that way around here," Duane said, stating the obvious. The morning's gale had given way to an intense sultriness. Though it was seven in the evening, the temperature was one hundred and six. The sun appeared to have stalled in its descent. It hung just above ground level, cooking the hundreds of people who had crammed themselves into the little grandstand, many of whom already looked well cooked.

Duane was still a little hung over from the papaya punch. He didn't feel like talking, or listening, either, a fact which deterred no one. Several people were talking to him at once, expecting him not only to listen but to produce sensible decisions as well.

Old Man Balt was the immediate subject of controversy. He sat just behind Duane, atop a large sorrel horse named Dobbs.

As Hardtop County's oldest living pioneer, Mr. Balt was about to open the evening's entertainment by riding around the arena carrying the American flag. It was the old man's moment of glory, one hundred years in the making. Karla sat beside him, on Willie Nelson. She was to ride the colors with him, carrying the Texas flag.

Old Man Balt sat impassively atop Dobbs, chewing tobacco. At the last minute Jenny had stuck a Buffalo Bill wig on his head. She had procured a gross or two of pioneer wigs from an outfitter in Old Tucson. Mr. Balt's wig was held in place by a large cowboy hat.

The old man looked ready, but he wasn't saying much. Now and again he bent over and spat tobacco juice. It was the spitting that had everybody worried.

"Daddy spits about every two minutes," Beulah said. "He's been chewin' and spittin' for ninety years now. He's so in the habit of spittin' I guess he'd spit ever' two minutes even if he didn't have any tobacco juice in his mouth."

"That's what scares me," Jenny said. "What if he leans over to spit and falls off? He'll break into a million pieces."

"He fell out of a moving car and didn't break a single bone," Duane reminded her.

"He don't have much of a grip," Buster Lickle pointed out. "He might drop the flag. If Old Glory gets besmirched on opening night we're in for some bad publicity."

Bobby Lee, man of dark visions, had wandered over to listen. His mere presence irritated Duane.

"He might drop the flag and spit on it too," Bobby Lee said. "He'll never get no letter from the President if word of that gets out."

"Shut up and go away," Duane said. "I don't want any unsolicited opinion right now."

"If you can't stand the heat get off the pot," Bobby Lee said, unimpressed.

"Hellzapoppin!" Old Man Balt said. It was evidently an expression he had learned long ago.

"Nobody's ever got hurt riding Dobbs," Duane pointed out.

Dobbs, a retired kid pony, had been chosen after much research as the horse most likely to carry Old Man Balt safely around the arena. His reputation for stability was countywide.

Often as many as five children had ridden him in parades, all safely. Dobbs, nearly thirty, had been Dickie's kid pony, and Nellie's as well.

"There's no better horse for the job," Duane said.

Various members of the committee still looked irritatingly dubious.

"Okay, then I'll wire him on!" Duane said. He found some baling wire in the back of a pickup and wired Old Man Balt's feet securely in the stirrups. The old man seemed to be napping.

"I never heard of anybody being wired to a horse," Bobby Lee said. "What if the horse falls down and squashes the poor old soul?"

"Fuck you," Duane said. "Start the show."

To stifle further debate he climbed quickly up into the announcer's booth. Sonny was there, testing the sound system. The stands on both sides of the arena were packed, and hundreds of people lined the fences or sat on the hoods of pickups. The sun had finally dropped, though its departure had not made the evening much cooler.

Across the calm encircling plain, Duane could see the lights beginning to wink on in little oilpatch communities fifteen and twenty miles away.

"Look at this crowd," Sonny said. "There's never been this many people in town at one time before."

For once he seemed genuinely cheerful. At the reunion he had been the one person who really seemed to be enjoying himself. He remembered everyone, and had even laughed out loud a time or two. It had been so long since anyone had heard Sonny laugh out loud that Duane had even mentioned it to Karla.

"It wasn't a natural laugh, Duane," Karla said. "It was the kind of laugh that makes you feel like crying, if you know the person real well."

"I don't think you know Sonny real well," Duane said. "I don't think anybody does."

"Don't talk to me about it right now or I won't sing good in the show," Karla said. "It makes me feel like crying and I can't sing good when I'm about to cry."

"There they go," Sonny said.

Sure enough, the colors were riding. Karla tried to set the pace, holding Willie Nelson to a sedate trot, but Old Man Balt wasn't interested in sedate trots. He had been equipped with a quirt, in case the lethargic Dobbs refused to move at all, and he began to beat Dobbs with it vigorously, kicking him at the same time.

Dobbs commenced a ponderous jog, which didn't satisfy Old Man Balt in the least. He began to try and hit Dobbs with the American flag. Dobbs ignored his efforts, trotting slowly along.

But Old Man Balt wasn't going to spend his moment of glory in a slow trot. He twisted around and managed to jab Dobbs in the flank with the little golden eagle on top of the American flag.

"Uh-oh," Duane said.

The jab was too much, even for Dobbs. He lifted his tail, farted loudly, and broke into a kind of run—perhaps the first he had indulged in for ten or fifteen years. The novelty of rapid motion seemed to inspire him—he ran even faster. Old Man Balt's big hat and Buffalo Bill wig at once blew off. Their loss made him appear to be headless, for the high pioneer collar with which he had been outfitted completely hid his small wizened head.

Karla, taken unawares, had to spur Willie Nelson in order to stay even with Dobbs's wild charge. The two riders crossed at the far end of the arena, flags fluttering. Old Man Balt was waving his flag about above his head, as if leading a cavalry charge.

"This is great," Sonny said. "Look at that old man go."

The crowd was equally impressed. Horns honked and people leaped to their feet, cheering. Dobbs thundered down the north side of the arena, directly under the announcer's booth. Several cowboys, lounging around the bucking chutes, looked up, saw him coming and automatically began climbing the fence, as surprised as if they had seen a rhino charging at them.

At the last second, just as the two horses were about to pass out of the arena, the excited Dobbs decided to go around again. Karla had to fling the Appaloosa back on its haunches to keep from being hit broadside.

"Oh, no, he's tilting," Duane said, as Old Man Balt started up the far side of the arena for a second time.

Sure enough, the saddle was slipping. Old Man Balt was leaning left, roughly in the ten o'clock position.

"Where's the pickup men?" Sonny asked. "They'll have to get him."

"This isn't a rodeo," Duane said. "There aren't any pickup men. Besides, he's wired to the saddle."

Karla had handed her flag to a cowboy. She loped alongside Dobbs, trying to decide how to proceed. Old Man Balt had already slipped to the nine o'clock position. He was sticking straight off the left side of the horse, parallel to the ground.

Duane dashed out of the announcer's booth and began to run down the grandstand steps. Just as he was approaching the ground a child carrying a Sno-Cone appeared, directly in front of him. Duane jumped over the child but fell hard against the arena fence. He got up and tried to climb the fence but felt a sharp stab of pain in his side. Looking through the wire he saw that Old Man Balt had slipped to eight o'clock. If he slipped to six he would undoubtedly be pulverized by Dobbs's huge hoofs.

Duane made another try and got over the fence, but when he landed he was in too much pain to move. It didn't matter, though; while he was getting over the fence Dickie had stopped flirting with his little group of cowboys' wives long enough to run out, catch his old kid pony and ease him to a stop. Old Man Balt slipped to six o'clock just as the horse stopped. Duane limped over and helped Karla unwire him. Dickie had even managed to catch the American flag and keep it from falling in the dirt. He stood patting Dobbs's neck, apparently not even particularly impressed with himself for having rescued the county's oldest living citizen.

"I'm in adrenaline shock from nearly being run over," Karla said. "Is that why you're so pale, Duane? Was you worried I'd be killed?"

"That, plus I think I might have broken one or two ribs when I jumped that kid with the Sno-Cone," Duane said.

CHAPTER 73

"IT'S IRONIC THAT YOU BROKE ALL YOUR RIBS JUST before we did the Adam and Eve skit," Jacy said. "I wonder what a psychiatrist would make of that."

"He'd probably just empty his wastebasket on his desk," Duane said.

Jacy gave him a tolerant smile. In general, she seemed to find him amusing.

"The psychiatrist wouldn't necessarily be a male," Jacy said. "There are women psychiatrists—good ones, too."

"Anyway, I didn't break all my ribs," Duane said. "I just broke three."

"That doesn't affect the irony, honey pie," Jacy said.

Duane had never been totally sure that he knew what irony was, but he didn't say so. The two of them sat in the little waiting room of the Thalia hospital, waiting for the doctor to come back and bandage Duane's ribs. The doctor had rushed up from the pageant and taken X-rays, but then he had to dash back and drive a horse and buggy around the arena in a skit honoring pioneer doctors.

Jacy still wore the body stocking she had worn as Eve. She had driven Duane to the hospital instead of Karla because Karla had to be in the square-dance exhibition. Jacy had nothing to do until it was time for her to sing the closing hymn.

"I wish we could go swimming," Jacy said. "This body stocking is hot."

Duane had on the bathing suit he had worn to play Adam, with a shirt thrown over his shoulders. The bathing suit sported a sewn-on fig leaf that flopped when he walked. The air conditioning in the waiting room seemed to have faltered— it was almost as sultry as it had been outdoors. Jacy had piled her long hair on top of her head but there were still beads of sweat on her neck. The body stocking was sweat-stained at the armpits and also between her breasts.

The crowd had loved the Garden of Eden skit, though. Duane had to do little more than hold his side and look surprised, while Jacy lounged under a small tree in her body stocking, pretending to get instructions from a rubber snake. Then she persuaded Adam to eat a bite of apple, at which point the sound system produced a crackling sound that was meant to signify God's displeasure. Then Adam and Eve walked hand in hand out of Eden, toward the bucking chutes.

The crowd had screamed and yelled for more, although groups of patriots and redcoats were already mustered behind the calf pens, ready to fight the American Revolution.

"You don't really have to wait around in this heat," Duane said. "You could go on back. The doctor can bring me when he gets me bandaged up."

"Eve's not supposed to run off and leave Adam just because it's summertime in the garden," Jacy said.

Duane wished the doctor would hurry. Being alone with Jacy made him slightly apprehensive. He often felt a similar apprehension when he was alone with Karla, but at least he knew why he was apprehensive: either Karla was mad at him already or she was likely to become mad if he made the slightest wrong move.

But Jacy was not mad, or very likely to become mad. Her behavior was friendly and considerate—loyal, even. She had already been waiting with him in the muggy room for forty-five minutes and had displayed neither impatience nor pique.

"I guess we're the only ones in the hospital," he said, thinking out loud.

"Yeah, and it's full of beds, too," Jacy said.

She smiled at him again, and then leaned back against the vinyl couch and yawned. She closed her eyes for a moment. She seemed to be about to doze, but then she opened her eyes again and looked at him.

"I don't want you to try and fuck me, Duane," she said.

"I wasn't going to," he protested quickly.

"No, you weren't, but you were going to tie yourself in knots thinking about it every time we're together," she said. "I can't enjoy you if you're sitting there mind-fucking, and you can't enjoy me either. If you'd just relax about it we could have a certain amount of fun."

"Okay," Duane said.

"Can't you do a little better than okay?" she asked.

"I don't guess I know what you would consider better," he said.

"Conversation, for starters," Jacy said, with some vehemence. "I get tired of starting every one we have. You start one for a change. When I had lovers I usually had to tell them every single thing I wanted done. Having to beg men to talk is just about as depressing, let me tell you."

"I guess I get scared I'll say something wrong," Duane said.

"You talk to every other woman within a fifty-mile radius," Jacy said. "But you won't talk to me because you're afraid you'll say something wrong. What if you did say something wrong? Do you think I'd banish you forever for some small conversational lapse?"

"I guess I must think that," Duane said.

Jacy chuckled.

"You sure do a lot of guessing," she said. "But not very bold guessing. At least not where I'm concerned. Why are you so timid with me, Duane?"

"I'm scared in some way," he said. "I don't know why, exactly."

"And you're not scared of Karla in the same way."

"Oh, I'm plenty scared of Karla," Duane said.

"But not scared in exactly the way you are with me," Jacy said.

"Karla and I have survived a lot of mistakes," he said. "I imagine we'll survive a lot more."

"Uh-huh, and you could probably even survive a few with me," Jacy said. "You *have* survived a few with me, in fact."

Duane felt painfully confused. When he wasn't with Jacy he sometimes imagined approaching her sexually, but in her company he immediately knew he wouldn't—couldn't. The timidity she complained of overcame him, blocking his desire.

And yet the moment she left him he felt filled with yearning and troubled by a sense that he had mishandled an opportunity, missing a chance to draw close to the woman he had once supposed he would spend his life being close to.

Now the timidity seemed to be increasing. His silly injury had presented him with a fine chance to talk to her, but he wasn't talking. He was just sort of mumbling. Even his desire to talk seemed to be blocked.

"I don't think my ribs need bandaging all that bad," he said, feeling at a loss. "Maybe we should just go on back to the pageant."

Jacy had been looking rather cheerful. The minute he spoke her face fell.

"Okay," she said, in a subdued voice.

Duane felt terrible. He knew he was doing virtually everything wrong.

"Why'd you take my family away?" he asked—it was the one thing he could think of to ask.

"They're fearless," Jacy said. "I need that. I thought some of it must have come from you, but now I don't know. Maybe it all came from Karla. You're sure not fearless. You're afraid to sit here with me. You're scared to death you might feel something you can't control."

She stood up, but instead of walking out of the hospital she went down the hall and turned a corner. Duane assumed she might have needed to use the bathroom, but several minutes passed and she didn't reappear.

Then the doctor popped in, dressed in a black frock coat, a stovepipe hat and fake side whiskers.

"Let's hurry and get you taped up," he said. "I have to get back in time for the doughboy skit."

Duane followed the doctor into the emergency room to be taped. There was still no sign of Jacy.

"The cowboys and Indians had a good scuffle," the doctor said. "The Alamo skit got pretty rough too. Some of the defenders didn't want to lie down and play dead. I wouldn't be surprised if we get an injury or two before all this is over."

He rushed off the second he finished the taping. Duane walked all through the empty hospital, but didn't find Jacy.

Stepping outside, he saw Shorty, who had ridden to the emergency room with them. Shorty was wiggling around on his back in the middle of the lawn, trying to bite his tail.

Jacy sat on the hood of the Mercedes, wrapped in a towel.

"I thought I'd lost you," Duane said.

"As you once pointed out, you never had me," she said.

"I meant just now," he said.

Jacy looked at him coldly.

"I thought maybe my sweat was repelling you, so I took a shower," she said. "You might be one of those men who gag if they have to smell a sweaty armpit or a bloody cunt."

"Nope," Duane said. "I was gagging on myself."

Jacy held the towel around her with one hand and offered him the other, so he could help her off the car. She walked around and opened the car door. The light from the car's interior shone on her white legs.

"Why aren't you in the market for love?" he asked.

"Because of my child," Jacy said, so sharply that Shorty immediately stopped wiggling on the lawn. He jumped to his feet and barked, as if he thought an invader might be attacking. Then he began to circle the hospital yard, his tail in the air.

"Your dead child?" Duane asked.

"His name was Benny," Jacy said. "I'm glad you at least acknowledged that I have a dead child. Your wife confronted that issue about two minutes after I met her. It took you several months but at last you've done it. Not great timing, though, because I have to go sing that hymn and I can't sing when I'm sad."

It was the second time that evening that the problem of sadness and singing had come up.

"Would you like me to drive?" he asked.

Jacy stood in silence for a moment, her face hidden in darkness, her legs white in the light. Her legs looked too thin. The sight of them made Duane suddenly sad.

Then she got in the car and started it. She looked out at him, her pale face framed in the car window. Her look was one of deep disappointment. Duane felt that he had either done something very wrong or had failed to do the slightest thing right. He had not given her something that she needed. He wanted to stop her from leaving, afraid that if he didn't he would be haunted by her disappointed look the rest of his life.

But he couldn't think of what to say.

Jacy backed the car in a half circle on the gravel and drove away. Shorty chased the car a few steps, gave up, and came back to Duane.

"I'm not doing too well tonight, Shorty," Duane said.

Shorty, thinking he had been complimented, began to try and climb his master's leg.

CHAPTER 74

D<small>UANE</small> <small>THOUGHT</small> <small>HE</small> <small>COULD</small> <small>PROBABLY</small> <small>CATCH</small> <small>A</small> ride back to the pageant, but apparently all the cars in town were already there. Ordinarily he would have felt silly walking through town in a bathing suit with a floppy fig leaf sewn to it, but he was so depressed at having disappointed Jacy that he gave his appearance no thought.

Passing the courthouse, he noticed Billie Anne and Junior. They sat on their mattress, smoking marijuana. The band that had been hired to play for the street dances was warming up. Over at the little carnival, a young woman was spinning sticks of cotton candy off a cotton-candy machine. A thin old man with tattoos on both arms tested the bumper cars.

"We're telling one another the story of our lives," Billie Anne said, as Duane walked past. "I'm just up to the fifth grade."

"Are you two still fasting?" he asked.

"No, we couldn't resist the barbecue," Junior said. "We may start over tomorrow."

Duane stopped at the Kwik-Sack and got himself beer on

412

credit. Genevieve was watching a Mary Tyler Moore rerun on the tiny TV behind the counter.

"Didn't you want to see the pageant?" he asked.

"Why? Life in this place has all been a pageant," Genevieve said.

Duane walked slowly down the street toward the arena, sipping his beer. Constant gunfire came over the loudspeaker—it was probably the Iwo Jima skit, he decided. That one had been hard to cast because no one in the county wanted to be Japs. Finally some junior high girls had been talked into it.

Cars and pickups were parked everywhere, along the road, on lawns, in alleys. Hundreds filled the parking lot and slopped over onto the adjacent baseball diamond. Duane had been half drunk when he parked his pickup, and was not sure he could even find it. He did come upon the truck that carried his pulling machine—the one Turkey Clay drove—and stopped to take a leak behind it.

While he was readjusting his fig leaf he heard Karla's voice over the loudspeaker. She had been chosen to read the names of the county's dead, from various wars. Twenty-six local boys had died in World War I, more than forty in World War II. Three had been killed in Korea, and thirteen in Viet Nam. Karla read the names carefully, pausing between each one.

Duane leaned against the fender of a parked Oldsmobile, listening. Five of the boys lost in Viet Nam had roughnecked for him before they were drafted. He remembered each of them well.

A gawky kid named Charlie Sears had worked hard, but was hopeless with wrenches. One hot summer night he had tried four different wrenches on a recalcitrant nut, and all had slipped. Duane finally loosened the nut himself.

"I hope I get the hang of these wrenches before I die," Charlie Sears said, embarrassed by his own ineptitude.

Duane had forgotten the remark, but when Karla said "Charles Eugene Sears, Thalia," he remembered it. Charlie's people had been oilfied trash, but they didn't buy bumper stickers saying they were proud of it. None of them could have imagined any other existence.

Charlie had always had a shock of long, dirty hair hanging

out from under his dozer cap. Duane had tried to keep him off the rig floor for fear his hair might somehow get caught in the pipestem. Despite his awkwardness, he had been a popular hand, often taking shifts for older roughnecks if they turned up too drunk to work.

Charlie Sears's name was the last Karla read. Duane noticed Shorty standing quizzically by a pickup, and realized the pickup was his. He limped over, let Shorty in, and climbed in himself. He felt like going home.

Before he started the pickup, Jacy began the closing hymn. Her rich voice floated out over the dark town. When he heard it, Shorty put his paws on the dashboard and looked around alertly, hoping to spot Jacy.

"Like the faint dawn of the morning,
Like the sweet freshness of dew . . ."

If sadness had threatened Jacy's singing voice, she had overcome it. Her voice poured out, over the crowd, the cars, the town, the shadowed plain.

The beauty of her voice gave Duane a feeling of great pride, but then he remembered her hurt look and the proud feeling gave way to one of deep forlornness.

He started the pickup and began to weave his way through the lines of parked cars. He didn't want to stay for the street dancing, the carnival, any of it. He wanted to leave.

As he passed the entrance to the arena, he caught a glimpse of Jacy, standing on the dusty turf in a white dress, her hands on a microphone. A row of little junior high girls dressed as Japanese soldiers knelt on the goal line, listening to her sing.

Duane drove slowly out of town, Jacy's voice fading behind him:

"Hope is an action to keep us . . ."

He was almost two miles out before the hymn ended. The dust his wheels threw up was as white as the Milky Way. To the west, heat lightning flickered, licking the horizon with its white snake's tongue. He bumped over his cattle guard and parked beneath the twins' basketball goal.

Looking toward town, he could see the circle of lights above the arena, and the tiny colored arc of the Ferris wheel. Shorty whined to be let out. When the door was opened he scrambled across Duane's lap and trotted off on a tour of inspection.

Duane couldn't stop thinking of Charlie Sears. The boy had never been to a dentist. One of his molars had come in crooked —it bulged over the gum line. His upper lip didn't quite cover it. Except for the one bulging tooth, he was a good-looking boy, with a lazy, self-mocking grin. Duane had offered to advance him the money to get his teeth fixed, but Charlie never took him up on the offer, nor had he ever got the hang of wrenches, before he died.

CHAPTER 75

DUANE AWOKE TO A RAIN OF SOFT BLOWS. HE opened his eyes and discovered that his family had returned. The blows were the work of Little Mike, who was hitting him in the head with a stuffed dog.

"That's the stuff," Karla said. "Wake up Grandpa. He's been sleeping long enough."

Karla sat on the edge of the bed in an Elvis T-shirt. She poured a big glob of expensive cream into one hand and rubbed it up and down her calf. Barbette lay on the bed beside Karla, sucking a pacifier and looking solemn.

"Other women's makeup always seems more interesting," Jacy said. She was at Karla's big dressing table, experimenting with some of Karla's innumerable shades of eye shadow.

Duane caught the stuffed dog and threw it across the bedroom. Little Mike looked surprised. He decided it must be a game, slid off the bed and went to retrieve the dog.

"Hello, Duane," Karla said. "I hope you weren't having a nice dream."

Duane realized he was almost naked. Fortunately the bedsheet had wadded itself more or less around his middle. Little Mike, stuffed dog in hand, climbed back on the bed and began to hit him with the dog again. Once Little Mike started a game, he was reluctant to stop. Duane threw the dog across the room again and held Little Mike by both ankles, hoping he would realize that the game was over. Little Mike began to struggle and squeal.

"Why'd you stay away from the dance, Duane?" Karla asked.

"Probably because I gave him a hard time at the hospital," Jacy said. "He probably spent the evening feeling guilty and wishing he knew how to treat women."

Minerva walked in and abruptly whacked Little Mike on the behind with the morning paper. He had stopped struggling and was practicing spitting off the bed.

"Them Mexican eggs are ready," she announced.

"It's a good thing Dickie stayed," Jacy said. "He's far and away the best dancer in town."

"Yeah, but it don't do me no good," Karla said. "The little fucker won't dance with his own mother."

She had finished rubbing cream onto her calves, and wiped her hands on Duane's stomach.

"Are you grumpy this morning, Duane?" she asked. "We thought you'd be glad to see a little life around here for a change."

"Let's eat, I'm starving," Jacy said.

"Eye shadow can cause brain tumors," Minerva pointed out.

"Bullshit," Jacy said.

"I guess Duane enjoys sulking around by himself," Karla said. "I don't think he's very glad to see us."

She stood up and began doing little dance steps around the bedroom, humming to herself.

"Let him alone, he's still sensitive because of the hard time I gave him," Jacy said. She picked up Barbette and left the room. Minerva left too. Little Mike grabbed the newspaper and ran over and hit the stuffed dog with it.

"What did happen at the dance?" Duane asked.

He was very glad to have them back—Karla, especially. The sound of her voice, familiar, energetic, uncompromising, made him feel that living another day might be interesting.

418 / Larry McMurtry

"Jacy danced all night with Dickie and I made do with whatever drunken slobs I could get," Karla said. She had stripped
off her T-shirt and was riffling rapidly through the hundreds
that hung in her walk-in closet.

"I gotta get me some more Elvis T-shirts," she said. "That
one's about faded out."

"I've about faded out too," Duane said, hoping for sympathy.

"Oh, you always liked to stay home and hide from the world,
Duane," Karla said. "You'd have been a recluse long ago if it
hadn't been for me."

She took a plain black T-shirt out of the closet and put it on.

"Aren't you ever going to wear any of the T-shirts with words
on them again?" he asked.

"Not until I stop being depressed, *if* I stop being depressed," Karla said.

"You don't look depressed," Duane said.

"Maybe you don't know me very well anymore," Karla said.
"Sometimes husbands and wives just grow apart."

She danced out of the bedroom but immediately popped
back in.

"If you want any huevos rancheros you better shake a leg,"
she said. "I brought a few people home so the house wouldn't
seem so gloomy."

"Like who, for example?" he asked.

"Oh, just people who didn't want the dance to be over,"
Karla said. "Bobby Lee, for one."

"I could have guessed Bobby Lee," Duane said. "He's never
wanted any dance to be over."

Karla sat down on the bed.

"I could have probably married Bobby Lee," she remarked.

"Every woman he's ever met can say that," Duane said.

"I know, but it's interesting to think about what your life
would have been like if you'd married another person instead
of the one you did marry," Karla said. "Don't you ever wonder
what your life would have been like if you'd married Jacy?"

"It would have been about the same, except for the month or
two before we got divorced," Duane said. "Then I would have
married you and we'd have still ended up sitting on this bed
wondering what to do next."

"Let's sell the house," Karla said. "We don't really need this two-million-dollar son-of-a-bitch. Do you think there's anyone around still rich enough to buy it?''

"Some lawyers, maybe," Duane said. "Bankruptcy lawyers. If they're not rich enough now, they soon will be."

He suddenly remembered his debt. It seemed to him a big note was due. Maybe it had even been due yesterday. For at least a year he had thought about the debt several times a day, every day. Nothing had been able to distract him from it until the past few days. But in the past few days he had almost forgotten about it. The debt—the only thing in his life that had seemed crucial—had abruptly stopped seeming crucial.

"I forgot how in debt we are," he said, surprised that he had been able to forget the one thing that had dominated his thinking for a year.

"Maybe it's because you're falling in love with Jacy," Karla suggested. "Love's the one thing that'll take money troubles off your mind."

"I'm not falling in love with her," Duane said.

"She don't think so either, but I'm the one who's lived with you twenty-two years," Karla said. "I know better. You do too. You're just too scared to admit it."

Duane thought it might be true that Jacy had helped distract him from the debt. Suzie Nolan had helped distract him too. But a capacity to be distracted was not quite the same as falling in love.

"I stop myself from falling in love before I start," he said. "One minute I wish I could fall in love and the next minute I'm glad I don't have to. I get scared."

Karla was looking at him thoughtfully.

"I'm too middle-aged to be in love," Duane said. "I'm lucky I have you to keep me moving."

Karla grinned. "You hit that one on the button," she said. "You're real lucky you have me to keep you moving."

"Only now you're keeping Jacy moving," he said. "You've left me to grind to a halt."

"That's right," Karla said. She got up and slid open the big sliding glass doors. Duane looked out and saw a surprising sight. Toots Burns, the sheriff, was on the deck trying to boogie with his bride, the teenage runaway.

The phone rang and Karla picked it up.

"Hi, Ruth," she said.

Duane got up and started for the bathroom. Before he got there he heard Karla say, "Uh-oh."

She motioned him to her side. Duane could tell from the alarm on her face that something bad had happened.

"Okay," Karla said. "Let's look on the bright side. At least the little girls weren't hurt. We'll come right on in."

She hung up, looking older and more tired than she had only moments earlier.

"What'd Dickie do now?" he asked.

"It wasn't Dickie, it was Sonny," Karla said. "He just drove his car right through the front wall of the Stauffers' house."

CHAPTER 76

"I HAD TWO HUSBANDS WHO WERE CRAZY," JACY said, on the ride into town. "I didn't want to admit that they were crazy and neither did they. We kept changing shrinks and trying to pretend they were just temporarily a little abnormal. Big mistake. I spent about twelve years being worried every minute. I lied to my kids, trying to come up with normal explanations for the things their fathers did."

"What kinds of things did they do?" Karla asked.

Jacy shrugged. "Self-destructive things," she said. "Sometimes very inventive, but always self-destructive. I used to hope that I'd just meet one man in my life who wasn't out to do himself in."

"Maybe Sonny was just tired from dancing all night," Duane said.

"He didn't dance all night," Karla said. "I don't think he danced at all."

"Maybe he was drunk," Duane said. "His hand could have slipped off the wheel."

"He's crazy," Jacy said. "You better just face it. His timing gear's broken, or something. He thinks it's 1954."

The house Sonny crashed into had once been Ruth Popper's house. She had lived in it for over fifteen years with her husband, the late coach. In those years the house—an ordinary small frame house—had had a carport at the back, opening into the kitchen.

But the Stauffers, who bought the house from Ruth, had a growing family. When their last girl was born they decided they needed extra rooms worse than they needed a carport. They built two small rooms in the area where the carport had once been.

It was one of those rooms that Sonny had driven into. Fortunately both little girls had been outside when Sonny's car hit the house.

"Sonny won't look at me," Jacy said. "I noticed that the first time I went into that depressing little store to buy magazines. He doesn't really look at me."

"He's shy with me, too," Karla said.

"It's not shyness," Jacy said. "I like shyness. In fact, as I get older, I like it more and more. With Sonny it's something else. He wants me in the golden past, and if I hang around reading magazines too long and he has to contemplate the present me, it fucks up his fantasy or something."

"He don't take very good magazines, either," Bobby Lee complained. He was riding in the back seat with Jacy; her proximity made him so nervous that he was scrunched over against one door.

"Lock that door or you'll fall out, the way you're scrunched up against it," Karla said.

"Don't pick on him," Duane said. Bobby Lee looked fragile. One testy word from Karla might send him plummeting into depression.

"Why's he scrunched up against the door like that?" Karla asked.

"Because he's a rabbit," Jacy said.

Bobby Lee accepted that description without protest.

"Jacy says worse things to him than I do," Karla said.

"I think the town should raise taxes," Bobby Lee said.

"Why?" Duane asked.

"They need to build a couple more quiet rooms onto the

hospital," Bobby Lee said. "Lester hogs that one they got. Now Sonny needs one and I might need one any day."

"You're a working man," Duane reminded him. "You can't afford to sit around in a quiet room having nervous breakdowns."

Jacy and Karla laughed.

"What's funny about me having a nervous breakdown?" Bobby Lee asked.

"It's just a funny thought," Karla said.

"This is a democracy, I can have one if I want to," Bobby Lee said. "If I do it'll be because mean women drove me to it."

Duane felt his spirits lift a little. It was pleasant to be riding around in the morning with Karla and Jacy, idly picking on Bobby Lee. The women seemed to be in a good mood too, and Bobby Lee had not yet plummeted into depression, although he continued to scrunch against the door.

The only threat to rising spirits was having to actually go see Sonny. In no time they were in town. Duane exchanged glances with the women. He wondered if they were thinking what he was thinking, which was that it would be nice to postpone actually seeing Sonny. It was on the tip of his tongue to ask them, but he didn't.

"Let's don't go to the hospital yet," Karla said.

"Why not?" Duane asked.

"Duane, you don't want to either," Karla said. "Let's just go see how much damage he did to the house."

The house proved to be a sobering sight. A crowd of onlookers, most of them dressed in pioneer garb, stood in the street, evidently sobered by it too. No one was saying much.

Sonny's car was firmly embedded in one of the new rooms that had been built where the carport once stood. The two little girls who ordinarily lived in the rooms were cheerfully giving lemonade to the hung-over celebrants in pioneer clothes who had come to see the damage.

The parents, Ed and Josie Stauffer, who ran the hardware store, were far less cheerful. They were too uncheerful even to stand on their feet. Both sat glumly in lawn chairs.

"How's it look from the inside?" Duane asked.

"It looks like something you don't even want to think about," Josie Stauffer said. "Go see for yourself."

Just as Duane went inside, Shiny Miller roared up in his huge tow truck. Shiny specialized in towing trucks, buses or other large vehicles. He rarely bothered with cars, but had apparently decided to make an exception for one embedded in a house.

Bobby Lee gingerly followed Duane inside.

Sonny's car almost filled the little girl's bedroom. The bed was crushed under its front wheels. A shelf of stuffed animals had fallen through the car window into the front seat. The car was slightly longer than the room. Its front bumper had gone through the north wall.

"It takes a lot of luck to survive around here," Bobby Lee said.

"A lot of luck," Duane said.

"Do you think he thought he was just driving up to see Ruth, back when there was a carport here?" Bobby Lee asked.

"I have no idea what he thought," Duane said.

Suddenly there was the roar of a heavy engine, and the whole house began to shake.

"Uh-oh," Duane said. "Go stop Shiny. He's pulling the house off the foundation."

Before Bobby Lee could move, the refrigerator in the kitchen crashed over, right in front of him.

"Oh, shit!" he said.

As he was crawling over the refrigerator the cabinet doors swung open and all the glasses and plates slid out of the cabinets and began to break.

"Why doesn't somebody tell him to stop?" Duane said.

Bobby Lee scrambled over the fallen refrigerator, Duane right behind him. Several drawers shot out of the kitchen cabinet, scattering knives and forks amid the broken crockery. A tide of canned goods shook off the pantry shelves and flowed into the kitchen. Duane turned his ankle on a rolling can of butter beans.

Fortunately it was a small house, and they were able to struggle outside. Most of the crowd, having witnessed a tumbleweed stampede and a dazzling centennial pageant in less than twenty-four hours, were too jaded to react strongly to the sight of a small house being pulled off its foundations by a large tow truck. The Stauffers still sat in their lawn chairs, watching it all dully. Karla and Jacy were jumping up and down on the sidewalk, yelling at Shiny, but Shiny smiled down at them from his high cab as if he thought they were encouraging them to keep on trucking. The roar of his huge engine drowned out their words.

The little house had already been turned at right angles to its former position. Instead of facing the street, it now faced its neighbor's dog kennels. It was being watched closely by two mournful bird dogs.

Sonny's car, which was what the tow truck was actually attached to, had not budged from its position.

Duane hobbled across the lawn and managed to climb up to the level of the truck cab. Between his broken ribs and his newly turned ankle, it was all he could do.

"Stop, Shiny!" he yelled. "It's not working!"

"I ain't got her in grandma yet, either," Shiny said.

"No, you're towing the house!" Duane yelled.

Shiny stuck his head out the window and looked back down his tow cable.

"Oh, my lord!" he said, instantly slackening the cable.

The house, partially off its foundation, tipped slightly. One corner rested on the ground.

"What do you reckon I ought to do now, Duane?" Shiny asked.

Duane looked at the tipped house with Sonny's car still firmly embedded in it. Canned goods from the pantry were rolling out the front door.

"I don't know, Shiny," he said. "I think if I were you I might just move to Mexico."

CHAPTER 77

"I WANT TO LIVE IN THE JAIL," SONNY SAID. "IT'S
just a block from my room, and it's cleaner than my room. On
days when I feel in control I can ask Toots to let me out."

They were in the Dairy Queen, talking the situation over.
Certain amends had already been made. Sonny owned four
smallish rent houses in Thalia. He had offered to give the
Stauffers one of them in settlement for the damages done to
their home.

The Stauffers had quickly accepted. They were beginning to
adapt to their own celebrity. Lots of people, already grown
bored with the more historical aspects of the centennial, had
straggled over to see the house that had been nailed by a Plymouth and then pulled off its foundation by a tow truck. Some
took snapshots of it. Josie Stauffer, more resilient than her husband, had already begun to look on it as a lucky day. Both her
daughters were alive, and she had just been given a new and
larger house.

Ed Stauffer, more pessimistic, continued to sit in his lawn
chair, wondering what would happen next.

"I expect a bolt of lightning will come down from the sky before the day's over," he said, several times.

Jacy had had an attack of revulsion at the thought of seeing Sonny and had gone back to Los Dolores.

"I just don't want to see him," she said. "Something about him makes my skin crawl. It happened the day I married him, too. My skin started crawling. That's why we never fucked."

"Was it because he just had one eye?" Duane asked.

"Naw, that didn't bother me," Jacy said. "It's his willingness to be unhappy, or something. It gave me the creeps then, and it gives me the creeps now."

Sonny knew that his car wreck had deeply depressed Duane and Karla. He thought his decision to live in the jail might please them, but as soon as he said it he saw that it didn't.

"It would actually improve the quality of life in the jail if I stayed there," he said. "I'm a pretty good cook. Besides, the deputies get lonesome sitting there night after night by themselves. I could play cards with them. I might cheer them up."

"What did you see in your head, when you ran into the house?" Karla asked.

"I didn't see the house," Sonny explained patiently. "There used to be a carport there. Ruth and I parked in it hundreds of times when I took her home. I just turned into it exactly like I used to."

"It's just lucky those little girls were outside," Duane said, remembering the crushed bed.

"Maybe you better come and live at our house," Karla said. "Sitting in the hot tub's real good therapy. At least it works for me."

Duane didn't say anything, but he felt uneasy at the thought of Sonny living with them. They had two grandchildren at home, after all. It was not likely that he would do anything to harm them, but then it had not seemed likely that he would try to drive through a house, either.

"Oh, no," Sonny said. "I don't think I could live in a house where there's lots of people."

"I think you better see another doctor," Duane said. "Whatever that first one gave you isn't getting the job done."

"There's really nothing wrong with living in a jail," Sonny

said. "I'd pay a reasonable rent. It would save the county money."

"It's not a hospital, though," Duane said. "We'd like to see you cured, and you won't get cured sitting in that old jail."

"What if I'm never cured?" Sonny said, in a different tone. He sounded almost belligerent, for a moment.

"You've just been to one doctor," Karla pointed out. "There's lots of doctors. The next one might cure you in no time."

Sonny shook his head. His brief anger, if it had been anger, had passed, and a flat, sad look came on his face.

"The jail's the best solution," he said. "I'll keep it clean and help with the cooking. I'll even give up my driver's license, if that would help. That way I couldn't possibly hurt anybody. I don't need to drive. All my businesses are here. If I did need to go to Wichita Falls I could just hitchhike."

"We've got a lot of room in that big house," Karla said. "Junior Nolan lived with us and we never even noticed him."

But she said it hopelessly. She seemed about to cry.

Various survivors of the first night of the centennial sat in the Dairy Queen, several of them so hung over that it seemed a second night might kill them.

Sonny got up, scattered some change on the table and went out. Through the window they could see him walk slowly up the hot street.

Karla was tearing her napkin into little pieces. It was a habit Duane hated. Partly he hated it because he just hated it, and partly he hated it because she only did it when she was very angry or very sad.

"Don't do that," he said.

Karla continued to tear the napkin into minute squares.

"I hate this place," she said. "Why won't he live in our house?"

"You're going to Italy," he reminded her. "What would I do with him while you're gone?"

"He could just watch TV with Minerva," Karla said. "He could if he wasn't so stubborn. I don't want him to go away to some hospital. He's lived here all his life. It wouldn't be the same town without him."

Duane watched her tear the napkin into small bits. He couldn't think of anything to say.

"I know you don't want him living with us," Karla said. "You didn't back me up one bit."

"It would just be one more person to watch," Duane said. "You might decide you like Europe and stay for months. I can't watch everybody."

"I don't want him to go away," Karla said. "I'll build him a house out by us. That way he won't get on your nerves."

"He's already gone away, honey," Duane said. "He's just gone away to the past."

Karla finished tearing up the napkin.

"I don't care," she said. "It's not as bad as thinking about him living in a hospital among strangers."

She got up and hurried outside to cry in the car. Duane decided to give her five minutes. He sipped his cold coffee. Buster Lickle came clipping down the road in a buggy, ready to give people buggy rides from the Dairy Queen to Old Texasville, on the courthouse lawn.

Several customers stared at the buggy malevolently, as if it were responsible for their headaches. No one went out to take a ride, although Buster, dressed as a riverboat gambler, sat waiting hopefully.

CHAPTER 78

"OKAY, LET HIM LIVE HERE," DUANE SAID, FINALLY. "I'll be bankrupt and won't have anything to do anyway. I can sit around all day and watch him and Barbette and Little Mike."

After her cry, Karla descended into a cold silence. They drove home in silence. At home they tried to take a nap but neither could sleep. Karla hadn't uttered a sound for twenty minutes. They both lay on their backs on the waterbed, fully clothed, staring at the ceiling.

Duane wished she would say something, even something bitter and horrible. She didn't. Eventually he decided that having Sonny live with them would be less nerve-wracking than trying to endure even two more minutes of Karla's silence.

On the way home they had stopped to get the mail. The only interesting thing in it was a short letter from C. L. Sime, of Odessa, Texas.

Duane read the letter while stopped at the red light:

DEAR DUANE,

As we have done business several times I hope you will not mind if I address you by your first name.

I have read your well-typed proposition. It is a fair proposition but I am going to say no. The reason is, I try not to encumber myself with rigs or other hardware.

There's good production in Norway. It's a chilly place, tho not as bad as Amarillo.

Politely yours,
C. L. SIME

"The light's green," Karla said, her last words for twenty minutes.

Duane tucked the letter in his pocket. He could not remember why he had ever supposed his proposition would really interest C. L. Sime.

"At least I had a little vacation from thinking about bankruptcy," he said.

Karla said nothing.

"I think our sex life's over," she said, resuming the conversation only after he had broken down and offered to let Sonny come and live with them.

"You've said that before and been wrong," he reminded her.

"Sonny's your oldest friend," Karla said.

"What's that got to do with our sex life?" Duane asked.

"Plenty," Karla said, although she didn't expand on the comment.

"I said he could stay," Duane said.

"Yeah, an hour late," Karla said. "If you'd backed me up at the Dairy Queen we could have already had him moved in."

"It still doesn't have anything to do with our sex life," Duane said.

"Yeah, it does," Karla said. "You weren't loyal to your oldest friend, so we aren't going to have one anymore. Not that we were having one anyway. It was just within the realm of possibility then, and now it's not."

"Oldest friend doesn't mean best friend," Duane pointed out. "You can wear a friendship out."

"That's right," Karla said. "Just like a sex life."

Duane gave up and went to town. Karla's colder angers could last for days. He felt that he had tried his best—his efforts had just failed.

As he passed the square he noticed that the baseball throw had drawn a huge crowd. Lester Marlow sat on a plank above a tank of water. At least twenty people were lined up waiting their chance to throw balls at the bull's-eye and duck Lester. Someone had evidently already hit the bull's-eye, because Lester was soaking wet.

Duane started to stop at his office. He wanted to talk to Ruth. But after a moment's hesitation, he decided that he wanted, even more, to see Suzie Nolan. Probably Dickie would be there, but there was always the chance that he wouldn't.

To his relief, no Porsche was in the driveway. Suzie was in her den, watching a soap opera.

"Did you really buy Dickie that Porsche?" Duane asked.

"Oh, I just put my name on the note," Suzie said. She wrinkled her nose at him good-humoredly, as if to indicate that it wasn't any of his business.

"Why?" Duane asked.

Suzie laughed.

"You'd know why if you'd ever been to bed with him," Suzie said. "That little rat's just a prize."

Duane decided he should have settled for a talk with Ruth. Suzie's preference for Dickie was so obvious that it made him feel out of place. His spirits, low already, slipped a little lower.

"Duane," Suzie said, "can I give you a hug?"

"A hug?" he asked. "Why?"

"Because I just want to," Suzie said. "You're a real sweet man and you look sad enough to die."

Duane stretched out on the couch in her arms. They were very comfortable arms. Somehow he had never been able to lie down comfortably with Janine. They endlessly adjusted their limbs, posture, heads. But with Suzie he felt immediately comfortable, however he happened to fall.

Lulled by the comfort, he soon dozed off. He dreamed he was in Odessa, talking with C. L. Sime. It was a pleasant conversation. Duane had the blissful sense that Mr. Sime was going to buy his rigs.

When he awoke the blissful sense vanished. He felt he had slept much too long. Outside the sky was white, meaning the sun was blazing straight down. It must be almost noon. He started to rise, but he was still enfolded in Suzie Nolan's arms, and they held him no less comfortably than they had when he lay down. Suzie just tightened them a little when he tried to sit up.

"Lay still," she said. "You're just the jumpiest man."

Duane accepted her mild command. She smoothed his hair, arranging it around his ears in a way that pleased her. Her touch felt easy and relaxing, but not just relaxing. He felt sleepy and excited both. Once in a while Suzie slipped her hand inside his shirt and caressed him. Duane liked the combination of relaxation and excitement so much that for a moment he felt like marrying her. It was the first time the notion of marrying someone had crossed his mind for twenty-two years. He dimly remembered how desperate he had been to marry Karla. He had felt that he might as well die if she refused him. Without her there could be no happiness in life.

Fortunately Karla had married him, and life had been exciting and lucky. Now it felt neither exciting nor lucky. He still loved Karla, but he couldn't imagine lying in her arms for two hours. He couldn't imagine being either very excited or very relaxed by her touch. Perhaps the two of them should just let one another go.

"Would you ever marry me?" he asked.

Suzie laughed. "What's Karla gonna do, die?" she asked.

"Oh, no," Duane said. "Karla's gonna go on being Karla."

"Then nobody's gonna marry you," Suzie said.

"Karla and I have been happy for a long time," Duane said. "But we might be losing our happiness."

"You just need a little pussy, sweetie," Suzie said.

"No, I need a different life," he said.

Suzie shrugged her gown off her shoulders. "Pussy is a different life," she said. "At least it is if it's mine you're getting."

Duane felt an awkward confusion of feelings. The casualness of her sexual preparations aroused him and yet her calm also reminded him of Junior's tension. He realized that he was not doing much better in relation to Karla than Junior had in relation to Suzie. It made him sad that his wife had to wear suggestive T-shirts—sad and guilty. But the low truth was that he was capable of ignoring his own beautiful, vivacious wife but incapable of ignoring Suzie, who was already moving over him, inexorably arranging him to her liking.

"You didn't answer my question," he said, after Suzie had proceeded to prove her point.

"What question?" Suzie asked, yawning.

"Would you marry me?"

"I might under certain conditions," Suzie said.

Pleasure changed her eyes. They remained large and brown, but a keenness came into them after sex. At such moments, looking into her eyes, he felt that he was probably underestimating her, neglecting to credit her with her full intelligence.

She was unusually comfortable with herself, and because she was he slipped into the habit of thinking of her as a dreamy, unambitious woman, with nothing to distinguish her except an unusual sexual responsiveness. But the way she looked at him after lovemaking made him feel shallow. He came to her because it was easy, uncomplicated and very exciting. But her eyes convinced him that the uncomplicated part could easily change.

"What conditions?" he asked.

"We'd have to wait until Dickie finds himself a nice girl," Suzie said. "I wouldn't want to do anything to hurt Dickie—such as marrying his daddy."

"Why don't you marry him?" Duane asked. "You seem to love him a lot. I think you'd be real good for him."

"I am very good for him," Suzie said. "It's child's play to be good for a kid like Dickie."

"I don't know why you even sleep with me, if he's such a prize," Duane said.

"I like to," Suzie said. "Two things don't have to be equal to be good. Besides, you need me and I usually go where the need is."

"Junior thinks he needs you," he reminded her.

Suzie smiled and ruffled his hair.

"That's like hinting that you're gonna get divorced," she said. "You're not gonna get divorced, and Junior don't need me. Sitting on that mattress trying to do a hunger fast is the

most interesting thing he's done in his life. If I stay out of his
way he might develop into something yet.

"Junior's an addict, and I was his drug," she added. "But I
got tired of being a drug for a man who never even smiles.

"It makes a lot of difference, if someone just smiles," she
said.

Duane looked again into her smart, mysterious eyes.

"You're the most interesting woman in this town," he said.
He meant it, although he was aware even as he said it that if
Karla were hearing him say it he would be in deep trouble.

Suzie looked amused—the compliment did not overwhelm
her.

"It took you long enough to figure that out," she said, rubbing his chest lightly.

Duane thought of Dickie, his lucky son, whom Suzie regarded so fondly. Would the day come when Dickie realized
what an exceptional woman had loved him when he was
twenty-one? How old would he be when that realization
struck? There was no knowing, but Duane felt a moment's
sadness at the thought of the regret, and perhaps the longing,
awaiting his son on some day far in the future, when life turned
dull and he remembered Suzie Nolan.

Suzie got off the couch and bent to pick up her gown. Watching her, Duane felt sad. There was always something sad about
bodies after sex, he thought. Suzie's body was well-preserved
—a little skinny in the legs, but lovely. It would not be long
before it was old—his would be old, and Karla's, and
Jacy's.

He stood up too, and began to pick up his clothes, thinking
that if he moved he might avoid feeling even more sad.

"Dickie might live a long life and not find a woman who'll
be as good for him as you," he said, putting an arm around her
shoulders.

Suzie held her gown in her hands. She was looking out the
window at her bird feeders.

"Sad but true," she said.

CHAPTER 79

WHEN DUANE LEFT SUZIE HE DROVE OUT TO A large stock tank where he often fished. He didn't fish, though. Suzie had given him three nice tomatoes from her garden, and some salt in a Baggie. He sprinkled a little salt on the tomatoes and lunched on them. Then he stretched out under a large oak tree and napped. When he awoke he sat under the tree for another hour, watching the turtles' heads bobbing in the brown water.

Looking at water, even comparatively ugly water, usually made him feel peaceful, but this time it didn't. Questions that had begun to trouble him at Suzie's continued to trouble him. His family was planning to go away without him, something that had never happened before. It occurred to him that he could just get on a plane and leave before they left. He had always wanted to see a glacier and a rain forest—though not with his kids along. They would just fall off the glacier, or get lost in the rain forest.

He imagined how surprised everyone would be if he did just get on a plane and leave. The thought cheered him a little. The sinking sun was whittling at his shade, slowly moving it to the other side of the tree, so he got in his pickup and headed back to town. Riding along, he realized that he really missed Jack and Julie. They irritated him constantly, but he missed them anyway, and Karla too.

The thought of Karla made him apprehensive. It had occurred to him often in the past few weeks that most people in Thalia were disappointed with their lives. Falling oil prices hadn't caused the disappointment, though in some cases they might have exposed it. Lately he had begun to see disappointment in every face, but he had rarely seen it in his wife's face. Karla complained with such force and energy that he had taken her complaints at face value and assumed that she was complaining about what really bothered her.

He wondered, though. It was possible that from Karla's point of view he was a complete bust as a husband. The few hours he had spent in Suzie Nolan's assured embraces had somehow awakened his doubts about himself. After all, Karla had left. She was essentially living with Jacy now. Was it because Jacy needed her, or because she needed Jacy, or because they needed one another more than either of them needed him?

He hurried to his office, hoping to ask Ruth's opinion. He had lost all confidence in his ability to assess his own record as a person, but he hadn't lost confidence in Ruth's ability. Ruth was never loath to assess people's records, particularly his.

When he opened the office door he thought for a moment that someone in town had died. Ruth had put the cover on her typewriter. She sat stiffly in her chair, her few belongings in a cardboard box at her feet.

"What's the matter?" he asked, forgetting Karla, his doubts, and everything else. He had never seen Ruth look so sad.

"They closed the bank today," Ruth said. "I turned the phone off to keep people from driving me crazy."

"Oh, shit!" Duane said. "What'd Lester do?"

"Well, he got ducked eleven times in a row," Ruth said. "That little pitcher from Iowa Park showed up. They say he hit the bull's-eye eleven times in a row. I guess having the bank closed on top of all those duckings was the last straw for Lester."

"Did he kill himself?" Duane asked.

"Of course not," Ruth said. "He just jumped in his Lincoln sopping wet and headed out of town doing about ninety."

"People are always racing out of this town," Duane said. "I guess they think they can go fast enough to escape gravity and get in orbit somewhere else. But mostly they just turn around and come back."

"That wasn't the sad part," Ruth said. "The sad part is that Sonny jumped out of his room at the hotel."

"His room was just on the second floor," Duane said apprehensively. "That little fall wouldn't kill him."

"It wasn't a suicide attempt," Ruth said. "He thought he was jumping on some Indian who was stealing his horse. He just skinned his knees a little and broke his wrist."

"If nobody's dead, why are you packed up to leave?" Duane asked.

"You're broke, that's why," Ruth said. "You're absolutely broke. You can't afford to pay me and there's nothing left to do anyway. This business is dead."

"It ain't dead," Duane said. "I've still got three rigs working."

"I don't see why you won't face it, Duane," Ruth said. "You're broke."

"When you came to work for me oil was about three dollars a barrel," Duane reminded her. "Now it's sixteen. That's not as good as thirty, but it's a lot better than three."

"When I came to work for you you weren't twelve million dollars in debt," Ruth said. "And sixteen is just the price today. It's going to go a lot lower before it stops going lower."

"Okay," Duane said, discouraged suddenly. "You win. Leave if you want to."

He walked into his dark office and raised the shades. Briscoe sat on the windowsill, as if he had been waiting for the shade to be raised so he could stare at Duane. He immediately began to peck at the window in an annoyed but persistent way. His pecking reminded Duane of Ruth's typing. He had grown used to hearing her type while he sat in his office, brooding. With the typewriter silent and no potbellied oil promoters standing around—with no one standing around, not even Bobby Lee— the office was a lonely place.

"Don't sit there and look like that," Ruth said. She stood in the doorway.

"I didn't think you'd quit me," he said.

Ruth came in and sat down in the chair where the potbellied oil promoters usually sat.

"I can't take a salary from you when you don't have any money," Ruth said. "My conscience won't let me. You've been very good to me."

Duane remembered that he had been going to ask her what she thought of him as a husband, since the conviction that he was a failure as a husband had been rapidly growing on him. The conviction was starting to weigh him down, but other weights were accumulating so swiftly that that one was already way down in the pile.

"Where's Sonny now?" he asked.

"At my place," Ruth said. "He's going to live with me."

"It's really swift, this life," Duane said. "I just left town to go fishing for an hour or two, and now the bank's closed, and Lester's left town, and Sonny jumped out a window, and you quit."

"I'll stay if you just want me around, Duane," Ruth said. "But I won't take a salary. That wouldn't really be right."

"Do you think I've lost Karla?" he asked.

Ruth looked at him solemnly.

"Do you want to keep her?" she asked.

"I'll put it another way," he said, sighing. "Do you think I've been a bad husband?"

"Do you want to keep her?" Ruth asked again.

Duane shook his head. One of his major pet peeves was people who replied to questions with other questions. He didn't want to tell Ruth it was one of his pet peeves, though. If he did she might get up and leave and he'd never see her again.

"Let's pass that problem," he said. "Why is Sonny at your place? Why do you think you can live with someone who's crazy?"

"He's a very mild person, and he loved me once," Ruth said. "I would have been dead long ago if Sonny hadn't loved me. I think it's my place to take him in."

"You're getting awful Christian in your old age," Duane said. "Too Christian. Sonny's getting sicker. Last week he just thought he *saw* movies that weren't there. This week he thinks he's *in* movies that aren't there. He's way past being helped by amateurs like us."

"You don't know that," Ruth said. There were tears on her cheeks.

"I wish you could have seen his face," she said. "He was just so shocked when he realized there was no movie, and no Indian, and no horse."

"What if he's living in your trailer and he thinks he's in a movie and it's *The Boston Strangler?*" Duane asked.

Ruth took out a Kleenex and wiped her cheeks.

"I wish you'd just let me try this, Duane," she said. "I'm an old woman. Nobody would care much if he strangled me."

"I'd care," Duane said. "I'd kill him if he hurt you."

Ruth looked at him a moment. Then she shut her purse in a businesslike way.

"Well, maybe he won't," she said. She got up and went back to her desk. Duane put his finger against the glass of the window to see if Briscoe would peck it. Briscoe ignored it.

In a moment he heard Ruth begin to type. Duane got his cap and started to leave. When he stepped out of his office, she stopped, waiting for him to pass through. She looked at him and smiled.

"Would you like to try the question about Karla again?" he asked.

Ruth resumed her typing. She typed at a furious clip. Duane had to resist an impulse to lean over and see what she was typing.

"You should have stayed clear of Suzie Nolan," Ruth said, pausing for a second. "I told you to stay clear of her but you never listen to me. Suzie's not like most of the women around here, and now you've got a taste for her. I don't know where it will end."

"I was asking if you thought I'd lost Karla," Duane reminded her.

Ruth resumed her typing. She finished a page, laid it face down on her desk and rapidly rolled another sheet of paper into the typewriter.

"I don't know why you ask me questions if you aren't going to listen to me when I give you advice," she said, and started typing again.

CHAPTER 80

DUANE DROVE BY THE BANK TO SEE IF IT WAS really closed, and discovered that virtually everyone else in town wanted to find out too. There was both a traffic jam and a people jam in front of the bank. The only parking place he could find was several blocks away, beside the Byelo-Baptist church. He pulled in next to a pickup whose rear end was filled with brooms. G. G. Rawley leaned on the tailgate, looking happily at the brooms.

"Going in the broom business?" Duane asked.

"No, but I plan to sweep away a heap of sin, starting tonight," G.G. said.

"I didn't know sin would sweep," Duane said. "I thought it was more like an indelible stain."

"You're gonna wish you hadn't grown up to be so mockful," G.G. said.

Duane managed to get close enough to get a good look at the bank. Several unfamiliar men in suits were visible through the plate-glass walls. They seemed to be trying to ignore all the worried people who clustered around the building.

He heard a car, almost at his elbow, and looked around to see Jacy's Mercedes. Jacy, Jack, Julie and Shorty were in the front seat. All but Shorty wore sunglasses. Duane went around and got in the back seat.

Jacy was already wearing the body stocking she used in the Adam and Eve skit, which was due to start in only forty-five minutes.

"I guess that bank's really closed," Duane said.

"Momma says those banker men have been calling you all day," Julie said. "She says you'll have to live like a communist now."

"Not like a communist, like a guerrilla," Jacy said.

"That'll be easy, I already live like a gorilla," Duane said.

"They're gonna take everything we own, as soon as they catch you," Jack said. He was popping his knuckles, something he was apt to do if cooped up in a car, plane or movie theater too long.

"Stop popping your knuckles, Jack," Duane said.

"*Please* stop popping your knuckles, Jack," Jacy said, glancing at Duane. He realized she was correcting his manners, not beseeching his son.

"They're not taking my new bike," Jack said.

"Mine neither," Julie said. "Let's get a parrot."

"I hate parrots," Jack said. "That parrot in the pet shop bit me, remember?"

"That's because you said the fuck word to it," Julie said. "Birds don't like to hear the fuck word."

"I don't particularly like to hear it either, Julie," Jacy said.

She whipped into the rodeo grounds and parked in the shade of the bleachers. The minute she stopped the twins got out, slamming the door in Shorty's face. He immediately jumped out the window and chased after them.

"We may not get much of a crowd tonight," Duane said. "A bank closing puts people off. No mon, no fun."

"That's not how it works at all," Jacy said. "The less bread, the more circuses—that's how it works."

She opened a small makeup kit and propped a mirror on the dashboard, studying her face a little wearily. She seemed indifferent to, even a little disdainful of, the face she saw in the mirror, and sat for a while with her hands in her lap, doing nothing about her makeup.

"Did you hear about Sonny?" Duane asked.

Jacy looked around at him. "You can sit in the front seat if you want to," she said. "At least you can if you'll talk to me about something besides Sonny."

Duane moved to the front seat. His mind was mainly on the closed bank. He wondered if it would be taken over by a big city bank, and if so, which one.

"You look kind of cute when you're depressed," Jacy said. "You have a kind of hangdog charm. It's when you're feeling cocky that you're intolerable."

"Dickie's cocky and he's not intolerable," Duane said. "All you women love him to death."

"Of course we do," Jacy said. "Cockiness is cute in a kid that age. But when a man your age is cocky it's something to avoid. It means the man hasn't learned a thing."

"I must have learned something in forty-eight years," Duane said. "I can't put my finger on what, though."

Jacy took a lipstick out of the makeup bag, then dropped it back in and took out some eye liner. She began to do her eyes.

"When you're at your most hangdog I sometimes have the impulse to hug you," she said. "I may hug you sometime, but if I do it's not something you should misinterpret."

"I wouldn't dare interpret anything with you women," Duane said.

"Stop saying 'you women'—I'm the only woman here," Jacy said.

She did her makeup as the stands filled. Her prediction proved to be right. The stands soon filled; the crowd seemed even larger than it had the first night. Pageant performers straggled in the bleacher area and began to put on sombreros or gun belts or pioneer sunbonnets.

"You're not pulling your weight, Duane," Jacy said. "You're not talking to me about anything. Try and make a little conversation."

"Do you think I've lost Karla?" he said, deciding to use the question he could not get Ruth Popper to answer.

"Why, do you really want to keep her?" Jacy asked, blotting her lipstick.

"Yeah," Duane said. "I do."

Jacy gave him a disdainful look.

"You males like to get things settled, don't you?" Jacy said. "You're anxious for conclusions—nice firm ones that will last forever. I keep Karla. I lose Karla. No gray areas, no uncertainty."

"It's nice to know what's happening," Duane said.

"You mean it's nice to know who's gonna take care of you," Jacy said.

Duane had begun to wish he hadn't used the question.

"What do you really want to know, Duane?" Jacy said. "Whether Karla and I lick one another's cunts?"

"I didn't ask anything like that," Duane protested.

"No, but only because you're gutless," Jacy said. "You're scared to find out what you really want to know, which is whether I seduced your wife, or she seduced me, or in general what's going on with the cunts you have an interest in."

She closed her makeup kit and seemed for a moment ready to get out of the car.

"I wish you wouldn't leave," he said.

"Why?"

"Because if you go off mad I'll really be miserable," Duane said.

"You should learn to distinguish between anger and contempt," Jacy said.

"Why contempt?" he said. "I just asked a question. I don't really need to know what goes on between you and Karla."

"I think you're feeling guilty about something," Jacy said. "Otherwise you wouldn't be wondering if you'd lost your wife."

"Well, no guiltier than I've felt for about the last ten years," Duane said. "I am guilty of a lot of things, but I've learned to carry along a certain amount of guilt."

"I can too, come to think of it," Jacy said. "I ran around like crazy when I was married. Guilt didn't really slow me down."

The arena lights came on. Karla and Old Man Balt rode into the arena, getting ready to ride the colors. The western sky was still bright, but the Mercedes was in deep shadow.

"You better get your bathing suit on, Adam," Jacy said. "It's nearly time for us to go out there and start the human race."

"Oh, shit," Duane said. "I left it in the pickup. We'll have to go get it."

"Oh, do the show in your underwear," Jacy said. "Who cares?"

"I care," Duane said. "I'm not going out there in my underwear. I'd never live it down."

"It's interesting that I've started picking on you," Jacy said. "Karla says you make a good all-purpose scapegoat, and she's right. You're just guilty enough to make a good scapegoat, and you don't seem to be tough enough to be dangerous in a fight."

"Fighting back just gets you picked on worse," Duane said.

"Maybe you enjoy being picked on," Jacy said. "Maybe it gives you the illusion that you're involved, or about to be involved, or something."

"Let's go get my bathing suit," Duane said. The fear of having to play Adam in his underwear was making him more and more nervous, obscuring more major fears, such as fear of bankruptcy or fear of losing his wife.

"You go get it," Jacy said. "I have to help sing the 'Battle Hymn of the Republic.' It's my favorite part of the show."

Duane slid under the wheel and started the car. Jacy hadn't walked away. She stood right by the car door, so close that he could have put an arm around her. He glanced up and saw that she was watching him. Though she was close enough that he could feel the heat of her body, her face was in shadow. He couldn't see her eyes.

"I don't know about you, Duane," Jacy said. "It's possible that you're really pretty nice. You're just a little too attached to the linear principle, or something."

He raced to the pickup, grabbed his bathing suit and put it on in the restroom of the filling station. When he came out, the strains of the "Battle Hymn" could be heard all over the quiet town.

CHAPTER 81

"SOMEBODY OUGHT TO TELL THAT STUPID BAND TO stop playing rumbas," Karla said. "Where do they think they are, Acapulco?"

Duane was glad to be told that he was supposed to be doing a rumba. They were in the middle of the street dance—hundreds of booted feet shuffled over the asphalt, making it difficult to hear the band. Duane only occasionally caught a bar or two of the music.

"I guess they're just trying to provide a little variety," Duane said.

"That little bass player's real cute," Karla said. "He can provide me with some variety any time he's willing to be caught. You wouldn't begrudge me a bass player, would you, Duane?"

"Not unless he tries to put in a garbage disposal and fucks up," Duane said.

"It looks like you'd be over that by now, Duane," Karla said. "That was years ago."

"Jenny's taking a long time to cry herself out," he observed. Jenny sat on an ice chest by one of the concession booths, sobbing bitterly. Charlene and Lavelle stood by her, occasionally giving her a pat on the back.

"I don't blame her," Karla said. "The pageant was awful tonight, plus Lester ran off in despair."

There was no denying that the pageant had been a shambles. The Iwo Jima skit had to be scratched because the teenage girls who had agreed to play Japanese soldiers had decided to go roller-skating instead. The Civil War and World War I had to be omitted because of a terrible brawl between the defenders of the Alamo, led by Eddie Belt, and Santa Anna's army, led by Bobby Lee. Quite a few loungers and drunks had jumped the fence and rushed to the defense of the Alamo. Santa Anna's army had been forced to flee through the roping pens to keep from being beaten to a pulp.

"Duane, slide your feet more," Karla commanded.

"I wish you'd come home," Duane said. "You could bring Jacy. There's lots of room."

"That would make it easy for you, wouldn't it?" Karla said. "You'd have us both under the same roof."

"It was just a suggestion," Duane said.

"Why would you even want me back home?" Karla asked. "We never have sex and we argue all the time."

"I miss the comedy," Duane said.

Karla's tone had been neutral—not exactly hostile, not exactly friendly—but she smiled when he said he missed the comedy.

Just then there was a commotion on the courthouse lawn. A number of men with brooms were moving through the crowd, followed by a number of men in uniform. The men with brooms seemed to be swatting at people. Duane saw G. G. Rawley swat at Bobby Lee. A beer cup rose in the air like a pop fly. Bobby Lee looked astonished, but only for a second. He flung himself at G.G. but was immediately collared by two large young officers.

"Duane, they're arresting Bobby Lee," Karla said.

"G.G.'s got himself a broom brigade," Duane said. "It's his idea of how to sweep away sin. I guess those cops are from the Liquor Control. I never saw them before."

Little melees began to break out all over the place. G.G. and his volunteers had the advantage of surprise. Most of the beer drinkers were unaware that the broom brigade was attacking until the moment when they started to raise a can or a cup to their lips. Many were too drunk to be quite sure what was happening—even when the can or cup got swatted out of their hands. Those alert enough to realize what had occurred frequently showed fight and were immediately collared by teams of officers.

Duane went to help Bobby Lee, who had already been stuffed into a large cattle truck that was serving as a temporary detention pen. Bobby Lee was not taking his detention passively, though. He was kicking dirt and dried cow chips at the two officers who guarded the rear of the truck.

"What is this?" Duane said. "You can't throw people in a cattle truck just for drinking free beer."

"Oh, we ain't gettin' 'em for drinking," one officer assured him. "We're just gettin' 'em for fighting."

"I wasn't fighting until that fuckhead knocked my beer out of my hands," Bobby Lee said. "He started it, why ain't anybody locking him up?"

"That's all right, honey, I'll get revenge for you," Karla said, turning on her heel.

Duane was torn between his desire to try and reason with the officers and a sense that he ought to keep Karla in sight. He decided in favor of keeping Karla in sight.

Karla borrowed a can of beer from the first ice chest she saw and began to stalk G.G.

"What are you gonna do?" Duane asked.

"If you can keep up with me you'll find out," Karla said, walking up behind G.G., who was flanked by a large young cop. The cop smiled in a friendly way when he saw Karla.

"Hi, G.G., having fun?" Karla asked, putting a hand on G.G.'s shoulder.

G.G. turned in surprise. As he did Karla grabbed his trousers at the waist. She pulled them out as far as she could and stuffed the beer can, open end down, into his pants.

G.G. jumped as the cold beer flooded his loins.

"Oh, my lord, little lady, what'd you do that for?" the young officer asked.

"I just didn't want the preacher's skin to go to bed thirsty tonight," Karla said, giving the officer her most winning smile.

"Arrest her, she's one of the worst sinners in town," G.G. said.

"Come on, G.G.," Duane said. "There's no law against Karla pouring beer down your pants."

G.G. was trying to get the beer can out, but with Karla staring straight at him he fumbled the job. The can slipped into one of his pants legs and beer began to trickle down his leg and into his shoe.

"By God, there's a law against public disorder," G.G. said.

"Yeah, but I wasn't disorderly," Karla said. "I poured the beer right where I wanted it to go."

She turned and walked away.

"You could have thought of that trick, Duane," she said when he caught up with her.

As they were crossing the street they saw Dickie slip into the cab of the cattle truck. He had been dancing with Jacy on the sidewalk in front of the old picture show.

Before the officers guarding the truck knew what was happening, Dickie started the truck and whipped it around the corner. The officers ran in pursuit, but they were easily outdistanced. Dickie drove the truck a few blocks down the street and stopped. He and the dozen or so detainees jumped out and disappeared up a dark street. By the time the officers got to the truck most of the culprits were back in the crowd, drinking beer again.

P. L. Jolly, the local highway patrolman, stood with Karla and Duane a minute, laughing and coughing. P.L. remained one of Dickie's staunchest fans.

"That little sucker, he fooled them agin," P.L. said. "I don't know what the town would do without him."

CHAPTER 82

"INSTEAD OF HAVING HIM NEUTERED, WE SHOULD have had his barker taken out," Karla said, referring to Shorty. "Maybe if he could fuck he wouldn't bark so much."

Shorty stood thirty feet away, on the shore of the lake, barking at a turtle. He had been barking at it steadily for ten minutes, during which time the turtle had not moved an inch.

"Back the car up," Karla said. "Your dog's making me deaf."

They were in Jacy's Mercedes, waiting for her to finish her morning swim. The sun had been up only a few minutes. Jacy was so far out in the lake that they couldn't see her.

"At least he concentrates on one thing at a time," Duane said, in Shorty's defense. But he backed the Mercedes up about fifty yards.

"He thinks he's cornered that turtle," Duane said. "He's a funny dog."

"I don't want to talk about your dog anymore, Duane," Karla said. "Do you think Sonny will sue anybody, or what?"

Duane had begun to hate the subject of Sonny almost as much as Jacy hated it. At four o'clock in the morning, when only Jacy and Dickie, Nellie and little Joe Coombs, and a few other diehard dancers were still boogieing, he and Karla had walked down to the Kwik-Sack to see how Sonny was feeling.

"I think I may sue the town," Sonny said, the minute they walked in. He had the belligerent air that he had had that morning at the Dairy Queen.

"I think the town's responsible for all my trouble," Sonny said. "It's driven me crazy and I think I should sue."

Neither Duane nor Karla could think of a word to say. They both smiled nervously, as if they thought he had made a joke. Karla bought some Fritos and jalapeño dip and began to eat the Fritos.

"I've lived here all my life," Sonny said. "If I'm crazy it must be because the town's done it to me. I think it's done it to you, too. I think we're all crazy now. There's not a sane person left in town. We should get up a class-action suit and sue the town for a lot of money."

"I don't think I'm crazy," Karla said. "I'll admit just about everybody else is."

"Sure you're crazy," Sonny said. "You go to Dallas and spend thousands on things you don't need."

"That's not crazy, that's bored," Karla said.

"You have tacky boyfriends and Duane has tacky girl-friends," Sonny said. "You're both crazy."

"I should have brought the vodka," Karla said, looking depressed.

"It's also crazy to drink vodka by the gallon just because I said your boyfriends were tacky," Sonny said angrily.

Duane felt like hitting him, but didn't.

"Boy, you're in a bad mood," Karla said. "I drink vodka because I like vodka, for your information. As for tacky boyfriends, sometimes it's tacky or nothing. Your problem is you choose nothing instead of making do with a little bit of tacky, like the rest of us do."

"See, you think I've gone crazy because I don't have a tacky girlfriend," Sonny said. "Anyone who doesn't make stupid compromises is crazy in your book."

Duane and Karla exchanged looks. Neither of them really knew what to say. They had never seen Sonny in such a mood.

In the background Dr. Ruth was talking about premenstrual
syndrome. Duane half wanted to listen so he could pass along
any tips to Janine, who suffered from deep premenstrual de-
spairs. But he couldn't really listen, with Sonny so hostile and
strange.

"We're all crazy and life in this town is what's done it,"
Sonny said. "It's cost us our sanity. We should all sue together."

"But we are the town," Duane said. "If we're crazy, we made
ourselves crazy. There's no point in suing ourselves."

"It's really just the centennial that did it," Sonny said.
"Maybe I should just sue the Centennial Committee."

The belligerence left his face and his voice. The old sad look
came back, and the tone of polite defeat.

"But you're on the Centennial Committee," Duane reminded him. "And I'm on it."

"You're on it but you never took it seriously," Sonny said.
"You don't care about the past. But I care about it. I started
thinking about it, and now I can't stop. I thought the centennial
would really be about the past, but it isn't. It's just a gimmick
to get people to come here and buy souvenirs. It doesn't have
anything to do with the real past."

"A centennial's just mostly entertainment," Karla said. "It's
pretty silly, but that's no reason to go crazy."

"It didn't make me go crazy," Sonny said. "It made me realize I've always been crazy, or I wouldn't have wasted my life
here. I should have left right after high school."

"I thought you loved Thalia," Duane said, very surprised.
Sonny was one of the few people who, over the years, had
always talked about what a nice place Thalia was. He had been
president of the Chamber of Commerce four or five times.

"I used to love it," Sonny said. "The centennial made me
hate it. That's another reason to sue."

Duane wished they had never come to the Kwik-Sack. He
didn't know what to say to Sonny's criticisms.

"It's a wonder we were ever best friends," Sonny said, looking at him sadly.

"Why?" Duane asked.

"You're the town success," Sonny said. "I'm the town failure. It's been that way ever since high school. You wouldn't think a winner and a loser could ever be best friends."

Duane started to remind Sonny that he owned several prosperous businesses, not to mention other property. He started to point out that he had served well in virtually every city office. He started to tell Sonny that virtually everyone in town respected him—as indeed, almost everyone did.

But he didn't say any of it. He really wanted to leave the Kwik-Sack and never set foot in it again. Karla could shop there if she wanted to. He was through.

"Jacy's right about him," he said to Karla, as they were walking back to the square. "He's a loser and he likes being a loser."

Karla looked very depressed, but not depressed enough to give up on Sonny.

"You two are too hard on him," she said.

CHAPTER 83

WATCHING THE SUN BURN THE MORNING MIST OFF the brown lake, Karla came back to the subject of winners and losers.

"I could be considered a loser myself, Duane," she said. "I haven't really ever done that much."

"You're not a loser, though," Duane said.

"If the only reason I'm not is because I'm married to a winner, then I am a loser," Karla said.

Duane felt like shaking her.

"Stop calling yourself a loser!" he said. "You're not a loser. You're a beautiful, wonderful woman."

"Are you getting mad, Duane?" Karla asked.

"Yes," Duane said. "I don't want to hear you talking like Sonny."

"If I'm so beautiful and wonderful, how come you sleep with tacky girlfriends instead of me?" Karla asked. She was rubbing Blistex onto her lips in preparation for the blazing day ahead.

Duane sighed. Another thing he hated was conversations

that worked their way around to why he was sleeping with somebody, or not sleeping with somebody.

"We've been married twenty-two years," he said. "Let's say we fucked two hundred times a year for the first ten years. That's two thousand times. Then maybe a hundred and fifty times a year for another five years. That's another seven fifty. I don't know what it would be for the last six or seven years, but it must be at least a couple of hundred more times. That's about three thousand times, not counting before we got married."

"We got married right after we met," Karla said. "I doubt we slept together even fifty times while we were dating."

"It's still three thousand times," Duane pointed out.

"It depresses me to think about love in terms of numbers, Duane," Karla said.

"It might not be romantic but it explains why I have girl-friends," Duane said. "You were just talking about variety last night yourself."

"When I talk about it I'm usually just showing off," Karla said. "When you talk about it you actually go out and get it. I guess that's the difference between a winner and a loser."

"If you call yourself a loser one more time I'm gonna strangle you," Duane said.

"Actually, you just get it and don't talk about it," Karla said. "That's even worse."

"You never look on the bright side," Duane said.

"That's a lie," Karla said. "I usually look on the bright side. I've spent most of my life just cheering you up."

Duane did not deny it.

"Which is the bright side, in our case?" Karla asked, a minute later.

"Three thousand first-rate fucks," Duane said. "That's probably about as good a sex life as anybody gets."

"Don't brag, Duane," Karla said. "Not every single one was first-rate."

"Most of them were from my point of view," Duane said. "Ninety percent, at least."

"That still leaves ten percent that were just so-so," Karla pointed out.

"Most people would settle for ninety percent," Duane said. "Why are you so stubborn?"

"What makes you think I'm stubborn?" Karla asked.

"You just seem stubborn," he said. "I wish Jacy would come back."

"Yeah, because it upsets you when I ask questions, or talk about sex," Karla said. "I'm only forty-six, you know. I'm not ready to just quit."

"Nobody said you had to quit," Duane said.

"I do, or else I have to have tacky boyfriends," Karla said. "The only reason you said that about three thousand times was to let me know you think your duty's done."

"I don't look on it as a duty," Duane said. "I used to spend all day at the rig, thinking about you. I'd think about what we might do when I got home."

"That's sweet, but it won't help me now that I'm forty-six and you never give me a thought," Karla said. "What about the rest of our lives?"

"I guess we'll just plod along," Duane said.

"Fuck plodding along," Karla said. "I'll go off to Europe and get in a lot of trouble and it'll be your fault for letting me go off horny."

"I wish Jacy would come back," Duane said again. "If she came back at least we'd have to change the subject."

"It's my favorite subject," Karla said. "I don't want to change it."

"Right, because you enjoy making me feel like a jerk," Duane said.

Besides feeling like a jerk he also felt tired and old and at a loss. Such conversations always left him feeling tired, old and at a loss. What *would* they do with the rest of their lives? He had no idea, but whatever it was, it seemed all too likely that they would do it less well than what they had done so far—a depressing prospect.

The same conversation seemed to have the opposite effect on Karla, who suddenly looked younger, beautiful and energized. She was shuffling through Jacy's collection of tapes, a keen look in her eye. At times she looked her age, but at that moment she could have passed for thirty-three or thirty-four.

Her capacity to reclaim her youthful qualities for several hours at a time had always amazed him. He didn't understand what made it happen. Certainly no one would ever mistake him for thirty-three, even for three seconds.

"You look wonderful," he said. "You look just beautiful."

Karla grinned. "It don't make your dick get hard, though—does it, Duane?" she said. "I guess beautiful and smart and feisty's still not enough for you, Mr. Hard to Please."

"I'm not hard to please," he insisted. "I guess I'm just getting old faster than you are. It's not my fault."

"I guess hard to get hard's not quite the same as hard to please," Karla said. "It's because you work all the time that you aged so quick."

"I'm glad you're in a good humor again," he said.

"Just because I'm in one don't mean I'll stay in one," she said.

"Karla, I know that."

"You'd think a person who's beautiful and smart and feisty would always get what she wants," Karla said. "They do on TV. It's a peculiar world if a person with my drive can't get what she wants."

"Think of it in terms of baseball," Duane said. "The best hitters around just don't bat much more than three hundred."

"To hell with that," Karla said. "I want to bat six or seven hundred at least."

She popped a Pink Floyd tape into the tape player.

The mud turtle Shorty had been barking at began to walk into the water. Shorty tried to nip at its legs. Every time he nipped, the turtle stopped and withdrew into its shell. The minute it stopped Shorty began to yip at it again. His yips, even at a distance, were almost as penetrating as the music of Pink Floyd. Then Shorty noticed a killdeer and ran over and put it to flight. While he was gone the turtle hurried into the water and disappeared.

"I bet it's a relief not to have a dog like Shorty barking into your shell," Karla said.

"You bark into my shell," Duane said.

"I hope you're not going to start feeling sorry for yourself just because you're bankrupt and have a mean wife," Karla said.

"I'm not bankrupt," Duane said. "Not yet."

"I don't know about your values, Duane," Karla said. "How come you're more worried about going bankrupt than you are about me going to Europe and getting in trouble?"

"I'm worried sick about both," Duane said.

"It's hard to think when the music's that loud," he added, yawning.

They saw Jacy swim slowly up to the little boat dock and rest a moment by the ladder before pulling herself out. Shorty raced to greet her. He ran around in circles on the dock.

"If I tried to swim as far as she does I'd get cramps and drown," Karla said.

"Do you think she'll ever marry again?" Duane asked.

"No, and I wouldn't either, if you got killed," Karla said.

"You would too," Duane said. "At least I hope you would."

"You better not hope any such thing," Karla said, giving him a fierce look.

"I just said that accidentally," Duane said. "I've never given any thought to what you might do if I die."

"Just because I look for trouble doesn't mean I want any husband but you," Karla said. "What made you say that?"

"I don't know," Duane said. "I have no idea why I said it. I'm retreating as fast as I can."

Jacy came walking up, a large blue towel around her shoulders. Shorty ran ahead of her, barking loudly.

"He thinks he's my police escort," Jacy said.

Shorty, in a delirium of happiness, began to run in circles around the Mercedes. Jacy stood by the window on Karla's side and dried her legs.

"Duane said he hoped I'd get married again, if he died," Karla informed her.

"He did, did he?" Jacy said, getting in the back seat.

Duane felt that he hadn't retreated either far enough or fast enough. Having Karla beside him and Jacy behind him made him nervous. He could smell the lake on Jacy—the odor of a wet towel and a wet bathing suit on a wet woman. He glanced in the rearview mirror and met her eye. She had been waiting for his glance. She looked amused.

Duane felt a moment of desire, an urge to kiss her. It seemed sad and strange to him that he felt it for the wet woman in the back seat rather than the radiant woman in the front seat. Jacy fingered her wet hair.

He remembered that he was already in trouble because of what he had said about Karla marrying, if he died. He was not sure why the women thought it had been such a bad thing to say.

"I was just thinking of your happiness," he said to Karla.

Both women laughed.

He felt Jacy looking at him in the mirror again, waiting for his eyes.

CHAPTER 84

ON HIS WAY HOME, KARLA BLITHELY INFORMED HIM
that he had to get dressed up because the three of them had to
judge the centennial art show.

"You have to wear a sports coat, at least, and it wouldn't
really hurt you to wear a tie," she said.

"I could wear all the ties I own and it wouldn't help me
judge an art show," he said. The art show was the one centennial event he thought he had no responsibility for. It had been
Jenny's idea, and Jenny, Karla and Lester were supposed to
judge it.

"I know Lester's run off but Jenny hasn't run off," he said.
"Why can't you three judge it?"

"We need a man on the panel to make it more balanced,"
Karla said.

"Stop trying to get out of everything, Duane," Jacy said. "It's
not going to hurt you to judge a little art show."

"You don't know what might hurt me," Duane said. He felt
picked on.

At home, Karla and Jacy put away huge breakfasts, stoking

their already lavish energies. Duane ate a bowl of cereal. His stomach felt nervous.

"Are you sick?" Minerva asked. She herself was fantasizing stomach cancer.

"No," Duane said.

"You look subdued," Minerva observed.

"I am subdued," Duane said. "These two subdued me."

He nodded at Karla and Jacy, who were too busy eating to pick on him, for the moment. He felt sure they would start again as soon as their meal was finished.

"He said he wanted me to marry again if he dies," Karla informed Minerva, between bites.

Minerva shrugged. "Par for the course," she said. "When you have stomach cancer they take out your whole stomach."

"I'd rather they just take out your tongue," Duane remarked.

"I take that back," he said immediately, as silence fell around the table. "I wouldn't want you to lose your tongue."

"You didn't subdue him enough," Minerva said to Karla. "Imagine a man saying a thing like that to an eighty-six-year-old woman."

"What do you expect from someone who wants me to go get married the minute he dies?" Karla asked.

Duane got Barbette and sat by the pool with her for thirty minutes while Karla and Jacy got dressed. Jacy came out first, carrying a selection of ties in her hand. She held two or three of them against his collar to see how they worked.

"I don't want to wear a tie," he said. "I don't want to judge an art show, either."

"I have a feeling you just want to sulk," Jacy said. "That's all you seem to be doing. But that's okay with me. It adds to your hangdog charm."

"Why is it so bad that I said I wanted Karla to marry again if I die?" Duane asked.

"Because it means you wouldn't care if somebody else fucked her," Jacy said.

"If I was dead, I *wouldn't* care," he pointed out.

"The fact that you'd be dead is totally irrelevant," Jacy said. "Wear this tie with the white spots. It makes you look sort of Las Vegas."

"I hate that tie," Duane said. "Somebody gave it to me for Christmas. Somebody like Bobby Lee."

Barbette began to cry and stretch her arms out to Jacy, who took her. Barbette immediately stopped crying.

"You're so sulky you upset your grandbaby," Jacy said.

The art show covered the sidewalk all the way around the courthouse and slopped over onto the sidewalk between the courthouse and the jail. Duane, under duress, had put on the tie with the white spots.

"I never felt sillier in my life," he whispered several times, walking along the rows and rows of oils with Jacy and Karla.

"Duane, hush, we don't care if you feel silly," Karla said.

The people who had painted the pictures, almost all of whom he knew, stood behind their canvases. Duane was extremely surprised to see some of the people who stood behind canvases —he had not suspected that so many of his neighbors and colleagues entertained artistic impulses.

It was apparent, though, that they not only entertained the impulses, they had high hopes for the results. He had been intending just to walk through the art show and vote for whatever pictures Karla and Jacy said should win. At once he saw that it wasn't going to be that simple. Each painter expected him to come to a full stop and give his or her picture the attention it deserved. He started to walk past an oil of a red pickup parked at a filling station—painted by Bud Wardholt, who ran the local filling station—and glanced at Bud to say hi. Bud was a jovial man, usually, with a wad of chewing tobacco tucked into his jaw. He had a kind of juicy grin. He still had the chewing tobacco, but not the grin. Duane realized, in the nick of time, that Bud was waiting for him to stop and actually look at the picture. He stopped and looked. It was a picture of a red Chevrolet pickup with a gas nozzle stuck in its gas tank.

"That pickup looks familiar," Duane said, looking more closely.

Bud Wardholt relaxed, and the juicy grin came back.

"I thought you'd recognize it," he said. "It's that old Chevy Dickie used to have."

"My gosh," Duane said. "When'd you take up oil painting?"

"Years ago," Bud said, looking slightly insulted.

"That's real pretty," Duane said. "You can almost read the license plate on the pickup."

He moved on to an oil painting of a fat little blob with blue eyes. The painting was titled "Our Little Darling." It sat beside two other virtually identical paintings of blue-eyed blobs. One was titled "Our First Grandbaby," and the other "Just a Little Bundle of Love." The artist was old lady Collins, who with her husband ran a little bait shop out by the lake. They specialized in stink bait, but also sold worms and minnows. Their daughter Cindy, mother of the three little bundles of love, had been in trouble several times for writing hot checks.

Duane felt like strangling Lester Marlow for running off at such a time and sticking him with yet another thankless job. As he walked along the sidewalk, trying to think of something to say about each picture, his annoyance with Lester increased.

"That's real pretty," which was what he said in most cases, plainly didn't satisfy the artists.

Various roughnecks were exhibiting, and almost all of them had done pictures of oil rigs at sunset. The many exhibiting farmers had either done pictures of tractors or dairy cows, though one who ran a pig farm had attempted a picture of his prize pig. The cowboys submitted pictures of their horses, or portraits of Willie Nelson. The fishermen painted fish, the hunters deer. Lady artists, of which there were many, favored fields of bluebonnets, ponds at sunset—the latter outnumbered oil rigs at sunset by a slim margin. Buster Lickle had done a watercolor of his Dairy Queen. Numerous grandchildren were represented, a few grandfathers, several brides, at least thirty cats and many dogs.

Duane had been in an art museum once, briefly, in Fort Worth. His only thought during the visit had been to try and keep Jack from destroying any of the art objects. He had kept his eyes on his son most of the time and saw almost nothing of the art, except for a sculpture of a frog, which Jack destroyed despite him, somehow knocking it off its pedestal. No one could understand how he did it, because the sculpture weighed six hundred pounds and Jack only about sixty at the time, but he did it. Duane expected to have to pay millions in damages, but the museum officials were so relieved that the

frog hadn't squashed Jack that they didn't charge Duane anything.

As he walked through the show, Duane grew increasingly
nervous. Not having to pay for a broken frog represented his
only experience with the art world. How was he supposed to
choose between so many little bundles of love and oil rigs at
sunset? They all looked more or less alike to him.

He saw Junior Nolan looking at a picture with a sad expression on his face. Duane was startled to see that the picture he
was looking at was a portrait of Dickie, sitting with his shirt off,
on an orange couch. Almost before he realized it was Dickie,
Duane recognized the couch. It was Suzie Nolan's couch, the
one they had made love on the day before. It must be Suzie's
painting.

Junior undoubtedly recognized the couch too. He looked
sad, but not entirely sad. There was a kind of pride in his
look.

"Suzie could have been an artist," Junior said quietly.
"Suzie could have been anything."

Duane looked at the picture again. It did seem to be better
than most of the other paintings in the show. There was Dickie,
in all his youth and beauty, with a kind of softness in his face
that Duane only rarely saw.

Jacy and Karla walked up behind him as he was looking at
the painting. Junior smiled at them without losing his sad
expression. Duane felt very awkward. Neither woman said
anything. They just stood looking at the painting. The look
on their faces resembled, for a moment, the look on Dickie's
face.

Duane would have liked to look at the painting longer. He
would have liked to look at it alone. Looking at it with Karla
and Jacy and Junior made him feel embarrassed. The painting
made him realize that Suzie did love Dickie very much. It
made him feel, again, that he had been misjudging her, not
taking her seriously enough. It also made him wonder why she
allowed him in her life.

The next picture he came to was Sonny's. Duane remembered that there had been a time when Sonny tried his hand at
painting. Mainly, as Duane remembered, Sonny had done

paintings of buildings around the square. A few of them had been sold at the drugstore. A few still hung in the old hotel, and one or two were in the Dairy Queen.

This painting was different. Duane had never seen anything quite like it. For one thing, it was much larger than most of the paintings in the show. In an upper corner the red light blinked over an empty street. In another corner was a high school letter jacket—empty, just the jacket, with a "For Thalia" on it. In one of the lower corners a boy with a cap on was sweeping the street in front of the picture show. In the final corner an old man bent over a pool table in an empty poolroom. The center of the picture showed a football field, a smudge of crowd in the stands. On the green field a football player embraced a home-coming queen. The painting was called "Hometown." Duane looked at it a long time, taking in the details. Some of them were tiny. There was even the name of a movie on the marquee of the picture show. It was "The Kid from Texas," a movie Duane had never heard of.

Eddie Belt was a few yards away, standing proudly behind a picture of his bird dog, Monroe. Duane was well aware of how much Eddie thought of Monroe, because he talked about him all the time. Monroe was a skinny pointer with big sad eyes and ears that had been chewed to shreds by coyotes and other dogs. Eddie's passion for Monroe was, in Duane's view, totally irrational, for as a bird dog Monroe had his failings, the princi-pal one being a habit of immediately devouring any bird that fell to Eddie's gun. Duane and Eddie often whiled away idle hours at the rig by arguing the relative merits of Shorty and Monroe. Eddie's position, frequently reiterated, was that Mon-roe was by far the most valuable pet.

"At least Monroe does *something!*" Eddie said. "He points them birds. That's something. Shorty don't do nothing."

"Shorty does plenty," Duane maintained.

"What?"

"He bites people I don't like," Duane said.

"Yeah, and people you do like, too," Eddie said.

Duane had to admit that Eddie had skill with the brush. His portrait of Monroe was far more realistic than any of the other animal portraits in the show. He had caught Monroe's mangled ears perfectly, Duane thought, and also his big sad eyes and protruding ribs.

"I never knew I had such a talented artist working for me," he said. "I thought you mainly just doodled dirty pictures on the backs of envelopes."

Eddie seemed quietly pleased with the compliment.

Jacy and Karla came over and studied the portrait of Monroe.

"That dog looks like he's starving," Jacy said. "If you'd feed him maybe his ribs wouldn't stick out."

"I feed him," Eddie said testily. "Bird dogs are just naturally skinny."

"He looks a little too much like one of those Ethiopian children," Karla said. "I like it, though. I think I'm gonna vote for it."

"Which category?" Duane said. He too was considering voting for it, both for diplomatic reasons and because he considered it an excellent likeness of Monroe.

There were only two categories in the centennial art show, Portraits and General.

"General, I guess," Karla said. "I guess dog pictures would have to go in General."

Eddie Belt instantly gave her a black look.

"I'll have you know that ain't no general dog," Eddie said. "That's Monroe. I raised that dog from a pup. This is a portrait. Anybody can see that."

Karla and Jacy both smiled as if they thought Eddie was bats. While it was possible that they were right, and that he was bats, he was also subject to wild mood swings, as Duane knew better than anyone alive except Nelda, Eddie's long-suffering wife.

Duane thought he saw a mood swing coming on. Eddie was silent, but swollen and red in the face. There was no question but that he would fight anyone in sight if he thought Monroe's honor was being besmirched in the smallest degree.

"I think the judges had better consult," Duane said. He took each woman by the arm and attempted to lead them a few steps away. Both immediately jerked their arms free. They were obviously ready to do combat over anything smacking of sexist treatment, such as being led by the arm by a male.

"Now look," Duane said. "What we've got here is a man in love with his bird dog. I think we better put Monroe in Portraits."

"No," Karla said. "It's a real good picture. I'd a lot rather vote for it than all those paintings of oil rigs and bluebonnets. If we leave it in General he could take Monroe home a blue ribbon."

"Why can't we vote it first prize in the portraits?" Duane asked.

"Because it's not the best portrait," Jacy said. "That woman's portrait of Dickie is much the best portrait."

"Besides, you can't go giving a dog portrait first prize when there's portraits of people's grandbabies in the show," Karla said. "All those people with grandbabies would take us out and hang us if we voted a dog portrait first prize."

Duane sighed. "Now you see, this is the kind of thing you get into when you start having art shows," he said.

"I guess Dickie must really sleep with Suzie Nolan," Karla said. "I didn't believe it until I saw that picture. She makes him look real sweet."

"He *is* real sweet," Jacy said.

"I wish she hadn't put it in the show, though," Duane said.

Both women looked at him appraisingly.

"Why not?" Jacy said. "She had a perfect right to put it in the show."

"I just said I wish she hadn't," Duane said.

"What's it to you, one way or the other, Duane?" Karla asked.

"She's forty-five years old," Duane said.

"Is that supposed to explain something?" Jacy asked.

Both women were still looking at him appraisingly. Duane knew that even the most innocent remarks could sometimes get you in trouble, but it was beginning to seem that any remark got him in trouble.

"She's forty-five and let's say she's having an affair with Dickie and he's twenty-one," Duane said. "If we give that painting first prize in the portrait category it's gonna upset the Christian contingent."

"Tough shit," Karla said. "I'm voting for it for first prize."

"Me too," Jacy said.

Duane sighed again. "Okay," he said. "Where does that leave Monroe the bird dog?"

"Maybe we can talk Eddie into letting us put Monroe in General," Jacy said. "That way he can have a blue ribbon."

"I don't know," Karla said. "Eddie's a worse sulker than Duane."

"I think Lester Marlow ought to have to go to jail for having thought up this art show," Duane said.

"Duane, it doesn't hurt to have a little culture with a centennial," Karla said.

Eddie Belt, whose principles were as rock, at least where his bird dog was concerned, refused absolutely to let Monroe's portrait be judged in the general category.

"I have to look that dog in the eye every day," he said.

"Eddie, Monroe's not gonna know which category his portrait got put in," Karla said. She had lavished quite a bit of charm on Eddie in an attempt to change his mind, and was annoyed to find failure staring her in the face.

"That dog knows more than lots of people know," Eddie said. "That's a real sensitive dog."

"Don't argue with Eddie," Duane said. "He'll argue for weeks."

"It's your fault, Duane," Karla said.

"My fault?" he said. "Why?"

"It just is," Karla said.

"What are we gonna tell people in the portrait category whose grandbabies didn't get judged as high as your bird dog?" Duane asked Eddie.

"I never told you to be a judge," Eddie said.

In the end they left Monroe in Portraits. Suzie got first prize, Eddie second, and a dairy farmer third. The dairy farmer had done a recognizable rendering of John Wayne. The blue ribbon in the general category went to a painting of the Alamo, the red to a painting of a calf roper, and the white to a painting of a farmer on a tractor.

Duane suggested giving Sonny's picture of the town an honorable mention, but all it got him was hard looks from his fellow judges.

"It's morbid," Jacy said. "I felt like putting my foot through it."

"He didn't even put me in it," Karla said. "Who does he think's been his friend all these years? Besides, he was real rude to me last night, telling me I drink too much vodka and have tacky boyfriends."

"Aren't we just supposed to judge them as art?" Duane asked.

"You didn't take up for me either, when he was rude," Karla said.

"Well, I started to hit him," Duane said, "but the last time I hit him I put out his eye, remember?"

"No, because I didn't live here then," Karla said icily. "It's interesting you hit him over Jacy but didn't hit him over me."

"I didn't think you'd want me to hit him over you," Duane said. "You've been so protective of him, I figured you'd divorce me if I hit him over you."

"There's good reasons and bad reasons for hitting people, Duane," Karla said.

"My God," Duane said. He felt worse by the second. "Talking to you women's like handling a live wire. I can't say anything without one of you jumping down my throat."

"Duane, don't use the plural when you're just addressing me," Karla said coolly.

Duane had used the plural because he thought he was addressing Jacy too. She was in earshot of the argument, but didn't seem to be listening. She stared, expressionless, at Suzie Nolan's portrait of Dickie. While she stared the twins tootled up on their new mountain bikes and stopped a moment with Jacy to look at the painting.

"I don't see what's so hot about Dickie," Julie said.

"Dickie's a puke face," Jack said.

Jacy smiled and put her arms around them for a moment, almost tipping over their bikes. The twins soon disengaged themselves and rode on, and Jacy and Karla walked off.

Karla gave Duane a final, icy look as she was leaving, but didn't say a word.

CHAPTER 85

DUANE WENT OVER AND SAT DOWN ON THE STEPS OF the courthouse. He felt terrible. He had never given any thought to having a nervous breakdown, but suddenly he felt that he might be having one. He wished he were home so he could shoot at the doghouse for several hours. The crashing sound of the big bullets might shut out the world for a while. He tried to remind himself that nothing that was happening was really so bad, but his mind wouldn't listen to its own counsels. Why had it become such a desperate strain to talk to anyone, particularly Karla?

The day before, Minerva had needed some rags and had torn up an old sheet to make them. Duane watched, thinking nothing of it. The sheet had been washed many times and was very thin. Minerva tore it apart as if she were tearing paper. The sheet might have been twenty years old. He and Karla, or perhaps the older children, must have slept on it hundreds of times. And yet in five minutes it stopped being a sheet and became rags.

His companionship with Karla was only a little older than

the sheet, and now it seemed to be tearing too. A few more weeks and they might only have the rags of a marriage. His children also seemed to be separating from him—easily, soundlessly—the two older ones because of age, the twins for no reason at all. They were just going.

Everything, it seemed, had been washed too many times, had worn too thin. His friendships and his little romances all seemed sad and fragile to him. They had once been the comfortable and reliable fabric that was his life. But the fabric became too old to bear the weight of all the bodies and personalities and needs of the people who tossed and turned on it. At some point a toenail or an elbow had poked through, and now it was all tearing.

Duane felt people looking at him. He didn't know how he looked, but he didn't want people staring at him. He got up and went in the courthouse. His legs were weak and he felt very confused. He remembered the courtrooms on the second floor of the courthouse. The courts weren't in use at the time. A courtroom might be a peaceful place to hide.

He climbed the stairs to the second floor, holding on to the varnished banisters as he went. When he got to the second floor he was surprised to hear typing coming from one of the courtrooms. The door was closed and the Court in Session sign hung on the door. That was odd. Duane knew perfectly well there was no court in session. He opened the door a crack and peeped in. Janine Wells was at the court reporter's table, typing away on a small portable typewriter. Lester Marlow, his hair wilder than ever, sat on a sleeping bag in front of the jury box, scribbling on a legal pad. They both heard the door open and looked around in surprise.

"It's just me," Duane said, feeling foolish.

"Don't stand there holding the door open, come in," Janine said, testily.

Duane did as he was told.

"How'd the art show go?" Lester asked amicably.

"Well, it went," Duane said. "Have you been hiding in here all the time? Jenny's half crazy from worrying about you."

"That's an improvement then," Lester said. "She's two thirds crazy when I'm around."

"He's writing a book and I'm typing it up for him," Janine said.

"Yeah, my autobiography," Lester said. "I thought I'd just write it in the courtroom. Maybe I'll be finished by the time my trial starts. When the judge asks me if I have anything to say in my own defense I'll just read my autobiography to the jury. I think they'll realize I meant well."

Duane didn't know what to say. It looked as if Janine and Lester had been living in the courtroom for weeks. One of Janine's lavender negligees was draped over a chair, and Lester's shaving kit was on the counsel's table. They even had a hot plate with a coffeepot on it.

"Well," Duane said. "I guess a courtroom wouldn't be a bad place to write a book."

"If I were you I'd leave town, Duane," Lester said. "A Dallas bank's taking over the bank. Those Dallas bankers are just waiting for the centennial to be over to start grabbing stuff. Your stuff will be the first stuff they grab, too."

Duane was thinking how radiant Janine looked. She gave Lester a dreamy little smile, very different from the smiles she had once given him.

"Want some gum?" she asked, offering him a package of spearmint.

"Oh, no, thanks," Duane said.

"What are you doing up here, anyway?" Janine asked.

"I was looking for a place to have a nervous breakdown," Duane said. He realized he didn't feel nearly as close to a nervous breakdown as he had a few minutes earlier.

"Oh, be serious," Janine said, though it was clear she didn't really care whether he was serious or unserious. She wanted him to leave so she could get on with typing Lester's autobiography.

After assuring them that he wouldn't reveal their whereabouts, he went back downstairs. His shaky mood had passed. On the sidewalk he noticed a number of people looking at Suzie's blue ribbon portrait of Dickie.

There had not been a word of dissent when the picture was awarded first prize. Several of the artists who had painted their grandbabies stood looking at the portrait solemnly.

"She got the hands right," one elderly woman said. "That ain't easy. I can do the eyes, but I had a real hard time getting the hands right."

Junior Nolan was squatting under an oak tree nearby, listening to people praise his wife's portrait of Dickie Moore. The blue ribbon hung beside it. Junior no longer looked sad. He just looked proud.

CHAPTER 86

IN THE STREET, DUANE RAN INTO THE VERY PERSON he least wanted to see, namely Buster Lickle. Buster saw him before he could duck into his pickup. He dashed across the street and grabbed Duane's arm.

"Duane, we're in trouble," Buster said, his face sweaty and despairing.

"Oh, you mean because the bank's closed?" Duane asked.

"No, the souvenirs!" Buster said, almost shouting. "There's no business. The goddamn past just ain't selling. We've only sold forty ashtrays and the damn centennial's just got one more day to run."

"Forty out of how many?" Duane asked.

"Forty out of three thousand," Buster said. "We just sold a hundred T-shirts, and all of them Smalls."

"You act like you think I'm supposed to do something about it," Duane said, disengaging his arm from Buster's anguished grip.

"You gotta do something about it!" Buster said. "I'm losing my ass on this centennial. Nobody wants to buy ashtrays, and you can't even give away buggy rides in this heat."

"I don't see what I'm supposed to do about it," Duane said.

"Go on TV," Buster pleaded. "Get one of the TV stations in Wichita to put you on."

"Go on TV and do what?"

"Tell people they ought to love their glorious heritage more," Buster said. "Tell them the past belongs to all of us and they better get over here and learn about it while there's still time."

"The past may belong to all of us, but the ashtrays and T-shirts belong to you," Duane said. "The city offered to go fifty-fifty on the souvenirs but you wanted it all for yourself."

"But what am I gonna do with three thousand ashtrays?" Buster said. "Five thousand T-shirts. We got salt and pepper shakers and centennial pillows and place mats with the courthouse on 'em. What am I gonna do with all that shit? I can't return it."

"If I were you I'd start discounting the past about ninety percent, real quick," Duane said, getting in his pickup.

He started to back out of his parking place, but Buster grabbed the stanchions to the rearview mirror and hung on. He had a desperate look—a look that had become increasingly common in Thalia, Duane thought.

"Just do a TV show," Buster said. "Just do one, Duane. People trust you. Talk about the Alamo and Sam Houston and longhorn cattle. And remind them that the souvenir shop's open from seven A.M. till midnight on the last day of the centennial."

"Buster, I'm an oilman," Duane said. "I don't know anything about longhorn cattle."

"Just talk about this glorious heritage," Buster said.

"Seems to me it's so glorious it's just about driven us all crazy," Duane said. He wanted to go, but Buster still clung to his rearview mirror. When he finally let go he stood in the hot street looking so hopeless that Duane felt his headache starting again, just from having to look at Buster in his despair.

"I don't know what to think of people anymore," Buster said. "They ain't even buying the centennial key rings. Now you know everybody needs a new key ring, once in a while."

He turned in defeat and walked back across the street, wiping his dripping face on his shirtsleeve.

CHAPTER 87

DUANE HURRIED HOME, HOPING EVERYONE WOULD be absent as usual. If they were absent as usual he could shoot at the doghouse for a while, unobserved. The doghouse was so ugly that shooting at it had seemed natural the first few times he did it. There could not be much wrong with shooting at an ugly doghouse, particularly if there were no dogs in it.

Now that the thought that he might be capable of having a nervous breakdown had crossed his mind, it occurred to him that he probably ought to reassess the business of shooting at the doghouse. A casual bystander might think it a rather odd thing for a grown person to do. His own family had never questioned him about it, but it was possible that even they might regard it as odd.

Once or twice he had awakened Barbette by shooting at the doghouse. When he reflected on the matter, he realized that it might not be good for a baby girl to be awakened by the sound of a .44 Magnum. Duane didn't want to be a bad grandparent, whatever else he might be, so the last few times he had gone out to the hot tub with his gun he had contented himself with merely putting on his earmuffs and staring at the doghouse. He left the gun unloaded. That way he avoided being a bad grandparent, but otherwise he didn't feel very pleased.

He didn't really care about the doghouse, ugly though it was. What he wanted was to hear the sound the gun made—though not all the sound. The earmuffs not only kept him from being deafened, they civilized the sound of the gun, rendering it almost musical. With the shooting muffs on, he could be on perfect terms with the sound. It retained its strength, but not its power to punish. It had a force like a powerful wave; with the muffs on he could move in it but not be drowned by it.

When he walked in, his whole family, Dickie excepted, was sitting around the kitchen table. They all had felt pens in their hands and blank pieces of paper in front of them. Little Mike sat in Karla's lap, grasping a Crayola as if it were a hunting knife. Little Joe Coombs sat by Nellie. Everyone except Little Mike looked solemn. The twins had on their mirror sunglasses.

Duane went and got his earmuffs, which hung in a little gun closet. He put them around his neck and went back to the kitchen. If the earmuffs could civilize the sound of a .44 Magnum, it was possible they could also civilize the sound of his family. And if they couldn't civilize it, perhaps they could obliterate it.

"If anybody says one mean thing to me I'm putting on my earmuffs," he said, looking at Karla.

"Duane, we're just gonna write out our prophecies and hopes for the next hundred years," Karla said. "They're gonna seal the time capsule tomorrow."

"My hope is that nobody says anything mean to me for the next hundred years," Duane said, getting himself a beer. "It's not my prophecy, though."

"He's been snappish lately, ain't he?" Minerva said.

Duane spread the earmuffs and held them a half inch from his ears.

"Go on," he said. "Just say something mean."

"Duane, if you want to participate and be part of the family, just sit down and behave," Karla said.

Duane sat down and stared for a bit into the mirror sunglasses of the twins. He saw four images of himself, one in each lens, but could not gain a glimmering of what kind of mood the twins might be in.

"My other hope is that I'll never have to judge another art show," Duane said.

"Duane, just hush, you did real good," Karla said. "You voted exactly the way Jacy and I told you to."

"I was gonna do a portrait of Linda Lovelace, I think she's a victim," Minerva said.

"Why didn't you?" Duane asked.

"They never run that *Deep Throat* show no more and I've forgotten what she looks like," Minerva said.

"I've forgotten what all of you look like," Duane said. "You don't stay home long enough for me to remember."

Just as he said it Jacy walked into the kitchen. She looked as if she'd been crying. Duane felt his remark might disturb her —she might think he was accusing her of depriving him of his family. But Jacy showed no sign that she'd heard him. She took a bottle of white wine out of the refrigerator, a glass out of the cabinet, put a couple of ice cubes in the glass and left without a word.

"Her little boy was younger than me and he got killed," Jack said, once Jacy was gone.

No one had anything to say to that.

"I'd never get killed," Jack said, kicking the table leg nervously.

"Hush, it's bad luck to talk about it," Karla said.

"I seen a man get killed yesterday," little Joe Coombs remarked. The sound of his voice, which only Nellie had really been privileged to hear—and she not often—startled everyone.

"Who? You never told me," Nellie said reproachfully.

"A crop duster," little Joe said, embarrassed now that all eyes were on him. "His plane went down instead of up. He was dead on impact."

"You never told me," Nellie repeated.

"Didn't want to upset you," little Joe murmured. "It was in the paper.

"Anybody can always get killed," he added, becoming more and more nervous. Everyone was watching him.

"It's just a matter of sheer luck," he said. "It can happen any time of the day or night."

"Shut up, Joe, you're getting on my nerves," Karla said. "Talk about something else. We're all trying to think of cheerful hopes for the time capsule."

"Don't pick on him, Momma!" Nellie said. "You're always wanting him to talk more when we're on the phone and now he came all the way out here and he's trying to take part in the conversation and you tell him to shut up."

"I wasn't picking on him," Karla said loudly. "I just want him to shut up if all he can think of to talk about is how easy it is to get killed."

"It was a cable on the movie set that killed her little boy," Julie said. "It wasn't covered up like it was supposed to be. He just brushed against it but it was so full of electricity he never had a chance."

Duane noticed her lip quivering, beneath the mirror sunglasses. A moment later she threw herself in his arms, crying so loudly that Little Mike looked up, astonished. He had been stabbing the table with his Crayola.

"Now look what you've started, Joe!" Karla said. She too seemed on the verge of tears.

"Jack started it, actually," Duane said, hugging Julie.

Even Jack looked morose. He took off his sunglasses and flung them on the table.

"I wouldn't have brushed against the cable," Jack said. "I watch for things like that."

Julie stopped sobbing long enough to scream at him.

"You shut up!" she said. "You've never even been to a movie set. You don't know what you'd do."

Jack pretended his felt pen was a dart. He threw it at Little Mike. As usual, his aim was unerring. The felt pen hit Little Mike in the middle of his forehead, making a blue mark. Little Mike opened his mouth in surprise.

"You could have put that baby's eye out!" Karla yelled, jumping out of her chair.

"It was just a felt pen," Jack said.

Julie wiggled out of Duane's arms, grabbed the sugar bowl and dumped all the sugar right on Jack's head.

"You've never even been on a movie set!" she yelled. "You don't know what you'd do. You might be killed in five seconds."

"You fuckerface asshole!" Jack said, jumping up. He started to pummel his sister, a dust of sugar raining from his hair, but he saw his mother coming and turned and raced for the back door.

Julie slumped back in Duane's arms, sobbing even more wildly.

"I'll whip your little butt if I catch you!" Karla yelled at Jack, but instead of going after him she burst into tears and ran out of the kitchen in the opposite direction.

"You never take up for yourself!" Nellie yelled at Joe. "You just let Momma walk all over you! It's making me crazy!"

Joe turned beet red and looked as if he too might cry.

"Goin' home for a while," he mumbled, hurrying for the back door.

"I'm going with you, I can't live in this house, it's making me crazy!" Nellie said. She followed Joe out the back door. Julie wiggled loose and ran after them.

"Where are you going?" Duane asked.

"To beat up Jack, he shouldn't say he knows what to do on a movie set," Julie said.

"Sweet family you got," Minerva said, when the kitchen had emptied. Little Mike, left behind, was trying to stab the cat with his Crayola.

"Not too stable, though," she added.

"Well, who is too stable?" Duane asked.

"Me," Minerva said. "When you've beat the odds as many times as I have it stables you down."

"I don't think I've beaten the odds a single time this year," Duane remarked.

Barbette was fretting, disturbed by all the tears and commotion. He picked up the felt pen Jack had thrown at Little Mike, put the top on it and handed it to Barbette to play with. She popped it into her mouth.

Duane walked out the back door, worried that Jack and Julie might be hitting one another with rocks. They were over by the pickups, arguing fiercely, but not endangering one another's lives. Shorty came over and stuck his head between Duane's legs. He liked to hide his eyes during periods of tension.

Duane went back in and wandered around his huge house, thinking about how much he hated it. He knew he should go try and comfort Karla, but he felt too nervous and kept putting it off. He wandered into the living room, which contained, among other things, two grand pianos and a stuffed Kodiak bear. The reason for the pianos was that Karla occasionally fantasized that the twins would become concert pianists.

The Kodiak bear loomed over one corner of the living room. He was mounted on his hind legs and stood over ten feet tall. He had been shot by a car dealer in Fort Worth. The dealer, who aspired to seduce Karla, threw in the Kodiak bear in a package deal one time near the height of the boom, when they had bought his-and-hers Cadillacs.

Everyone hated the Kodiak bear, even Karla, who confessed later that she had only taken it to punish Arthur, her architect, after he had proved so disappointing romantically.

"He's probably still vomiting at the thought that there's a Kodiak bear in the precious living room he designed," she said.

"How'd he find out about it?" Duane asked.

"I told him. How would you think he'd find out, Duane?" Karla said. "Arthur hates me now."

"Well, you hate him too," Duane said. "You're even."

"He was sweet at the beginning, though," Karla said. "You'd be surprised how many men are sweet at the beginning."

"Was I sweet at the beginning?" he asked.

"No, you were pitiful, just like you are now," Karla said.

Duane sat down at one of the huge pianos and played "Chopsticks" with one finger. He felt it would be nice to play the piano. Playing music might be better than shooting at the doghouse. His music could drown out the world, and he wouldn't have to wear the earmuffs, which could become uncomfortably hot.

"Why the fuck are you playing 'Chopsticks'?" Jacy asked. She was watching him from the doorway, a glass of wine in her hand.

"No reason," Duane said, stopping at once.

Jacy walked over and stood looking at the Kodiak bear for a moment. She squatted down near it and looked more closely.

"Where's its dick?" she asked.

Duane came over and looked too. He had never paid much attention to the Kodiak bear, or the living room, either, for that matter. The bear did seem to lack genitals.

"No dick and no balls," Jacy said. "I guess your bear's been censored."

"It's not my bear," Duane said. "Some car dealer from Fort Worth fell in love with Karla and threw it in with a couple of Cadillacs."

"I hope you beat him up," Jacy said. "In the first place he shouldn't be shooting harmless bears and in the second place he shouldn't be bothering your wife."

"I don't know that he bothered her," Duane said. He had not beaten up the car dealer—in fact, had not even met him.

Jacy strolled out of the room and Duane followed. She went down the hall and into one of the numerous guest rooms. She seemed to be living in it. There was an overnight bag by the bed, a pile of compact disks on the floor, a Walkman, a scattering of magazines. On the TV a game show was in progress, but the sound was turned off.

Jacy sat down on the bed. She looked dejected. Duane stopped in the doorway, not sure that he was welcome even that close. But he remembered how her eyes had sought his in the rearview mirror. He remembered wanting to kiss her.

She looked up at him sourly.

"Forget it, if that's what you're thinking," she said.

Duane didn't say anything. He started to go away.

"Duane," she said, after he had already turned.

He looked in again.

"Could you just bring me that bottle of white wine?" she asked.

He went to the kitchen and got it for her.

"I'm sorry I bit your head off," she said when he returned and handed her the wine bottle.

"It wasn't much of a bite, compared to some," he said.

Jacy scooted over, indicating that he was to sit on the bed.

"I'm still sorry," she said. "I doubt you were thinking anything. You look more miserable than I feel. But there's no point in your coming around me wanting love. You're not going to get any, and I don't want you trying to give it, either. I haven't got the energy to reject people graciously right now. I've got enough to feel bad about without having to engineer considerate rejections."

Duane smiled. "Don't worry," he said. "I'm used to the inconsiderate kind."

Jacy smiled too, though a little wanly. She put a hand to her breast.

"There's a cavity here," she said. "You think of it as being filled with a normal woman's heart, but that's not how I think of it. I think of it as being more like a washing machine. Things swirl around. Sometimes I'm on a slow cold cycle, and other days I'm on a hot fast cycle. If I load the washer carefully and just clean one thing at a time I do fairly well. I'll never get all the grief out but if I'm careful and don't overload the washer it'll be a stain I might live with, someday."

She got up, walked around the bed, and pulled the curtain back from the window. It was around a hundred and six degrees outside—the landscape was gray-white with heat.

"Italy's no place to do that kind of laundry," she said, sitting back down. She offered him a sip of her wine, but he shook his head.

"Too pretty?" he asked.

"Too responsive," Jacy said. "There's too much that tempts you to love."

She looked at him—not angrily—and then out the window again.

"I just wanta wash my clothes, and I came to the right place to do it," she said. "This place looks exactly like I feel—dirty, bleak, hot and empty. There's no discrepancy between what I see outside and what's swirling around in the washer—which is good."

Duane started to put his arm around her but decided against it.

"Go pay your wife some attention," Jacy said. She leaned off the bed and began to rummage through the compact disks.

"Anyway, I love you," he said, standing up to go. Immediately, he regretted saying it. He expected a cold response, or else an angry one, but Jacy, her hands filled with compact disks, just looked quizzical.

"Anyway, you love me?" she said. "What does the anyway mean?"

Duane didn't know what to say. What *had* he meant, by putting it that way? Why had he said it at all? He was not sure it was even true. His life was already too complicated—he didn't really want to love her or have her in love with him. But the words had popped out.

"Anyway, I love you," Jacy said, testing the statement thoughtfully. "Anyway I love you. Anyway *I* love you. Anyway, I love *you*."

Duane felt profoundly silly, but was relieved, at least, that he hadn't made her angry.

"We've got quite a few possibilities to choose from here, haven't we, honey pie?" Jacy said. "I guess I'll have to ponder them for a while. I'm too tired to choose right now."

She stood up, yawning, and waved with her hand for him to go. When he left she closed the door behind him.

CHAPTER 88

DUANE EXPECTED TO FIND KARLA DESOLATE, BUT instead found her cheerful. She sat at her dressing table, writing furiously on a note pad. He flopped on the waterbed, feeling discouraged. Why was he going around telling women he loved them just because he liked them? Wasn't there a difference?

"What's the matter with you now?" Karla asked.

Duane didn't answer. He bobbed on the waterbed for a while. Mainly he felt an urge to go out to the rig and not come back, but for the moment he was too tired to convert his feelings into action.

Karla continued to write, glancing over at him from time to time.

"Duane, it's hard to concentrate when you're in such a bad mood," she said.

"What makes you think I'm in a bad mood?" he asked.

Karla put down her pen and came and sat on the bed. She had a lively look in her eye. Duane was afraid he knew what it meant. He felt gloomy and doubtful. Why must she always be

485

so energized when he felt too tired to lift a hand in his own defense?

"Let's try making love," Karla said, beginning to unbutton his pants. "I wanta see if we can get to three thousand and one."

"Not a chance," Duane said. "We'd just get to three thousand and a half."

"That's fine, as long as I'm the half that gets off," Karla said, pulling her T-shirt over her head.

Duane put a pillow on his face.

"I read an article that said some men are scared of tits," Karla said. "Maybe that's your whole problem."

"It's not my whole problem, or any part of my problem," Duane said.

"You could be scared of tits and not want to admit it," Karla said. She continued to work at the buttons on his jeans, winced and looked ruefully at a bent fingernail.

"Now look what you've done, Duane," she said. "I've asked you a million times to buy those Levi's with zippers."

"I always forget," Duane said.

Karla got off the bed. Duane peeped over his pillow, expecting her to go tend to her wounded fingernail. Instead, she finished undressing. She stood by the bed, her panties in one hand, as if debating with herself. Then she grabbed the pillow he had been peeping over and dropped her panties on his face. Duane immediately threw them on the floor.

"You could have sniffed once or twice," Karla said. "It said in an article I read that the smell of women's undergarments is very exciting to most men."

"You read too much," Duane said. He felt slightly less tired, though. It was interesting to see what lengths Karla would go to in order to get what she wanted. There was something appealing about her determination. He had once been every bit as determined where she was concerned, and she had been the hesitant one.

He put the pillow under his head, rather than over his face. Then he noticed something odd: Karla didn't seem to have as much pubic hair as she had had the last time he looked.

"What happened to you?" he asked.

"I shaved," Karla said. She bent over him and carefully finished unbuttoning his pants. Then she hurried over to her dressing table and scribbled a sentence or two more, before returning to the bed. Duane looked again at her pubis. She had definitely shaved. She still had some pubic hair, but not much.

"Why'd you do that?" he asked.

"Boredom," Karla said. "I just did it one day in the bathtub."

"Oh," Duane said.

Karla got another pillow and put it over his feet. Then she lay on top of him, her head at his feet and her heels beside his head. She wiggled a little, getting comfortable, and then she just lay there.

"Karla, did you read about this in *Playgirl?*" he asked. "Did some writer think your husband would get wildly excited if you lay on top of him?"

"Are you wildly excited, Duane?" she asked.

"I'm totally squashed," Duane said.

"I partly shaved out of boredom but it was partly because I bought one of those bathing suits like Nellie has," Karla said. "Those bathing suits barely hide your pussy."

"I've noticed that," Duane said.

"I don't get along too well with Nellie," Karla said. "I guess I'm jealous because she's young and beautiful and has all those boyfriends chasing her and I'm old and don't even have you chasing me."

"I might chase you if I wasn't squashed," Duane remarked.

"I wish I knew what other women were like in bed," Karla said, lifting one leg briefly in order to scratch a chigger bite on her calf. "I used to have confidence that I was as interesting as anybody but now I've lost my confidence. Maybe there are women who are twice as interesting. Ever since I had that thought my mind hasn't been at rest."

"I don't want you wearing one of those bathing suits like Nellie has," Duane said.

"Why not?"

"It wouldn't hide enough," he said.

"You sleep with other women and you could tell me if I'm as interesting but you never say a word that would put my mind at rest," Karla said.

"You aren't listening," Duane said, a little annoyed. "I told you those bikinis like Nellie wears don't hide enough."

"That's just a matter of point of view," Karla said.

"I'm looking right at what one would have to hide and I'm telling you it wouldn't hide enough, not for a woman your age," Duane said.

He looked straight up his wife's body, between her breasts, and met her eyes. Karla looked quizzical, as Jacy had when he told her he loved her anyway.

"Oh," Karla said. "Now that you've fucked it three thousand times and had four nice babies out of it, you want me to hide it. Is that right, Duane? Nellie's your own daughter but just because she's young you don't care if she shows hers off."

"I never have been crazy about her showing it off," he said, rolling out from under her.

"No, but it don't offend you, it's just looking at my old one that she came out of that offends you," Karla said.

She started to roll off the bed but Duane caught her.

"It don't offend me one bit," Duane said. He had caught her just on the edge of the bed and was trying to pull her back into the center but the waterbed exerted a kind of suction and it wasn't easy. The two of them were wedged against the side of the bed.

"Duane, don't lie, you're just trying to be nice because you know I'm upset," Karla said.

"I'm not trying to be nice, I'm trying to fuck you but I'm stuck to this stupid waterbed," he said.

"It's not good sexual ethics to pretend you want to fuck your wife just because you were rude and insensitive and upset her," Karla said, still trying to crawl out of the bed.

"Sexual what?" Duane asked.

"Sexual ethics," Karla said. "Didn't you see that paperback I had called *Sexual Ethics*? I left it in the bathroom and it disappeared. I thought you might be reading it."

Duane managed to kiss her, something he had not done in he couldn't remember when. It was a novel and pleasant sensation, partly because Karla opened her mouth to continue her discussion of sexual ethics just as they kissed. She had clearly not expected to be kissed, and reacted hesitantly, ready to go on with the conversation if he stopped.

"You're not supposed to make it seem like a favor," she said, during a break in the kiss.

"Karla, it's not a favor," he said, annoyed both by the waterbed and her reluctance to believe that his desire was sincere. Then he became annoyed with himself for not having heeded her advice to buy Levi's with zippers. The waterbed exerted such suction that it was almost impossible to undress. He had to get off it to struggle out of his pants. He remembered what Jacy had said about the swirling inside her, a hot swirling and a cold. He felt an unusual swirling too and was afraid it would stop too soon. Memories of his joyful youth with Karla got mixed with his anxiety.

"Gosh, that was an intense orgasm, thanks, Duane," Karla said, later. Her doubts about his sincerity were gone—she was rubbing cream on his lower abdomen, which had been slightly chafed by a particularly bristly area of her newly shaven pubis.

"It wasn't a favor and you're not supposed to thank me," Duane said. "Didn't that book teach you anything?"

"What book?" she asked nonchalantly.

"The one on sexual ethics," he said.

"Oh, I didn't read it. Why would I need to read it?" she said.

"To learn about sexual ethics, I guess," he said.

Karla lifted her breasts and rubbed a little deodorant under them.

"I got good sexual ethics, they're instinctive," she said. "Do unto others whatever you can get them to do unto you. I bought that book for you to read, but I bet the twins stole it."

He decided one reason he had stayed married to Karla was because she was the one woman he could sleep with and not feel depressed later. She was at her most delightful after a little sex. There was no telling what she would say or do, postcoitum —not that there was much telling at any other time. He decided he must be crazy for not making love to her more often.

He had been feeling relaxed and virtuous, but the thought that the twins would soon be embarking on their sex lives caused his sense of virtue to tail off a little.

"I'm not ready to think about the twins' sex lives just yet," he said.

"Which had you least rather think about, the twins' sex lives or how much money you owe?" Karla asked.

Out the window Duane could see the twins, who were in the pool. For once they were not trying to drown one another. They were even taking turns diving. Both of them dove beautifully. They seemed very young, but there was no getting around the fact that Jack was constantly stealing oils and creams from Karla's dressing table, to be used in secret practices.

"Once those two get into sex lives we won't have no youngsters anymore," Duane said.

"That's right," Karla said. She looked out the window at the twins. He couldn't tell from her face whether her thoughts were happy or sad. She poured a little more cream in her hand and rubbed it on his abdomen.

"What'll we do then?" Karla asked.

"Shave ourselves in the bathtub, I guess," Duane said.

Karla smiled serenely.

"You think we'll even be together?" she asked.

"Didn't we just start our comeback?" he said.

Karla twisted around to try and see a mole that grew on the back of her arm, high up.

"Yes, Duane, it was a real sexy comeback," she said.

"So why wouldn't we be together?"

Karla went to her table and got a mirror. She held it so she could get a better look at her mole.

"One little sexy comeback don't mean you can say for sure," she said. "You put some of me at peace but you haven't said a word that would put my mind at peace."

Duane tried to think of a lie about sexual skills that might put her mind at peace. He couldn't think of one. Karla had always been appealing sexually. She had also always been generous and competent. He would have considered her more or less without peer had he not stumbled into bed with Suzie Nolan, whose qualities in that sphere were on a level beyond competence. But of course, Suzie was new. He had only slept with her a few times—not thousands of times, as he had with Karla. It was not fair to compare them. If he continued with Suzie for twenty years she might cease to seem so advanced.

"Penny for your thoughts, Duane," Karla said, returning to the bed.

Duane decided not to launch into any lies. That would just destroy what was left of his sense of virtue. He wrenched himself loose from the waterbed and picked up his Levi's.

"I wish you'd go get that mole taken off," he said. "That would sure help *my* peace of mind."

CHAPTER 89

JACY TOOK ADVANTAGE OF THE FACT THAT IT WAS
their last performance to vamp up the Adam and Eve skit. Instead of languorously eating an apple, she sidled up to him and
kissed him. Duane was deeply ill at ease and embarrassed,
though the crowd went wild.

"My God, you're stodgy," Jacy said, when the skit was over.
"I was just updating my homecoming queen kiss. I figure I
should get to kiss you in the rodeo arena at least once every
thirty years."

The people continued to cheer as they walked off the field,
but Duane didn't care. He was sick of the pageant, the centennial, the crowds of people. He listened to the women rock
through the "Battle Hymn of the Republic," and then got in
his pickup and headed for the lake. Shorty, who had been
snoozing in the pickup, was happy to be going along.

He got to the boat dock a few minutes before sunset, only to
discover that his boat was gone. A red Porsche was parked on
the dock.

Duane felt annoyed. Dickie was supposed to let him know if

he wanted to borrow the boat. He loved being on the lake just after sunset and felt frustrated at having to mope around on land. He got in the pickup and honked his horn for several minutes, hoping Dickie would get the message. Then he began to get his fishing tackle together. He felt in the mood to lay a trot line and had bought plenty of bait.

The western reaches of the lake were already in shadow, and he couldn't spot the boat. He walked along the shoreline and cast a time or two with a plug to pass the time. With the sun down, the surface of the lake was silvery—he enjoyed watching the wiggling plug as he reeled in the line. He wasn't really expecting a strike, and was surprised when a fish hit the line—a fish with some fight, too, judging from the zing of the line. He was just about to start playing the bass when he heard Dickie laugh. A second later he heard a splash that was too large to be a fish. Duane looked up and saw his boat. It had drifted out of the shadows, forty yards away. The splash had been Dickie diving overboard. He was swimming rapidly toward the dock. A woman wearing only a shirt—Duane saw that it was Suzie—stood in the boat, bending over the motor. A second later it started and she turned the boat slowly toward the dock, staying a good distance behind the swimmer.

Duane forgot his fish until it was too late. The line went slack. He was in shadow himself—Suzie hadn't seen him. The boat putted past, only a few yards away, just as Dickie climbed out on the dock. Suzie smiled when she saw Dickie, a smile so deeply pleased that Duane wished he was on the other side of the lake, or perhaps on another planet.

Though it was only a glimpse of a woman's smile, seen in the evening light, it was to haunt Duane for months and years. Suzie, smiling in the motorboat, played over and over again, like a few frames from a film, in waking and sleeping dreams throughout his life. It was the most compelling look he was ever to see on a woman's face, a look of keen and hungry happiness, drawn from no common level of affection or satisfaction. It was to become his image of what love was—images from his own experience quickly blurred by comparison. Shorty, who had been nervously pacing along the shore, came and stood close to him, ignoring several frogs.

Dickie, at whom the smile was directed, either didn't see it or was not particularly struck by it. He waited on the dock a little impatiently, eager for Suzie to dock the boat.

Duane saw Suzie handing Dickie their clothes and an ice chest. While they were clearing the boat he tiptoed deeper into the shadows. For the second time that evening he felt deeply embarrassed, without quite knowing why. In an age of back-yard hot tubs, skinny-dipping was no big deal. It never had been a big deal.

It was not their nakedness that had struck him to the heart—yet something had. He squatted by the lake, listening to the occasional frog plop into the water, remembering how Suzie Nolan had smiled at his son. Had any woman ever smiled at him that way? Perhaps Karla had, at some point in their lives, and he, like Dickie, had missed it.

Suzie and Dickie stood on the dock and dressed. Duane could hear them talking, but not what they said. Once Suzie stopped Dickie and kissed him. Then Dickie carried the small ice chest to the Porsche. Suzie picked up their towels and deposited a bag of trash in a trash barrel.

His pickup was sitting right next to the Porsche, so they must realize that he was around, but they went on casually chatting and packing the car.

Duane began to feel silly. He had known for a long time that Suzie loved Dickie. He had only got to know her himself because of a little riffle in their relations. He had no reason to hide in the darkness, listening to frogs jump in the water, but he stood a little longer before forcing himself to start back.

Suzie and Dickie stood by the Porsche, their arms around one another, when Duane walked up.

"Hey, Dad," Dickie said. "Where's the fish?"

"The fish got away," Duane said. "Hi, Suzie."

"Duane, can I get a ride?" she asked. "Dickie has to go to Wichita."

"Sure, I'll take you in," Duane said.

Dickie seemed a bit nervous. He stood on one foot and then the other.

"Aren't you coming to the dance?" Duane asked. "It's the last night of the centennial."

"Oh, I'm coming," Dickie said. "Jacy would skin me alive if I didn't show up to dance with her. I'm just going to run a little errand first."

After a nervous glance at Duane, he gave Suzie another kiss.

"You tell him," he said, and jumped in the Porsche. Shorty began to jump up in the air and yip.

"Take him with you," Duane said. "I think he wants to ride in a Porsche."

Dickie didn't complain. He snapped his fingers and Shorty jumped in. The Porsche was soon out of sight, trailing a cloud of dust.

"Tell me what?" Duane asked.

"We're getting married," Suzie said. "I'm gonna be your daughter-in-law, Duane."

"Naw, Suzie, come on," Duane said.

"Yep, I am," Suzie said. "He's gone to Wichita to get the engagement ring right now. Some of those jewelry stores in the mall stay open until nine."

"I think I'll drown myself," Duane said. "Or maybe I should drown you."

Suzie laughed. Neither threat impressed her.

"I'll be good for him, Duane," she said. "I've already got him to stop selling dope."

"How?" Duane asked, genuinely surprised. Dickie loved to sell marijuana.

"I bought him out," Suzie said. "It took the last of poor old Junior's money, but I told Dickie I loved him too much to risk anything bad happening to him."

"That's good, but it don't mean you need to marry him, does it?" Duane asked.

"He don't know about us, if that's what's worrying you," Suzie said.

"That's not what's worrying me," Duane said. "Everything's what's worrying me. Did you know Jenny thinks she's pregnant by him?"

"Sure," Suzie said. "That okay with me. Dickie will make a great daddy."

"Yeah, but now Janine's pregnant by Lester," Duane said. "They're hiding out in the courthouse. Bobby Lee thinks he's in love with Nellie. Junior's involved with Billie Anne, and she's still married to Dickie. Now you wanta marry Dickie, and you're not even divorced from Junior. It's too much. I don't know where we're gonna start, but we need to get a little sanity around here pretty soon."

"You haven't said anything about yourself, Duane," Suzie said. "You're just talking your head off about other people."

"Yeah, because other people's behavior is driving me crazy," Duane said. "It's hard enough facing bankruptcy without everybody I know marrying and divorcing once or twice a week."

"Why should you care? You're happily married," Suzie said.

"I don't know that I am," Duane said. "My own family left home and moved in with Jacy."

"They moved back though—didn't they?" Suzie asked.

"Yeah, but who knows if they'll stay," he said. "They're planning to go to Italy. I guess they'll come back, but I don't know. Maybe they won't."

The more he talked about it, the more confused and outraged he felt. Grown-up sensible people just seemed to have lost all balance.

"There don't seem to be no restraint at all anymore," he said. "People just do anything—and not just kids, either. Grown-up people, who ought to know better, just do anything that pops into their heads."

Suzie laughed and nudged him in the ribs.

"Look who's talking," she said. "Seems like I remember a couple of people having sex under the red light. If you're so big on restraint how come that happened?"

"It happened where it happened because you wouldn't let me drive around behind the post office," he said.

He was aware, though, that the force of his complaint had been somewhat weakened.

"Besides that, you'd do it again, if I wanted you to," Suzie said. "Wouldn't you?"

"Not a chance," Duane said.

"I think there's a chance," Suzie said, with a certain authority in her voice. "I think there's a hundred percent chance you'd do it again if I wanted you to."

"You're about to be my daughter-in-law," he said. "If I was to do it again I certainly wouldn't admire myself for it."

Suzie smiled—not the incandescent smile of love she had given Dickie, just the satisfied smile of a woman confident of her powers.

"I'm not gonna lose two minutes' sleep the rest of my life over whether you admire yourself or not, Duane," she said. "I just want you to admit you'd do it if I wanted you to."

"How about Junior?" he asked. "How's he gonna take this news?"

"He's already taken it," Suzie said. "I told him this morning. He said he didn't want to stand in the way of my happiness. Actually he's just tired of me getting in the way of his *unhap-piness.*"

The wind blew through the pickup, blowing Suzie's long hair across her face.

"I tried to give him happiness but there's just some people who won't take it," Suzie said. "Junior won't die, though. He seems like one of those people who don't really live, but I guess he lives, in his way. He'll mope around and get rich again someday, when things improve."

They came into town just in time to get ahead of a string of cars leaving the rodeo pens. The pageant had just ended.

"You staying for the dance?" he asked.

Suzie shook her head. "Take me home," she said.

Taking her home only took a few minutes. He pulled up to her driveway and killed the motor. They could faintly hear the sounds of the merry-go-round from the little carnival. Duane was in no hurry to leave, nor did Suzie seem to be in a hurry to get out. She was relaxed, but he wasn't. His sense that things were running wildly out of kilter kept returning.

"Dickie's young and he's fickle," Duane said. "You're my age. Have you ever thought of the long term?"

"Uh-huh," Suzie said. "I've thought about the long term of my old age."

"He's a good boy," Duane said, "but he's kind of a heart-breaker."

"Shut up, Duane," Suzie said. "It's not your job to keep me from getting hurt."

"I'd hate to see either one of you get hurt," Duane said.

"You better think about yourself," Suzie said. "You're gonna end up going crazy if you don't stop worrying about everybody you know. You're not ever gonna get people around here to settle down and do sensible things. They're just gonna do whatever they want to do. Why should you try and stop them?"

"I'm trying to stop you and Dickie because I think you're making a big mistake," he said.

"Are you fighting it because you want me for yourself?" she asked.

"It's not so much that," Duane said, unprepared for the question.

Suzie opened her door.

"If it's not that, then it's none of your business," she said. "I guess I'll see you at the wedding, after we all get our divorces."

"I could never have had you for myself," he said, made uncomfortable by her hostile tone. "You were too much in love with Dickie all along."

"Head over heels in love with him," Suzie said with a smile. "I'm just trying to get you to be honest about what you want, but you're never going to be because you don't know how to be honest and you don't know what you want, either."

She got out and started for her house, but then stopped and came around to his side of the pickup. She gestured for him to bend down, and gave him a little kiss.

"That's okay, sweetie," she said. "I don't care if you don't know what you want. I'm glad I'm getting you for a father-in-law. We might have some interesting family reunions one of these days."

"I just hope he stays with you long enough for there to be time for reunions," Duane said.

"Duane, you keep harping on the wrong things," Suzie said. "Something doesn't have to last a hundred years to be beautiful."

"I guess it's the marrying part I don't understand," Duane said. "It don't seem necessary. Why don't you just keep doing what you're doing?"

Suzie seemed hurt by the comment. She stepped back from the pickup and the look she gave him was indignant.

"I can't wait to start calling you Daddy Duane," she said in an angry tone. "You act like a Daddy all the time now."

"Suzie, I didn't mean to hurt your feelings," he said.

"My feelings are fine," Suzie said. "They're real healthy feelings. If you had a few like them you'd have a lot better time at that dance."

Then she turned and went in her house.

CHAPTER 90

DUANE ARRIVED AT THE COURTHOUSE IN A TROU-
bled state. It had become his usual, almost his only, state. He
decided on the short ride from Suzie's house that he would
give up talking to women. It seemed to be the only way to
avoid living in a troubled state, which was almost always the
result of things women said. Chance remarks that they flung
off effortlessly, without a thought, bounced around in his memory for hours or even days. He had the sense that his own
speech consisted almost entirely of stupid statements, the
equivalent of weak forehands, which didn't really represent his
game at its best. The women responded with conversational
smashes, drop shots, or stinging volleys, according to their
bent.

No matter what shot he chose to hit, he was left with a sense
of being out of position. They all contented themselves with
pointing out that he had the wrong attitude toward life, but
none of them bothered to supply him with an attitude that he
could replace his old one with.

The streets were so thronged with revelers come to dance

away the final night of the Hardtop County Centennial that he was forced to park seven blocks from the courthouse, a new record.

He had hardly stepped on the courthouse lawn—and the crowd was so thick it was hard even to get to the courthouse lawn—when he was seized by Bobby Lee, who had a nose-bleed and a split lip but seemed invigorated nonetheless.

"What happened to you?" Duane asked.

"I got into it with G.G. The son-of-a-bitch keeps knocking beer cans out of my hands," Bobby Lee said. "They're arresting us fighting drunks left and right, but there's only ten or twelve of them and there's thousands of us. Come on, hurry."

"Hurry where?" Duane asked.

"Over to the carnival," Bobby Lee said. "Little Mike's up-staged the human fly."

Duane saw to his surprise that almost everyone crowded onto the courthouse lawn was gazing upward. Some were looking at the human fly, a well-known local performer named Jerry Cooper, who hailed from the small town of Megargel, Texas. Jerry, a rig painter, supplemented his modest income by doubling as a human fly, climbing courthouses, water towers and other lowly structures, generally in connection with rodeos or county fairs. He had performed in Thalia many times, climbing the water tower, courthouse or jail, as the mood struck him.

This time, what seemed to have struck him was panic. He was clinging to the side of the courthouse, midway between the second and third floors, going neither up nor down.

"What's wrong, Jerry?" Duane asked. He had always admired Jerry's skills and had been responsible for hiring him to make the centennial climb.

"This courthouse is a mean booger, Duane," Jerry said in a wan, discouraged voice. "I think it's gonna get me this time."

The crowd hooted. The courthouse was made of rough sandstone and looked easy to climb—or easy if one was a climber. Several drunks immediately started climbing it to show how easy it was. One of them reached the second floor in a matter of seconds but then grew overconfident, slipped and fell into some shrubbery. He did not appear to be hurt, but his fall didn't improve Jerry Cooper's mood.

"See what I mean," he said.

"But you've already climbed this courthouse five or six times," Duane said.

"I know, but that was in the daylight," Jerry said. "It's more slippery at night. Seems like these rocks kinda sweat."

The crowd booed mercilessly. It was plain they had little use for a human fly who couldn't climb a three-story courthouse.

"You just like one story being up," Duane said, to encourage him.

"The way I look at it, I like two stories being down," Jerry said, morosely. "I ain't going up."

Duane heard screams from behind him. A crowd of women were looking up at the Ferris wheel and screaming. Jacy, Jenny and several men stood under the Ferris wheel. The men had picked up Junior Nolan's mattress and were using it as a safety net. Seated on a stanchion, high atop the Ferris wheel, was Little Mike.

"Hang on, Jerry, we'll get you down in a minute," Duane said. He saw Karla and Nellie standing back a little way from the group of women. They were both yelling at Little Mike, but the crowd drowned out their yells.

Duane ran over to the Ferris wheel, which was stopped. It was also full. Many teenagers were suspended in midair. They seemed to be enjoying the excitement. The large man who operated the ride was leaning on the brake lever with a look of impatience.

"Meanwhile I'm losing business," he said to Karla, who had kicked off her dancing shoes and was preparing to climb up after her grandson.

"Now wait a minute," Duane said. "Let's think this through and not do anything rash."

The crowd screamed again. Little Mike, holding casually to a cable, had bent over to spit at the men with the mattress. The farther he bent, the louder the crowd screamed. In the quiet moments after the scream Duane heard Little Mike babbling happily to himself.

"Where have you been?" Karla asked, eyes flashing.

"Fishing," Duane said.

"Momma thinks he'll fall but I don't," Nellie said. "He's a real good little climber."

"Meanwhile I'm losing business," the Ferris wheel operator said.

"Duane, will you buy this Ferris wheel?" Karla asked, as she started her climb. "This profit-minded son-of-a-bitch is bugging me."

The operator looked startled. "Is she serious?" he asked.

"Now, Karla, hold on a minute," Duane said. Karla had quickly climbed to the first crossbar.

"Why?" Karla asked, peering down at him. "That's my grandbaby up there."

"He's just sitting there spitting," Duane pointed out.

"If she's serious you can have the whole carnival for sixty thousand," the operator said. "And that's installed wherever you want it installed."

"Duane, somebody's got to get him down," Karla said.

"He's got good balance, he might not fall," Jacy said. She too was looking upward, appraising the situation.

"He can tell when you're mad," Duane said to Karla. "That's why I don't think you should climb up after him. He might try to get away and fall accidentally."

"We're all trained volunteer firemen, we can catch him right on this mattress," Eddie Belt said.

"I wish Julie would hurry," Nellie said. "He'd come down if Julie told him to."

"Where is Julie?" Duane asked.

"Down at Ruth's, playing cards with Sonny," Karla said. She had paused in her ascent. Little Mike bent over and spat again, provoking more screams.

"I think Duane's got a point," Jacy said. "As long as you don't scare him he's probably safe enough."

"Safe enough? He's fifty feet in the air!" Karla said, but she didn't climb any higher. Several of the men holding the mattress, too drunk to be particularly interested in Little Mike, were not too drunk to enjoy looking up Karla's skirt.

"Fifty-five thousand and you install it yourself," the carnival operator said. "It'd fit in a good-sized backyard and then your kids would never be bored."

To his relief Duane saw the twins wheeling through the crowd on their bikes. They were taking their time, and appeared to be their nonchalant selves.

"Want me to climb up and shake the little dickface off?" Jack asked, not visibly disturbed by the plight of his nephew.

"No, we don't want him shook off," Duane said.

"And you watch your language, this is a public place," Karla said, crouching on her crossbar.

"These louts are looking at your snatch," Jacy informed her.

"Oh, let 'em dream," Karla said. "Julie, will you see if you can get Little Mike to come down?"

"Get down from there, you little showoff!" Julie yelled, not bothering to dismount from her bicycle.

Hearing the command of his goddess, Little Mike immediately began to climb down. Various people, including Duane, positioned themselves to catch him if he fell, but he made a smooth and rapid descent.

"That kid should be sent to reform school right now," Jack said jealously.

"Shut up, you fuckerface!" Julie said. They rode off together, arguing.

Little Mike avoided his irate grandmother and climbed directly down into his mother's arms.

"I forgot how I got up here," Karla said, still crouching on the crossbar.

"Just drop, we'll catch you in the mattress," Eddie Belt said. He was disappointed at not getting to exhibit his firefighting techniques.

"No way," Karla said.

"Why not? We're trained volunteer firefighters," Eddie said.

"Don't listen to them, they're just hoping to get a better look at your snatch," Jacy said.

"Duane, back the pickup under me and I'll drop onto the hood."

"You're just eight feet up," he said. "Dangle off the crossbar and I'll set you down."

That proved doable. Just as Duane was setting Karla down they heard a roar from the crowd on the courthouse lawn. Bobby Lee, another trained volunteer firefighter, was backing the city's one fire truck across the lawn. He had already raised the ladder and was preparing to rescue the distraught Jerry Cooper. The crowd reluctantly made room for the fire truck.

Bobby Lee had not bothered to remove his sombrero despite the fact that he could not see out from under it very well. Instead of backing up slowly, until Jerry Cooper could grab the ladder, Bobby Lee roared backward. The ladder struck the courthouse ten feet south of where Jerry clung, and went right through the wall of the building. The shock dislodged the luckless human fly, who plunged, unflylike, into the shrubbery.

"If we'd been over there instead of over here we might have caught him," Eddie observed. He and several other trained volunteer firefighters still held Junior's mattress.

"Oh, no," Karla said. "Now look. Bobby Lee's punctured the courthouse."

The sight struck Jacy as hilarious. She burst into peals of laughter.

"This centennial gets better with age," she said, gasping for breath.

Duane ran over to see if Jerry Cooper was hurt, but could find no trace of him. He had crept out through the shrubbery and left town. Several weeks later, curious as to what had become of him, Duane discovered that he had given up rig painting and was driving a beer truck. He felt rather bad about it— Jerry had once been a competent human fly. Perhaps it had been unfair to ask him to climb the courthouse at night.

Meanwhile the ladder had pierced the courtroom where Lester and Janine were hiding. Their startled faces appeared at a window. Neither of them appeared to be clothed.

"Hey, knock it off!" Lester yelled to an audience of hundreds of drunks.

Bobby Lee, conscious that his rescue effort had misfired and that he was an object of ridicule to most of the crowd, was trying to drive the fire truck off the lawn. But the crowd, now that life and death were no longer at stake, went back to their drinking. What Bobby Lee hadn't noticed was that the ladder was stuck to the courthouse. When it had opened to its fullest length, the truck stopped. Bobby Lee put it in low and gave it all he had, but the truck wouldn't budge. It was stuck to the courthouse as firmly as Sonny's car had been stuck to the Stauffers' house.

The refusal of the ladder to come loose infuriated Bobby

Lee. He jumped out of the truck, threw his sombrero on the ground and stomped on it.

"He's ruined our one historic building," Jenny said. "What a terrible way to end our beautiful centennial."

Janine Wells had put on her nightgown. She leaned out of the window, looking bouncy. Several drunks were trying to persuade her to come down and dance with them.

"Look at Bobby Lee, he's having a fit," Karla said. "He's cute when he's mad, unlike you, Duane."

Nellie came over and handed Little Mike to Duane.

"Just hold him while I dance one dance with Joe," she said.

Duane carried Little Mike around for the next hour, during half of which Little Mike slept soundly on his shoulder. He searched through the crowd, hoping to find Minerva, but Minerva was nowhere in sight. The street was so thick with dancers that he could never even spot Nellie again, though Dickie had reappeared and was dancing with Jacy. After several circles of the courthouse, with Little Mike snoring on his shoulder, the only relative he encountered was Karla, who refused to take her grandson.

"Come on, take him for a while," Duane said. "Marriage is fifty-fifty."

"Marriage is the survival of the fittest, and I can't dance with a baby on my shoulder," Karla said, before allowing herself to be led off by Junior Nolan.

Finally Duane got a beer, sat down with his back against the courthouse, and put Little Mike face down on the grass, where he slept peacefully. Bobby Lee, having stomped his sombrero into straw, came and sat with him.

"I'll rest for a minute, then I'll get my second wind," Bobby Lee said.

While he was waiting for his second wind, he and Duane watched the dance. The twins were break-dancing with one another. They whipped in and out of groups of large shuffling drunks, gyrating, doing splits, whirling on their hands. Jacy and Dickie stopped dancing and clapped for them. Then Janine and Lester, who had just joined the revels, also stopped and clapped for them. Nellie and little Joe Coombs began to break-dance. To everyone's surprise, little Joe was a spectacular break-dancer, flinging his stocky body around with wild abandon.

"That Nellie, she's a beautiful dancer," Bobby Lee said, a throb of love in his voice.

"Not only that, her mother is too," Duane said.

Karla had joined the twins. She had tried dancing with Junior Nolan for a few minutes, but Junior soon wandered away, a puzzled look on his face. Jacy stepped in and started dancing with Karla. They tried to mimic the twins. Then they began to improvise and the twins mimicked them perfectly. Dickie stepped in and danced with Jacy and his mother.

"By God, I hate to think I'm the kind of man who'd sit around all night and watch other people dance," Bobby Lee said.

He took a deep breath, handed Duane his beer, and rushed into the street, where he began to shriek and shake, rotating his pelvis in imitation of Elvis Presley. He grabbed Nellie and spun her around five or six times. He imitated, in the space of a few seconds, virtually every dancing style Duane had ever seen. Impressed, Karla started dancing with him. Dickie went back to Jacy, and Nellie to little Joe. The twins, looking disgusted, got on their bikes and rode away.

Janine and Lester came over and sat down by him.

"Duane, you was always a wallflower," Janine said, offering him some gum.

"No, there are people still living who can remember when I was the life of the party," Duane said.

"I'm one of them," Lester said. "I can remember when you threatened to whip my ass in front of the Legion Hall."

"It's a good thing he didn't, I would never speak to him again if he had of, sweetie," Janine said, taking Lester's hand.

Lester seemed irritated by this remark.

"Sometimes your logic eludes me, honey," he said. He got up, wandered off and was soon dancing with Charlene Duggs. Janine watched, chewing her gum with increased intensity.

"What logic was he talking about?" she asked.

"I don't know," Duane said. "I sure haven't noticed any logic around here."

"Sometimes I think it was a mistake that we broke up," Janine said.

Bobby Lee had danced himself out. He came over and flopped down by them.

"Janine, would you get me a beer before I die of dehydration?" Bobby Lee asked.

"I'm certainly not getting beer for someone who hasn't even had the courtesy to ask me for one dance," Janine said.

Before Bobby Lee could reply, John Cecil walked up and politely asked Janine to dance. They were soon doing a lively two-step.

Bobby Lee got up and headed for the beer truck.

"Bring me one," Duane said. He felt a little left out and a little depressed. He really wanted to drive back out to Suzie's. Maybe he could apologize successfully and they could continue their talk. He hated it when conversations ended on an awkward note, as theirs had. He had a sense that Suzie was angry with him, and the sense held him in check in some way. He wanted to go back and talk out their differences, so as not to feel in check, but was afraid if he went back Dickie would arrive with the engagement ring while he was there.

He told himself he was silly to worry about it. It hadn't really been an argument, just a momentary disagreement. He could not even be sure what the issues were. Suzie had already probably forgotten the whole matter. In all likelihood she was happily reading a romance, or watching TV, while she waited for Dickie.

But Duane couldn't forget it. Jenny Marlow, dancing with Buster Lickle, waved frantically behind Buster's back for him to come dance with her. Duane pointed at the sleeping baby. Ordinarily he liked to dance. He could assign Bobby Lee, approaching with the beers, to watch Little Mike. But the thought of Suzie wouldn't leave his mind.

He looked around and saw G. G. Rawley, a sledgehammer in his hand, standing in front of the Texasville replica. He picked up Little Mike and walked over. Bobby Lee followed.

"It's a little late to start knocking down the saloon, G.G.," Duane said. "All the sinners are already drunk."

"The Lord don't expect me to win every battle," G.G. said. "He just expects me to keep fighting."

Just at that moment something fell into Bobby Lee's beer

cup from a considerable height. Most of the beer splashed into Bobby Lee's face, and some of it on Duane. Bobby Lee looked surprised. He wiped his dripping face on his shirtsleeve. But when he peeped into his cup he looked even more surprised. He reached in and fished out an egg.

"It rained an egg," he said, astonished.

G. G. Rawley raised his sledgehammer to start the demolition of Texasville, and as he did a shower of eggs fell on him, at least fifteen or twenty, splattering on his shoulders, chest and head.

As he stood, looking puzzled, a second egg shower fell. A few of the eggs missed and splattered on the ground, but several more hit their target.

G.G. was too startled to move. He looked cautiously into the heavens. Eggs were flying out of the dark skies. Some arched into the street, splattering the dancers. A dozen or so splatted onto the roof of Old Texasville. Some hit the roofs of cars.

"It's punishment time!" G.G. concluded, a happy light coming into his eyes. "The Lord's raining down egg bombs on this haven of sots."

As eggs continued to fall, the preacher became more excited, and also louder.

"He's set loose the crazy chickens!" he yelled. "He's freed the hens of hell!"

Duane thought otherwise. From high overhead he heard laughter, and it was the twins' laughter, not the Lord's. He tucked Little Mike under his arm and raced for the courthouse, wondering where they got the eggs.

CHAPTER 91

IN THE COURTHOUSE THE FIRST PERSON HE SAW WAS
Minerva. She sat on a bench outside the tax collector's office,
listening to her chest with a stethoscope. Minerva never traveled without her stethoscope. Listening to her own heart was
one of her favorite pastimes. Occasionally she claimed to be
able to pick up sounds from other organs as well.

"It sounds like I've got a spot on that left lung," she said,
when Duane appeared.

"I don't care where you've got a spot, take Little Mike," he
said, handing her the sleeping child.

"Why, are you too macho to take care of your own grandchild?" Minerva asked.

"I'm not too macho but I'm too confused," Duane said.

A stream of kids raced up and down the courthouse stairs.
Those going up carried numerous cartons of eggs. Outside he
heard shrieks from the direction of the dance, as dancers
sought cover from the egg showers.

"Where are you kids getting those eggs?" he asked a boy
with ten cartons in his arms. The boy ignored the question and
raced up the stairs.

"I didn't come here to baby-sit," Minerva informed him. "I was dancing before you were born, and I'm still dancing."

"The twins are throwing eggs off the roof," he pointed out. "They're throwing *lots* of eggs off the roof."

"Well, it's the last night of the centennial, I say let it rip," Minerva said.

The hens of hell, in the form of the twins, came racing down the stairs. Jack raced out the door but Duane managed to catch Julie's arm.

"Where are you getting those eggs?" he asked.

"From an egg truck," Julie said, as if answering a very stupid question. She twisted loose and ran after her brother.

Duane followed the twins outside, but not far out. The roof of the courthouse seemed to be ringed with children, all well supplied with eggs, which rained down like hail. Across the street he could see a semi, parked in front of Sonny's laundry-mat. A stream of children came and went from it like ants. The truck was clearly the source of the eggs, but why it was there he had no idea.

He ran up to the roof and saw at once that the egg throwers had ammunition for a long siege. Hundreds of cartons of eggs were stacked on the roof, and more were coming. Virtually every child in town was there. He saw Lester and Jenny's two girls, and Suzie and Junior's handsome children.

Below there was confusion. Some of the dancers were too far away to be reached by the eggs. Some danced happily on, unaware that anything out of the ordinary was happening. On the sidewalk across the street, Dickie was still dancing with Jacy.

Just as he thought the egg rain might be confined to the courthouse lawn, he saw the twins racing toward the dancers on their bikes, their bike pouches filled with eggs. Other kids followed, on other bikes. Jack and Julie sped by the dancers like Comanches, guiding their bikes by balance. They lobbed eggs over their heads like grenades, or casually flipped them under the dancers' feet. Soon dancers began to slip and fall. Many were victims of direct hits. The twins disappeared into the darkness, only to reappear moments later, egg pouches re-plenished. Jack, still wearing his mirror sunglasses, bore down on the dancers at top speed. He only veered aside at the last moment, when his victims were frozen with panic. Then he raced along the sidewalk, flinging eggs far out into the dance. Julie, just as fast, came right behind him, flinging hers at the ground as if she were skipping stones.

Many of the dancers were confused. The kids appeared only for seconds, and then vanished into the night. Most of the dancers were so drunk they never saw them. Eggs that seemed to come out of nowhere hit them and ran down their clothes. After watching for a few minutes, Duane decided to leave town. If enough people realized that his kids were the leaders of the egg bombers he would probably be beaten to a pulp—and even if he weren't he would certainly have to listen to complaints he would rather not hear.

The question was how to escape the courthouse without being covered with eggs. He found a janitor's closet and borrowed a couple of large garbage bags. He meant to loan Minerva one, but when he came back to the lobby Minerva and Little Mike were nowhere to be seen.

Duane slipped one of the garbage bags over his head, poked a couple of eyeholes in it and ran out the door. Several eggs hit the garbage bag, but in seconds he was in the street and out of range. Looking back, he saw kids with cartons of eggs getting on the Ferris wheel.

As he turned to go to his pickup, he saw Toots Burns standing by his police car in a very eggy state. He looked as if he had been hit by at least a hundred eggs.

"This is getting a little wild, ain't it, Sheriff?" Duane said.

"Yep," Toots said affably. "I just got gang-egged, or egg-banged or something."

"Where'd the egg truck come from?" Duane asked.

Toots shrugged. "It's got Iowa plates," he said. "That ol' boy that's driving it picked a hell of a bad time to go for a walk."

"The driver went for a walk?"

"Yep, he just parked her and walked off," Toots said. "He's in for a big surprise when he comes back."

There were screams from the carnival area. Showers of eggs were flying off the Ferris wheel, pelting down on kids driving bumper cars. They splattered on the merry-go-round and caused people to flee the cotton-candy stand.

"See you later, Toots," Duane said. "Don't get too stressed. It's just eggs."

"I'm not stressed," Toots said. "Ain't raw eggs supposed to be good for your complexion? I might get even prettier than I am already."

"That's what I call looking on the bright side," Duane said.

CHAPTER 92

WALKING TO HIS PICKUP, HE SAW KARLA AND JACY. They sat on the fenders of Karla's BMW, having a drink. An ice chest with two fruit jars full of liquor sat on the hood of the car.

"Got anything that don't have papaya juice in it?" he asked.

"Duane, the whole centennial's nearly gone by and you haven't danced a single dance with either one of us," Karla pointed out.

"I would have, but watching Dickie's given me an inferiority complex where dancing's concerned."

"I think you do have a massive inferiority complex," Jacy said. "You shouldn't blame it on Dickie though."

"Why not, when the whole town's in love with him?" Duane asked.

"Duane, just because you're a little bit inferior is no reason to get depressed," Karla said. She got off the fender and poured him a huge drink.

"I asked if it had papaya juice in it," he reminded her.

"Oh, don't be so picky," Jacy said.

"For your information it's grapefruit," Karla said. "Minerva

514

forgot the papaya." She refilled Jacy's drink and handed it back to her.

Duane wished he had walked up another street. The women had seemed very peaceful, sitting on the car together. They seemed to share a quiet or serenity or something that he could never share with them. They even shared a mutual appetite for picking on him. Their picking on him was just a form of joking, he knew. Mostly it was even affectionate. The problem with it was that it prompted his agreement; he would start picking on himself, only he wouldn't be joking. The more the two women joked, the more he would doubt himself. The very bond that they had formed left him out, though he was glad, very glad, that they had become friends.

Through the years, thinking about Jacy, he had often fantasized that she would come back someday and become friends with Karla. In his fantasies it was a way of having them both. For years it had been one of his pleasantest daydreams.

Now Jacy had come back, and she and Karla were friends, but the central part of the daydream hadn't happened. Instead of having them both, he had neither of them. He felt they had become much closer to one another than either of them was to him. It was warming to see that they provided one another with such easy, relaxed companionship; but where, in the years ahead, was *his* support to come from?

"Honey pie, I'm sorry," Jacy said. "Don't look so sad. You're such an easy victim, I guess we just can't resist."

"Don't baby that man," Karla said. "He's suckered me for twenty-two years with those sad looks of his."

"I don't think it's an act," Jacy said. "I think we're looking at a sad man."

"Duane, are you?" Karla asked.

"No," Duane said.

Jacy's remark startled him. In his whole life he could not remember anyone describing him as sad. He had heard hundreds of other people described as sad, but never himself.

"You shouldn't get drunk if you're sad," Karla said. "It'll just make you worse."

"I'm not drunk and I'm not sad," he insisted.

"You shouldn't lie about how you feel, either," Jacy said.

"You might fool one of us but you could never fool both of us. We know you too well."

"I don't think either one of you know me very well," Duane said angrily.

The women were silent a moment. They exchanged looks.

"My lord, you're grumpy," Karla said. "We were just joking. I remember when you had a sense of humor, Duane."

"I still have a sense of humor," Duane insisted.

At the moment, however, nothing seemed funny, though it should have. The children of Thalia were bombarding their elders with eggs, which had been made available for no reason by a trucker from Iowa who happened to park his truck in the worst possible place at the worst possible time. G. G. Rawley had been hit by twenty-five eggs which he thought came from the hens of hell. But G.G. didn't seem funny, and neither did Toots Burns, normally a comical sight even when he wasn't covered with raw eggs. None of it affected Duane as strongly as the sight of the two women sitting on the car, so self-possessed and quiet.

"Dickie's coming in a minute," Karla said. "It's hard to dance on all those broken eggs. We're gonna go out to Aunt Jimmie's and dance to the jukebox. You want to come with us?"

"Don't pressure him," Jacy said. "If he'd rather stay here and feel left out, let him."

"Duane, is it a midlife crisis or what?" Karla asked.

"I guess I'm just tired of the centennial," he said. "It seems like it's been going on for a hundred years."

"I think you're threatened by your own child," Jacy said. "You practically said that yourself. It's a common human experience—you don't have to be defensive about it. Just admit it."

"I think I'll take a walk," Duane said. "Maybe I'll run into that truck driver and tell him he's losing his eggs."

He drained his drink and pitched the cup back in the ice chest.

Jacy got off the car and put her arms around him.

"Come on, honey pie, go dancing with us," she said. "We'll make up for all the mean things we said."

"You didn't say any mean things," Duane said.

"No, but we hurt your tender feelings somehow," she said.

"He's too stubborn to have fun with us," Karla said. "If we take him he'll just sit there and be gloomy and none of us will have any fun."

"Somebody responsible needs to stick around here," Duane said. "The twins started this egg fight. They might get arrested or something."

"See, he's always got some excuse for not having fun," Karla said.

Duane felt undecided. Part of him wanted to go dancing. On the other hand, he agreed with Karla's appraisal of the situation. If he went dancing, in the mood he was in, none of them would have as much fun as they might have if he didn't go.

"I think I'll just take a walk," he said.

Jacy let him go without another word. When he looked back, from half a block down the street, he saw Jacy and Karla standing by the car door, looking in his direction.

Beyond them, beneath the blinking red light and in the streets around the courthouse, there were signs of a general melee. It was no longer just the children who were throwing eggs. Everyone seemed to be throwing eggs.

While Duane watched, Dickie drove up in the Porsche and stopped by Karla and Jacy. He parked the Porsche and got in the BMW. A moment later the three of them sped past. They all waved at him gaily, but didn't slow down to see if he had changed his mind about going dancing.

Duane could not decide what he would have done if they had stopped.

CHAPTER 93

Duane rarely walked. Floating in his boat was his main form of relaxation. He could not remember when he had taken a walk through Thalia at night. Though it was a very small town, there were parts of it he had not been through in years—not since Dickie and Nellie's first teenage years, when Karla was constantly forcing him to get out of bed and go look for them. They never came home from parties or ball games when they were supposed to, and in looking for them he had once poked through every small alley or lover's lane in town.

At first, walking, he felt a kind of disgust with himself for not having accepted the women's invitation to go dancing. He didn't really know why he hadn't, except to some extent he felt like an intruder in Karla's life when she was with Jacy, and in Jacy's when she was with Karla. If either of them alone had asked him to go dancing, he would have accepted, but they had come to seem like a couple, and their closeness was a barrier he was unwilling to try and penetrate. It was more relaxing not to have to tilt with the vibes they gave off when they were together.

Knowing that Dickie was safely gone for the night, he decided to walk to Suzie Nolan's house. To avoid the egg fight, he walked along the western edge of town. He passed the little Thalia cemetery, a place he normally only came to in the capacity of a pallbearer, every year or two. Both his parents were buried there. His father had been killed overseas, in World War II; his body had been shipped back and buried when Duane was five. His mother had died in her early sixties, mainly, so far as Duane could tell, because she had little interest in living. A few roughnecks he had worked with were buried there, a few old-timers he had liked, and several classmates who had died in accidents.

It struck him, walking past the cemetery, that there was no one buried in it whom he had ever been close to. He had never really known his father, and had had only a formal relationship with his mother. All his main workmates and drinking buddies were still alive, as were all the women he had cared about, and all his children. He had lived almost half a century without death touching him. The only person buried in the cemetery for whose passing he had felt any grief was Charlie Sears, the buck-toothed kid killed in Viet Nam; and that, he knew, was a small grief. He had only known the boy a few short months.

The thought struck him, walking past the cemetery, that his own death might be the first that would really affect him. It was a novel thought, and one of the few he had ever had about death. It was obvious, as Joe Coombs had pointed out, that it could happen to anyone, anytime, but, though Duane had worked all his life at a dangerous trade, he had never come really close to it and had rarely been even momentarily scared.

He felt, with no sense of fear, a sudden mild curiosity about his own removal from the texture of daily life. "Life goes on . . . ": he had heard it said after every funeral, every fatal accident. He knew it would be true in his family's case, if he were killed; their energies might be blunted for a time, but not for a long time.

But what of his own energies? Except for Karla, he had always been the most energetic person he knew. He had always been able to do more work and, while doing it, maintain a higher level of attention, than any of his rivals in the oil patch. It occurred to him that if something was really lost from his life, making him, as Jacy had suggested, a sad person, it was energy. For most of the past fifteen months he had worried much of the night about money, not sleeping the deep sleep that had for so long been his as a gift. He slept tired, woke tired, worked tired. The sense that he possessed an almost absolute energy was gone. He could still work, but in contrast to what he had once done routinely, his capacity seemed paltry. It was like the difference between floating in deep water and floating in the shallows. A buoyancy had been lost, but only by himself. Dickie, Karla, the twins, still had absolute energy. They were always wanting to go dancing or water-skiing, to play football, to have sex, to do something—when mainly what he wanted was to take a really satisfying nap.

It was a new thought to realize that he had reached an age when he would have to balance his energies as well as his checkbook—leave a little in the account for family life, some for his business, some for a girlfriend, if he could keep one. Karla alone necessitated keeping a substantial reserve.

Suzie Nolan's house was totally dark when he approached it. Duane hesitated—he didn't want to startle or frighten her. He felt he should probably just go away. He could call her on the phone and apologize the next day. It was probably silly to bring it up. Weren't women always accusing him of trying to settle things that couldn't be settled?

But he didn't want to go away, however silly his feeling was. He let himself into her kitchen and turned on the light. Then he sat at the kitchen table, wondering how to wake Suzie without frightening her.

"Dickie?" she said. A light came on in the hall.

"No, it's just me," Duane said.

Suzie came into the kitchen in her nightgown. She looked sleepy and a little worried.

"Have you seen my kids?" she asked. "They're not home."

"They're up at the courthouse throwing eggs," he said.

Suzie looked puzzled. "Why are they throwing eggs?" she asked.

"Hundreds of people are throwing eggs," Duane said. "Some idiot parked an egg truck right by the laundrymat and the kids got into it somehow."

Suzie sat down at the table, looking at him sleepily.

"Just me?" she said. "I was gonna start calling you Daddy Duane, but maybe I'll call you 'Just Me.' What do you want, 'Just Me?'"

"To be back in your good graces," he said.

"Go find my kids for me then," she said. "I'm the kind of mother that don't sleep good unless her kids are home. I've just been tossing and turning, waiting for them to come in."

"Finding two kids in an egg fight is a hard task," he said.

"It's the shortest route to my good graces, though," Suzie said.

"Where's your car keys?" he asked.

She pointed to a nail by the back door. Just as she did, the screen door opened and her two tall, grinning children stepped in. Both were almost as egg-drenched as Toots Burns had been.

"Stop!" Suzie said, snapping awake.

She left the kitchen briefly and returned with two bathrobes.

"Go outside and undress," she said. "Leave those slimy clothes on the porch. And take showers. You both got egg in your hair."

In a minute the children, in their bathrobes, slipped through the kitchen. They were good-looking kids, as lively and full of mischief as their mother could be in certain moods. Both said polite goodnights, calling him "Mr. Moore."

The thought that Dickie would soon be their stepfather seemed strange to him, but he let it be. He felt he had been foolish to return. Suzie looked at him as she might at an unthreatening stranger—far from being angry with him, she seemed almost to have forgotten him. It didn't bother her that he was in her kitchen in the middle of the night, but it didn't interest her, either. Her need for sleep, plus the fact that her kids were home, erased him as a factor in her life. She poured herself a glass of ice water and stood by the refrigerator drinking it. Though almost asleep, she seemd to be savoring each swallow. There was something deeply appealing about her as she drank—a way she had of making the simplest physical act, such as drinking cold water, seem as satisfying and as necessary as an intimate touch.

Though stirred, Duane merely hung the car keys on the back

of the door. She had erased him, but then he had been erased before. With Suzie, her body was always apt to take over and assert a demand to which there was no appeal. It might be for food, for sleep, for sex or just for a cold drink of water, but whatever it was for, that need became the only thing with any real existence to Suzie, for a time. He had learned a few things about her bodily needs, one of which was not to try and talk to them. Erased for now did not mean erased forever.

" 'Night," he said.

"Duane, you could sleep on the couch," she said, setting down her water glass.

"No, thanks," he said. "I got kids too. I better go see what *mine* are doing."

" 'Bye," Suzie said, turning off the kitchen light.

CHAPTER 94

GETTING BACK TO THE COURTHOUSE PROVED TO be no simple matter. The streets around the square, covered with the slime of thousands of broken eggs, were as slippery as ice.

Surveying the scene from the comparative safety of the filling station, Duane was not sure he really wanted to go back. For one thing, the egg war still raged, though the number of participants had diminished. The band had given up, a fact which hadn't discouraged a few die-hard dancers, who might not even have noticed it. All around the square piles of egg cartons were heaped up like shell casings.

The main battle now raged around Old Texasville, which had become the Alamo of the drinking faction. Forty or fifty cases of beer had been stacked in front of it as a barricade. Santa Anna and General Travis, or Bobby Lee and Eddie Belt, had joined forces to fight their common enemy, G. G. Rawley, who had recruited a large group of strong-armed Byelo-Baptist farm boys.

Bobby and Eddie had only a few allies, all very drunk, and

ammunition was evidently running low. They also had Shorty. From time to time, at Bobby Lee's urging, Shorty would jump up on the barricade of beer cases and pace about nervously. The plan seemed to be to have Shorty draw the Baptists' fire, but the Baptists were too short of ammunition to waste it on a dog. They had only about a dozen cartons of eggs left. The defenders of Texasville only risked an egg when they thought they could make an easy hit.

Duane managed to tiptoe across the street, walking when possible on the thousands of beer cans that mingled with egg slime on every approach to the square.

Just as he reached the cover of the hot-dog stand he saw Jack and Julie pass under the red light in a golf cart. It was Lester and Jenny's golf cart and their girls rode in it with the twins. Several kids came behind them on lawn tractors.

Unlike the Baptists, the kids had plenty of eggs. Julie drove the golf cart, and Jack, the strike-out pitcher, began to drill egg after egg at the outflanked Byelo-Baptists, who wasted a whole carton in fruitless retaliation. Jack's aim was deadly—almost every egg splattered against a face, chest or crotch.

Seeing that the enemy was caught in a crossfire, Bobby and Eddie rushed out in front of the barricade and flung several eggs at G. G. Rawley. Shorty was yipping his loudest, causing friend and foe alike to wince. Some of the Baptist farm boys tried to rush the kids, but the footing was treacherous and most of them fell down.

Jack rearmed himself in mid-flight, taking cartons of eggs from the ammunition train of lawn tractors. His accuracy was something to see. Duane indulged in a brief but vivid fantasy in which Jack struck out the last man in the last game of the World Series, in Yankee Stadium.

The farm boys were stubborn foes, however. Though smacked time after time with eggs, they still struggled through the slime, saving their last few eggs until they were at point-blank range. Jack threw faster, hoping to slow their advance, but they weren't slowing, and were almost through the region of slime.

Jack decided it was time for a strategic retreat. Julie whipped the golf cart into an alley and sped into the night. The rear guard, on the sluggish lawn tractors, which maneuvered poorly on a terrain of beer cans and broken eggs, tried to get away but were overtaken by the farm boys and pelted savagely.

"Let's call a truce, G.G.," Bobby Lee said. "We ain't got many more eggs."

"I ain't truce-ing with no heathen sots," G.G. said. Though little more than a walking column of albumen, he had not lost one whit of his fighting spirit. He threw his last three eggs, all of which splattered against the front of Old Texasville.

Bobby Lee had only one egg left and he dropped it. Shorty, who had become convinced that it was his duty to destroy eggs, pounced on it and crunched it before Bobby Lee could pick it up. Eddie Belt took a couple of last throws at G.G. but missed by several yards.

"It's a good thing your life don't depend on hitting somebody with an egg," Bobby Lee remarked.

Duane walked over and reduced the barricade by one beer.

"Where was you when we was fighting the good fight?" Bobby Lee asked.

"Well out of range," Duane said. It seemed as if the whole front of the courthouse, not to mention the lawn and the surrounding streets, was covered with egg.

"I'm so tired I'm about to drop," Eddie Belt said, yawning.

"Go on and drop, who'd miss you?" Bobby Lee said unsentimentally. The combat seemed to have invigorated him. "Wonder if anybody's left out at Aunt Jimmie's who'd like to dance with me?" he asked.

The egg truck was still parked by the laundrymat, its rear doors swinging open. Duane walked over and looked in it. It contained not a single egg.

A faint light was visible down the highway to the east. The curb behind the truck was the only spot around free of eggs, so he sat down on it, to sip his beer and wait for the dawn.

Bobby Lee, who was far from free of egg, came and joined him.

"We don't have to work today, do we?" he asked.

"Sure, we have to work today," Duane said. "We have to set pipe on that second well. Just because you drunk beer and threw eggs all night don't give you the right to be lazy."

It grew a little lighter. They saw a man come walking along the street, a rolled-up sleeping bag over his shoulder.

"That might be our truck driver," Duane said.

He was right. When the man was a block and a half away he slipped on some egg slime. Up to that point he had apparently not noticed the carnage ahead of him in the street. He noticed then, however. In front of some stores, empty egg cartons were heaped almost as high as the tumbleweeds had been.

The man tried to run to his truck and immediately fell down. He picked himself up and struggled forward, slipping repeatedly. When he finally reached the truck he was both aghast and out of breath.

"What happened here?" he asked.

"Well, it was just kind of a celebration," Duane said.

"Celebration!" the man said. He was about sixty, thin and sandy-haired. "My eggs are gone! I had five thousand dozen eggs in that truck! Sixty thousand eggs!"

"You probably shouldn't have gone off and left them," Duane suggested.

"I took a nap," the truck driver said. He seemed a little embarrassed.

"I drove all the way down from Ottumwa, Iowa," he added. "You got such nice lawns down here in Texas. I don't care for motels. I'd rather just walk around in these peaceful little towns and find me a nice lawn to stretch out on. Sleep under the stars. It's more restful."

He kept looking in his truck, as if unable to believe that the eggs which had traveled with him all the way from Ottumwa, Iowa, were no longer there.

"I never once dreamed that anything like this could happen," he said. "What kind of maniacs could break sixty thousand eggs?"

"It was Libyan terrorists that started it," Bobby Lee said, in his most reasonable voice. "They slipped in dressed like Baptist preachers, and the next thing we knew eggs were just flying everywhere."

"It's our centennial," Duane said. "Things like this don't happen but once every hundred years."

"Them eggs was grade double A large," the driver said. He

looked increasingly stunned. Spotting the lone pay phone on the corner across the street, he started toward it.

"I got to call my boss," he said. "He's not hardly gonna know what to think about this."

"Just send the bill to the town," Duane said. "We're not thieves. We'll pay for your eggs. Send it to Thalia, Texas. The zip is 76359."

The man carefully wrote the zip code down on a checkbook and slipped and slid his way across the street to the pay phone.

"You're too easy on people," Bobby Lee said. "I would have let the dumb son-of-a-bitch figure out the zip code for himself. Look at him. He hasn't even learned that you make faster progress stepping on the beer cans than you do stepping on the eggs."

"He's in shock," Duane said. "You would be too if you lay down to take a nap on a nice lawn and came back to discover you'd lost sixty thousand eggs."

"I personally wouldn't have sixty thousand eggs to lose," Bobby Lee said. "I rarely eat an egg."

CHAPTER 95

THE TRUCKER FROM IOWA MADE HIS CALL AND
went on his way. He was only out of sight a few minutes when
they spotted the delivery truck that dropped off the newspapers every morning. It was coming fast. Duane jumped
up and waved his dozer cap, hoping the driver would slow
down, but the driver came right on. He hit the egg slick going about fifty. The truck slid sideways for half a block,
crunching beer cans by the score. It came to a stop only a few
yards from where Duane and Bobby Lee stood. Shorty picked
his way into the street on a bridge of beer cans and began to
bark at it.

The driver was a stout boy in his late teens. He started to
step out of the truck, but thought better of it. The bundle of
papers he had to deliver dangled from one hand.

"I don't see no place I can set these down," he said.

Duane walked over and took them from him.

"Did an egg truck spill, or what?" the young man asked.

"It didn't exactly spill but it did lose quite a few eggs,"
Duane said.

"I hope I don't have a flat," the boy said. "I'd hate to change a flat in a place like this."

He started his truck and drove carefully away.

"We got a good vantage point here," Bobby Lee said. "I wonder who'll come along next."

It happened to be the twins, who appeared out of the gray dawn. They had only one carton of eggs left.

"I hope they ain't thinking of chunking us," Bobby Lee said. "You raised a couple of fine little chunkers there."

Julie went in the courthouse, where she had hidden her bike, and Jack contented himself with throwing the twelve eggs, one by one, across the street, into the shattered shell of the old picture show's ticket window. One high throw hit the dusty marquee, but the rest of the eggs passed through the ticket office and splattered against the wall where the popcorn machine had once stood.

When the carton was empty, Jack went into the courthouse, got his bike and rode off after his sister. Both kids negotiated the wasteland of eggs and beer cans without a slip.

"I wonder what those kids will grow up to be?" Bobby Lee said.

"I have no idea," Duane replied.

"They'll be something," Bobby Lee said. "They won't have quite as far to go as you did."

"That might just make it harder on them," Duane said. "If you have a long way to go, you just go. You don't have as big a chance of having an identity crisis as kids do nowadays."

"Your wife wouldn't agree," Bobby Lee said. "She just told me yesterday you were having an identity crisis."

"Have you ever had one?" Duane asked.

"No, I'm planning to have mine at the same time I have my mid-life crisis," Bobby Lee said. "Kill two birds with one stone."

In the east the horizon was pink. It was at its brightest just where the long straight highway met the horizon. Duane noticed Sonny's *Wall Street Journal* on top of the pile of newspapers. He pulled it out and opened it.

"OIL HITS FOURTEEN YEAR LOW," the headline said. "Oil Minister Says Saudis Unwilling to Slow Production."

The first paragraph of the story informed him that West Texas Intermediate Crude had closed at $8.89 a barrel. Experts expected it to go even lower before bottoming out. Some said $7, some said $6, and a few thought it might even sink to $5.

Duane refolded the *Journal* and stuck it back with the other newspapers.

"I guess you'll get your day off, after all," he told Bobby Lee. "You might get the rest of the year off, too."

"How come?" Bobby Lee asked, surprised.

"I might as well let that oil stay where it is," Duane said. "I'm not going to bring it up just to give it away, even if I could afford to. Dickie can bring it up, or Little Mike."

"How come them Saudis can afford to, if we can't?" Bobby Lee asked.

"They've got more of it," Duane said.

"Nobody's supposed to have more of anything than Americans have," Bobby Lee said. "It's unconstitutional. Shit, let's get the Supreme Court after them."

Duane had not opened the *Journal* expecting to read of rising oil prices. He knew which direction they were going. But the figure still stunned him. The price had dropped five dollars a barrel in less than a week. The old figure was severe, but not conclusive. The old figure would have daunted investors, weeded out amateurs, destroyed the most hopelessly debt-ridden. Over the long haul it might have had a cleansing effect, purging the business of poseurs and incompetents, forcing the professionals to work harder, stay alert and produce what they produced more economically.

But the new figure had no bright side for those throughout the oil patch who lived off small oil. Duane imagined the tens of thousands of pumps across the vast plain, from the Permian Basin east to the swamps of Louisiana, that worked the little three-and-four-barrel-a-day stripper wells. He had seen the pumps working all his life, like patient, domesticated insects, bringing up their three or four barrels every day: not enough to make anyone rich, but enough to give the old folks a little edge on their social security, or to keep the kids in school. As long as they kept pumping, pumpers would be hired to pump them, well-service crews to clean out the wells, truckers to haul the oil and equipment, welders to fix what broke down.

Now much of that life would stop. The pumps would cease to peck at the stained plains. Little businesses would fold, and little lives.

Duane felt tired and sad, thinking about it. But he didn't feel persecuted. He knew quite well that it could easily have happened sooner, and that there was still plenty of room for it to get worse.

Bobby Lee pulled the *Journal* off the stack and glanced at it.

"I've never been out of work a day in my life," he said. "Do you think it'll get worse than the Depression?"

"I wasn't alive in the Depression," Duane said. "Basically, I've had forty-eight years of prosperity. One thing I don't mean to do is start complaining."

"You wouldn't lay me off, would you, after all we've been through together?" Bobby Lee asked, staring gloomily at the *Journal*.

"I'd lay you off last, I'll promise you that," Duane said. "The bank may lay *me* off, you know."

"Those motherfuckers, we should have thrown all these eggs in there," Bobby Lee said.

They saw a Lincoln edging around the square. It stopped, and Lester and Jenny got out of it. Both of them carried cameras.

"What happened to Janine?" Duane asked, surprised to see Lester with his wife.

"Janine caught Lester kissing Lavelle," Bobby Lee said. "I guess if you're headed for prison you try to get all you can get."

Duane imagined a sad Janine, alone in her little house, getting more and more pregnant. He imagined himself going to see her, too.

"If you're worried about Janine, forget it," Bobby Lee said. "Worry about me if you want to worry about somebody."

"Why not worry about Janine?"

"She took up with Junior Nolan," Bobby Lee said. "He beat me to her, if you want to know the truth. Janine's improved in the last few years. I think me and her'd get along real well now.

"It's hard for people around here to decide who they want to live with," he added.

"But what became of Billie Anne?" Duane asked.

"Oh, she went back to Benson, Arizona," Bobby Lee said. "She said it was too tame around here."

Lester and Jenny walked over. It was not quite light enough to take good pictures. Both of them looked perky.

"This is a miracle," Lester said, happily surveying the scene. "When I show the judge pictures of this scene and he realizes I had to try and run a bank in a town that does things like this he'll dismiss all the charges."

"The whole centennial's just been real successful, all except the souvenir sales," Jenny said.

They walked off and stood under the red light, focusing their cameras.

Bobby Lee threw *The Wall Street Journal* into the nearest pile of egg goop.

"I hate reading things that depress me," he said.

They saw a black Mercedes approaching from the west. At first Duane thought it was Jacy's, but it was a much newer model.

"Those folks picked a bad shortcut, if they're trying to take a shortcut," he said.

The Mercedes came into town at a fast clip. When it hit the slime it duplicated the behavior of the delivery truck. It slid sideways for half a block, spun around three times and came to a stop.

After a moment, two smoked windows on the curb side slowly lowered. A longhaired sleepy man wearing a leather hat looked out of the back seat, but the sight of sixty thousand broken eggs mixed with several thousand beer cans evidently did not strike him as unusual or worthy of note. Without so much as raising an eyelid he put his window back up.

The other traveler had more curiosity. He had red hair, wore a headband and had a beard that was mostly gray. He opened the door of the Mercedes and stepped out a minute, grinning a shy grin. He was wearing running shoes, which didn't prevent him from slipping in the egg slime. He managed to keep himself from falling by grabbing the car door, but the slithery nature of the footing discouraged him from further exploration. He held on to the door and looked around a minute, obviously more impressed by what he saw than was his colleague. He looked at Duane and Bobby Lee and grinned.

"My lord," he said. "You folks must have had a pretty good ratfuck around here last night."

"We sure did," Duane said.

The traveler got back in the Mercedes and the Mercedes edged between Lester and Jenny, who were still taking pictures. The car disappeared into the sunrise.

"I think that was Willie Nelson," Bobby Lee said cautiously.

"You might be right," Duane said.

CHAPTER 96

THE THOUGHT THAT HE HAD JUST SPOKEN TO WIL-
lie Nelson filled Bobby Lee with a kind of awe. For several
minutes he was too awed to speak, but once he regained the
use of his tongue he gave way to wild speculation. Perhaps
Willie had decided to settle in Thalia. Perhaps he was thinking
of buying Jacy's house—the house Steve McQueen was said to
have visited. Perhaps he would be coming back to town later
in the day. He might give Bobby Lee an autograph. He might
eat a meal at the Dairy Queen.

"He might and he might not," Duane said. He was getting a
headache. He knew he ought to get up and head straight for
Dallas to try and find a decent bankruptcy lawyer. None of the
miracles that might have saved him from that distasteful expe-
dient had happened. He didn't want to go bankrupt, but his
only alternative was to let the bank take everything he had and
hope it satisfied them.

Besides that little personal problem, there was a civic problem: what to do about sixty thousand broken eggs. The red rim
of the sun was just about to break the eastern horizon. It was

an August sun, too. In a couple of hours Thalia was going to look like the world's biggest omelet.

"It's a pity you stuck the fire truck to the courthouse," he said. "It'd be a lot easier to clean up this mess if we had a fire truck."

He saw Briscoe racing across the courthouse lawn with an egg in his mouth. It was probably the only unbroken egg left in town.

"There's a simple solution to the problem of the fire truck," Bobby Lee said reasonably. "It's not the truck that's stuck to the courthouse, it's the ladder. All we gotta do is chop off the ladder and we'll have us a usable fire truck."

Before Duane could critique that solution he saw the BMW streaking back into town from the direction of Aunt Jimmie's Lounge. He immediately ran down the sidewalk, waving his arms and trying to slow the car. If Dickie was driving his usual eighty-five, bad things were going to happen when the car hit the egg slick.

But Dickie wasn't driving, or even in the car. Karla was driving, and no one was with her but Jacy. She stopped well clear of the eggy area.

Duane picked his way to the car, Bobby Lee close at his heels.

"Willie Nelson was just here," Bobby Lee said breathlessly.

"You're lying," Karla said. "You're just trying to make me feel bad, as usual."

"He was here, livin', breathin' Willie Nelson," Bobby Lee insisted.

"Oh, get in, we're starving," Karla said. "Let's go to the Dairy Queen."

"I'm not shitting you, Karla," Bobby Lee said. "Your biggest idol in the world passed right through town. I think he's thinking of buying a house here."

"Just ignore him, he was the one spread the rumor about Steve McQueen, too," Karla said to Jacy.

Duane got in. Both women were in high spirits. They had started to put on lipstick, then had decided to trade lipsticks and were admiring their new looks.

"What's wrong with you, gloom puss?" Karla asked.

"You'll know when you read the paper," Duane said. "Today's the day we finally went broke."

"Duane, you just need a good breakfast," Karla said. "There's people in the oil business who've been broke five or six times. It's no big deal."

"Karla, Willie Nelson spoke to me," Bobby Lee said.

Jacy reached back and gave Duane a pat on the knee, the only part of him she could reach.

"Cheer up, honey pie," she said. "It's a beautiful day and you're riding around with the two best-looking women in Texas. That's something."

"It sure is," Duane admitted. "I never intended to go broke, though."

"Well, things don't always work out," Karla said. "Hitch up your belt, Duane. You're just forty-eight. You got plenty of time to get rich again."

The women's high spirits were irresistible. Duane felt a lot better, just being with them. Probably he *could* get rich again, if he could figure out a way to steal some of their energy.

"He seemed like a real modest man," Bobby Lee said. "He grinned his little grin."

"Yeah, and I'm gonna kick your little dick if you don't shut up," Karla said. "Willie's too much of a gentleman to come to town the one time I wouldn't be here to meet him."

They parked at the Dairy Queen. Several bleary-eyed celebrants were standing around in the parking lot, scraping egg off their Levi's with pocketknives.

As they were at the door, Ruth Popper whirled into the parking lot in her dusty old Volkswagen. Her hair was wet and she looked distraught.

"I've lost Sonny," she said. "He snuck out while I was showering."

"Oh, well," Duane said, "I doubt he'll go far. Come in and eat breakfast with us."

"No, I have to look for him," Ruth said. "I just don't know what he might do, and I'd never forgive myself if anything happened to him."

"Okay, I'll come with you," Duane said. "The rest of you go on and eat."

"Let's all go look," Karla said. "I can't eat on a worried stomach. Sonny might need a good breakfast too. We'll find him and all eat together."

"He's not at the hotel or the Kwik-Sack," Ruth said. "Genevieve hasn't seen him."

"Maybe he went back to the rodeo arena," Jacy said. "He might have forgotten something last night."

"He could have even left with Willie," Bobby Lee said.

The women looked at him sternly.

"I'll ride with Ruth," Duane said.

CHAPTER 97

ON THE TOP SEAT OF THE BLEACHERS, ABOVE THE empty arena, Sonny was watching movies on the great silver screen of the dawn.

He was watching *Rio Bravo*. The great gun battle at the end would soon begin. An exchange of prisoners was about to take place. He saw Dean Martin step into the dusty wagon yard, blinking in the bright sunlight. He saw Dean Martin, he *was* Dean Martin. He was Dude. He started walking toward the distant adobe buildings, where John Wayne and Ricky Nelson waited. Joe was walking to meet him. Joe was the killer he was being exchanged for. Dude saw a broken adobe wall to his left. It gave him an idea. He had a chance to redeem himself, to make things up to his friends. He would tackle Joe and roll him behind the wall before the gunmen in the warehouse could shoot. He hunched forward a little. Joe was only a few steps away. Joe was sneering. He thought he had won. Dude got ready to tackle him. Another second and Joe would be in reach.

Then Duane caught his arm. Ruth Popper caught his other arm. Dude tried to struggle. They were ruining everything.

The picture was fading. He would never be redeemed unless he could tackle Joe, but Joe was gone. The only images left were wisps—they were little clouds. Duane and Ruth wouldn't let him tackle Joe.

Then the screen was the sky over Thalia, over the courthouse, over the plains. Sonny felt hopeless. The movie was lost. His chance was lost. He began to cry from disappointment.

"Just sit down a minute, honey," Ruth said. "Sit down and rest."

"I'm not tired," Sonny said. He saw two women climbing into the bleachers, Karla and Jacy. He didn't know why everyone had come back to the arena. The pageant had ended the night before.

"We're starving," Duane said. "Let's all go eat breakfast."

"You want to, Luke?" Karla asked.

Sonny felt a little better. It was nice that they had all come to take him to breakfast. Karla and Jacy looked beautiful, so beautiful that it made him feel shy to look at them. Ruth's hair was wet and stringy. She seemed upset. Duane still held his arm.

"Okay," Sonny said. "I am a little hungry. I guess it's breakfast time."

CHAPTER 98

"DID YOU THINK HE WAS ABOUT TO JUMP?" JACY asked, as Ruth and Karla led Sonny to the BMW. They were talking to him quietly.

"Well, he was kind of crouching," Duane said. "I guess he might have jumped."

"Karla's never going to believe Willie Nelson was here," Bobby Lee said. His failure to convince her of the miraculous visit worried him more than Sonny Crawford's problems.

"Oh, get off it about Willie Nelson," Jacy said. "Who cares about Willie Nelson?"

Bobby Lee looked hurt.

"Anybody in their right mind would care about seeing Willie," he said.

Sonny got in the back seat of the BMW, with Ruth on one side of him and Karla on the other.

Duane was about to get in and drive when he looked up the street and saw the twins. They were on their bikes and coming like blazes, preceded by a blue blur that proved to be Shorty.

"Oops, they're after your dog," Bobby Lee said. Jacy turned to look.

The twins were definitely after Shorty. Their aim seemed to be to catch his tail and flip him over. The threat was not lost on Shorty, fleeing down the dusty road for all he was worth, his ears flattened against his head. Duane had never seen him run so fast, but more than that, he had never seen the twins ride as they were riding. It was as if they had trained as a precision biking team for months, honing the techniques that would be necessary to catch a small blue dog.

Racing into the open, empty acres of the parking lot, Shorty began a series of brilliant, desperate maneuvers. He ran in tight circles, he doubled back on himself, he ducked, he dodged, he executed figure eights. No matter what he did, the twins hung tight on either side of him, a hand's length behind. When he circled, they circled. Several times Jack almost had his tail—Shorty, sensitive to the peril, kept it tucked tightly between his hind legs. Spotting the cars, he stopped dodging and raced for them with a last blazing burst of speed. The twins came on relentlessly, right at his heels, blinding glints shooting from their mirror sunglasses.

"Look at those kids!" Jacy said. "Look at those kids!"

She stood just behind Duane, watching the race.

"Oh, look at those kids!" she said a third time, with a breaking note in her voice.

To Duane's surprise she suddenly flung her arms around him, from behind. He felt her lips against his neck, then her teeth—her sudden tears wet his skin. She bit his neck as she cried, sobbing and sobbing. Bobby Lee turned away, shocked and embarrassed. Duane didn't move. Shorty slid to safety under the BMW, the twins parting at the last second, one going on one side of the car, one on the other. They coasted far out into the empty parking lot.

Jacy stopped biting, her crying slowed, it was only her lips he felt against his wet neck. He put his hands over her hands.

"I need them so, Duane," Jacy said, her face still tightly pressed against his neck. "It's like Benny's here—it makes me feel something of him's alive when I see kids doing things like that. All children don't die—maybe the ones that live carry the lives of the ones that die. You know what I mean?"

"Can I turn around?" Duane asked.

He turned and hugged her, and, as he did, saw his wife

watching through the rear window of the car. Karla's face was partly in shadow. He could not tell what she might be thinking, and he would have liked to know.

"Of course you don't know what I mean," Jacy whispered. "Your little boy and your little girl are right here. It's just that for a second now and then, when I see your kids, I feel like Benny's here too. You don't know how precious that is to me."

She hid her face against his chest. The twins wheeled up. From the back seat, Karla still watched. Julie wheeled up and looked in the car.

"What's wrong with Uncle Sonny?" she asked.

It didn't seem unusual to either twin that their father was hugging Jacy.

"I guess he's a little tired in his mind," Duane said.

Julie got off her bike and crawled into the car. Through the window he saw her get in Sonny's lap. Karla put her arm around them both.

Jack sat on his bike, watching Shorty, whose head was just visible under the BMW, his tongue hanging out.

"If he makes a run for it now I'll get him at once," Jack said, with a brilliant smile.

"I don't thinks he plans to make a run for it," Duane said.

Jacy stepped back from him, wiping her eyes.

"These centennials are awesome," Jack said. "I think we should have one every year."